#1 *New York Times*
bestselling author

NORA
ROBERTS

R E U N I O N

D0034012

GRIFFIN

**Also available from
#1 *New York Times*
bestselling author**

NORA ROBERTS

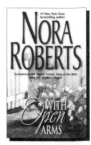

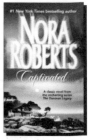

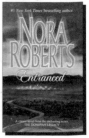

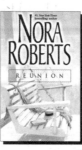

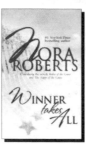

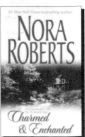

ISBN 0-373-28505-1

9 780373 285051

50799

EAN

PSNR1204IFC

Dear Reader,

In this special volume of classic novels, not widely available for over ten years, the amazing Nora Roberts shows her mastery of romance. *Reunion* features two compelling, sensual tales of reunited lovers who find love is better the second time around.

In *Once More with Feeling,* musician/composer Brandon Carstairs had left Raven Williams five years ago, without a word. Now he wants the talented singer back—to work with him on a project. Can Raven perform side by side with an old flame without getting burned? Or will their passion consume them both?

Desperate to complete her father's work, Kate Hardesty asks Ky Silver for his help. Kate knows her old boyfriend is the only one who can uncover the sunken ship and the booty buried within. Will they discover the greatest treasure of all is in each other's arms, in *Treasures Lost, Treasures Found.*

Fun Nora fact: If you place all the Nora Roberts's books end to end, they would stretch from New York to Los Angeles ten times!

Enjoy!

The Editors
Silhouette Books

NORA ROBERTS

REUNION

Published by Silhouette Books
America's Publisher of Contemporary Romance

SILHOUETTE BOOKS

REUNION

Copyright © 2004 by Harlequin Books S.A.

ISBN 0-373-28505-1

The publisher acknowledges the copyright holder of the individual works as follows:

ONCE MORE WITH FEELING
Copyright © 1983 by Nora Roberts

TREASURES LOST, TREASURES FOUND
Copyright © 1986 by Nora Roberts

Visit Silhouette Books at www.eHarlequin.com

Printed in U.S.A.

CONTENTS

ONCE MORE WITH FEELING

To Ran,
for all the songs yet unwritten,
for all the songs yet unsung.

Chapter 1

He stood out of view as he watched her. His first thought was how little she had changed in five years. Time, it seemed, hadn't rushed or dragged but had merely hung suspended.

Raven Williams was a small, slender woman who moved quickly, with a thin, underlying nervousness that was unaccountably appealing. She was tanned deep gold from the California sun, but at twenty-five her skin was as smooth and dewy soft as a child's. She pampered it when she remembered and ignored it when she forgot. It never seemed to make any difference. Her long hair was thick and straight and true black. She wore it simply, parted in the center. The ends brushed her hips and it swirled and floated as she walked.

Her face was pixielike, with its cheekbones well-defined and the chin slightly pointed. Her mouth smiled easily, but her eyes reflected her emotions. They were smoky gray and round. Whatever Raven felt would be reflected there. She had an overwhelming need to love and be loved. Her own need was one of the reasons for her tremendous success. The other was her voice—the rich, dark, velvet voice that had catapulted her to fame.

Raven always felt a little strange in a recording studio: insulated, sealed off from the rest of the world by the glass and the soundproofing. It had been more than six years since she had cut her first record, but she was still never completely comfortable in a studio. Raven was made for the stage, for the live audience that pumped the blood and heat into the music. She considered the studio too tame, too mechanical. When she worked in the studio, as she did now, she thought of it exclusively as a job. And she worked hard.

The recording session was going well. Raven listened to a playback with a single-mindedness that blocked out her surroundings. There was only the music. It was good, she decided, but it could be better. She'd missed something in the last song, left something out. Without knowing precisely what it was, Raven was certain she could find it. She signaled the engineers to stop the playback.

"Marc?"

A sandy-haired man with the solid frame of a lightweight wrestler entered the booth. "Problem?" he said simply, touching her shoulder.

"The last number, it's a little…" Raven searched for the word. "Empty," she decided at length. "What do you think?" She respected Marc Ridgely as a musician and depended on him as a friend. He was a man of few words who had a passion for old westerns and Jordan almonds. He was also one of the finest guitarists in the country.

Marc reached up to stroke his beard, a gesture, Raven had always thought, that took the place of several sentences. "Do it again," he advised. "The instrumental's fine."

She laughed, producing a sound as warm and rich as her singing voice. "Cruel but true," she murmured, slipping the headset back on. She went back to the microphone. "Another vocal on 'Love and Lose,' please," she instructed the engineers. "I have it on the best authority that it's the singer, not the musicians." She saw Marc grin before she turned to the mike. Then the music washed over her.

Raven closed her eyes and poured herself into the song. It was a slow, aching ballad suited to the smoky depths of her voice. The lyrics were hers, ones she had written long before. It had only been recently that she had felt strong enough to sing them publicly. There was only the music in her head now, an arrangement of notes she herself had produced. And as she added her voice, she knew that what had been missing before had been her emotions. She had restricted them on the other recordings, afraid to risk them. Now she let them out. Her voice flowed with them.

An ache passed through her, a shadow of a pain buried for years. She sang as though the words would bring her relief. The hurt was there, still with her when the song was finished.

For a moment there was silence, but Raven was too dazed to note the admiration of her colleagues. She pulled off the headset, suddenly sharply conscious of its weight.

"Okay?" Marc entered the booth and slipped his arm around her. He felt her tremble lightly.

"Yes." Raven pressed her fingers to her temple a moment and gave a surprised laugh. "Yes, of course. I got a bit wrapped up in that one."

He tilted her face to his, and in a rare show of public affection for a shy man, kissed her. "You were fantastic."

Her eyes warmed, and the tears that had threatened were banished. "I needed that."

"The kiss or the compliment?"

"Both." She laughed and tossed her hair behind her back. "Stars need constant admiration, you know."

"Where's the star?" a backup vocalist wanted to know.

Raven tried for a haughty look as she glanced over. "You," she said ominously, "can be replaced." The vocalist grinned in return, too used to Raven's lack of pretentions to be intimidated.

"Who'd carry you through the session?"

Raven turned to Marc. "Take that one out and shoot him," she requested mildly, then looked up at the booth. "That's a wrap," she called out before her eyes locked on the man now standing in full view behind the glass.

The blood drained from her face. The remnants of emotion from the song surged back in full force. She nearly swayed from the power of it. "Brandon." It was a thought to be spoken aloud but only in a whisper. It was a dream she thought had finally run its course. Then his eyes were on hers, and Raven knew it was real. He'd come back.

Years of performing had taught her to act. It was always an effort for her to slip a mask into place, but by the time Brand Carstairs had come down from the booth, Raven wore a professionally untroubled face. She'd deal with the storm inside later.

"Brandon, it's wonderful to see you again." She held out both hands and tilted her face up to his for the expected, meaningless kiss of strangers who happen to be in the same business.

Her composure startled him. He'd seen her pale, seen the shock in her eyes. Now she wore a façade she'd never had before. It was slick, bright and practiced. Brand realized he'd been wrong; she *had* changed.

"Raven." He kissed her lightly and took both her

hands. "You're more beautiful than anyone has a right to be." There was the lightest touch of brogue in his speech, a mist of Ireland over the more formal British. Raven allowed herself a moment to look at him, really look at him.

He was tall and now, as always, seemed a bit too thin. His hair was as dark as her own but waved where hers was needle straight. It was thick and full over his ears and down to the collar of his shirt. His face hadn't changed; it was still the same face that drove girls and women to scream and swoon at his concerts. It was raw-boned and tanned, more intriguing than handsome, as the features were not altogether even. There was something of the dreamer there, from his mother's Irish half. Perhaps that was what drew women to him, though they were just as fascinated by the occasional British reserve. And the eyes. Even now Raven felt the pull of his large, heavy-lidded aquamarine eyes. They were unsettling eyes for as easygoing a man as Brand Carstairs. The blue and green seemed constantly at odds. But it was the charm he wore so easily that tilted the scales, Raven realized. Charm and blatant sex appeal were an irresistible combination.

"You haven't changed, have you, Brandon?" The question was quiet, the first and only sign of Raven's distress.

"Funny." He smiled, not the quick, flashing grin he was capable of, but a slow, considering smile. "I thought the same of you when I first saw you. I don't suppose it's true of either of us."

"No." God, how she wished he would release her hands. "What brings you to L.A., Brandon?"

"Business, love," he answered carelessly, though his eyes were taking in every inch of her face. "And, of course, the chance to see you again."

"Of course." Her voice was coldly polite, and the smile never reached her eyes.

The sarcasm surprised him. The Raven he remembered hadn't known the meaning of the word. She saw his brow lift into consideration. "I do want to see you, Raven," Brand told her with his sudden, disarming sincerity. "Very much. Can we have dinner?"

Her pulse had accelerated at his change of tone. Just reflex, just an old habit, she told herself and struggled to keep her hands passive in his. "I'm sorry, Brandon," she answered with perfect calm. "I'm booked." Her eyes slipped past him in search of Marc, whose head was bent over his guitar as he jammed with another musician. Raven could have sworn with frustration. Brand followed the direction of her gaze. Briefly his eyes narrowed.

"Tomorrow, then," he said. His tone was still light and casual. "I want to talk to you." He smiled as to an old friend. "I'll just drop by the house awhile."

"Brandon," Raven began and tugged on her hands.

"You still have Julie, don't you?" Brand smiled and held on to her hands, unaware of—or ignoring—her resistance.

"Yes, I..."

"I'd like to see her again. I'll come by around four.

I know the way." He grinned, then kissed her again, a quick, friendly brushing of lips before he released her hands, turned and walked away.

"Yes," she murmured to herself. "You know the way."

An hour later Raven drove through the electric gates that led to her house. The one thing she hadn't allowed Julie or her agent to thrust on her was a chauffeur. Raven enjoyed driving, having control of the low, sleek foreign car and indulging from time to time in an excess of speed. She claimed it cleared her head. It obviously hadn't done the job, she thought as she pulled up in front of the house with a short, peevish squeal of the brakes. Distracted, she left her purse sitting on the seat beside her as she sprang from the car and jogged up the three stone steps that led to the front door. It was locked. Her frustration only mounted when she was forced to go back and rip the keys from the ignition.

Slamming into the house, Raven went directly to the music room. She flung herself down on the silk-covered Victorian sofa and stared straight ahead without seeing anything. A gleaming mahogany grand piano dominated the room. It was played often and at odd hours. There were Tiffany lamps and Persian rugs and a dime-store flowerpot with a struggling African violet. An old, scarred music cabinet was filled to overflowing. Sheet music spilled onto the floor. A priceless Fabergé box sat next to the brass unicorn she had found in a thrift shop and had fallen in love with. One wall was crowded with awards: Grammys, gold and platinum records, plaques and statues and the keys to a few cities. On another was the framed sheet music from the first song she had written and a breathtaking Picasso. The sofa on which she sat had a bad spring.

It was a strange hodgepodge of cultures and tastes and uniquely Raven's own. She would have thought *eclectic* a pretentious word. She had allowed Julie her exacting taste everywhere else in the house, but here she had expressed herself. Raven needed the room the same way she needed to drive her own car. It kept her sane and helped her remember exactly who Raven Williams was. But the room, like the drive, hadn't calmed her nerves. She walked to the piano.

She pounded out Mozart fiercely. Like her eyes, her music reflected her moods. Now it was tormented, volatile. Even when she'd finished, anger seemed to hover in the air.

"Well, I see you're home." Julie's voice, mild and unruffled, came from the doorway. Julie walked into the room as she had walked into Raven's life: poised and confident. When Raven had met her nearly six years before, Julie had been rich and bored, a party-goer born into old money. Their relationship had given them both something of importance: friendship and a dual dependence. Julie handled the myriad details attached to Raven's career. Raven gave Julie a purpose that the glittery world of wealth had lacked.

"Didn't the recording go well?" Julie was tall and

blond, with an elegant body and that exquisitely casual California chic.

Raven lifted her head, and the smile fled from Julie's face. It had been a long time since she'd seen that helpless, ravaged look. "What happened?"

Raven let out a long breath. "He's back."

"Where did you see him?" There was no need for Julie to ask for names. In all the years of their association only two things had had the power to put that look on Raven's face. One of them was a man.

"At the studio." Raven combed her fingers through her hair. "He was up in the booth. I don't know how long he'd been there before I saw him."

Julie pursed her lightly tinted lips. "I wonder what Brand Carstairs is doing in California."

"I don't know." Raven shook her head. "He said business. Maybe he's going to tour again." In an effort to release the tension, she rubbed her hand over the back of her neck. "He's coming here tomorrow."

Julie's brows rose. "I see."

"Don't turn secretary on me, Julie," Raven pleaded. She shut her eyes. "Help me."

"Do you want to see him?" The question was practical. Julie, Raven knew, was practical. She was organized, logical and a stickler for details—all the things Raven wasn't. They needed each other.

"No," Raven began almost fiercely. "Yes…" She swore then and pressed both hands to her temples. "I don't know." Now her tone was quiet and weary.

"You know what he's like, Julie. Oh, God, I thought it was over. I thought it was finished!"

With something like a moan, she jumped from the stool to pace around the room. She didn't look like a star in jeans and a simple linen blouse. Her closet held everything from bib overalls to sables. The sables were for the performer; the overalls were for her.

"I'd buried all the hurts. I was so sure." Her voice was low and a little desperate. It was still impossible for her to believe that she had remained this vulnerable after five years. She had only to see him again, and she felt it once more. "I knew sooner or later that I'd run into him somewhere." She ran her fingers through her hair as she roamed the room. "I think I'd always pictured it would be in Europe—London—probably at a party or a benefit. I'd have expected him there; maybe that would have been easier. But today I just looked up and there he was. It all came back. I didn't have any time to stop it. I'd been singing that damn song that I'd written right after he'd left." Raven laughed and shook her head. "Isn't that wild?" She took a deep breath and repeated softly, wonderingly, "Isn't that wild?"

The room was silent for nearly a full minute before Julie spoke. "What are you going to do?"

"Do?" Raven spun back to her. Her hair flew out to follow the sudden movement. "I'm not going to *do* anything. I'm not a child looking for happy-ever-after anymore." Her eyes were still dark with emotion, but her voice had grown gradually steadier. "I was barely twenty when I met Brandon, and I was blindly in love with his talent. He was kind to me at a time when I badly needed kindness. I was overwhelmed by him and with my own success.''

She lifted a hand to her hair and carefully pushed it behind her shoulders. ''I couldn't cope with what he wanted from me. I wasn't ready for a physical relationship.'' She walked to the brass unicorn and ran a fingertip down its withers. ''So he left,'' she said softly. ''And I was hurt. All I could see—maybe all I wanted to see—was that he didn't understand, didn't care enough to want to know why I said no. But that was unrealistic.'' She turned to Julie then with a frustrated sigh. ''Why don't you say something?''

''You're doing fine without me.''

''All right, then.'' Raven thrust her hands in her pockets and stalked to the window. ''One of the things I've learned is that if you don't want to get hurt, you don't get too close. You're the only person I've never applied that rule to, and you're the only one who hasn't let me down.'' She took a deep breath.

''I was infatuated with Brandon years ago. Perhaps it was a kind of love, but a girl's love, easily brushed aside. It was a shock seeing him today, especially right after I finished that song. The coincidence was...'' Raven pushed the feelings away and turned back from the window. ''Brandon will come over tomorrow, and he'll say whatever it is that he has to say, then he'll go. That'll be the end of it.''

Julie studied Raven's face. ''Will it?''

"Oh, yes." Raven smiled. She was a bit weary after the emotional outburst but more confident. She had regained her control. "I like my life just as it is, Julie. He's not going to change it. No one is, not this time."

Chapter 2

Raven had dressed carefully, telling herself it was because of the fittings she had scheduled and the luncheon meeting with her agent. She knew it was a lie, but the smart, sophisticated clothes made her feel confident. Who could feel vulnerable dressed in a St. Laurent?

Her coat was white silk and full cut with batwing sleeves that made it seem almost like a cape. She wore it over matching pants with an orchid cowlneck blouse and a thick, gold belt. With the flat-brimmed hat and the carefully selected earrings, she felt invulnerable. You've come a long way, she had thought as she had studied herself in the bedroom mirror.

Now, standing in Wayne Metcalf's elaborate fitting room, she thought the same thing again—about both of them. Wayne and Raven had started the rise to fame together, she scratching out a living singing in seamy clubs and smoky piano bars and he waiting tables and sketching designs no one had the time to look at. But Raven had looked and admired and remembered.

Wayne had just begun to eke out a living in his trade when plans had begun for Raven's first concert tour. The first professional decision she made without advice was the choice of her costume designer. She had never regretted it. Like Julie, Wayne was a friend close enough to know something about Raven's early personal life. And like Julie, he was fiercely, unquestionably loyal.

Raven wandered around the room, a much plusher room, she mused, than the first offices of Metcalf Designs. There'd been no carpet on that floor, no signed lithographs on laquered walls, no panoramic view of Beverly Hills. It had been a cramped, airless little room above a Greek restaurant. Raven could still remember the strange, heavy aromas that would seep through the walls. She could still hear the exotic music that had vibrated through the bare wood floor.

Raven's star had not risen with that first concert tour, it had rocketed. The initial taste of fame had been so heady and so quick, she had hardly had the time to savor it all: tours, rehearsals, hotel rooms, reporters, mobs of fans, unbelievable amounts of money and impossible demands. She had loved it, although the traveling had sometimes left her weak and disoriented and

the fans could be as frightening as they were wonderful. Still she had loved it.

Wayne, deluged with offers after the publicity of
that first tour, had soon moved out of the one-room
office above the *moussaka* and *souvlaki*. He'd been
Raven's designer for six years, and although he now
had a large staff and a huge workload, he still saw to
every detail of her designs himself.

While she waited for him, Raven wandered to the
bar and poured herself a ginger ale. Through all the
years of luncheon meetings, elegant brunches and recording sessions, she had never taken more than an
occasional drink. In this respect, at least, she would
control her life.

The past, she mused, was never very far away, at
least not while she still had to worry about her mother.
Raven shut her eyes and wished that she could shut
off her thoughts as easily. How long had it been that
she had lived with that constant anxiety? She could
never remember a life without it. She had been very
young when she had first discovered that her mother
wasn't like other mothers. Even as a little girl, she had
hated the oddly sweet smell of the liquor on her
mother's breath that no mints could disguise, and she
had dreaded the flushed face, the first slurred, affectionate, then angry tones that had drawn mocking
stares or sympathetic glances from friends and neighbors.

Raven pressed her fingers against her brow. So
many years. So much waste. And now her mother had

disappeared again. Where was she? In what sordid hotel room had she holed herself up in to drink away what was left of her life? Raven made a determined effort to push her mother out of her mind, but the terrible images, the frightful scenes, played on in her mind.

It's my life! I have to get on with it, Raven told herself, but she could feel the bitter taste of sorrow and guilt rise in her throat. She started when the door across swung open and Wayne walked in.

He leaned against the knob. "Beautiful!" he said admiringly, surveying her. "Did you wear that for me?"

She made a sound that was somewhere between a laugh and a sob as she moved across the room to hug him. "Of course. Bless you!"

"If you were going to dress up for me, you might at least have worn something of mine," he complained but returned the embrace. He was tall, a thin reed of a man who had to bend over to give her the quick kiss. Not yet thirty, he had a scholarly attractive face with hair and eyes the same rich shade of brown. A small white scar marred his left eyebrow and gave him, he preferred to think, a rakish profile.

"Jealous?" Raven grinned and drew away from him. "I thought you were too big for that."

"You're never too big for that." He released her, then made his way across to the bar. "Well, at least take off your hat and coat."

Raven obliged, tossing them aside with a careless-

ness that made Wayne wince. He gazed at her for a
long moment as he poured out a Perrier. She grinned
again and did a slow model's turn. "How am I holding up?" she demanded.

"I should have seduced you when you were eighteen." He sighed and drank the sparkling water.
"Then I wouldn't be constantly regretting that you
slipped through my fingers."

She came back for her ginger ale. "You had your
chance, fella."

"I was too exhausted in those days." He lifted his
scarred brow in a practiced gesture that always
amused her. "I get more rest now."

"Too late," she told him and touched her glass to
his. "And you're much too busy with the model-of-
the-week contest."

"I only date all those skinny girls for the publicity." He reached for a cigarette and lit it elegantly.
"I'm basically a very retiring man."

"The brilliance of the pun I could make is terrify-
ing, but I'll pass."

"Wise," he concluded, then blew out a delicate
trail of smoke. "I hear Brand Carstairs is in town."

Raven's smile fled, then returned. "He never could
keep a low profile."

"Are you okay?"

She shrugged her shoulders. "A minute ago I was
beautiful, now you have to ask if I'm okay?"

"Raven." Wayne laid a hand on top of hers. "You
folded up when he left. I was there, remember?"

"Of course I remember." The teasing note left her voice. "You were very good to me, Wayne. I don't think I would have made it without you and Julie."

"That's not what I'm talking about, Raven. I want to know how you feel now." He turned her hand over and laced his fingers through hers. "I could renew my offer to go try to break all his bones, if you like."

Touched and amused, she laughed. "I'm sure you're a real killer, Wayne, but it isn't necessary." The straightening of her shoulders was unconscious, a gesture of pride that made Wayne smile. "I'm not going to fold this time."

"Are you still in love with him?"

She hadn't expected such a direct question. Dropping her gaze, she took a moment to answer. "A better question is, Did I ever love him?"

"We both already know the answer to that one," Wayne countered. He took her hand when she would have turned away. "We've been friends a long time. What happens to you matters to me."

"Nothing's going to happen to me." Her eyes were back on his, and she smiled. "Absolutely nothing. Brandon is the past. Who knows better than I that you can't run away from the past, and who knows better how to cope with it?" She squeezed his hand. "Come on, show me the costumes that are going to make me look sensational."

After a quick, final glance at her face, Wayne walked over to a gleaming Chippendale table and pushed the button on an intercom. "Bring in Ms. Williams's designs."

Raven had approved the sketches, of course, and the fabrics, but still the completed designs took her by surprise. They had been created for the spotlights. She knew she'd sparkle on stage. It felt odd wearing blood red and silver sequins in Wayne's brightly lit, elegant room with mirrors tossing her image back at her from all angles. But then, she remembered, it was an odd business.

Raven stared at the woman in the mirrors and listened with half an ear to Wayne's mumbling as he tucked and adjusted. Her mind could not help but wander. Six years before, she'd been a terrified kid with an album shooting off the top of the charts and a whirlwind concert tour to face. It had all happened so fast: the typical overnight success—not counting the years she had struggled in smoke-choked dives. Still, she'd been young to make a name for herself and determined to prove she wasn't a one-shot fluke. The romance with Brand Carstairs, while she had still been fresh, hot news, hadn't hurt her career. For a brief time it had made her the crown princess of popular music. For more than six months their faces appeared on every magazine cover, dominating the newsstands. They'd laughed about it, Raven remembered, laughed at the silly, predictable headlines: "Raven and Brand Plan Love Nest"; "Williams and Carstairs Make Their Own Music."

Brand had complained about his billing. They had

ignored the constant flare and flash of cameras because they had been happy and saw little else but each other. Then, when he had gone, the pictures and headlines had continued for a long time—the cold, cruel words that flashed the intimacies of private hurts for the public eye. Raven no longer looked at them.

Over the months and years, she had grown from the crown princess to a respected performer and celebrity in her own right. That's what's important, she reminded herself. Her career, her life. She'd learned about priorities the hard way.

Raven slipped into the glistening black jumpsuit and found it fit like a second skin. Even her quiet breathing sent sequins flashing. Light streaked out from it at the slightest movement. It was, she decided after a critical survey, blisteringly sexy.

"I'd better not gain a quarter of an ounce before the tour," she remarked, turning to view her slim, sleek profile. Thoughtfully, she gathered her hair in her hand and tossed it behind her back. "Wayne…" He was kneeling at her feet, adjusting the hem. His answer was a grunt. "Wayne, I don't know if I have the nerve to wear this thing."

"This thing," he said mildly as he rose to pluck at the sleeve, "is fantastic."

"No artistic snub intended," she returned and smiled as he stepped back to survey her up and down in his concentrated, professional gaze. "But it's a bit…" She glanced at herself again. "Basic, isn't it?"

"You've got a nice little body, Raven." Wayne ex-

amined his creation from the rear. "Not all my clients
could wear this without a bit of help here and there.
Okay, take it off. It's perfect just as it is."

"I always feel like I've been to the doctor when
I've finished here," she commented as she slipped
back into her white slacks and orchid blouse. "Who
knows more about our bodies' secrets than our dress-
makers?"

"Who else knows more about *your* secrets, darling?" he corrected absently as he made notes on each
one of the costumes. "Women tend to get chatty when
they're half-dressed."

"Oh, what lovely gossip do you know?" Fastening
her belt, Raven walked to him, then leaned companionably on his shoulder. "Tell me something wonderfully indiscreet and shocking, Wayne."

"Babs Curtin has a new lover," he murmured, still
intent on his notes.

"I said shocking," Raven complained. "Not predictable."

"I've sworn an oath of secrecy, written in dress-
maker's chalk."

"I'm very disappointed in you." Raven left his side
to fetch her coat and hat. "I was certain you had feet
of clay."

"Lauren Chase just signed to do the lead in *Fantasy*."

Raven stopped on her way to the door and whirled.
"What?" She dashed back across the room and
yanked the notebook from Wayne's hand.

"Somehow I thought that would get your attention," Wayne observed dryly.

"When? Oh, Wayne," she went on before he could answer. "I'd give several years of my young life for a chance to write that score. Lauren Chase…oh, yes, she's so right for it. Who's doing the score, Wayne?" Raven gripped his shoulders and closed her eyes. "Go ahead, tell me, I can take it."

"She doesn't know. You're cutting off the circulation, Raven," he added, disengaging her hands.

"Doesn't know!" she groaned, crushing the hat down on her head in a way that made Wayne swear and adjust it himself. "That's worse, a thousand times worse! Some faceless, nameless songwriter who couldn't possibly know what's right for that fabulous screenplay is even now sitting at a piano making unforgivable mistakes."

"There's always the remote possibility that whoever's writing it has talent," he suggested and earned a lethal glare.

"Who's side are you on?" she demanded and flung the coat around her shoulders.

He grinned, grabbed her cheeks and gave her a resounding kiss. "Go home and stomp your feet, darling. You'll feel better."

She struggled not to smile. "I'm going next door and buy a Florence DeMille," she threatened him with the name of a leading competitor.

"I'll forgive you that statement," Wayne said with

a hefty sigh. "Because along with my feet of clay I've
a heart of gold."

She laughed and left him with her rack of costumes
and his notebook.

The house was quiet when Raven returned. The
faint scent of lemon oil and pine told her that the
house had just been cleaned. As a matter of habit, she
peeked into her music room and was satisfied that
nothing there had been disturbed. She liked her dis-
organization just as it was. With the idle thought of
making coffee, Raven wandered toward the kitchen.

She had bought the house for its size and rambling
openness. It was the antithesis of the small, claustro-
phobic rooms she had grown up in. And it smelled
clean, she decided. Not antiseptic; she would have
hated that, but there was no lingering scent of stale
cigarettes, no sickly sweet odor of yesterday's bottle.
It was her house, as her life was hers. She'd bought
them both with her voice.

Raven twirled once around the room, pleased with
herself for no specific reason. I'm happy, she thought,
just happy to be alive.

Grabbing a rose from a china vase, she began to
sing as she walked down the hall. It was the sight of
Julie's long, narrow bare feet propped up on the desk
in the library that stopped her.

Raven hesitated, seeing Julie was on the phone, but
was quickly gestured inside.

"I'm sorry, Mr. Cummings, but Ms. Williams has

a strict policy against endorsements. Yes, I'm sure it's a marvelous product.'' Julie lifted her eyes from her pink-tinted toenails and met Raven's amused grin. She rolled her eyes to the ceiling, and Raven settled cross-legged in an overstuffed leather chair. The library, with its warm, mahogany paneling and stately furnishings, was Julie's domain. And, Raven thought, snuggling down more comfortably, it suited her.

"Of course, I'll see she gets your offer, but I warn you, Ms. Williams takes a firm stand on this." With one last exasperated glance at the ceiling, Julie hung up. "If you didn't insist on being nice to everybody who calls you, I could have thought of a few different words for that one," Julie snapped.

"Trouble?" Raven asked, sniffing her rose and smiling.

"Get smart and I'll tell them you'll be thrilled to endorse his Earth Bubble Shampoo." She laced her fingers behind her head as she made the threat.

"Mercy," Raven pleaded, then kicked off her elegant, orchid-toned shoes. "You look tired," she said, watching Julie stretch her back muscles. "Been busy?"

"Just last-minute nonsense to clear things for the tour." A shrug dismissed the complications she had handled. "I never did ask you how the recording went. It's finished, isn't it?"

"Yeah." Raven took a deep breath and twirled her rose by the stem. "It went perfectly. I haven't been happier with a session since the first one. Something just clicked.''

''You worked hard enough on the material,'' Julie remarked, thinking of the endless nights Raven had spent writing and arranging.

''Sometimes I still can't believe it.'' She spoke softly, the words hardly more than thoughts. ''I listen to a playback, and it's all there, the strings, the brass, the rhythm and backups, and I can't believe it's me. I've been so incredibly lucky.''

''Talented,'' Julie corrected.

''Lots of people have talent,'' Raven reminded her. ''But they're not sitting here. They're still in some dreary piano bar, waiting. Without luck, they're never going to be anywhere else.''

''There are also things like drive, perseverance, guts.'' Raven's persistent lack of self-confidence infuriated Julie. She'd been with her almost from the beginning of Raven's start in California six years before. She'd seen the struggles and the disappointments. She knew about the fears, insecurities and work behind the glamour. There was nothing about Raven Williams that Julie didn't know.

The phone interrupted her thoughts on a lecture on self-worth. ''It's your private line,'' she said as she pressed the button. ''Hello.'' Raven tensed but relaxed when she saw Julie smile. ''Hi, Henderson. Yes, she's right here, hold on. Your illustrious agent,'' Julie stated as she rose. She slipped her feet back into her sandals. Raven got up from her chair just as the door-bell chimed.

"I guess that's Brandon." With admirable ease, she flopped into the chair that Julie had just vacated. "Would you tell him I'll be along in a minute?"

"Sure." Julie turned and left as Raven's voice followed her down the hall.

"I left it where? In your office? Henderson, I don't know why I ever bother carrying a purse."

Julie smiled. Raven had a penchant for losing things: her purse, her shoes, her passport. Vital or trivial, it simply didn't matter. Music and people filled Raven's thoughts, and material objects were easily forgotten.

"Hello, Brand," Julie said as she opened the front door. "Nice to see you again." Her eyes were cool, and her mouth formed no smile.

"Hello, Julie."

There was warmth in his greeting. She sensed it and ignored it. "Come in," she invited. "Raven's expecting you; she'll be right out."

"It's good to be here again. I've missed this place."

"Have you?" Her tone was sharp.

His grin turned into a look of appraisal. Julie was a long-stemmed woman with a sleek cap of honey-blond hair and direct brown eyes. She was closer to Brand's age than Raven's and was the sort of woman he was usually attracted to: smart, sophisticated and coolly sexy. Yet, there could never have been anything between them but friendship. She was too fiercely devoted to Raven. Her loyalty, he saw, was unchanged.

"Five years is a long time, Julie."

"I'm not sure it's long enough," she countered. Old resentments came simmering back to the surface. "You hurt her."

"Yes, I know." His gaze didn't falter at the confession, and there was no plea for understanding in his eyes. The lack of it touched off respect in Julie, but she dismissed it. She shook her head as she looked at him.

"So," she said softly, "you've come back."

"I've come back," he agreed, then smiled. "Did you think I wouldn't?"

"She didn't," Julie retorted, annoyed with herself for warming to him. "That's what matters."

"Julie, Henderson's sending over my purse." Raven came down the hall toward them in her quick, nervous stride. "I told him not to bother; I don't think there's anything in it but a comb and an expired credit card. Hello, Brandon." She offered her hands as she had at the recording studio, but now she felt more able to accept his touch.

She hadn't bothered to put her shoes back on or to repaint her mouth. Her smile was freer, more as he remembered it. "Raven." Brand brought her hands to his lips. Instantly she stiffened, and Brand released her. "Can we talk in the music room?" His smile was easy, friendly. "I was always comfortable in there."

"Of course." She turned toward the doorway. "Would you like something to drink?"

"I'd have some tea." He gave Julie his quick, charming grin. "You always made a good cup of tea."

"I'll bring it in." Without responding to the grin, Julie moved down the hall toward the kitchen. Brand followed Raven into the music room.

He touched her shoulder before she could cross to the sofa. It was a gesture that asked her to wait. Turning her head, Raven saw that he was giving the room one of his long, detailed studies. She had seen that look on his face before. It was a curious aspect of what seemed like a casual nature. There was an intensity about him at times that recalled the tough London street kid who'd once fought his way to the top of his profession. The key to his talent seemed to be in his natural gift for observation. He saw everything, remembered everything. Then he translated it into lyric and melody.

The fingers on her shoulder caressed once, almost absently, and brought back a flood of memories. Raven would have moved away, but he dropped the hand and turned to her. She had never been able to resist his eyes.

"I remember every detail of this room. I've pictured it from time to time when I couldn't do anything but think of you." He lifted his hand again to brush the back of it against her cheek.

"Don't." She shook her head and stepped away.

"It's difficult not to touch you, Raven. Especially here. Do you remember the long evenings we spent here? The quiet afternoons?"

He was moving her—with just his voice, just the steady spell of his eyes. "It was a long time ago, Brandon."

"It doesn't seem so long ago at the moment. It could be yesterday; you look the same."

"I'm not," she told him with a slight shake of her head. He saw her eyes darken before she turned away. "If I had known this was why you wanted to see me, I wouldn't have let you come. It's over, Brandon. It's been over for a long time."

"Is it?" Raven hadn't realized he was so close behind her. He turned her in his arms and caught her. "Show me, then," he demanded. "Just once."

The moment his mouth touched hers, she was thrown back in time. It was all there—the heat, the need, the loving. His lips were so soft, so warm; hers parted with only the slightest pressure. She knew how he would taste, how he would smell. Her memory was sharper than she had thought. Nothing was forgotten.

He tangled his fingers in the thickness of her hair, tilting her head further back as he deepened the kiss. He wanted to luxuriate in her flavor, in her scent, in her soft, yielding response. Her hands were trapped between their bodies, and she curled her fingers into the sweater he wore. The need, the longing, seemed much too fresh to have been dormant for five years. Brand held her close but without urgency. There was a quiet kind of certainty in the way he explored her mouth. Raven responded, giving, accepting, remembering. But when she felt the pleasure drifting toward passion, she resisted. When she struggled, he loosened his hold but didn't release her. Raven stared up at him with a look he well remembered but had never been able to completely decipher.

"It doesn't seem it's altogether finished after all," he murmured.

"You never did play fair, did you?" Raven pushed out of his arms, furious and shaken. "Let me tell you something, Brandon. I won't fall at your feet this time. You hurt me before, but I don't bruise so easily now. I have no intention of letting you back into my life."

"I think you will," he corrected easily. "But perhaps not in the way you mean." He paused and caught her hair with his fingers. "I can apologize for kissing you, Raven, if you'd like me to lie."

"Don't bother. You've always been good at romance. I rather enjoyed it." She sat down on the sofa and smiled brightly up at him.

He lifted a brow. It was hardly the response he had expected. He drew out a cigarette and lit it. "You seem to have grown up in my absence."

"Being an adult has its advantages," Raven observed. The kiss had stirred more than she cared to admit, even to herself.

"I always found your naiveté charming."

"It's difficult to remain naive, however charming, in this business." She leaned back against the cushion, relaxing deliberately. "I'm not wide-eyed and twenty anymore, Brandon."

"Tough and jaded are you, Raven?"

"Tough enough," she returned. "You gave me my first lesson!"

He took a deep drag on his cigarette, then considered the glowing tip of it. "Maybe I did," he murmured. "Maybe you needed it."

"Maybe you'd like me to thank you," she tossed back, and he looked over at her again.

"Perhaps." He walked over, then dropped down beside her on the sofa. His laugh was sudden and unexpected. "Good God, Raven, you've never had this bloody spring fixed."

The tension in her neck fled as she laughed with him. "I like it that way." She tossed her hair behind her back. "It's more personal."

"To say nothing of uncomfortable."

"I never sit on that spot," she told him.

"You leave it for unsuspecting guests, I imagine." He shifted away from the defective spring.

"That's right. I like people to feel at home."

Julie brought in a tea tray and found them sitting companionably on the sofa. Her quick, practiced glance found no tension on Raven's face. Satisfied, she left them again.

"How've you been, Brandon? Busy, I imagine." Raven crossed her legs under her and leaned over to pour the tea. It was a move Brandon had seen many times. Almost savagely, he crushed out his cigarette.

"Busy enough." He understated the five albums he had released since she'd last seen him and the three grueling concert tours. There'd been more than twenty songs with his name on the copyright in the past year.

"You've been living in London?"

"Mostly." His brow lifted, and she caught the gesture as she handed him his tea.

"I read the trades," she said mildly. "Don't we all?"

"I saw your television special last month." He sipped his tea and relaxed against the back of the sofa. His eyes were on her, and she thought them a bit more green than blue now. "You were marvelous."

"Last month?" She frowned at him, puzzled. "It wasn't aired in England, was it?"

"I was in New York. Did you write all the songs for the album you finished up yesterday?"

"All but two." Shrugging, she took up her own china cup. "Marc wrote 'Right Now' and 'Coming Back.' He's got the touch."

"Yes." Brand eyed her steadily. "Does he have you, too?" Raven's head whipped around. "I read the trades," he said mildly.

"That comes under a more personal heading." Her eyes were dark with anger.

"More bluntly stated, none of my business?" he asked, sipping again.

"You were always bright, Brandon."

"Thanks, love." He set down his cup. "But my

question was professional. I need to know if you have any entanglements at the moment.''

''Entanglements are usually personal. Ask me about my dancing lessons.''

''Later, perhaps. Raven, I need your undivided devotion for the next three months.'' His smile was engaging. Raven fought his charm.

''Well,'' she said and set her cup beside his. ''That's bluntly stated.''

''No indecent proposal at the moment,'' he assured her. Settling back in the hook of the sofa's arm, he sought her eyes. ''I'm doing the score for *Fantasy*. I need a partner.''

Chapter 3

To say she was surprised would have been a ridiculous understatement. Brand watched her eyes widen. He thought they were the color of peat smoke. She didn't move but simply stared at him, her hands resting lightly on her knees. Her thoughts had been flung in a thousand different directions, and she was trying to sit calmly and bring them back to order.

Fantasy. The book that had captured America's heart. A novel that had been on the bestseller list for more than fifty weeks. The sale of its paperback rights had broken all records. The film rights had been purchased as well, and Carol Mason, the author, had written the screenplay herself. It was to be a musical; *the* musical of the nineties. Speculation had been buzzing for months on both coasts as to who would write the score. It would be the coup of the decade, the chance of a lifetime. The plot was a dream, and the reigning box-office queen had the lead. And the music... Raven already had half-formed songs in her head. Carefully she reached back and poured more tea. Things like this don't just fall in your lap, she reminded herself. Perhaps he means something entirely different.

"You're going to score *Fantasy*," she said at length, cautiously. Her eyes met his again. His were clear, confident, a little puzzled. "I just heard that Lauren Chase had been signed. Everywhere I go, people are wondering who's going to play Tessa, who's going to play Joe."

"Jack Ladd," Brand supplied, and the puzzlement in Raven's eyes changed to pure pleasure.

"Perfect!" She reached over to take his hand. "You're going to have a tremendous hit. I'm very happy for you."

And she was. He could see as well as hear the absolute sincerity. It was typical of her to gain genuine pleasure from someone else's good fortune, just as it was typical of her to suffer for someone else's misfortune. Raven's feelings ran deep, and he knew she'd never been afraid to show emotion. Her unaffectedness had always been a great part of her appeal. For the moment, she had forgotten to be cautious with Brand. She smiled at him as she held his hands.

"So that's why you're in California," she said. "Have you already started?"

"No." He seemed to consider something for a moment, then his fingers interlaced with hers. Her hands were narrow-boned and slender, with palms as soft as a child's. "Raven, I meant what I said. I need a partner. I need you."

She started to remove her hands from his, but he tightened his fingers. "I've never known you to need anyone, Brandon," she said, not quite succeeding in making her tone light. "Least of all me."

His grip tightened quickly, causing Raven's eyes to widen at the unexpected pain. Just as quickly, he released her. "This is business, Raven."

She lifted a brow at the temper in his voice. "Business is usually handled through my agent," she said. "You remember Henderson."

He gave her a long, steady look. "I remember everything." He saw the flash of hurt in her eyes, swiftly controlled. "Raven," his tone was gentler now. "I'm sorry."

She shrugged and gave her attention back to her tea. "Old wounds, Brandon. It does seem to me that if there was a legitimate offer, Henderson would have gotten wind of it."

"There's been an offer," Brand told her. "I asked him to let me speak to you first."

"Oh?" Her hair had drifted down, curtaining her face, and she flipped it behind her back. "Why?"

"Because I thought that if you knew we'd be working together, you'd turn it down."

"Yes," she agreed. "You're right."

"And that," he said without missing a beat,

"would be incredibly soft-headed. Henderson knows that as well as I do."

"Oh, does he?" Raven rose, furious. "Isn't it marvelous the way people determine my life? Did you two decide I was too feeble-brained to make this decision on my own?"

"Not exactly." Brand's voice was cool. "We did agree that left to yourself, you have a tendency to be emotional rather than sensible."

"Terrific. Do I get a leash and collar for Christmas?"

"Don't be an idiot," Brand advised.

"Oh, so now I'm an idiot?" Raven turned away to pace the room. She had the same quicksilver temper he remembered. She was all motion, all energy. "I don't know how I've managed all this time without your pretty compliments, Brandon." She whirled back to him. "Why in the world would you want an emotional idiot as a collaborator?"

"Because," Brandon said and rose, "you're a hell of a writer. Now shut up."

"Of course," she said, seating herself on the piano bench. "Since you asked so nicely."

Deliberately he took out another cigarette, lit it and blew out a stream of smoke, all the while his eyes resting on her face. "This is an important project, Raven," he said. "Let's not blow it. Because we were once very close, I wanted to talk to you face to face, not through a mediator, not through a bloody telephone wire. Can you understand that?"

She waited a long moment before answering. "Maybe."

Brand smiled and moved over to her. "We'll add stubborn to those adjectives later, but I don't want you mad again."

"Then let me ask you something before you say anything I'll have to get mad about." Raven tilted her head and studied his face. "First, why do you want a collaborator on this? Why share the glory?"

"It's also a matter of sharing the work, love. Fifteen songs."

She nodded. "All right, number two, then. Why me, Brandon? Why not someone who's scored a musical before?"

He answered her by walking around her and slipping down on the piano bench beside her. Without speaking, he began to play. The notes flooded the room like ghosts. "Remember this?" he murmured, glancing over and into her eyes.

Raven didn't have to answer. She rose and walked away. It was too difficult to sit beside him at the same piano where they had composed the song he now played. She remembered how they had laughed, how warm his eyes had been, how safe she had felt in his arms. It was the first and only song they had written and recorded together.

Even after he had stopped playing, she continued to prowl the room. "What does 'Clouds and Rain' have to do with anything?" she demanded. He had touched a chord in her; he heard it in the tone of her voice. He felt a pang of guilt at having intentionally peeled away a layer of her defense.

"There's a Grammy over there and a gold record, thanks to that two minutes and forty-three seconds, Raven. We work well together."

She turned back to look at him. "We did once."

"We will again." Brand stood and came to her but this time made no move to touch her. "Raven, you know how important this could be to your career. And you must realize what you'd be bringing to the project. *Fantasy* needs your special talents."

She wanted it. She could hardly believe that something she wanted so badly was being offered to her. But how would it be to work with him again, to be in constant close contact? Would she be able to deal with it? Would she be sacrificing her personal sanity for professional gain? But I don't love him anymore, she reminded herself. Raven caught her bottom lip between her teeth in a gesture of indecision. Brand saw it.

"Raven, think of the music."

"I am," she admitted. "I'm also thinking of you—of us." She gave him a clear, candid look. "I'm not sure it would be healthy for me."

"I can't promise not to touch you." He was annoyed, and his voice reflected it in its crisp, concise tone. "But I can promise not to push myself on you. Is that good enough?"

Raven evaded the question. "If I agreed, when would we start? I've a tour coming up."

"I know, in two weeks. You'll be finished in six, so we could start the first week in May."

"I see." Her mouth turned up a bit as she combed her fingers through her hair. "You've looked into this thoroughly."

"I told you, it's business."

"All right, Brandon," she said, conceding his point. "Where would we work? Not here," she said quickly. There was a sudden pressure in her chest. "I won't work with you here."

"No, I thought not. I have a place," he continued when Raven remained silent. "It's in Cornwall."

"Cornwall?" Raven repeated. "Why Cornwall?"

"Because it's quiet and isolated, and no one, especially the press, knows I have it. They'll be all over us when they hear we're working together, especially on this project. It's too hot an item."

"Couldn't we just rent a small cave on the coast somewhere?"

He laughed and caught her hair in his hand. "You know how poor the acoustics are in a cave. Cornwall's incredible in the spring, Raven. Come with me."

She lifted a hand to his chest to push back, not certain if she was about to agree or decline. He could still draw too much from her too effortlessly. She needed to think, she decided; a few days to put it all in perspective.

"Raven."

She turned to see Julie in the doorway. "Yes?"

"There's a call for you."

Vaguely annoyed, Raven frowned at her. "Can't it wait, Julie? I..."

"It's on your private line."

Brand felt her stiffen and looked down curiously. Her eyes were completely blank.

"I see." Her voice was calm, but he detected the faintest of tremors.

"Raven?" Without thinking, he took her by the shoulders and turned her to face him. "What is it?"

"Nothing." She drew out of his arms. There was something remote about her now, something distant that puzzled him. "Have some more tea," she invited and smiled, but her eyes remained blank. "I'll be back in a minute."

She was gone for more than ten, and Brand had begun to pace restlessly through the room. Raven was definitely no longer the malleable young girl she had been five years before; he knew that. He wasn't at all certain she would agree to work with him. He wanted her—for the project and yes, for himself. Holding her, tasting her again, had stirred up much more than memories. She fascinated him and always had. Even when she had been so young, there had been an air of secrecy about her. There still was. It was as if she kept certain parts of herself locked in a closet out of reach. She had held him off five years before in more than a physical sense. It had frustrated him then and continued to frustrate him.

But he was older, too. He'd made mistakes with her before and had no intention of repeating them. Brand knew what he wanted and was determined to get it. Sitting back at the piano, he began to play the song he had written with Raven. He remembered her voice, warm and sultry, in his ear. He was nearly at the end when he sensed her presence.

Glancing up, Brand saw her standing in the doorway. Her eyes were unusually dark and intense. Then he realized it was because she was pale, and the contrast accentuated the gray of her irises. Had the song disturbed her that much? He stopped immediately and rose to go to her.

"Raven..."

"I've decided to do it," she interrupted. Her hands were folded neatly in front of her, her eyes direct.

"Good." He took her hand and found it chilled. "Are you all right?"

"Yes, of course." She removed her hands from his, but her gaze never faltered. "I suppose Henderson will fill me in on all the details."

Something about her calm disturbed him. It was as if she'd set part of herself aside. "Let's have dinner, Raven." The urge to be with her, to pierce her armor, was almost overwhelming. "I'll take you to the Bistro; you always liked it there."

"Not tonight, Brandon, I...have some things to do."

"Tomorrow," he insisted, knowing he was pushing but unable to prevent himself. She looked suddenly weary.

"Yes, all right, tomorrow." She gave him a tired

smile. "I'm sorry, but I'll have to ask you to leave now, Brandon. I didn't realize how late it was."

"All right." Bending toward her, he gently kissed her. It was an instinctive gesture, one that demanded no response. He felt the need to warm her, protect her. "Seven tomorrow," he told her. "I'm at the Bel-Air; you only have to call me."

Raven waited until she heard the front door shut behind her. She pressed the heel of her hand to her brow and let the tide of emotions rush through her. There were no tears, but a blinding headache raged behind her eyes. She felt Julie's hand on her shoulder.

"They found her?" Julie asked, concerned. Automatically she began kneading the tension from Raven's shoulders.

"Yes, they found her." She let out a long, deep breath. "She's coming back."

Chapter 4

The sanitarium was white and clean. The architect, a good one, had conceived a restful building without medical overtones. The uninformed might have mistaken it for an exclusive hotel snuggled in California's scenic Ojai. It was a proud, elegantly fashioned building with several magnificent views of the countryside. Raven detested it.

Inside, the floors were thickly carpeted, and conversation was always low-key. Raven hated the controlled silence, the padded quiet. The staff members wore street clothes and only small, discreet badges to identify themselves, and they were among the best trained in the country, just as the Fieldmore Clinic was the best detoxification center on the west coast. Raven had made certain of its reputation before she had brought her mother there for the first time over five years before.

Raven waited in Justin Karter's paneled, book-lined, tasteful office. It received its southern exposure through a wide, thick-paned window. The morning sunlight beamed in on a thriving collection of leafy green plants. Raven wondered idly why her own plants seemed always to put up only a halfhearted struggle for life, one they usually lost. Perhaps she should ask Dr. Karter what his secret was. She laughed a little and rubbed her fingers on the nagging headache between her brows.

How she hated these visits and the leathery, glossy smell of his office. She was cold and cupped her elbows, hugging her arms across her midriff. Raven was always cold in the Fieldmore Clinic, from the moment she walked through the stately white double doors until long after she walked out again. It was a penetrating cold that went straight to the bone. Turning away from the window, she paced nervously around the room. When she heard the door open, she stopped and turned around slowly.

Karter entered, a small, youthful man with a corn-colored beard and healthy pink cheeks. He had an earnest face, accentuated by tortoise-rimmed glasses and a faint smattering of freckles. Under other circumstances, Raven would have liked his face, even warmed to it.

"Ms. Williams." He held out a hand and took hers in a quick, professional grip. It was cold, he realized, and as fragile as he remembered. Her hair was pinned up at the nape of her neck, and she looked young and pale in the dark tailored suit. This woman was far different from the vibrant, laughing entertainer he had watched on television a few weeks before.

"Hello, Dr. Karter."

It always amazed him that the rich, full-toned voice belonged to such a small, delicate-looking woman. He had thought the same years before when she had been hardly more than a child. He was an ardent fan but had never asked her to sign any of the albums in his collection. It would, he knew, embarrass them both.

"Please sit down, Ms. Williams. Could I get you some coffee?"

"No, please." She swallowed. Her throat was always dry when she spoke to him. "I'd like to see my mother first."

"There are a few things I'd like to discuss with you."

He watched her moisten her lips, the only sign of agitation. "After I've seen her."

"All right." Karter took her by the arm and led her from the room. They walked across the quiet, carpeted hallway to the elevators. "Ms. Williams," he began. He would have liked to have called her Raven. He thought of her as Raven, just as the rest of the world did. But he could never quite break through the film of reserve she slipped on in his presence. It was, Karter knew, because he knew her secrets. She trusted him to keep them but was never comfortable with him.

She turned to him now, her great, gray eyes direct and expressionless.

"Yes, Doctor?" Only once had Raven ever broken down in his presence, and she had promised herself she would never do so again. She would not be destroyed by her mother's illness, and she would not make a public display of herself.

"I don't want you to be shocked by your mother's appearance." They stepped into the elevator together, and he kept his hand on her arm. "She had made a great deal of progress during her last stay here, but she left prematurely, as you know. Over the past three months, her condition has...deteriorated."

"Please," Raven said wearily, "don't be delicate. I know where she was found and how. You'll dry her out again, and in a couple of months she'll leave and it'll start all over. It never changes."

"Alcoholics fight a continuing battle."

"Don't tell me about alcoholics," she shot back. The reserve cracked, and the emotion poured through. "Don't preach to me about battles." She stopped herself, then, shaking her head, pressed her fingers to the concentrated source of her headache. "I know all about alcoholics," she said more calmly. "I haven't your dedication or your optimism."

"You keep bringing her back," he reminded Raven softly.

"She's my mother." The elevator doors slid open, and Raven walked through them.

Her skin grew colder as they moved down the hallway. There were doors on either side, but she refused to think of the people beyond them. The hospital flavor was stronger here. Raven thought she could smell the antiseptic, the hovering medicinal odor that always made a hint of nausea roll in her stomach. When Karter stopped in front of a door and reached for a knob, Raven laid a hand on top of his.

"I'll see her alone, please."

He sensed her rigid control. Her eyes were calm, but he had seen the quick flash of panic in them. Her fingers didn't tremble on his hand but were stiff and icy. "All right. But only a few minutes. There are complications we need to discuss." He took his hand from the knob. "I'll wait for you here."

Raven nodded and twisted the knob herself. She took a moment, struggling to gather every ounce of strength, then walked inside.

The woman lay in a hospital bed on good linen sheets, dozing lightly. There was a tube feeding liquid into her through a needle in her arm. The drapes were drawn, and the room was in shadows. It was a comfortable room painted in soft blue with an ivory carpet and a few good paintings. With her fingers dug into the leather bag she carried, Raven approached the bed.

Raven's first thought was that her mother had lost weight. There were hollows in her cheeks, and her skin had the familiar unhealthy yellow cast. Her dark hair was cropped short and streaked liberally with gray. It had been lovely hair, Raven remembered, glossy and full. Her face was gaunt, with deathly cir-

cles under the eyes and a mouth that seemed dry and
pulled in. The helplessness stabbed at Raven, and for
a minute she closed her eyes against it. She let them
fall while she looked down on the sleeping woman.
Without a sound, without moving, the woman in bed
opened her eyes. They were dark and gray like her
daughter's.

"Mama." Raven let the tears roll freely. "Why?"

By the time Raven got to her front door, she was
exhausted. She wanted bed and oblivion. The headache was still with her, but the pain had turned into a
dull, sickening throb. Closing the door behind her, she
leaned back on it, trying to summon the strength to
walk up the stairs.

"Raven?"

She opened her eyes and watched Julie come down
the hall toward her. Seeing Raven so pale and beaten,
Julie slipped an arm around her shoulders. Her concern took the form of a scolding. "You should have
let me go with you. I should never have let you go
alone." She was already guiding Raven up the stairs.

"My mother, my problem," Raven said tiredly.

"That's the only selfish part of you," Julie said in
a low, furious voice as they entered Raven's bedroom.
"I'm supposed to be your friend. You'd never let me
go through something like this alone."

"Please, don't be angry with me." Raven swayed
on her feet as Julie stripped off the dark suit jacket.

"It's something I feel is my responsibility, just mine. I've felt that way for too long to change now."

"I am angry with you." Julie's voice was tight as she slipped the matching skirt down over Raven's hips. "This is the only thing you do that makes me genuinely angry with you. I can't stand it when you do this to yourself." She looked back at the pale, tired face. "Have you eaten?" Raven shook her head as she stepped out of the skirt. "And you won't," she concluded, brushing Raven's fumbling hands away from the buttons of the white lawn blouse. She undid them herself, then pushed the material from Raven's shoulders. Raven stood, unresisting.

"I'm having dinner with Brandon," Raven murmured, going willingly as Julie guided her toward the bed.

"I'll call him and cancel. I can bring you up something later. You need to sleep."

"No." Raven slipped between the crisp, cool sheets. "I want to go. I need to go," she corrected as she shut her eyes. "I need to get out; I don't want to think for a while. I'll rest now. He won't be here until seven."

Julie walked over to pull the shades. Even before the room was darkened, Raven was asleep.

It was some minutes past seven when Julie opened the door to Brandon. He wore a stone-colored suit with a navy shirt open at the throat. He looked casually elegant, Julie thought. The nosegay of violets was charming rather than silly in his hands. He lifted a brow at the clinging black sheath she wore.

"Hello, Julie. You look terrific." He plucked one of the violets out of the nosegay and handed it to her. "Going out?"

Julie accepted the flower. "In a little while," she answered. "Raven should be down in a minute. Brand..." Hesitating, Julie shook her head, then turned to lead him into the music room. "I'll fix you a drink. Bourbon, isn't it? Neat."

Brand caught her arm. "That isn't what you were going to say."

She took a deep breath. "No." For a moment longer she hesitated, then began, fixing him with her dark brown eyes. "Raven's very important to me. There aren't many like her, especially in this town. She's genuine, and though she thinks she has, she hasn't really developed any hard edges yet. I wouldn't like to see her hurt, especially right now. No, I won't answer any questions," she said, anticipating him. "It's Raven's story, not mine. But I'm going to tell you this: She needs a light touch and a great deal of patience. You'd better have them both."

"How much do you know about what happened between us five years ago, Julie?" Brandon asked.

"I know what Raven told me."

"One day you ought to ask me how I felt and why I left."

"And would you tell me?"

"Yes," he returned without hesitation. "I would."

"I'm sorry!" Raven came dashing down the stairs in a filmy flutter of white. "I hate to be late." Her hair settled in silky confusion over the shoulders of the thin voile dress as she stopped at the foot of the stairs. "I couldn't seem to find my shoes."

There was a becoming blush of color on her cheeks, and her eyes were bright and full of laughter. It passed through Brand's mind quickly, and then was discarded, that she looked a little too bright, a little too vibrant.

"Beautiful as ever." He handed her the flowers. "I've never minded waiting for you."

"Ah, the golden Irish tongue," she murmured as she buried her face in the violets. "I've missed it." Raven held the flowers up to her nose while her eyes laughed at him over them. "And I believe I'll let you spoil me tonight, Brandon. I'm in a mood to be pampered."

He took her free hand in his. "Where do you want to go?"

"Anywhere. Everywhere." She tossed her head. "But dinner first. I'm starving."

"All right, I'll buy you a cheeseburger."

"Some things do stay the same," she commented before she turned to Julie. "You have fun, and don't worry about me." She paused a moment, then smiled and kissed her cheek. "I promise I won't lose my key. And say hello to..." She hesitated as she walked toward the door with Brandon. "Who is it tonight?"

"Lorenzo," Julie answered, watching them. "The shoe baron."

"Oh, yes." Raven laughed as they walked into the cool, early spring air. "Amazing." She tucked her arm through Brandon's. "Julie's always having some millionaire fall in love with her. It's a gift."

"Shoe baron?" Brand questioned as he opened the car door for Raven.

"*Mmm.* Italian. He wears beautiful designer suits and looks as though he should be stamped on the head of a coin."

Brand slid in beside her and in an old reflex gesture brushed the hair that lay on her shoulder behind her back. "Serious?"

Raven tried not to be moved by the touch of his fingers. "No more serious than the oil tycoon or the perfume magnate." The leathery smell of the upholstery reminded her abruptly of Karter's office. Quickly she pushed away the sensation. "What are you going to feed me, Brandon?" she asked brightly—too brightly. "I warn you, I'm starving."

He circled her throat with his hand so that she had no choice but to meet his eyes directly. "Are you going to tell me what's wrong?"

He'd always seen too much too quickly, she thought. It was one of the qualities that had made him an exceptional songwriter.

Raven placed her hand on top of his. "No questions, Brandon, not now."

She felt his hesitation. Then he turned his hand over

and gripped hers. Slowly, overriding her initial resistance, he brought her palm to his lips. "Not now," he agreed, watching her eyes. "I can still move you," he murmured and smiled as though the knowledge pleased him. "I can feel it."

Raven felt the tremors racing up her arms. "Yes." She drew her hand from his but kept her eyes steady. "You can still move me. But things aren't the same anymore."

He grinned, a quick flash of white teeth, then started the engine. "No, things aren't the same anymore."

As he pulled away, she had the uncomfortable impression that they had said the same words but meant two different things.

Dinner was quiet and intimate and perfect. They ate in a tiny old inn they had once discovered by chance. Here, Brand knew, there would be no interruptions for autographs, no greetings and drinks from old acquaintances. Here there would be just the two of them, a man and a woman amidst candlelight, wine, fine food, and an intimate atmosphere.

As the evening wore on, Raven's smile became more spontaneous, less desperate, and the unhappiness he had seen deep in her eyes before now faded. Though he noticed the transition, Brand made no comment.

"I feel like I haven't eaten in a week," Raven managed between bites of the tender roast beef that was the house speciality.

"Want some of mine?" Brand offered his plate.

Raven scooped up a bit of baked potato; her eyes seemed to laugh at him. "We'll have them wrap it up so I can take it home. I want to leave room for dessert. Did you see that pastry tray?"

"I suppose I could roll you to Cornwall," Brand considered, adding some burgundy to his glass.

Raven laughed, a throaty sound that appealed and aroused. "I'll be a bag of bones by the time we go to Cornwall," she claimed. "You know what those whirlwind tours can do." She shook her head as he offered her more wine.

"One-night stands from San Francisco to New York." Brand lifted his glass as Raven gave him a quizzing look. "I spoke to Henderson." He twirled a strand of her hair around his finger so absently, Raven was certain he was unaware of the gesture. She made no complaint. "If it's agreeable with you, I'll meet you in New York at the end of the tour. We'll fly to England from there."

"All right." She took a deep breath, having finally reached her fill of the roast beef. "You'd better set it up with Julie. I haven't any memory for dates and times. Are you staying in the States until then?"

"I'm doing a couple of weeks in Vegas." He brushed his fingers across her cheek, and when she would have resisted, he laid his hand companionably over hers. "I haven't played there in quite a while. I don't suppose it's changed."

She laughed and shook her head. "No. I played

there, oh, about six months ago, I guess. Julie won a bundle at the baccarat table. I was a victim of the slots.''

"I read the reviews. Were you as sensational as they said?'' He smiled at her while one finger played with the thin gold bracelet at her wrist.

"Oh, I was much more sensational than they said,'' she assured him.

"I'd like to have seen you.'' His finger drifted lazily to her pulse. He felt it jump at his touch. "It's been much too long since I've heard you sing.''

"You heard me just the other day in the studio,'' she pointed out. She took her hand from his to reach for her wine. He easily took her other one. "Brandon,'' she began, half-amused.

"I've heard you over the radio as well,'' he continued, "but it's not the same as watching you come alive at a concert. Or,'' he smiled as his voice took on that soft, intimate note she remembered, "listening to you when you sing just for me.''

His tone was as smooth as the burgundy she drank. Knowing how easily he could cloud her brain, she vowed to keep their conversation light. "Do you know what I want right now?'' She lowered her own voice as she leaned toward him, but he recognized the laughter in her eyes.

"Dessert,'' he answered.

"You know me so well, Brandon.'' She smiled.

She wanted to go dancing. By mutual consent, when they left the restaurant they avoided the popular, trendy spots in town and found a crowded, smoky hole-in-the-wall club with a good band, much like the dozens they had both played in at the beginnings of their respective careers. They thought they wouldn't be recognized there. For almost twenty minutes they were right.

"Excuse me, aren't you Brand Carstairs?" The toothy young blond stared up at Brand in admiration. Then she glanced at Raven. "And Raven Williams."

"Bob Muldroon," Brand returned in a passable Texas drawl. "And my wife Sheila. Say howdy, Sheila," he instructed as he held her close and swayed on the postage-sized dance floor.

"Howdy," Raven said obligingly.

"Oh, Mr. Carstairs." She giggled and thrust out a cocktail napkin and a pencil. "Please, I'm Debbie. Could you write, 'To my good friend Debbie'?"

"Sure." Brand gave her one of his charming smiles and told Raven to turn around. He scrawled quickly, using her back for support.

"And you, too, Raven," Debbie asked when he'd finished. "On the other side."

It was typical of her fans to treat her informally. They thought of her as Raven. Her spontaneous warmth made it difficult for anyone to approach her with the awe normally reserved for superstars. Raven wrote on her side of the napkin when Brand offered his back. When she had finished, she noted that Debbie's eyes were wide and fixed on Brand. The pulse in her throat was jumping like a jackhammer. Raven knew what fantasies were dancing in the girl's mind.

"Here you are, Debbie." She touched her hand to bring the girl back to reality.

"Oh." Debbie took the napkin, looked at it blankly a moment, then smiled up at Brand. "Thanks." She looked at Raven, then ran a hand through her hair as if she had just realized what she had done. "Thanks a lot."

"You're welcome." Brand smiled but began to edge Raven toward the door.

It was too much to expect that the incident had gone unnoticed or that no one else would recognize them. For the next fifteen minutes they were wedged between the crowd and the door, signing autographs and dealing with a barrage of questions. Brand made certain they weren't separated from each other as he slowly maneuvered a path through the crowd.

They were jostled and shoved a bit but he judged the crowd to be fairly civilized. It was still early by L.A. standards, and there hadn't been too much drinking yet. Still he wanted her out. This type of situation was notoriously explosive; the mood could change abruptly. One overenthusiastic fan and it could all be different. And ugly. Raven signed and signed some more while an occasional hand reached out to touch her hair. Brand felt a small wave of relief as he finally drew her out into the fresh air. Only a few followed them out of the club, and they were able to make their way to Brand's car with just a smattering of extra autographs.

"Damn it. I'm sorry." He leaned across her to lock her door. "I should have known better than to have taken you there."

Raven took a long breath, combing her hair back from her face with her fingers as she turned to him. "Don't be silly; I wanted to go. Besides, the people were nice."

"They aren't always," he muttered as the car merged with Los Angeles traffic.

"No." She leaned back, letting her body relax. "But I've been pretty lucky. Things have only gotten out of hand once or twice. It's the hype, I suppose, and it's to be expected that fans sometimes forget we're flesh and blood."

"So they try to take little chunks of us home with them."

"That," Raven said dryly, "can be a problem. I remember seeing a film clip of a concert you gave, oh, seven or eight years ago." She leaned her elbow on the back of the seat now and cupped her cheek in her palm. "A London concert where the fans broke through the security. They seemed to swallow you whole. It must have been dreadful."

"They loved me enough to give me a couple of broken ribs."

"Oh, Brandon." She sat up straight now, shocked. "That's terrible. I never knew that."

He smiled and moved his shoulders. "We played it

down. It did rather spoil my taste for live concerts for a while. I got over it.'' He turned, heading toward the hills. "Security's tighter these days.''

"I don't know if I'd be able to face an audience after something like that.''

"Where else would you get the adrenaline?'' he countered. "We need it, don't we? That instant gratification of applause.'' He laughed and pulled her over beside him. "Why else do we do it, Raven? Why else are there countless others out there scrambling to make it? Why did you start up the road, Raven?''

"To escape,'' she answered before she had time to think. She sighed and relaxed against his shoulder when he didn't demand an explanation. "Music was always something I could hold on to. It was constant, dependable. I needed something that was wholly mine.'' She turned her head a bit to study his profile. "Why did you?''

"For most of the same reasons, I suppose. I had something to say, and I wanted people to remember I said it.''

She laughed. "And you were so radical at the start of your career. Such pounding, demanding songs. You were music's bad boy for some time.''

"I've mellowed,'' he told her.

"'Fire Hot' didn't sound mellow to me,'' she commented. "Wasn't that the lead cut on your last album?''

He grinned, glancing down at her briefly. "I have to keep my hand in.''

"It was number one on the charts for ten consecutive weeks," she pointed out. "That isn't bad for mellow."

"That's right," he agreed as if he'd just remembered. "It knocked off a little number of yours, didn't it? It was kind of a sweet little arrangement, as I recall. Maybe a bit heavy on the strings, but..."

She gave him an enthusiastic punch on the arm.

"Raven," Brand complained mildly. "You shouldn't distract me when I'm driving."

"That sweet little arrangement went platinum."

"I said it was sweet," he reminded her. "And the lyrics weren't bad. A bit sentimental, maybe, but..."

"I like sentimental lyrics," she told him, giving him another jab on the arm. "Not every song has to be a blistering social commentary."

"Of course not," he agreed reasonably. "There's always room for cute little ditties."

"Cute little ditties," Raven repeated, hardly aware that they had fallen back into one of their oldest habits by debating each other's work. "Just because I don't go in for showboating or lyrical trickery," she began. But when he swung off to the side of the road, she narrowed her eyes at him. "What are you doing?"

"Pulling over before you punch me again." He grinned and flicked a finger down her nose. "Showboating?"

"Showboating," she repeated. "What else do you call that guitar and piano duel at the end of 'Fire Hot'?"

"A classy way to fade out a song," he returned, and though she agreed with him, Raven made a sound of derision.

"I don't need the gadgetry. My songs are..."

"Overly sentimental."

She lifted a haughty brow. "If you feel my music is overly sentimental and cute, how do you imagine we'll work together?"

"Perfectly," he told her. "We'll balance each other, Raven, just as we always did."

"We're going to have terrible fights," she predicted.

"Yes, I imagine we will."

"And," she added, failing to suppress a smile, "you won't always win."

"Good. Then the fights won't be boring." He pulled her to him, and when she resisted, he cradled her head on his shoulder again. "Look," he ordered, pointing out the window, "why is it cities always look better at night from above?"

Raven looked down on the glittering Los Angeles skyline. "I suppose it's the mystique. It makes you wonder what's going on and you can't see how fast it's moving. Up here it's quiet." She felt his lips brush her temple. "Brandon." She drew away, but he stopped her.

"Don't pull away from me, Raven." It was a low, murmured request that shot heat up her spine. "Don't pull away from me."

His head lowered slowly, and his lips nibbled at

hers, hardly touching, but the hand at the back of her neck was firm. He kept her facing him while he changed the angle of the kiss. His lips were persuasive, seductive. He kissed the soft, dewy skin of her cheeks, the fragile, closed eyelids, the scented hair at her temple. She could feel herself floating toward him as she always had, losing herself to him.

Her lips parted so that when his returned, he found them inviting him to explore. The kiss deepened, but slowly, as if he savored the taste of her on his tongue. Her hand slid up his chest until she held him and their bodies touched. He murmured something, then pressed his mouth against the curve of her neck. Her scent rose and enveloped him.

She moaned when he took her breast, a sound of both hunger and protest. His mouth came back to hers, plundering now as he responded to the need he felt flowing from her. She was unresisting, as open and warm as a shaft of sunlight. Her body was yearning toward him, melting irresistibly. She thought his hand burned through the thin fabric of her dress and set fire to her naked skin. It had been so long, she thought dizzily, so long since she had felt anything this intensely, needed anything this desperately. Her whole being tuned itself to him.

"Raven." His mouth was against her ear, her throat, the hollow of her cheek. "Oh, God, I want you." The kiss was urgent now, his hands no longer gentle. "So long," he said, echoing her earlier thought. "It's been so long. Come back with me. Let me take you back with me to the hotel. Stay with me tonight.''

Passion flooded her senses. His tongue trailed over her warmed skin until he came again to her mouth. Then he took possession. The heat was building, strangling the breath in her throat, suffocating her. There was a fierce tug of war between fear and desire. She began to struggle.

''No.'' She took deep gulps of air. ''Don't.''

Brand took her by the shoulders and with one quick jerk had her face turned back up to his. ''Why?'' he demanded roughly. ''You want me, I can feel it.''

''No.'' She shook her head, and her hands trembled as she pushed at his chest. ''I don't. I can't.'' Raven tried to deepen her breathing to steady it. ''You're hurting me, Brandon. Please let me go.''

Slowly he relaxed his fingers, then released her. ''The same old story,'' he murmured. Turning away from her, he carefully drew out a cigarette and lit it. ''You still give until I'm halfway mad, then pull away from me.'' He took a long, deep drag. ''I should have been better prepared for it.''

''You're not fair. I didn't start this; I never wanted...''

''You wanted,'' he tossed back furiously. ''Damn it, Raven, you wanted. I've had enough women to know when I'm holding one who wants me.''

She stiffened against the ache that was speeding through her. ''You're better off with one of your many women, Brandon. I told you I wouldn't fall at your feet this time, and I meant it. If we can have a professional relationship, fine." She swallowed and straightened the hair his fingers had so recently caressed. "If you can't work with things on that level, then you'd best find another partner."

"I have the one I want." He tossed his cigarette through the open window. "We'll play it your way for a while, Raven. We're both professionals, and we both know what this musical's going to do for our careers." He started the engine. "I'll take you home."

Chapter 5

Raven hated to be late for a party, but there was no help for it. Her schedule was drum tight. If it hadn't been important that she be there, to rub elbows with Lauren Chase and a few other principals from the cast and crew of *Fantasy,* she'd have bowed out. There were only two days left before the start of her tour.

The truth was, Raven had forgotten about the party. Rehearsals had run over, then she had found herself driving into Beverly Hills to window shop. She hadn't wanted to buy anything but had simply wanted to do something mindless. For weeks there had been nothing but demand after demand, and she could look forward only to more of the same in the weeks to come. She would steal a few hours. She didn't want to think about her mother and the clean white sanitarium or

song lists and cues or her confusion over Brand as she
browsed through the treasures at Neiman-Marcus and
Gucci. She looked at everything and bought nothing.

Arriving home, she was met by a huge handwritten
note from Julie tacked on her bedroom door.

Party at Steve Jarett's. I know—you forgot.
IMPORTANT! Get your glad rags together,
babe, and go. Out with Lorenzo for dinner, we'll
see you there. J.

Raven swore briefly, rebelled, then capitulated before she stalked to the closet to choose an outfit. An
hour later she was cruising fast through the Hollywood Hills. It was important that she be there.

Steve Jarett was directing *Fantasy*. He was, at the
moment, the silver screen's boy wonder, having just
directed three major successes in a row. Raven wanted
Fantasy to be his fourth as much as he did.

The party would be crowded, she mused, and
looked wistfully at the open, star-studded sky. And
noisy. Abruptly she laughed at herself. Since when did
a noisy, crowded party become a trial by fire? There
had been a time when she had enjoyed them. And
there was no denying that the people who haunted
these parties were fascinating and full of incredible
stories. Raven could still be intrigued. It was just
that... She sighed, allowing herself to admit the real
reason she had dragged her feet. Brandon would be
there. He was bound to be.

Would he bring a date? she wondered. Why wouldn't he? She answered herself shortly, downshifting as she took a curve. Unless he decided to wait and take his pick from the women there. Raven sighed again, seeing the blaze of lights that told her she was approaching Jarett's house. It was ridiculous to allow herself to get tied up in knots over something that had ended years before.

Her headlights caught the dull gleam of sturdy iron gates, and she slowed. The guard took her name, checked his list, then admitted her. She could hear the music before she was halfway up the curving, palm-lined drive.

There was a white-jacketed teenager waiting to hand her out of the Lamborghini. He was probably a struggling actor or an aspiring screenwriter or cinematographer, Raven thought as she smiled at him.

"Hi, I'm late. Do you think I can slip in without anybody noticing?"

"I don't think so, Ms. Williams, not looking like that."

Raven lifted her brows, surprised that he had recognized her so quickly in the dim light. But even if he had missed the face and hair, she realized, he would never have mistaken the voice.

"That's a compliment, isn't it?" she asked.

"Yes, ma'am," he said so warmly that she laughed.

"Well, I'm going to do my best, anyway. I don't like entrances unless they're on stage." She studied the sprawling, white brick mansion. "There must be a side door."

"Around to the left." He pointed. "There's a set of glass doors that lead into the library. Go through there and turn left. You should be able to slip in without being noticed."

"Thanks." She went to take a bill out of her purse, discovered she had left it in the car and leaned in the window to retrieve it. After a moment's search, she found a twenty and handed it to him.

"Thank *you!* Raven," he enthused as she turned away. Then he called to her, "Ms. Williams?" Raven turned back with a half smile. "Would you sign it for me?"

She tossed back her hair. "The bill?"

"Yeah."

She laughed and shook her head. "A fat lot of good it would do you then. Here." She dug into her bag again and came up with a slip of paper. One side was scrawled on, a list of groceries Julie had given her a few weeks before, but the other side was blank. "What's your name?" she demanded.

"Sam, Sam Rheinhart."

"Here, Sam Rheinhart," she said. Dashing off a quick line on the paper, she gave him the autograph. He stared after her, the twenty in one hand and the grocery list in the other, as she rushed off.

Raven found the glass doors without trouble. Though they were closed, the sounds of the party came clearly through. There were groups of people out back listening to a very loud rock band and drifting around by the pool. She stayed in the shadows. She wore an ankle-length skirt and a dolman-sleeve pullover in a dark plum color with silver metallic threads running through which captured the moonlight. Entering through the library, she gave herself a moment to adjust to the darkness before groping her way to the door.

There was no one in the hall immediately outside. Pleased with herself, Raven stepped out and gravitated slowly toward the focus of noise.

"Why, Raven!" It was Carly Devers, a tiny blond fluff of an actress with a little-girl voice and a rapier sharp talent. Though they generally moved in different circles, Raven liked her. "I didn't know you were here."

"Hi, Carly." They exchanged obligatory brushes of the cheek. "Congratulations are in order, aren't they? I heard you were being signed as second lead in *Fantasy*."

"It's still in the working stage, but it looks like it. It's a gem of a part, and of course, working with Steve is *the* thing to do these days." As she spoke, she gave Raven a piercing look with her baby blue eyes. "You look fabulous," she said. Raven knew she meant it. "And of course, congratulations are in order for you as well, aren't they?"

"Yes, I'm excited about doing the score."

Carly tilted her head, and a smile spread over her face. "I was thinking more about Brand Carstairs than

the score, darling.'' Raven's smile faded instantly.
''Oops.'' Carly's smile only widened. ''Still tender.''
There was no malice in her amusement. She linked
her arm with Raven's. ''I'd keep your little collaboration very tight this time around, Raven. I'm tempted
to make a play for him myself, and I guarantee I'm
not alone.''

''What happened to Dirk Wagner?'' Raven reminded herself to play it light as they drew closer to
the laughter and murmurs of the party.

''Old news, darling, do try to keep up.'' Carly
laughed, a tinkling bell of a sound that Raven could
not help but respond to. ''Still, I don't make it a habit
to tread on someone else's territory.''

''No signs posted, Carly,'' Raven said carelessly.

''*Hmm.*'' Carly tossed back a lock of silver-blond
hair. A waiter passed by with a tray of glasses, and
she neatly plucked off two. ''I've heard he's a marvelous lover,'' she commented, her eyes bright and
direct on Raven's.

Raven returned the look equably and accepted the
offered champagne. ''Have you? But then, I imagine
that's old news, too.''

''Touché,'' Carly murmured into her glass.

''Is Brandon here?'' she asked, trying to prove to
herself and her companion that the conversation meant
nothing.

''Here and there,'' Carly said ambiguously. ''I
haven't decided whether he's been trying to avoid the
flocks of females that crawl around him or if he's

seeking them out. He doesn't give away much, does he?''

Raven uttered a noncommittal sound and shrugged. It was time, she decided, to change the subject. ''Have you seen Steve? I suppose I should fight my way through and say hello.''

It was a typical enough party, Raven decided. Clothes ranged from Rive Gauche to Salvation Army. There was a steady drum beat from the band by the pool underlying the talk and laughter. The doors to the terrace were open wide, letting out the clouds of smoke and allowing the warm night air to circulate freely. The expansive lawns were ablaze with colored lights. Raven was more interested in the people but gave the room itself a quick survey.

It was decorated stunningly in white—walls, furniture, rugs—with a few vivid green accents slashed here and there. Raven decided it was gorgeous and that she couldn't have lived in it in a million years. She'd never be able to put her feet up on the elegant, free-form glass coffee table. She went back to the people.

Her eyes sought out Julie with her handsome Italian millionaire. She spotted Wayne with one of his bone-thin models hanging on his arm. Raven decided that the rumors that he would design the costumes for *Fantasy* must be true. There were others Raven recognized: producers, two major stars whom she had watched countless times in darkened theaters, a choreographer she knew only by face and reputation, a screenwriter she had met before socially and several others whom she knew casually or not at all. She and Carly were both drawn into the vortex of the party.

There were dozens of greetings to exchange, along with hand-kissing and cheek-brushing, before Raven could begin to inch her way back toward the edges. She was always more comfortable with one or two people at a time than with a crowd, unless she was onstage. At a touch on her arm, she turned and found herself facing her host.

"Well, hello." Raven smiled, appreciating the chance for a tête-à-tête.

"Hi. I was afraid you weren't going to make it."

Raven realized she shouldn't have been surprised that he had noticed her absence in the crowds of people. Steve Jarett noticed everything. He was a small, slight man with a pale, intense face and dark beard who looked ten years younger than his thirty-seven years. He was considered a perfectionist, often a pain when shooting, but the maker of beautiful films. He had a reputation for patience—enough to cause him to shoot a scene over and over and over again until he got precisely what he wanted. Five years before, he had stunned the industry with a low-budget sleeper that had become the unchallenged hit of the year. His first film had received an Oscar and had opened all the doors that had previously been firmly shut in his face. Steve Jarett held the keys now and knew exactly which ones to use.

He held both of her hands and studied her face. It

was he who had insisted on Brand Carstairs as the writer of the original score for *Fantasy* and he who had approved the choice of Raven Williams as collaborator. *Fantasy* was his first musical, and he wasn't going to make any mistakes.

"Lauren's here," he said at length. "Have you met her?"

"No, I'd like to."

"I'd like you to get a real feel for her. I've copies of all of her films and records. You might study them before you begin work on the score."

Raven's brow rose. "I don't think I've missed any of her movies, but I'll watch them again. She is the core of the story."

He beamed suddenly, unexpectedly. "Exactly. And you know Jack Ladd."

"Yes, we've worked together before. You couldn't have picked a better Joe."

"I'm making him work off ten pounds," Jarett said, plucking a canape from a tray. "He has some very unflattering things to say about me at the moment."

"But he's taking off the ten pounds," Raven observed.

Jarett grinned. "Ounce by ounce. We go to the same gym. I keep reminding him Joe's a struggling writer, not a fulfilled hedonist."

Raven gave a low, gurgling laugh and popped a bite of cheese into her mouth. "Overweight or not, you're assembling a remarkable team. I don't know how you

managed to wrangle Larry Keaston into choreograph-
ing. He's been retired for five years."

"Bribes and perseverance," Jarett said easily,
glancing over to where the trim, white-haired former
dancer lounged in a pearl-colored armchair. "I'm talking him into doing a cameo." He grinned at Raven
again. "He's pretending dignified reluctance, but he's
dying to get in front of the cameras again."

"If you can even get him to do a time step on film,
you'll have the biggest coup of the decade," Raven
observed and shook her head. And he'd do it, she
thought. He has the touch.

"He's a big fan of yours," Jarett remarked and
watched Raven's eyes widen.

"Of mine? You're joking."

"I am not." He gave Raven a curious look. "He
wants to meet you."

Raven stared at Jarett, then again at Larry Keaston.
Such things never ceased to amaze her. How many
times, as a child, had she watched his movies on fuzzy
black and white TV sets in cramped rooms while she
had waited for her mother to come home? "You don't
have to ask me twice," she told Jarett. She linked her
arm in his.

Time passed quickly as Raven began enjoying herself. She talked at length with Larry Keaston and discovered her girlhood idol to be personable and witty.
He spoke in a string of expletives delivered in his posh
Boston accent. Though she spoke briefly with Jack

Ladd, she had yet to meet Lauren Chase when she spotted Wayne drinking quietly in a corner.

"All alone?" she asked as she joined him.

"Observing the masses, my dear," he told her, sipping lightly from his whiskey and soda. "It's amazing how intelligent people will insist on clothing themselves in inappropriate costumes. Observe Lela Marring," he suggested, tilting his head toward a towering brunette in a narrow, pink minidress. "I have no idea why a woman would care to wear a place mat in public."

Raven suppressed a giggle. "She has very nice legs."

"Yes, all five feet of them." He swerved his line of vision. "Then, of course, there's Marshall Peters, who's trying to start a new trend. Chest hair and red satin."

Raven followed the direction of his gaze and this time did giggle. "Not everyone has your savoir-faire, Wayne."

"Of course not," he agreed readily and took out one of his imported cigarettes. "But surely, taste."

"I like the way you've dressed your latest protégée," Raven commented, nodding toward the thin model speaking to a current hot property in the television series game. The model was draped in cobwebby black and gold filigree lace. "I swear, Wayne, she can't be more than eighteen. What do you find to talk about?"

He gave Raven one of his long, sarcastic looks. "Are you being droll, darling?"

She laughed in spite of herself. "Not intentionally."

He gave her a pat on the cheek and lifted his glass again. "I notice Julie has her latest conquest with her, a Latin type with cheekbones."

"Shoes," Raven said vaguely, letting her eyes drift around the room. They rested in disbelief on a girl dressed in skin-tight leather pants and a spangled sweatshirt who wore heart-shaped glasses over heavily kohl-darkened eyes. Knowing Wayne would be horrified, she started to call his attention to her when she spotted Brand across the room.

His eyes were already on hers. Raven realized with a jolt that he had been watching her for some time. It had been at just such a party that they had first met, with noise and laughter and music all around them. Their eyes had found each other's then also.

It had been Raven's first Hollywood party, and she had been unashamedly overwhelmed. There had been people there whom she had known only as voices over the radio or faces on the screen. She had come alone then, too, but in that case it had been a mistake. She hadn't yet learned how to dodge and twist.

She remembered she had been cornered by an actor, though oddly she couldn't recall his name or his face. She hadn't had the experience to deal with him and was slowly being backed against the wall when her eyes had met Brand's. Raven remembered how he had been watching her then, too, rather lazily, a half smile on his mouth. He must have seen the desperation in her eyes, because his smile had widened before he had started to weave his way through the crowd toward her. With perfect aplomb, Brand had slid between Raven and the actor, then had draped his arm over her shoulders.

"Miss me?" he had asked, and he had kissed her lightly before she could respond. "There're some people outside who want to meet you." He had shot the actor an apologetic glance. "Excuse us."

Before another word could be exchanged, he had propelled Raven through the groups of people and out to a terrace. She could still remember the scent of orange blossoms that had drifted from an orchard nearby and the silver sprinkle of moonlight on the flagstone.

Of course Raven had recognized him and had been flustered. She had managed to regain her poise by the time they were alone in the shadows on the terrace. She had brushed a hand through her hair and smiled at him. "Thanks."

"You're welcome." It had been the first time he had studied her in his direct, quiet fashion. She could still remember the sensation of gentle intrusion. "You're not quite what I expected."

"No?" Raven hadn't known exactly how to take that.

"No." He'd smiled at her. "Would you like to go get some coffee?"

"Yes." The agreement had sprung from her lips before she had given it a moment's thought.

"Good. Let's go." Brand had held out his hand. After a brief hesitation, Raven had put hers into it. It had been as simple as that.

"Raven…Raven."

She was tossed back into the present by the sound of Wayne's voice and his hand on her arm.

"Yes…what?" Blandly Raven looked up at him.

"Your thoughts are written all over your face," he murmured. "Not a wise move in a room full of curious people." Taking a fresh glass of champagne from a tray, he handed it to her. "Drink up."

She was grateful for something to do with her hands and took the glass. "I was just thinking," she said inadequately, then made a sound of frustration at Wayne's dry look. "So," she tried another tactic, "it seems we'll be working on the same project."

"Old home week?" he said with a crooked grin.

She shot him a direct look. "We're professionals," she stated, aware that they both knew whom she was speaking of.

"And friends?" he asked, touching a finger to her cheek.

Raven inclined her head. "We might be; I'm a friendly sort of person."

"*Hmm.*" Wayne glanced over her shoulder and watched Brand approach. "At least he knows how to dress," he murmured, approving of Brand's casual but perfectly cut slate-colored slacks and jacket. "But are you sure Cornwall's necessary? Couldn't you try Sausalito?''

Raven laughed. ''Is there anything you don't know?''

''I certainly hope not. Hello, Brand, nice to see you again.''

Raven turned, smiling easily. The jolt of the memory had passed. ''Hello, Brandon.''

''Raven.'' His eyes stayed on her face. ''You haven't met Lauren Chase.''

With an effort Raven shifted her eyes from his. ''No.'' She smiled and looked at the woman at his side.

Lauren Chase was a slender wisp of a woman with a thick mane of dark, chestnut hair and sea-green eyes. There was something ethereal about her. Perhaps, Raven thought, it was that pale, almost translucent skin or the way she had of walking as though her feet barely touched the ground. She had a strong mouth that folded itself in at the corners and a long, slender neck that she adorned with gold chains. Raven knew she was well into her thirties and decided she looked it. This was a woman who needn't rely on dewy youth for her beauty.

She had been married twice. The first divorce had become an explosive affair that had received a great deal of ugly press. Her second marriage was now seven years old and had produced two children. Raven recalled there was little written about Lauren Chase's current personal life. Obviously, she had learned to guard her privacy.

"Brand tells me you're going to put the heart in the music." Lauren's voice was full and rich.

"That's quite a responsibility." Raven shot Brand a glance. "Generally Brand considers my lyrics on the sentimental side; often I consider him a cynic."

"Good." Lauren smiled. "Then we should have a score with some meat in it. Steve's given me final word on my own numbers."

Raven lifted a brow. She wasn't altogether certain if this had been a warning or a passing remark. "Then I suppose we should keep you up to date on our progress," she said agreeably.

"By mail and phone," Lauren said, slanting a glance at Brand, "since you're traipsing off halfway around the world to write."

"Artistic temperament," Brand said easily.

"No question, he has it," Raven assured her.

"You should know, I suppose." Lauren lifted a shoulder. Abruptly she fixed Raven with a sharp, straight look. "I want a lot out of this score. This is the one I've been waiting for." It was both a challenge and a demand.

Raven met the look with a slow nod. Lauren Chase was, she decided, the perfect Tessa. "You'll get it."

Lauren touched her upper lip with the tip of her tongue and smiled again. "Yes, I do believe I will at that. Well," she said, turning to Wayne and linking her arm through his, "why don't you get me a drink and tell me about the fabulous costumes you're going to design for me?''

Raven watched them move away. "That," she murmured, toying with the stem of her glass, "is a woman who knows what she wants."

"And she wants an Oscar," Brand remarked. Raven's eyes came back to his. "You'll remember she's been nominated three times and edged out three times. She's determined it isn't going to happen again." He smiled then, fingering the dangling amethyst Raven wore at her ear. "Wouldn't you like to bag one yourself?"

"That's funny, I'd forgotten we could." She let the thought play in her mind. "It sounds good, but we'd better get the thing written before we dream up an acceptance speech."

"How're rehearsals going?"

"Good. Very good." She sipped absently at her champagne. "The band's tight. You leave for Vegas soon, don't you?"

"Yes. Did you come alone?"

She glanced back at him, confused for a moment. "Here? Why, yes. I was late because I'd forgotten about it altogether, but Julie left me a note. Did she introduce you to Lorenzo?"

"No, we haven't crossed paths tonight." As she had begun to search the crowd for Julie, Brand took her chin to bring her eyes back to his. "Will you let me take you home?"

Her expression shifted from startled to wary. "I have my car, Brandon."

"That isn't an answer."

Raven felt herself being drawn in and struggled. "It wouldn't be a good idea."

"Wouldn't it?" She sensed the sarcasm before he smiled, bent down and kissed her. It was a light touch—a tease, a promise or a challenge? "You could be right." He touched her earring again and set it swinging. "I'll see you in a few weeks," he said with a friendly grin, then turned and merged back into the crowd.

Raven stared after him, hardly realizing she had touched her lips with her tongue to seek his taste.

Chapter 6

The theater was dark and quiet. The sound of Raven's footsteps echoed, amplified by the excellent acoustics. Very soon the quiet would be shattered by stagehands, grips, electricians, all the many backstage people who would put together the essential and hardly noticed details of the show. Voices would bounce, mingling with hammering and other sounds of wood and metal. The noise would have a hollow, empty tone, almost like her footsteps. But it was an important sound, an appealing sound, which Raven had always enjoyed.

But she enjoyed the quiet, too and often found herself roaming an empty theater long before she was needed for rehearsals, hours before the fans started to line up outside the main doors. The press would be there then, with their everlasting, eternal questions. And Raven wasn't feeling too chummy with the press at the moment. Already she'd seen a half dozen different stories about herself and Brandon—speculation about their pending collaboration on *Fantasy* and rehashes of their former relationship. Old pictures had been dredged up and reprinted. Old questions were being asked again. Each time it was like bumping the same bruise.

Twice a week she put through a call to the Fieldmore Clinic and held almost identical conversations with Karter. Twice a week he transferred her to her mother's room. Though she knew it was foolish, Raven began to believe all the promises again, all the tearful vows. She began to hope. Without the demands of the tour to keep her occupied and exhausted, she knew she would have been an emotional wreck. Not for the first time in her life, she blessed her luck and her voice.

Mounting the stage, Raven turned to face an imaginary audience. The rows of seats seemed to roll back like a sea. But she knew how to navigate it, had known from the first moment of her first concert. She was an innate performer, just as her voice was natural and untrained. The hesitation, the uncertainty she felt now, had to do with the woman, not the singer. The song had hovered in her mind, but she still paused and considered before bringing it into play. Memories, she felt, could be dangerous things. But she needed to prove something to herself, so she sang. Her voice lifted, drifting to the far corners of the theater; her only accompaniment was her imagination.

Through the clouds and the rain
You were there,
And the sun came through to find us.

Oversentimental? She hadn't thought so when the words had been written. Now Raven sang what she hadn't sung in years. Two minutes and forty-three seconds that bound her and Brand together. Whenever it had played on the radio, she had switched it off, and never, though the requests had been many, had she ever incorporated it in an album or in a concert. She sang it now as a kind of test, remembering the drifting, almost aching harmony of her own low tones combined with Brand's clean, cool voice. She needed to be able to face the memory of working with him if she was to face the reality of doing so. The tour had reached its halfway point. There were only two weeks remaining.

It didn't hurt the way she had been afraid it would; there was no sharp slap across the face. There was more of a warm ache, almost pleasant, somehow sexual. She remembered the last time she had been in Brand's arms in the quiet car in the hills above L.A.

"I've never heard you sing that."

Caught off-guard, Raven swung around to stage right, her hand flying in quick panic to her throat. "Oh, Marc!" On a laugh, she let out a long breath.

"You scared the wits out of me. I didn't know anyone was here."

"I didn't want you to stop. I've only heard the cut you and Carstairs made of that." He came forward now out of the shadows, and she saw he had an acoustic guitar slung over his shoulder. It was typical; she rarely saw him without an instrument in his hands or close by. "I've always thought it was too bad you never used it again; it's one of your best. But I guess you didn't want to sing it with anyone else."

Raven looked at him with genuine surprise. Of course, that had been the essential reason, but she hadn't realized it herself until that moment. "No, I guess I didn't." She smiled at him. "I guess I still don't. Did you come here to practice?"

"I called your room. Julie said you'd probably be here." He walked to her, and since there were no chairs, he sat on the floor. Raven sat with him. She crossed her legs in the dun-colored trousers and let her hair fall over the soft shoulders of her topaz angora sweater. She was relaxed with him, ready to talk or jam like any musician.

Raven smiled at Marc as he went through a quick, complicated lick. "I'm glad you came by. Sometimes I have to get the feel of the theater before a performance. They all begin to run together at this part of a tour." Raven closed her eyes and tilted her head, shaking her hair back. "Where are we, Kansas City? God, I hate the thought of getting back on that airplane. Shuttle here, shuttle there. It always hits me like this at the halfway point. In a couple of days I'll have my second wind.''

Marc let her ramble while he played quick, quiet runs on the guitar. He watched her hands as they lay still on her knees. They were very narrow, and although they were tanned golden brown, they remained fragile. There was a light tracing of blue vein just under the skin. The nails were not long but well-shaped and painted in some clear, hardening polish with a blush of pink. There were no rings. Because they were motionless, he knew she was relaxed. Whatever nerves he had sensed when he had first spoken to her were stilled now.

"It's been going well, I think," she continued. "The Glass House is a terrific warm-up act, and the band's tight, even though we lost Kelly. The new bass is good, don't you think?"

"Knows his stuff," Marc said briefly. Raven grinned and reached over to tug his beard.

"So do you," she said. "Let me try."

Agreeably Marc slipped the strap over his head, then handed Raven his guitar. She was a better-than-average player, although she took a great deal of ribbing from the musicians in her troupe whenever she attempted the guitar. Periodically she threatened them with a bogus plan to incorporate her semiskillful playing into the act.

Still she liked to make music with the six strings. It soothed her. There was something intimate about holding an instrument close, feeling its vibrations against your own body. After hitting the same wrong note twice, Raven sighed, then wrinkled her nose at Marc's grin.

"I'm out of practice," she claimed, handing him back his Gibson.

"Good excuse."

"It's probably out of tune."

He ran quickly up and down the scales. "Nope."

"You might be kind and lie." She changed position, putting her feet flat on the floor and lacing her hands over her knees. "It's a good thing you're a musician. You'd have made a lousy politician."

"Too much traveling," he said as his fingers began to move again. He liked the sound of her laughter as it echoed around the empty theater.

"Oh, you're right! How can anyone remain sane going from city to city day after day? And music's such a stable business, too."

"Sturdy as a crap table."

"You've a gift for analogy," she told him, watching the skill of his fingers on the strings. "I love to watch you play," she continued. "It's so effortless. When Brandon was first teaching me, I..." but the words trailed off. Marc glanced up at her face, but his fingers never faltered. "I—it was difficult," she went on, wondering what had made her bring up the matter, "because he was left-handed, and naturally his guitar was, too. He bought me one of my own, but watching him, I had to learn backwards." She laughed, pleased with the memory. Absently she lifted a hand to toy with the thick, dangling staff of her earring. "Maybe that's why I play the way I do. I'm always having to twist it around in my head before it can get to my fingers."

She lapsed into silence while Marc continued to play. It was soothing and somehow intimate with the two of them alone in the huge, empty theater. But his music didn't sound lonely as it echoed. She began to sing with it quietly, as though they were at home, seated on a rug with the walls close and comforting around them.

It was true that the tour had tired her and that the midway point had her feeling drained. But the interlude here was lifting her, though in a different way than the audience would lift her that night. This wasn't the quick, dizzying high that shot endurance back into her for the time she was on stage and in the lights. This was a steadying hand, like a good night's sleep or a home-cooked meal. She smiled at Marc when the song was over and said again, "I'm glad you came."

He looked at her, and for once his hands were silent on the strings. "How long have I been with you, Raven?"

She thought back to when Marc had first become a semiregular part of her troupe. "Four—four and a half—years."

"Five this summer," he corrected. "It was in August, and you were rehearsing for your second tour. You had on baggy white pants and a T-shirt with a rainbow on it. You were barefoot. You had a lost look in your eyes. Carstairs had gone back to England about a month before.''

Raven stared at him. She had never heard him make such a long speech. ''Isn't it strange that you would remember what I was wearing? It doesn't sound very impressive.''

''I remember because I fell in love with you on the spot.''

''Oh, Marc.'' She searched for something to say and found nothing. Instead, she reached up and took his hand. She knew he meant exactly what he said.

''Once or twice I've come close to asking you to live with me.''

Raven let out a quick breath. ''Why didn't you?''

''Because it would have hurt you to have said no and it would have hurt me to hear it.'' He laid the guitar across his lap and leaning over it, kissed her.

''I didn't know,'' she murmured, pressing both of his hands to her cheeks. ''I should have. I'm sorry.''

''You've never gotten him out of your head, Raven. It's damn frustrating competing with a memory.'' Marc squeezed her hands a moment, then released them. ''It's also safe. I knew you'd never make a commitment to me, so I could avoid making one to you.'' He shrugged his well-muscled shoulders. ''I think it always scared me that you were the kind of woman who would make a man give everything because you asked for nothing.''

Her brows drew together. ''Am I?''

''You need someone who can stand up to you. I'd

never have been able to. I'd never have been able to say no or shout at you or make crazy love. Life's nothing without things like that, and we'd have ended up hurting each other.''

She tilted her head and studied him. ''Why are you telling me all this now?''

''Because I realized when I watched you singing that I'll always love you but I'll never have you. And if I did, I'd lose something very special.'' He reached across to touch her hair. ''A fantasy that warms you on cold nights and makes you feel young again when you're old. Sometimes might-have-beens can be very precious.''

Raven didn't know whether to smile or to cry. ''I haven't hurt you?''

''No,'' he said so simply she knew he spoke the truth. ''You've made me feel good. Have I made you uncomfortable?''

''No.'' She smiled at him. ''You've made me feel good.''

He grinned, then rose and held out a hand to her. ''Let's go get some coffee.''

Brand changed into jeans in his dressing room. It was after two in the morning, but he was wide-awake, still riding on energy left over from his last show. He'd go out, he decided, and put some of it to use at the blackjack table. He could grab Eddie or one of the other guys from the band and cruise the casinos.

There'd be women. Brand knew there'd be a throng

of them waiting for him when he left the privacy of his dressing room. He could take his pick. But he didn't want a woman. He wanted a drink and some cards and some action; anything to use up the adrenaline speeding through his system.

He reached for his shirt, and the mirror reflected his naked torso. It was tight and lean, teetering on being thin, but there were surprising cords of muscles in the arms and shoulders. He'd had to use them often when he'd been a boy on the London streets. He always wondered if it had been the piano lessons his mother had insisted on that had saved him from being another victim of the streets. Music had opened up something for him. He hadn't been able to get enough, learn enough. It had been like food, and he had been starving.

At fifteen Brand had started his own band. He was tough and cocky and talked his way into cheap little dives. There had been women even then; not just girls, but women attracted by his youthful sexuality and arrogant confidence. But they'd only been part of the adventure. He had never given up, though the living had been lean in the beer-soaked taverns. He had pulled his way up and made a local reputation for himself; both his music and his personality were strong.

It had taken time. He had been twenty when he had cut his first record, and it had gone nowhere. Brand had recognized that its failure had been due to a combination of poor quality recording, mismanagement and his own see-if-I-care attitude. He had taken a few steps back, found a savvy manager, worked hard on arrangements and talked himself into another recording session.

Two years later he had bought his family a house in the London suburbs, pushed his younger brother into a university and set off on his first American tour.

Now, at thirty, there were times he felt he'd never been off the merry-go-round. Half his life had been given over to his career and its demands. He was tired of wandering. Brand wanted something to focus his life, something to center it. He knew he couldn't give up music, but it wasn't enough by itself anymore. His family wasn't enough, and neither was the money or the applause.

He knew what he wanted. He had known five years before, but there were times he didn't feel as sure of himself as he had when he had been a fifteen-year-old punk talking his way past the back door of a third-rate nightclub. A capacity crowd had just paid thirty dollars a head to hear him, and he knew he could afford to take every cent he made on that two-week gig and throw it away on one roll of the dice. He had an urge to do it. He was restless, reckless, running on the same nerves he had felt the night he'd taken Raven home from their dinner date. He'd only seen her once after that—at Steve Jarett's house. Almost immediately afterward he had flown to Las Vegas to begin polishing his act.

It was catching up with him now—the tension, the

anger, the needs. Not for the first time, Brand wondered whether his unreasonable need for her would end if he could have her once, just once. With quick, impatient movements, he thrust the tail of his shirt into the waist of his jeans. He knew better, but there were times he wished it could be. He left the dressing room looking for company.

For an hour Brand sat at the blackjack table. He lost a little, won a little, then lost it again. His mind wasn't on the cards. He had thought the noise, the bright lights, the rich smell of gambling was what he had wanted. There was a thin, intense woman beside him with a huge chunk of diamond on her finger and sapphires around her neck. She drank and lost at the same steady rhythm. Across the table was a young couple he pegged as honeymooners. The gold band on the girl's finger looked brilliantly new and untested. They were giddy with winning what Brand figured was about thirty dollars. There was something touching in their pleasure and in the soft, exchanged looks. All around them came the endless chinkity-chink of the slots.

Brand found himself as restless as he had been an hour before in his dressing room. A half-empty glass of bourbon sat at his elbow, but he left it as he rose. He didn't want the casino, and he felt an enormous surge of envy for the man who had his woman and thirty dollars worth of chips.

When he entered his suite, it was dark and silent, a sharp contrast to the world he had just left. Brand didn't bother hitting the switches as he made his way into the bedroom. Taking out a cigarette, he sat on the bed before lighting it. The flame made a sharp hiss and a brief flare. He sat with the silence, but the adrenaline still pumped. Finally he switched on the small bedside lamp and picked up the phone.

Raven was deep in sleep, but the ringing of the phone shot panic through her before she was fully awake. Her heart pounded in her throat before the mists could clear. She'd grown up with calls coming in the middle of the night. She forgot where she was and fumbled for the phone with a sense of dread and anticipation.

"Yes…hello."

"Raven, I know I woke you. I'm sorry."

She tried to shake away the fog. "Brandon? Is something wrong? Are you all right?"

"Yes, I'm fine. Just unbelievably inconsiderate."

Relaxing, Raven sank back on the pillows and tried to orient herself. "You're in Vegas, aren't you?" The dim light told her it was nearing dawn. He was two hours behind her. Or was it three? She couldn't for the life of her remember what time zone she was in.

"Yes, I'm in Vegas through next week."

"How's the show going?"

It was typical of her, he mused, not to demand to know why the hell he had called her in the middle of the night. She would simply accept that he needed to talk. He drew on the cigarette and wished he could touch her. "Better than my luck at the tables."

She laughed, comfortably sleepy. The connection was clean and sharp; he didn't sound hundreds of miles away. "Is it still blackjack?"

"I'm consistent," he murmured. "How's Kansas?"

"Where?" He laughed, pleasing her. "The audience was fantastic," she continued, letting her mind wander back to the show. "Has been straight along. That's the only thing that keeps you going on a tour like this. Will you be there in time for the show in New York? I'd love you to hear the warm-up act."

"I'll be there." He lay back on the bed as some of the superfluous energy started to drain. "Cornwall is sounding more and more appealing."

"You sound tired."

"I wasn't; I am now. Raven..."

She waited, but he didn't speak. "Yes?"

"I missed you. I needed to hear your voice. Tell me what you're looking at," he demanded, "what you see right now."

"It's dawn," she told him. "Or nearly. I can't see any buildings, just the sky. It's more mauve than gray and the light's very soft and thin." She smiled; it had been a long time since she had seen a day begin. "It's really lovely, Brandon. I'd forgotten."

"Will you be able to sleep again?" He had closed his eyes; the fatigue was taking over.

"Yes, but I'd rather go for a walk, though I don't think Julie would appreciate it if I asked her to come along."

Brand pried off his shoes, using the toe of one foot,

then the other. "Go back to sleep, and we'll walk on the cliffs one morning in Cornwall. I shouldn't have woken you."

"No, I'm glad you did." She could hear the change; the voice that had been sharp and alert was now heavy. "Get some rest, Brandon. I'll look for you in New York."

"All right. Good night, Raven."

He was asleep almost before he hung up. Fifteen hundred miles away, Raven laid her cheek on the pillow and watched the morning come.

Chapter 7

Raven tried to be still while her hair was being twisted and knotted and groomed. Her dressing room was banked with flowers; they had been arriving steadily for more than two hours. And it was crowded with people. A tiny little man with sharp, black eyes touched up her blusher. Behind her, occasionally muttering in French, was the nimble-fingered woman who did her hair. Wayne was there, having business of his own here in New York. He'd told Raven that he'd come to see his designs in action and was even now in deep discussion with her dresser. Julie opened the door to another flower delivery.

"Have I packed everything? You know, I should have told Brandon to give me an extra day in town for shopping. There're probably a dozen things I need.'' Raven turned in her seat and heard the swift French oath as her partially knotted hair flew from the woman's fingers. ''Sorry, Marie. Julie, did I pack a coat? I might need one.'' Slipping the card from the latest arrangement of flowers, she found it was from a successful television producer with whom she'd worked on her last TV special. ''They're from Max.... There's a party tonight. Why don't you go?'' She handed the card to Julie and allowed her lip liner to be straightened by the finicky makeup artist.

''Yes, you packed a coat, your suede, which you could need this early in the spring. And several sweaters,'' Julie said distractedly, checking her list. ''And maybe I will.''

''I can't believe this is it, the last show. It's been a good tour, hasn't it, Julie?'' Raven turned her head and winced at the sharp tug on her hair.

''I can't remember you ever getting a better response or deserving one more....''

''And we're all glad it's over,'' Raven finished for her.

''I'm going to sleep for a week.'' Julie found space for the flowers, then continued to check off things in her notebook. ''Not everyone has your constant flow of energy.''

''I love playing New York,'' she said, tucking up her legs to the despair of her hairdresser.

''You must hold still!''

''Marie, if I hold still much longer, I'm going to explode.'' Raven smiled at the makeup artist as he fussed around her face. "You always know just what to do. It looks perfect; I feel beautiful."

Recognizing the signal, Julie began nudging people from the room. Eventually they went, and soon only Julie and Wayne were left. The room quieted considerably; now the walls hummed gently with the vibrations of the warm-up act. Raven let out a deep sigh.

"I'll be so glad to have my face and body and hair back," she said and sprawled in the chair. "You should have seen what he made me put all over my face this morning."

"What was it?" Wayne asked absently as he smoothed the hem of one of her costumes.

"Green," she told him and shuddered.

He laughed and turned to Julie. "What are you going to do when this one takes off to the moors?"

"Cruise the Greek Islands and recuperate." She pushed absently at the small of her back. "I've already booked passage on the ninth. These tours are brutal."

"Listen to her." Raven sniffed and peered at herself critically in the glass. "She's the one who's held the whip and chair for four weeks. He certainly makes me look exotic, doesn't he?" She wrinkled her nose and spoiled the effect.

"Into costume," Julie commanded.

"See? Orders, orders." Obediently Raven rose.

"Here." Wayne lifted the red and silver dress from the hanger. "Since I nudged your dresser along, I'll be your minion."

"Oh, good, thanks." She stepped out of her robe

and into the dress. "You know, Wayne," she continued as he zipped her up, "you were right about the black number. It gets a tremendous response. I never know if they're applauding me or the costume after that set."

"Have I ever let you down?" he demanded as he tucked a pleat.

"No." She turned her head to smile at him over her shoulder. "Never. Will you miss me?"

"Tragically." He kissed her ear.

There was a brief, brisk knock at the door. "Ten minutes, Ms. Williams."

She took a long breath. "Are you going to go out front?"

"I'll stay back with Julie." He glanced over at her, lifting a brow in question.

"Yes, thanks. Here, Raven, don't forget these wonderfully gaudy earrings." She watched Raven fasten one. "Really, Wayne, they're enough to make me shudder, but they're fabulous with that dress."

"Naturally."

She laughed, shaking her head. "The man's ego," she said to Raven, "never ceases to amaze me."

"As long as it doesn't outdistance the talent," he put in suavely.

"New York audiences are tough." Raven spoke quickly, her voice jumping suddenly with nerves and excitement. "They scare me to death."

"I thought you said you loved playing New York." Wayne took out a cigarette and offered one to Julie.

"I do, especially at the end of a tour. It keeps you sharp. They're really going to know if I'm not giving them everything. How do I look?"

"The dress is sensational," Wayne decided. "You'll do."

"Some help you are."

"Let's go," Julie urged. "You'll miss your cue."

"I never miss my cue." Raven fussed with the second earring, stalling. He'd said he'd be here, she told herself. *Why isn't he?* He could have gotten the time mixed up, or he could be caught in traffic. Or he could simply have forgotten that he'd promised to be here for the show.

The quick knock came again. "Five minutes, Ms. Williams."

"Raven." Julie's voice was a warning.

"Yes, yes, all right." She turned and gave them both a flippant smile. "Tell me I'm wonderful when it's over, even if I wasn't. I want to end the tour feeling marvelous."

Then she was dashing for the door and hurrying down the hall where the sounds of the warm-up band were no longer gentle; now they shook the walls.

"Ms. Williams, Ms. Williams! Raven!"

She turned, breaking the concentration she'd been building and looked at the harried stage manager. He thrust a white rose into her hand.

"Just came back for you."

Raven took the bud and lifted it, wanting to fill herself with the scent. She needed no note or message to tell her it was from Brand. For a moment she simply dreamed over it.

"Raven." The warm-up act had finished; the transition to her own band would take place on the darkened stage quickly. "You're going to miss your cue."

"No, I'm not." She gave the worried stage manager a kiss, forgetful of her carefully applied lipstick. Twirling the rose between her fingers, she took it with her. They were introducing her as she reached the wings.

Big build-up; don't let the audience cool down. They were already cheering for her. *Thirty seconds; take a breath.* Her band hit her introduction. Music crashed through the cheers. *One, two, three!*

She ran out, diving into a wave of applause.

The first set was hot and fast, staged to keep the audience up and wanting more. She seemed to be a ball of flame with hundreds of colored lights flashing around her. Raven knew how to play to them, play with them, and she pumped all her energy into a routine she had done virtually every night for four weeks. Enthusiasm and verve kept it fresh. It was hot under the lights, but she didn't notice. She was wrapping herself in the audience, in the music. The costume sizzled and sparked. Her voice smoked.

It was a demanding forty minutes, and when she rushed offstage during an instrumental break, she had less than three minutes in which to change costumes. Now she was in white, a brief, shimmering top covered with bugle beads matched with thin harem pants.

The pace would slow a bit, giving the audience time to catch their breath. The balance was in ballads, the slow trembling ones she did best. The lighting was muted, soft and moody.

It was during a break between songs, when she traditionally talked to the audience, that someone in the audience spotted Brand in their midst. Soon more people knew, and while Raven went on unaware of the disturbance, the crowd soon became vocal. Shielding her eyes, she could just make out the center of the commotion. Then she saw him. It seemed they wanted him up on stage.

Raven was a good judge of moods and knew the value of showmanship. If she didn't invite Brand on stage, she'd lose the crowd. They had already taken the choice out of her hands.

"Brandon." Raven spoke softly into the mike, but her voice carried. Though she couldn't see his eyes with the spotlight in her own, she knew he was looking at her. "If you come up and sing," she told him, lightly, "we might get you a refund on your ticket." She knew he'd grin at that. There was an excited rush of applause and cheers as he rose and came to the stage.

He was all in black: trim, well-cut slacks and a casual polo sweater. The contrast was striking as he stood beside her. It might have been planned. Smiling at her, he spoke softly, out of the range of the microphone. "I'm sorry, Raven, I should have gone backstage. I wanted to watch you from out front."

She tilted her head. It was, she discovered, more wonderful to see him than she had imagined. "You're the one being put to work. What would you like to do?"

Before he could answer, the demands sprang from the crowd. Once the idea formed, it was shouted over and over with growing enthusiasm. Raven's smile faded. "Clouds and Rain."

Brand took her wrist and lifted the rose she held. "You remember the words, don't you?"

It was a challenge. A stagehand rushed out with a hand mike for Brand.

"My band doesn't know it," she began.

"I know it." Marc shifted his guitar and watched them. The crowd was still shouting when he gave the opening chords. "We'll follow you."

Brand kept his hand on Raven's wrist and lifted his own mike.

Raven knew how it needed to be sung: face to face, eye to eye. It was a caress of a song, meant for lovers. The audience was silent now. Their harmony was close, intricate. Raven had once thought it must be like making love. Their voices flowed into each other. And she forgot the audience, forgot the stage and for a moment forgot the five years.

There was more intimacy in singing with him than she had ever allowed in any other aspect of their relationship. Here she could not resist him. When he sang to her, it was as if he told her there wasn't anyone else, had never been anyone else. It was more moving than a kiss, more sexual than a touch.

When they finished, their voices hung a moment, locked together. Brand saw her lips tremble before he brought her close and took them.

They might have been on an island rather than on stage, spotlighted for thousands. She didn't hear the tumultuous applause, the cheers, the shouting of their names. Her arms went around him, one hand holding the mike, the other the rose. Cameras flashed like fireworks, but she was trapped in a velvet darkness. She lost all sense of time; her lips might have moved on his for hours or days or only seconds. But when he drew her away, she felt a keener sense of loss than any she had ever known before. Brand saw the confusion in her eyes, the dazed desire, and smiled.

"You're better than you ever were, Raven." He kissed her hand. "Too bad about those sentimental numbers you keep sticking into the act."

Her brows rose. "Try to boost your flagging career by letting you sing with me, and you insult me." Her balance was returning as they took a couple of elaborate bows, hands linked.

"Let's see if you can carry the rest on your own, love. I've warmed them back up for you." He kissed her again, but lightly now, on the cheek, before he waved to the audience and strolled offstage left.

Raven grinned at his back, then turned to her audience. "Too bad he never made it, isn't it?"

* * *

Raven should have been wrung dry after the two hours were over. But she wasn't. She'd given them three encores, and though they clamored for more, Brand caught her hand as she hesitated in the wings.

"They'll keep you out there all night, Raven." He could feel the speed of her pulse under his fingers. Because he knew how draining two hours onstage could be, he urged her back down the hall toward her dressing room.

There were crowds of people jammed in together in the hallway, congratulating her, touching her. Now and then a reporter managed to elbow through to shoot out a question. She answered, and Brandon tossed off remarks with quick charm while steering her determinedly toward her dressing room. Once inside, he locked the door.

"I think they liked me," she said gravely, then laughed and spun away from him. "I feel so good!" Her eyes lit on the bucket of ice that cradled a bottle. "Champagne?"

"I thought you'd need to console yourself after a flop like that." Brand moved over and drew out the bottle. "You'll have to open the door soon and see people. Do try to put on a cheerful front, love."

"I'll do my best." The cork popped, and the white froth fizzed a bit over the mouth of the bottle.

Brand poured two glasses to the rim and handed her one. "I meant it, Raven." He touched his glass to hers. "You were never better."

Raven smiled, bringing the glass to her lips. Again,

he felt the painful thrust of desire. Carefully Brand took the glass from her, then set both it and his own down again. "There's something I didn't finish out there tonight."

She was unprepared. Even though he drew her close slowly and took his time bringing his mouth to hers, Raven wasn't ready. It was a long, deep, kiss that mingled with the champagne. His mouth was warm on hers, seeking. His hands ran over her hips, snugly encased in the thin black jumpsuit, but she could sense he was under very tight control.

His tongue made a thorough, lengthy journey through the moist recesses of her mouth, and she responded in kind. But he wanted her to do more than give; he wanted her to want more. And she did, feeling the pull of need, the flash of passion. She could feel the texture of his long, clever fingers through the sheer material of her costume, then flesh to flesh as he brought them up to caress the back of her neck.

Her head was swimming with a myriad of sensations: excitement and power still clinging from her performance; the heady, heavy scent of mixed flowers which crowded the air; the firm press of his body against her; and desire, more complex, more insistent than she had been prepared for.

"Brandon," she murmured against his lips. She wanted him, wanted him desperately, and was afraid.

Brand drew her away, then carefully studied her face. Her eyes were like thin glass over her emotions.

"You're beautiful, Raven, one of the most beautiful women I know."

She was unsteady and tried to find her balance without clinging to him. She stepped back, resting her hand on the table that held their glasses. "One of the most?" she challenged, lifting her champagne.

"I know a lot of women." He grinned as he lifted his own glass. "Why don't you take that stuff off your face so I can see you?"

"Do you know how long I had to sit still while he troweled this stuff on?" Moving to the dressing table, she scooped up a generous glob of cold cream. Her blood was beginning to settle. "It's supposed to make me glamorous and alluring." She slathered it on.

"You make me nervous when you're glamorous, and you'd be alluring in a paper sack."

She lifted her eyes to his in the mirror. His expression was surprisingly serious. "I think that was a compliment." She smeared the white cream generously over her face and grinned. "Am I alluring now?"

Brand grinned back, then slowly let his eyes roam down her back to focus on her snugly clad bottom. "Raven, don't fish. The answer is obvious."

She began to tissue off the cream and with it the stage makeup. "Brandon. It was good to sing with you again." After removing the last of the cream from her face, Raven toyed with the stem of her champagne glass. "I always felt very special when I sang with you. I still do." He watched her chew for a moment on her bottom lip as if she was unsure about what she should say. "I imagine they'll play up that duet in the papers. They'll probably make something else out of it, especially—especially with the way we ended it."

"I like the way we ended it." Brand came over and laid his hands on her shoulders. "It should always be ended that way." He kissed the back of her neck while his eyes smiled into hers in the glass. "Are you worried about the press, Raven?"

"No, of course not. But, Brandon…"

"Do you know," he interrupted, brushing the hair away from her neck with the back of his hand, "no one else calls me that but my mother. Strange." He bent, nuzzling his lips into the sensitive curve of her neck. "You affect me in an entirely different way."

"Brandon…"

"When I was a boy," he continued, moving his lips up to her ear, "and she called me Brandon, I knew that was it. Whatever crime I'd committed had been found out. Justice was about to strike."

"I imagine you committed quite a few crimes." She forced herself to speak lightly. When she would have moved away, he turned her around to face him.

"Too many to count." He leaned to her, but instead of the kiss she expected and prepared for, he caught her bottom lip between his teeth. She clutched at his shirt as she struggled for breath and balance. Their eyes were open and on each other's, but his face dimmed, then faded, as passion clouded her vision.

Brand released her, then gave her a quick kiss on the nose. Raven ran a hand through her hair, trying to steady herself. He was tossing her back and forth too swiftly, too easily.

"Do you want to change before we let anyone in?" he asked. When she could focus again, Raven saw he was drinking champagne and watching her. There was an odd look on his face, as if, she thought, he were a boxer checking for weaknesses, looking for openings.

"I—yes." Raven brought herself back. "Yes, I think I would, but..." She glanced around the dressing room. "I don't know what I did with my clothes."

He laughed, and the look was gone from his face. Relieved, Raven laughed with him. They began to search through the flowers and sparkling costumes for her jeans and tennis shoes.

Chapter 8

It was late when they arrived at the airport. Raven was still riding on post-performance energy and chattered about everything that came into her head. She looked up at a half-moon as she and Brand transferred from limo to plane. The private jet wasn't what she had been expecting, and studying the comfortably lush interior of the main cabin helped to allay the fatigue of yet one more flight.

It was carpeted with a thick, pewter-colored shag and contained deep, leather chairs and a wide, plush sofa. There was a padded bar at one end and a doorway at the other which she discovered led into a tidy galley. "You didn't have this before," she commented as she poked her head into another room and found the bath, complete with tub.

"I bought it about three years ago." Brand sprawled on the sofa and watched her as she explored. She looked different than she had a short time before. Her face was naked now, and he found he preferred it that way. Makeup seemed to needlessly gloss over her natural beauty. She wore faded jeans and sneakers, which she immediately pried off her feet. An oversize yellow sweater left her shapeless. It made him want to run his hands under it and find her. "Do you still hate to fly?"

Raven gave him a rueful grin. "Yes. You'd think after all this time I'd have gotten over it, but…" She continued to roam the cabin, not yet able to settle. If she had to, Raven felt she could give the entire performance again. She had enough energy.

"Strap in," Brand suggested, smiling at the quick, nervous gestures. "We'll get started, then you won't even know you're in the air."

"You don't know how many times I've heard that one." Still she did as he said and waited calmly enough while he told the pilot they were ready. In a few minutes they were airborne, and she was able to unstrap and roam again.

"I know the feeling," Brand commented, watching her. She turned in silent question. "It's as though you still have one last burst of energy to get rid of. It's the way I felt that night in Vegas when I called and woke you up."

She caught back her hair with both hands. "I feel I should jog for a few miles. It might settle me down."

"How about some coffee?"

"Yes." She wandered over to a porthole and pressed her nose against it. It was black as pitch outside the glass. "Yes, coffee would be nice, then you can tell me what marvelous ideas you have forming for the score. You've probably got dozens of them."

"A few." She heard the clatter of cups. "I imagine you've some of your own."

"A few," she said, and he chuckled. Turning away from the dark window, she saw him leaning against the opening between the galley and the main cabin. "How soon do you think we'll start to fight?"

"Soon enough. Let's wait at least until we're settled into the house. Is Julie going back to L.A., or have you tied up all your loose ends there?"

A shadow visited her face. Raven thought of the one brief visit she had paid to her mother since the start of the tour. They had had a day's layover in Chicago, and she had used the spare time to make the impossible flight to the coast and back. There had been the inevitable interview with Karter and a brief, emotional visit with her mother. Raven had been relieved to see that the cast had gone from her mother's skin and that there was more flesh to her face. There had been apologies and promises and tears, just as there always were, Raven thought wearily. And as she always did, she had begun to believe them again.

"I never seem to completely tie up the loose ends," she murmured.

"Will you tell me what's wrong?"

She shook her head. She couldn't bear to dwell on unhappiness now. "No, nothing, nothing really." The kettle sang out, and she smiled. "Your cue," she told him.

He studied her for a moment while the kettle spit peevishly behind him. Then, turning, he went back into the galley to fix the coffee. "Black?" he asked, and she gave an absent assent.

Sitting on the sofa, Raven let her head fall back while the energy began to subside. It was almost as if she could feel it draining. Brand recognized the signs as soon as he came back into the room. He set down her mug of coffee, then sipped thoughtfully from his own as he watched her. Sensing him, Raven slowly opened her eyes. There was silence for a moment; her body and her mind were growing lethargic.

"What are you doing?" she murmured.

"Remembering."

Her lids shuttered down, concealing her eyes and their expression. "Don't."

He drank again, letting his eyes continue their slow, measured journey over her. "It's a bit much to ask me not to remember, Raven, isn't it?" It was a question that expected no answer, and she gave it none. But her lids fluttered up again.

He didn't have her full trust, nor did he believe he had ever had it. That was the root of their problems. He studied her while he stood and drank his coffee. There was high, natural color in her cheeks, and her eyes were dark and sleepy. She sat, as was her habit, with her legs crossed under her and her hands on her knees. In contrast to the relaxed position, her fingers moved restlessly.

"I still want you. You know that, don't you?"

Again Raven left his question unanswered, but he saw the pulse in her throat begin to thump. When she spoke, her voice was calm. "We're going to work together, Brandon. It's best not to complicate things."

He laughed, not in mockery but in genuine amusement. She watched his eyes lose their brooding intensity and light. "By all means, let's keep things simple." After draining his coffee, he walked over and sat beside her. In a smooth, practiced move, he drew her against his side. "Relax," he told her, annoyed when she resisted. "Give me some credit. I know how tired you are. When are you going to trust me, Raven?"

She tilted her head until she could see him. Her look was long and eloquent before she settled into the crook of his shoulder and let out a long sigh. Like a child, she fell asleep quickly, and like that of a child, the sleep was deep. For a long moment he stayed as he was, Raven curled against his side. Then he laid her down on the sofa, watching as her hair drifted about her.

Rising, Brand switched off the lights. In the dark he settled into one of the deep cabin chairs and lit a cigarette. Time passed as he sat gazing out at a sprinkle of stars and listening to Raven's soft, steady breathing. Unable to resist, he rose, and moving to her, lay down beside her. She stirred when he brushed the hair from her cheek, but only to snuggle closer to him. Over the raw yearning came a curiously sweet satisfaction. He wrapped his arm around her, felt her sigh, then slept.

It was Brand who awoke first. As was his habit, his mind and body came together quickly. He lay still and allowed his eyes to grow accustomed to the darkness. Beside him, curled against his chest, Raven slept on.

He could make out the curve of her face, the pixie sharp features, the rain straight fall of hair. Her leg was bent at the knee and had slipped between his. She was soft and warm and tempting. Brand knew he had experience enough to arouse her into submission before she was fully awake. She would be drowsy and disoriented.

The hazy gray of early dawn came upon them as he watched her. He could make out her lashes now, a long sweep of black that seemed to weigh her lids down. He wanted her, but not that way. Not the first time. Asleep, she sighed and moved against him. Desire rippled along his skin. Carefully Brand shifted away from her and rose.

In the kitchen he began to make coffee. A glance at his watch and a little arithmetic told him they'd be landing soon. He thought rather enthusiastically about breakfast. The drive from the airport to his house would take some time. He remembered an inn along the way where they could get a good meal and coffee better than the instant he was making.

Hearing Raven stir, he came to the doorway and watched her wake up. She moaned, rolled over and unsuccessfully tried to bury her face. Her hand reached out for a pillow that wasn't there, then slowly, on a disgusted sigh, she opened her eyes. Brand watched the stages as her eyes roamed the room. First came disinterest, then confusion, then sleepy understanding.

"Good morning," he ventured, and she shifted her eyes to him without moving her head. He was grinning at her, and his greeting was undeniably cheerful. She had a wary respect for cheerful risers.

"Coffee," she managed and shut her eyes again.

"In a minute." The kettle was beginning to hiss behind him. "How'd you sleep?"

Dragging her hands through her hair, she made a courageous attempt to sit up. The light was still gray but now brighter, and she pressed her fingers against her eyes for a moment. "I don't know yet," she mumbled from behind her hands. "Ask me later."

The whistle blew, and as Brand disappeared back into the galley, Raven brought her knees up to her chest and buried her face against them. She could hear him talking to her, making bright, meaningless conversation, but her mind wasn't yet receptive. She made no attempt to listen or to answer.

"Here, love." As Raven cautiously raised her head, Brand held out a steaming mug. "Have a bit, then you'll feel better." She accepted with murmured thanks. He sat down beside her. "I've a brother who wakes up ready to bite someone's—anyone's—head off. It's metabolism, I suppose."

Raven made a noncommittal sound and began to take tentative sips. It was hot and strong. For some moments there was silence as he drank his own cream-cooled coffee and watched her. When her cup was half empty, she looked over and managed a rueful smile.

"I'm sorry, Brandon. I'm simply not at my best in the morning. Especially early in the morning." She tilted her head so that she could see his watch, made a brave stab at mathematics, then gave up. "I don't suppose it matters what time it actually is," she decided, going back to the coffee. "It'll take me days to adjust to the change, anyway."

"A good meal will set you up," he told her, lazily sipping at his own coffee. "I read somewhere where drinking yeast and jogging cures jet lag, but I'll take my chances with breakfast."

"Yeast?" Raven grimaced into her mug, then drained it. "I think sleep's a better cure, piles of it." The mists were clearing, and she shook back her hair. "I guess we'll be landing soon, won't we?"

"Less than an hour, I'd say."

"Good. The less time I spend awake on a plane, the less time I have to think about being on one. I slept like a rock." With another sigh, Raven stretched her back, letting her shoulders lift and fall with the movement. "I made poor company." Her system was starting to hum again, though on slow speed.

"You were tired." Over the rim of his cup he

watched the subtle movements of her body beneath the oversize sweater.

"I turned off like a tap," she admitted. "It happens that way sometimes after a concert." She lifted one shoulder in a quick shrug. "But I suppose we'll both be better today for the rest. Where did you sleep?"

"With you."

Raven closed her mouth on a yawn, swallowed and stared at him. "What?"

"I said I slept with you, here on the couch." Brand made a general gesture with his hand. "You like to snuggle."

She could see he was enjoying her dismayed shock. His eyes were deep blue with amusement as he lifted his cup again. "You had no right..." Raven began.

"I always fancied being the first man you slept with," he told her before draining his cup. "Want some more coffee?"

Raven's face flooded with color; her eyes turned dark and opaque. She sprang up, but Brand managed to pluck the cup from her hand before she could hurl it across the room. For a moment she stood, breathing hard, watching him while he gave her his calm, measuring stare.

"Don't flatter yourself," she tossed out. "You don't know how many men I've slept with."

Very precisely, he set down both coffee cups, then looked back up at her. "You're as innocent as the day you were born, Raven. You've barely been touched by a man, much less been made love to."

Her temper flared like a rocket. "You don't know anything about who I've been with in the last five years, Brandon." She struggled to keep from shouting, to keep her voice as calm and controlled as his. "It's none of your business how many men I've slept with."

He lifted a brow, watching her thoughtfully. "Innocence isn't something to be ashamed of, Raven."

"I'm not…" She stopped, balling her fists. "You had no right to—" She swallowed and shook her head as fury and embarrassment raced through her. "—While I was asleep," she finished.

"Do what while you were asleep?" Brandon demanded, lazing back on the sofa. "Ravish you?" His humor shimmered over the old-fashioned word and made her feel ridiculous. "I don't think you'd have slept through it, Raven."

Her voice shook with emotion. "Don't laugh at me, Brandon."

"Then don't be such a fool." He reached over to the table beside him for a cigarette, then tapped the end of it against the surface without lighting it. His eyes were fixed on hers and no longer amused. "I could have had you if I'd wanted to, make no mistake about it."

"You have colossal nerve, Brandon. Please remember that you're not privy to my sex life and that you wouldn't have had me because I don't want you. I choose my own lovers."

She hadn't realized he could move so fast. The indolent slouch on the sofa was gone in a flash. He reached up, seizing her wrist, and in one swift move had yanked her down on her back, trapping her body with his. Her gasp of surprise was swallowed as his weight pressed down on her.

Never, in all the time they had spent together past and present, had Raven seen him so angry. An iron taste of fear rose in her throat. She could only shake her head, too terrified to struggle, too stunned to move. She had never suspected he possessed the capacity for violence she now read clearly on his face. This was far different from the cold rage she had seen before and which she knew how to deal with. His fingers bit into her wrist while his other hand came to circle her throat.

"How far do you think I'll push?" he demanded. His voice was harsh and deep with the hint of Ireland more pronounced. Her breathing was short and shallow with fear. Lying completely still, she made no answer. "Don't throw your imaginary string of lovers in my face, or, by God, you'll have a real one quickly enough whether you want me or not." His fingers tightened slightly around her throat. "When the time comes, I won't need to get you drunk on champagne or on exhaustion to have you lie with me. I could have you now, this minute, and after five minutes of struggle you'd be more than willing." His voice lowered, trembling along her skin. "I know how to play you, Raven, and don't you forget it."

His face was very close to hers. Their breathing

mixed, both swift and strained, the only sound coming from the hum of the plane's engines. The fear in her eyes leaped out, finally penetrating his fury. Swearing, Brand pushed himself from her and rose. Her eyes stayed on his as she waited for what he would do next. He stared at her, then turned sharply away, moving over to a porthole.

Raven lay where she was, not realizing she was massaging the wrist that throbbed from his fingers. She watched him drag a hand through his hair.

"I slept with you last night because I wanted to be close to you." He took another long, cleansing breath. "It was nothing more than that. I never touched you. It was an innocent and rather sweet way to spend the night." He curled his fingers into a fist, remembering the frantic flutter of her pulse under his hand when he had circled it around her throat. It gave him no pleasure to know he had frightened her. "It never occurred to me that it would offend you like this. I apologize."

Raven covered her eyes with her hand as the tears began. She swallowed sobs, not wanting to give way to them. Guilt and shame washed over her as fear drained. Her reaction to Brand's simple, affectionate gesture had been to slap his face. It had been embarrassment, she knew, but more, her own suppressed longing for him that had pushed her to react with anger and spiteful words. She'd tried to provoke him and had succeeded. But more, she knew now she had hurt him. Rising from the sofa, she attempted to make amends.

Though she walked over to stand behind him, Raven didn't touch him. She couldn't bear the thought that he might stiffen away from her.

"Brandon, I'm so sorry." She dug her teeth into her bottom lip to keep her voice steady. "That was stupid of me, and worse, unkind. I'm terribly ashamed of the way I acted. I wanted to make you angry; I was embarrassed, I suppose, and…" The words trailed off as she searched for some way to describe the way she had felt. Even now something inside her warmed and stirred at the knowledge that she had lain beside him, sharing the intimacy of sleep.

Raven heard him swear softly, then he rubbed a hand over the back of his neck. "I baited you."

"You're awfully good at it," she said, trying to make light of what had passed between them. "Much better than I am. I can't think about what I'm saying when I'm angry."

"Obviously, neither can I. Look, Raven," Brand began and turned. Her eyes were huge, swimming with restrained tears. He broke off what he had been about to say and moved to the table for his cigarettes. After lighting one, he turned back to her. "I'm sorry I lost my temper. It's something I don't do often because it's a nasty one. And you've got a good aim with a punch, Raven, and it reminded me of the last time we were together five years ago."

She felt her stomach tighten in defense. "I don't think either of us should dwell on that."

"No." He nodded slowly. His eyes were calm

again and considering. Raven knew he was poking into her brain. "Not at the moment, in any case. We should get on with today." He smiled, and she felt each individual muscle in her body relax. "It seems we couldn't wait until we settled in before having a fight."

"No." She answered his smile. "But then I've always been impatient." Moving to him, Raven rose on her toes and pressed her lips tightly to his. "I'm really sorry, Brandon."

"You've already apologized."

"Yes, well, just remember the next time, it'll be your turn to grovel."

Brand tugged on her hair. "I'll make some more coffee. We should have time for one more cup before we have to strap in."

When he had gone into the galley, Raven stood where she was a moment. The last time, she thought, five years ago.

She remembered it perfectly: each word, each hurt. And she remembered that the balance of the fault then had also been hers. They'd been alone; he'd wanted her. She had wanted him. Then everything had gone wrong. Raven remembered how she had shouted at him, near hysteria. He'd been patient, then his patience had snapped, though not in the way it had today. Then, she remembered, he'd been cold, horribly, horribly cold. Comparing the two reactions, Raven realized she preferred the heat and violence to the icy disdain.

Raven could bring the scene back with ease. They'd been close, and the desire had risen to warm her. Then it was furnace hot and she was smothering, then shouting at him not to touch her. She'd told him she couldn't bear for him to touch her. Brand had taken her at her word and left her. Raven could easily remember the despair, the regret and confusion—and the love for him outweighing all else.

But when she had gone to find him the next morning, he had already checked out of his hotel. He had left California, left her, without a word. And there'd been no word from him in five years. No word, she mused, but for the stories in every magazine, in every newspaper. No word but for the whispered comments at parties and in restaurants whenever she would walk in. No word but for the constant questions, the endless speculation in print as to why they were no longer an item—why Brand Carstairs had begun to collect women like trophies.

So she had forced him out of her mind. Her work, her talent and her music had been used to fill the holes he had left in her life. She'd steadied herself and built a life with herself in control again. That was for the best, she had decided. Sharing the reins was dangerous. And, she mused, glancing toward the galley, it would still be dangerous. *He* would still be dangerous.

Quickly Raven shook her head. Brandon was right, she told herself. It was time to concentrate on today. They had work to do, a score to write. Taking a deep breath, she walked to the galley to help him with the coffee.

Chapter 9

Raven fell instantly in love with the primitive countryside of Cornwall. She could accept this as the setting for Arthur's Camelot. It was easy to imagine the clash of swords and the glint of armor, the thundering gallop of swift horses.

Spring was beginning to touch the moors, the green blooms just now emerging. Here and there was the faintest touch of pink from wild blossoms. A fine, constant drizzling mist added to the romance. There were houses, cottages really, with gardens beginning to thrive. Lawns were a tender, thin green, and she spotted the sassy yellow of daffodils and the sleepy blue of wood hyacinths. Brand drove south toward the coast and cliffs and Land's End.

They had eaten a country breakfast of brown eggs,

thick bacon and oat cakes and had set off again in the little car Brand had arranged to have waiting for them at the airport.

"What's your house like, Brandon?" Raven asked as she rummaged through her purse in search of something to use to secure her hair. "You've never told me anything about it."

He glanced at her bent head. "I'll let you decide for yourself when you see it. It won't be long now."

Raven found two rubber bands of differing sizes and colors. "Are you being mysterious, or is this your way of avoiding telling me the roof leaks."

"It might," Brand considered. "Though I don't recall being dripped on. The Pengalleys would see to it; they're quite efficient about that sort of thing."

"Pengalleys?" Raven began to braid her hair.

"Caretakers," he told her. "They've a cottage a mile or so off from the house. They kept an eye on the place, and she does a bit of housekeeping when I'm in residence. He does the repairs."

"Pengalley," she murmured, rolling the name over on her tongue.

"Cornishmen, tried and true," Brand remarked absently.

"I know!" Raven turned to him with a sudden smile. "She's short and a bit stout, not fat, just solidly built, with dark hair pulled back and a staunch, rather disapproving face. He's thinner and going gray, and he tipples a bit from a flask when he thinks she's not looking."

Brand quirked a brow and shot her another brief glance. "Very clever. Just how did you manage it?"

"It had to be," Raven shrugged as she secured one braid and started on the next, "if any gothic novel I've ever read had a dab of truth in it. Are there any neighbors?"

"No one close by. That's one of the reasons I bought it."

"Antisocial?" she asked, smiling at him.

"Survival instinct," Brand corrected. "Sometimes I have to get away from it or go mad. Then I can go back and slip into harness again and enjoy it. It's like recharging." He felt her considering look and grinned. "I told you I'd mellowed."

"Yes," she said slowly, "you did." Still watching him, Raven twisted the rubber band around the tip of the second braid. "Yet you've still managed to put out quite a bit. All the albums, the double one last year; all but five of the songs were yours exclusively. And the songs you wrote for Cal Ripley—they were the best cuts on his album."

"Did you think so?" he asked.

"You know they were," she said, letting the rubber band snap into place.

"Praise is good for the ego, love."

"You've had your share now." She tossed both braids behind her back. "What I was getting at was that for someone who's so mellow, you're astonishingly productive."

"I do a lot of my writing here," Brand explained.

"Or at my place in Ireland. More here, actually, because I've family across the channel, so there's visiting to be done if I'm there."

Raven gave him a curious look. "I thought you still lived in London."

"Primarily, but if I've serious work or simply need to be alone, I come here. I've family in London as well."

"Yes." Raven looked away again out into the misty landscape. "I suppose large families have disadvantages."

Something in her tone made him glance over again, but her face was averted. He said nothing, knowing from experience that any discussion of Raven's family was taboo. Occasionally in the past, he had probed, but she had always evaded him. He knew that she had been an only child and had left home at seventeen. Out of curiosity, Brand had questioned Julie. Julie knew all there was to know about Raven, he was certain, but she had told him nothing. It was yet another mystery about Raven which alternately frustrated and attracted Brand. Now he put the questions in the back of his mind and continued smoothly.

"Well, we won't be troubled by family or neighbors. Mrs. Pengalley righteously disapproves of show people, and will keep a healthy distance."

"Show people?" Raven repeated and turning back to him, grinned. "Have you been having orgies again, Brand?"

"Not for at least three months," he assured her and

swung onto a back road. "I told you I'd mellowed. But she knows about actors and actresses, you see, because as Mr. Pengalley tells me, she makes it her business to read everything she can get her hands on about them. And as for musicians, *rock* musicians, well..." He let the sentence trail off meaningfully, and Raven giggled.

"She'll think the worst, I imagine," she said cheerfully.

"The worst?" Brand cocked a brow at her.

"That you and I are carrying on a hot, illicit love affair."

"Is that the worst? It sounds rather appealing to me."

Raven colored and looked down at her hands. "You know what I meant."

Brand took her hand, kissing it lightly. "I know what you meant." The laugh in his voice eased her embarrassment. "Will it trouble you to be labeled a fallen woman?"

"I've been labeled a fallen woman for years," she returned with a smile, "every time I pick up a magazine. Do you know how many affairs I've had with people I've never even spoken to?"

"Celebrities are required to have overactive libidos," he murmured. "It's part of the job."

"Your press does yours credit," she observed dryly.

Brand nodded gravely. "I've always thought so. I heard about a pool going around London last year.

They were betting on how many women I'd have in a three-month period. The British,'' he explained, ''will bet on anything.''

Raven allowed the silence to hang for a moment. ''What number did you take?''

''Twenty-seven,'' he told her, then grinned. ''I thought it best to be conservative.''

She laughed, enjoying him. He would have done it, too, she reflected. There was enough of the cocky street kid left in him. ''I don't think I'd better ask you if you won.''

''I wish you wouldn't,'' he said as the car began to climb up a macadam drive.

Raven saw the house. It was three stories high, formed of sober, Cornish stone with shutters of deep, weathered green and a series of stout chimneys on the roof. She could just make out thin puffs of smoke before they merged with the lead-colored sky.

''Oh, Brandon, how like you,'' she cried, enchanted. ''How like you to find something like this.''

She was out of the car before he could answer. It was then that she discovered the house had its back to the sea. There were no rear doors, she learned as she dashed quickly to the retaining wall on the left side. The cliff sheared off too close to the back of the house to make one practical. Instead, there were doors on the sides, set deep in Cornish stone.

Raven could look down from the safety of a waist-high wall and watch the water foam and lash out at jagged clumps of rock far below. The view sent a thrill of terror and delight through her. The sea roared below, a smashing fury of sound. Raven stood, heedless of the chill drizzle, and tried to take it all in.

"It's fabulous. Fabulous!" Turning, she lifted her face, studying the house again. Against the stone, in a great tangle of vines, grew wild roses and honeysuckles. They were greening, not yet ready to bloom, but she could already imagine their fragrance. A rock garden had been added, and among the tender green shoots was an occasional flash of color.

"You might find the inside fabulous, too," Brand ventured, laughing when she turned her wet face to him. "And dry."

"Oh, Brandon, don't be so unromantic." She turned a slow circle until she faced the house again. "It's like something out of *Wuthering Heights.*"

He took her hand. "Unromantic or not, mate, I want a bath, a hot one, and my tea."

"That does have a nice sound to it," she admitted but hung back as he pulled her to the door. She thought the cliffs wonderfully jagged and fierce. "Will we have scones? I developed a taste for them when I toured England a couple years ago. Scones and clotted cream—why does that have to sound so dreadful?"

"You'll have to take that up with Mrs. Pengalley," Brand began as he placed his hand on the knob. It opened before he could apply any pressure.

Mrs. Pengalley looked much as Raven had jokingly described her. She was indeed a sturdily built woman with dark hair sternly disciplined into a sensible bun.

She had dark, sober eyes that passed briefly over Raven, took in the braids and damp clothing, then rested on Brandon without a flicker of expression.

"Good morning, Mr. Carstairs, you made good time," she said in a soft, Cornish burr.

"Hullo, Mrs. Pengalley, it's good to see you again. This is Ms. Williams, who'll be staying with me."

"Her room's ready, sir. Good morning, Miss Williams."

"Good morning, Mrs. Pengalley," said Raven, a trifle daunted. This, she was sure, was what was meant by "a formidable woman." "I hope I haven't put you to too much trouble."

"There's been little to do." Mrs. Pengalley's dark eyes shifted to Brand again. "There be fires laid, and the pantry's stocked, as you instructed. I've done you a casserole for tonight. You've only to heat it when you've a mind to eat. Mr. Pengalley laid in a good supply of wood; the nights're cool, and it's been damp. He'll be bringing your bags in now. We heard you drive up."

"Thanks." Brand glanced over, seeing that Raven was already wandering around the room. "We're both in need of a hot bath and some tea, then we should do well enough. Is there anything you want in particular, Raven?"

She glanced back over at the sound of her name but hadn't been attentive to the conversation. "I'm sorry. What?"

He smiled at her. "Is there anything you'd like before Mrs. Pengalley sees to tea?"

"No." Raven smiled at the housekeeper. "I'm sure everything's lovely."

Mrs. Pengalley inclined her head, her body bending not an inch. "I'll make your tea, then." As she swept from the room, Raven shot Brand a telling glance. He grinned and stretched his back.

"You continually amaze me, Brandon," she murmured, then went back to her study of the room.

It was, Raven knew, the room in which they would be doing most of their work over the next weeks. A grand piano, an old one which, she discovered on a quick testing run, had magnificent tone, was set near a pair of narrow windows. Occasional rag rugs dotted the oak-planked floor. The drapes were cream-colored lace and obviously handworked. Two comfortable sofas, both biscuit-colored, and a few Chippendale tables completed the furniture.

A fire crackled in the large stone fireplace. Raven moved closer to examine the pictures on the mantel.

At a glance, she could tell she was looking at Brand's family. There was a teenage boy in a black leather jacket whose features were the same as Brand's though his dark hair was a bit longer and was as straight as Raven's. He wore the same cocky grin as his brother. A woman was next; Raven thought her about twenty-five and astonishingly pretty with fair hair and slanted green eyes and a true English rose complexion. For all the difference in coloring, how-

ever, the resemblance to Brand was strong enough for
Raven to recognize his sister. She was in another picture along with a blond man and two boys. Both boys
had dark hair and the Carstairs mischief gleaming in
their eyes. Raven decided Brand's sister had her hands
full.

Raven studied the picture of Brand's parents for
some time. The tall, thin frame had been passed down
from his father, but it seemed only one of the children
had inherited his fair, English looks. Raven judged it
to be an old snapshot—twenty, perhaps twenty-five,
years old. It had been painstaking staged, with the man
and woman dead center, standing straight in their Sunday best. The woman was dark and lovely. The man
looked a bit self-conscious and ill at ease having to
pose, but the woman beamed into the camera. Her
eyes bespoke mischief and her mouth a hint of the
cockiness so easily recognized in her children.

There were more pictures: family groups and candid
shots, with Brand in several of them. The Carstairses
were very much a family. Raven felt a small stir of
envy. Shaking it off, she turned back to Brand and
smiled.

"This is quite a group." She flicked her fingers
behind her toward the mantel. "You're the oldest,
aren't you? I think I read that somewhere. The resemblance is remarkable."

"Sweeney genes from my mother's side," Brand
told her, looking beyond her shoulder at the crowded
grouping of frames. "The only one they slipped up

on a bit was Alison." He ran a hand through his damp hair and came to stand beside her. "Let me take you upstairs, love, and get you settled in. The grand tour can wait until we're dry." He slipped an arm around her. "I'm glad you're here, Raven. I've never seen you with things that are mine before. And hotel rooms, no matter how luxurious, are never home."

Later, lounging in a steaming tub, Raven thought over Brand's statement. It was part of the business of being an entertainer to spend a great many nights in hotel rooms, albeit luxury suites, in their positions, but they were hotel rooms nonetheless. Home was a place for between concerts and guest appearances, and to her, it had become increasingly important over the years. It seemed the higher she rose, the more she needed a solid base. She realized it was the same with Brand.

They'd both been on the road for several weeks. He was home now, and somehow Raven knew already that she, too, would be at home there. For all its age and size, there was something comforting in the house. Perhaps, Raven mused as she lazily soaped a leg, it's the age and size. Continuity was important to her, as she felt she'd had little of it in her life, and space was important for the same reason.

Raven had felt an instant affinity for the house. She liked the muffled roar of the sea outside her window and the breathtaking view. She liked the old-fashioned porcelain tub with the curved legs and the oval, mahogany-framed mirror over the tiny pedestal sink.

Rising from the tub, she lifted a towel from the heated bar. When she had dried herself, she wrapped a thick, buff-colored towel around her before letting down her hair. The two braids fell from where she had pinned them atop of her head. Absently, as she wandered back into the bedroom, she began to undo them.

Her luggage still sat beside an old brass chest, but she didn't give much thought to unpacking. Instead she walked to the window seat set in the south wall and knelt on the padded cushion.

Below her the sea hurled itself onto the rocks, tossed up by the wind. There was a sucking, drawing sound before it crashed back onto the shingles and cliffs. Like the sky, they were gray, except for where the waves crested in stiff, white caps. The rain drizzled still, with small drops hitting her window to trail lazily downward. Placing her arms on the wide sill, Raven rested her chin on them and lost herself in dreamy contemplation of the scene below.

"Raven."

She heard Brand's call and the knock and answered both absently. "Yes, come in."

"I thought you might be ready to go downstairs," he said.

"In a minute. What a spectacular view this is! Come look. Does your room face the sea like this? I think I could sit here watching it forever."

"It has its points," he agreed and came over to stand behind her. He tucked his hands into his pockets. "I didn't know you had such a fondness for the sea."

"Yes, always, but I've never had a room where I felt right on top of it before. I'm going to like hearing it at night." She smiled over her shoulder at him. "Is your house in Ireland on the coast, too?"

"No, it's more of a farm, actually. I'd like to take you there." He ran his fingers through her hair, finding it thick and soft and still faintly damp. "It's a green, weepy country, and as appealing as this one, in a different way."

"That's your favorite, isn't it?" Raven smiled up at him. "Even though you live in London and come here to do work, it's the place in Ireland that's special."

He returned the smile. "If it wasn't that there'd have been Sweeneys and Hardestys everywhere we looked, I'd have taken you there. My mother's family," he explained, "are very friendly people. If the score goes well, perhaps we can take a bit of a vacation there when we're done."

Raven hesitated. "Yes...I'd like that."

"Good." The smile turned into a grin. "And I like your dress."

Puzzled, Raven followed his lowered glance. Stunned, she gripped the towel at her breasts and scrambled to her feet. "I didn't realize...I'd forgotten." She could feel the color heating her cheeks. "Brandon, you might have said something."

"I just did," he pointed out. His eyes skimmed down to her thighs.

"Very funny," Raven retorted and found herself

smiling. "Now, why don't you clear out and let me change?"

"Must you? Pity." He hooked his hand over the towel where it met between her breasts. The back of his fingers brushed the swell of her bosom. "I was just thinking I liked your outfit." Without touching her in any other way, he brought his mouth down to hers.

"You smell good," he murmured, then traced just the inside of her mouth with his tongue. "Rain's still in your hair."

A roaring louder than the sea began in her brain. Instinctually she was kissing him back, meeting his tongue with hers, stepping closer and rising on her toes. Though her response was quick and giving, he kept the kiss light. She sensed the hunger and the strength under tight control.

Under the towel, his finger swept over her nipple, finding it taut with desire. Raven felt a strong, unfamiliar ache between her thighs. She moaned with it as each muscle in her body went lax. He lifted his face and waited until her eyes opened.

"Shall I make love to you, Raven?"

She stared at him, aching with the churn of rising needs. He was putting the decision in her hands. She should have been grateful, relieved, yet at that moment she found she would have preferred it if he had simply swept her away. For an instant she wanted no choice, no voice, but only to be taken.

"You'll have to be sure," he told her quietly. Lifting her chin with his finger, he smiled. His eyes were a calm blue-green. "I've no intention of making it easy for you."

He dropped his hand. "I'll wait for you downstairs, though I still think it's a pity you have to change. You're very attractive in a towel."

"Brandon," she said when he was at the door. He turned, lifting a brow in acknowledgment. "What if I'd said yes?" Raven grinned, feeling a bit more steady with the distance between them. "Wouldn't that have been a bit awkward with Mrs. Pengalley still downstairs?"

Leaning against the door, he said lazily, "Raven, if you'd said yes, I wouldn't give a damn if Mrs. Pengalley and half the country were downstairs." He shut the door carefully behind him.

Chapter 10

Both Raven and Brand were anxious to begin. They started the day after their arrival and soon fell into an easy, workable routine. Brand rose early and was usually finishing up a good-sized breakfast by the time Raven dragged herself downstairs. When she was fortified with coffee, they started their morning stretch, working until noon and Mrs. Pengalley's arrival. While the housekeeper brought in the day's marketing and saw to whatever domestic chores needed to be seen to, Brand and Raven would take long walks.

The days were balmy, scented with sea spray and spring. The land was rugged, even harsh, with patches of poor ground covered with heather not yet in bloom. The pounding surf beat against towering granite cliffs. Hardy birds built their nests in the crags. Their cries could be heard over the crash of the waves. Standing high, Raven could see down to the village with its neat rows of cottages and white church spire.

They'd work again in the afternoon with the fire sizzling in the grate at their backs. After dinner they went over the day's work. By the end of the week they had a loosely based outline for the score and the completed title song.

They didn't work without snags. Both Raven and Brand felt too strongly about music for any collaboration to run smoothly. But the arguments seemed to stimulate both of them; and the final product was the better for them. They were a good team.

They remained friends. Brand made no further attempt to become Raven's lover. From time to time Raven would catch him staring intently at her. Then she would feel the pull, as sensual as a touch, as tempting as a kiss. The lack of pressure confused her and drew her more effectively than his advances could have. Advances could be refused, avoided. She knew he was waiting for her decision. Underneath the casualness, the jokes and professional disagreements, the air throbbed with tension.

The afternoon was long and a bit dreary. A steady downpour of rain kept Raven and Brand from walking the cliffs. Their music floated through the house, echoing in corners here and there and drifting to forgotten attics. They'd built the fire high with Mr. Pengalley's store of wood to chase away the dampness that seemed to seep through the windows. A tray of tea and biscuits that they had both forgotten rested on one of the Chippendale tables. Their argument was reaching its second stage.

"We've got to bring up the tempo," Raven insisted. "It just doesn't work this way."

"It's a mood piece, Raven."

"Not a funeral dirge. It drags this way, Brandon. People are going to be nodding off before she finishes singing it."

"Nobody falls asleep while Lauren Chase is singing," Brand countered. "This number is pure sex, Raven, and she'll sell it."

"Yes, she will," Raven agreed, "but not at this tempo." She shifted on the piano bench so that she faced him more directly. "All right, Joe's fallen asleep at the typewriter in the middle of the chapter he's writing. He's already believing himself a little mad because of the vivid dreams he's having about his character Tessa. She seems too real, and he's fallen in love with her even though he knows she's a product of his own imagination, a character in a novel he's writing, a fantasy. And now, in the middle of the day, he's dreaming about her again, and this time she promises to come to him that night."

"I know the plot, Raven," Brand said dryly.

Though she narrowed her eyes, Raven checked her temper. She thought she detected some fatigue in his voice. Once or twice she'd been awakened in the middle of the night by his playing. "'Nightfall' is hot,

Brandon. You're right about it being pure sex, and your lyrics are fabulous. But it still needs to move.''

"It moves.'' He took a last drag on his cigarette before crushing it out. "Chase knows how to hang on to a note.''

Raven made a quick sound of frustration. Unfortunately he was usually right about such things. His instincts were phenomenal. This time, however, she was certain that her own instincts—as a songwriter and as a woman—were keener. She knew the way the song had to be sung to reap the full effect. The moment she had read Brand's lyrics, she had known what was needed. The song had flowed, completed, through her head.

"I know she can hang on to a note, and she can handle choreography. She'll be able to do both and still do the song at the right tempo. Let me show you." She began to play the opening bars. Brand shrugged and rose from the bench.

Raven moved the tempo to *andante* and sang to her own accompaniment. Her voice wrapped itself around the music. Brand moved to the window to watch the rain. It was the song of a temptress, full of implicit, wild promises.

Raven's voice flowed over the range of notes, then heated when it was least expected until Brand felt a tight knot of desire in the pit of his stomach. There was something not quite earthy in the melody she had created. The quicker tempo made a sharp contrast, much more effective than the pace Brand had wanted.

She ended abruptly in a raspy whisper without any fade-out. She tossed her hair, then shot him a look over her shoulder.

"Well?" There was a half smile on her face.

He had his back to her and kept his hands tucked into his pockets. "You have to be right now and again, I suppose."

Raven laughed, spinning around on the bench until she faced the room. "You've a way with compliments, Brandon. It sets my heart fluttering."

"She doesn't have your range," he murmured. Then, making an impatient movement, he wandered over to the teapot. "I don't think she'll get as much out of the low scale as you do."

"*Mmm.*" Raven shrugged as she watched him pour out a cup of tea. "She's got tremendous style, though; she'll milk every ounce out of it." He set the tea down again without touching it and roamed to the fire. As she watched him, a worried frown creased Raven's brow. "Brandon, what's wrong?"

He threw another log on the already roaring fire. "Nothing, just restless."

"This rain's depressing." She rose to go to the window. "I've never minded it. Sometimes I like a dreary, sleepy day. I can be lazy without feeling guilty. Maybe that's what you should do, Brandon, be lazy today. You've got that marvelous chessboard in the library. Why don't you teach me to play?" She lifted her hands to his shoulders and feeling the tension, began to knead absently. "Of course, that might be hard work. Julie gave up playing backgammon with me. She says I haven't any knack for strategy.''

Raven broke off when Brand turned abruptly around and removed her hands from his shoulders. Without speaking, he walked away from her. He went to the liquor cabinet and drew out a bottle of bourbon. Raven watched as he poured three fingers into a glass and drank it down.

''I don't think I've the patience for games this afternoon,'' he told her as he poured a second drink.

''All right, Brandon,'' she said. ''No games.'' She walked over to stand in front of him, keeping her eyes direct. ''Why are you angry with me? Certainly not because of the song.''

The look held for several long moments while the fire popped and sizzled in the grate. Raven heard a log fall as the one beneath it gave way.

''Perhaps it's time you and I talked,'' Brandon said as he idly swirled the remaining liquor in the glass. ''It's dangerous to leave things hanging for five years; you never know when they're going to fall.''

Raven felt a ripple of disquiet but nodded. ''You may be right.''

Brand gave her a quick smile. ''Should we be civilized and sit down or take a few free swings standing up?''

She shrugged. ''I don't think there's any need to be civilized. Civilized fighting never clears the air.''

''All right,'' he began but was interrupted by the

peal of the bell. Setting down his glass, Brand shot
her a last look, then went to answer.

Alone, Raven tried to control her jitters. There was
a storm brewing, she knew, and it wasn't outside the
windows. Brand was itching for a fight, and though
the reason was unclear to her, Raven found herself
very willing to oblige him. The tension between them
had been glossed over in the name of music and peace.
Now, despite her nerves, she was looking forward to
shattering the calm. Hearing his returning footsteps,
she walked back to the tea tray and picked up her cup.

"Package for you." Brand gestured with it as he
came through the doorway. "From Henderson."

"I wonder what he could be sending me," she murmured, already ripping off the heavy packing tape.
"Oh, of course." She tossed the wrappings carelessly
aside and studied the album jacket. "They're sample
jackets for the album I'm releasing this summer."
Without glancing at him, Raven handed Brand one of
the covers, then turned to another to read the liner
notes.

For the next few minutes Brand studied the cover
picture without speaking. Again, a background of
white, Raven sitting in her habitual cross-legged fashion. She was looking full into the camera with only a
tease of a smile on her lips. Her eyes were very gray
and very direct. Over her shoulders and down to her
knees, her hair spilled—a sharp contrast against the
soft-focused white of the background. The arrangement appeared to be haphazard but had been cleverly

posed nonetheless. She appeared to be nude, and the effect was fairly erotic.

"Did you approve this picture?"

"Hmm?" Raven pushed back her hair as she continued to read. "Oh, yes, I looked over the proofs before I left on tour. I'm still not completely sure about this song order, but I suppose it's a bit late to change it now."

"I always felt Henderson was above packaging you this way."

"Packaging me what way?" she asked absently.

"As a virgin offering to the masses." He handed her the cover.

"Brandon, really…how ridiculous."

"I don't think so," he said. "I think it's an uncannily apt description: virgin white, soft focus, and you sitting naked in the middle of it all."

"I'm not naked," she retorted indignantly. "I don't do nudes."

"The potential buyer isn't supposed to know that, though, is he?" Brand leaned against the piano and watched her through narrowed eyes.

"It's provocative, certainly. It's meant to be." Raven frowned down at the cover again. "There's nothing wrong with that. I'm not a child to be dressed up in Mary Janes and a pink pinafore, Brandon. This is business. There's nothing extreme about this cover. And I'm more modestly covered than I would be on a public beach."

"But not more decently," he said coldly. "There's a difference."

Color flooded her face, now a mixture of annoyance and embarrassment. "It's not indecent. I've never posed for an indecent picture. Karl Straighter is one of the finest photographers in the business. He doesn't shoot indecent pictures."

"One man's art is another's porn, I suppose."

Her eyes widened as she lowered the jackets to the piano bench. "That's a disgusting thing to say," she whispered. "You're being deliberately horrible."

"I'm simply giving you my opinion," he corrected, lifting a brow. "You don't have to like it."

"I don't need your opinion. I don't need your approval."

"No," he said and crushed out his cigarette. "You bloody well don't, do you? But you're going to have it in any case." He caught her by the arm when she would have turned away. The power of the grip contrasted the cool tone and frosty eyes.

"Let go of me," Raven demanded, putting her hand on top of his and trying unsuccessfully to pry it from her arm.

"When I'm finished."

"You have finished." Her voice was abruptly calm, and she stopped her frantic attempts to free herself. Instead she faced him squarely, emotion burning in her eyes. "I don't have to listen to you when you go out of your way to insult me, Brandon. I won't listen to you. You can prevent me from leaving because you're stronger than I am, but you can't make me listen." She swallowed but managed to keep her voice steady. "I run my own life. You're entitled to your opinion, certainly, but you're not entitled to hurt me with it. I don't want to talk to you now; I just want you to let me go."

He was silent for so long, Raven thought he would refuse. Then, slowly, he loosened his grip until she could slip her arm from his fingers. Without a word she turned and left the room.

Perhaps it was the strain of her argument with Brand or the lash of rain against the windows or the sudden fury of thunder and lightning. The dream formed out of a vague montage of childhood remembrances that left her with impressions rather than vivid pictures. Thoughts and images floated and receded against the darkness of sleep. There were rolling sensations of fear, guilt, despair, one lapping over the other while she moaned and twisted beneath the sheets, trying to force herself awake. But she was trapped, caught fast in the world just below consciousness. Then the thunder seemed to explode inside her head, and the flash of lightning split the room with a swift, white flash. Screaming, Raven sat up in bed.

The room was pitch dark again when Brand rushed in; he found his way to the bed by following the sounds of Raven's wild weeping. "Raven. Here, love." Even as he reached her, she threw herself into his arms and clung. She was trembling hard, and her

skin was icy. Brand pulled the quilt up over her back
and cuddled her. "Don't cry, love, you're safe here."
He patted and stroked as he would for a child frightened of a storm. "It'll soon be over."

"Hold me." She pressed her face into his bare
shoulder. "Please, just hold me." Her breathing was
quick, burning her throat as she struggled for air. "Oh,
Brandon, such an awful dream."

He rocked her and laid a light kiss on her temple.
"What was it about?" The telling, he recalled from
childhood, usually banished the fear.

"She'd left me alone again," Raven murmured,
shuddering so that he drew her closer in response. The
words came out as jumbled as her thoughts, as tumbled as the dream. "How I hated being alone in that
room. The only light was from the building next
door—one of those red neon lights that blinks on and
off, on and off, so that the dark was never still. And
so much noise out on the street, even with the windows closed. Too hot…too hot to sleep," she murmured into his shoulder. "I watched the light and
waited for her to come back. She was drunk again."
She whimpered, her fingers opening and closing
against his chest. "And she'd brought a man with her.
I put the pillow over my head so I wouldn't hear."

Raven paused to steady her breath. It was dark and
quiet in Brand's arms. Outside, the storm rose in high
fury.

"She fell down the steps and broke her arm, so we
moved, but it was always the same. Dingy little

rooms, airless rooms that smelled always of gin no matter how you scrubbed. Thin walls, walls that might as well not have existed for the privacy they gave you. But she always promised that this time, this time it'd be different. She'd get a job, and I'd go to school…but always one day I'd come home and there'd be a man and a bottle.''

She wasn't clinging any longer but simply leaning against him as if all passion were spent. Lightning flared again, but she remained still.

''Raven.'' Brand eased her gently away and tilted her face to his. Tears were still streaming from her eyes, but her breathing was steadier. He could barely make out the shape of her face in the dark. ''Where was your father?''

He could see the shine of her eyes as she stared at him. She made a soft, quiet sound as one waking. He knew the words had slipped from her while she had been vulnerable and unaware. Now she was aware, but it was too late for defenses. The sigh she made was an empty, weary sound.

''I don't know who he was.'' Slowly she drew out of Brand's arms and rose from the bed. ''She didn't, either. You see, there were so many.''

Brand said nothing but reached into the pocket of the jeans he had hastily dragged on and found a pack of matches. Striking one, he lit the bedside candle. The light wavered and flickered, hardly more than a pulse beat in the dark. ''How long,'' he asked and shook out the match, ''did you live like that?''

Raven dragged both hands through her hair, then hugged herself. She knew she'd already said too much for evasions. "I don't remember a time she didn't drink, but when I was very young, five or six, she still had some control over it. She used to sing in clubs. She had big dreams and an average voice, but she was very lovely…once."

Pausing, Raven pressed her fingers against her eyes and wiped away tears. "By the time I was eight, she was…her problem was unmanageable. And there were always men. She needed men as much as she needed to drink. Some of them were better than others. One of them took me to the zoo a couple of times…."

She trailed off and turned away. Brand watched the candlelight flicker over the thin material of her nightgown.

"She got steadily worse. I think part of it was from the frustration of having her voice go. Of course, she abused it dreadfully with smoking and drinking, but the more it deteriorated, the more she smoked and drank. She ruined her voice and ruined her health and ruined any chance she had of making something of herself. Sometimes I hated her. Sometimes I know she hated herself."

A sob escaped, but Raven pushed it back and began to wander the room. The movement seemed to make it easier, and the words tumbled out quicker, pressing for release. "She'd cry and cling to me and beg me not to hate her. She'd promise the moon, and more often than not, I'd believe her. 'This time'—that was one of her favorite beginnings. It still is." Raven let out a shaky sigh. "She loved me when she wasn't drinking and forgot me completely when she was. It was like living with two different women, and neither one of them was easy. When she was sober, she expected an average mother-and-daughter relationship. Had I done my homework? Why was I five minutes late getting home from school? When she was drunk, I was supposed to keep the hell out of her way. I remember once, when I was twelve, she went three months and sixteen days without a drink. Then I came home from school and found her passed out on the bed. She'd had an audition that afternoon for a gig at this two-bit club. Later she told me she'd just wanted one drink to calm her nerves. Just one…" Raven shivered and hugged herself tighter. "It's cold," she murmured.

Brand rose and stooped in front of the fire. He added kindling and logs to the bed of coals in the grate. Raven walked to the window to watch the fury of the storm over the sea. Lightning still flashed sporadically, but the violence of the thunder and the rain were dying.

"There were so many other times. She was working as a cocktail waitress in this little piano bar in Houston. I was sixteen then. I always came by on payday so I could make certain she didn't spend the money before I bought food. She'd been pretty good then. She'd been working about six weeks straight and had an affair going with the manager. He was one of the better ones. I used to play around at the piano if the place was empty. One of my mother's lovers had been a musician; he'd taught me the basics and said I had a good ear. Mama liked hearing me play.'' Her voice had quieted. Brand watched her trail a finger down the dark pane of window glass.

''Ben, the manager, asked me if I wanted to play during the lunch hour. He said I could sing, too, as long as I kept it soft and didn't talk to the customers. So I started.'' Raven sighed and ran a hand over her brow. Behind her came the pop and crackle of flame. ''We left Houston for Oklahoma City. I lied about my age and got a job singing in a club. It was one of Mama's worst periods. There were times I was afraid to leave her alone, but she wasn't working then, and...'' She broke off with a sound of frustration and rubbed at an ache in her temple. She wanted to stop, wanted to block it all out, but she knew she had come too far. Pressing her brow against the glass, she waited until her thoughts came back into order.

''We needed the money, so I had to risk leaving her at night. I suppose we exchanged roles for a time,'' she murmured. ''The thing I learned young, but consistently forgot, was that an alcoholic finds money for a bottle. Always, no matter what. One night during my second set she wove her way into the club. Wayne was working there and caught onto the situation quickly. He managed to quiet her down before it got too ugly. Later he helped me get her home and into bed. He was wonderful: no lectures, no pity, no advice. Just support."

Raven turned away from the window again and wandered to the fire. "But she came back again, twice more, and they let me go. There were other towns, other clubs, but it was the same then and hardly matters now. Just before I turned eighteen I left her." Her voice trembled a bit, and she took a moment to steady it. "I came home from work one night, and she was passed out at the kitchen table with one of those half-gallon jugs of wine. I knew if I didn't get away from her I'd go crazy. So I put her to bed, packed a bag, left her all the money I could spare and walked out. Just like that." She covered her face with her hands a moment, pressing her fingers into her eyes. "It was like being able to breathe for the first time in my life."

Raven roamed back to the kitchen. She could see the vague ghost of her own reflection. Studying it, listening to the steady but more peaceful drum of rain, she continued. "I worked my way to L.A., and Henderson saw me. He pushed me. I'm not certain what my ambition was before I signed with him. Just to survive, I think. One day and then the next. Then there were contracts and recording sessions and the whole crazy circus. Doors started opening. Some of them were trap doors, I've always thought." She gave a quick, wondering laugh. "God, it was marvelous and scary and I don't believe I could ever go through those first few months again. Anyway, Henderson got me publicity, and the first hit single got me more. And then I got a call from a hospital in Memphis.''

Raven turned and began to pace. The light silk of her nightgown clung, then swirled, with her movements. ''I had to go, of course. She was in pretty bad shape. Her latest lover had beaten her and stolen what little money she had. She cried. Oh, God, all the same promises. She was sorry; she loved me. Never again, never again. I was the only decent thing she'd ever done in her life.'' The tears were beginning to flow again, but this time Raven made no attempt to stop them. ''As soon as she could travel, I brought her back with me. Julie had found a sanitarium in Ojai and a very earnest young doctor. Justin Randolf Karter. Isn't that a marvelous name, Brandon?'' Bitterness spilled out with the tears. ''A marvelous name, a remarkable man. He took me into his tasteful, leather-bound office and explained the treatment my mother would receive.''

Whirling, Raven faced Brand, her shoulders heaving with sobs. ''I didn't want to know! I just wanted him to do it. He told me not to set my hopes too high, and I told him I hadn't any hopes at all. He must have found me cynical, because he suggested several good organizations I could speak to. He reminded me that alcoholism is a disease and that my mother was a victim. I said the hell she was; *I* was the victim!'' Raven forced the words out as she hugged herself tightly. ''*I* was the victim; *I* had had to live with her and deal with her lies and her sickness and her men. It was so safe, so easy, for him to be sanctimonious and understanding behind that tidy white coat. And I *hated* her.'' The sobs came in short, quick jerks as she balled her hands and pressed them against her eyes. ''And I loved her.'' Her breath trembled in and out as everything she had pent up over the weeks of her mother's latest treatment poured through her. ''I still love her,'' she whispered.

Weary, nearly spent, she turned to the fire, resting her palms on the mantel. ''Dr. Karter let me shout at him, then he sat with me when I broke down. I went home, and they started her treatment. Two days later I met you.''

Raven didn't hear him move, didn't know he stood behind her, until she felt his hands on her shoulders. Without speaking she turned and went into his arms. Brand held her, feeling the light tremors while he stared down at the licking, greedy flames. Outside, the storm had become only a patter of rain against the windows.

''Raven, if you had told me, I might have been able to make things easier for you.''

She shook her head, then buried her face against his chest. ''No, I didn't want it to touch that part of my life. I just wasn't strong enough.'' Taking a deep breath, she pulled back far enough to look in his eyes. ''I was afraid that if you knew you wouldn't want anything to do with me.''

''Raven.'' There was hurt as well as censure in his voice.

"I know it was wrong, Brandon, even stupid, but you have to understand: everything seemed to be happening to me at once. I needed time. I needed to sort out how I was going to live my life, how I was going to deal with my career, my mother, everything." Her hands gripped his arms as she willed him to see through her eyes. "I was nobody one day and being mobbed by fans the next. My picture was everywhere. I heard myself every time I turned on the radio. You know what that's like."

Brand brushed her hair from her cheek. "Yes, I know what that's like." As he spoke, he could feel her relax with a little shudder.

"Before I could take a breath, Mama walked back into my life. Part of me hated her, but instead of realizing that it was a normal reaction and dealing with it, I felt an unreasonable guilt. And I was ashamed. No," she shook her head, anticipating him, "there's no use telling me I had no need to be. That's an intellectual statement, a practical statement; it has nothing to do with emotion. I don't expect you to understand that part of it. You've never had to deal with it. She's my mother. It isn't possible to completely separate myself from that, even knowing that the responsibility for her problem isn't mine." Raven gave him one last, long look before turning away. "And on top of everything that was happening to me, I fell in love with you." The flames danced and snapped as she watched. "I loved you," she murmured so quietly he strained to hear, "but I couldn't be your lover."

Brand stared at her back, started to reach for her, then dropped his hands to his sides. "Why?"

Only her head turned as she looked over her shoulder at him. Her face was in shadows. "Because then I would be like her," she whispered, then turned away again.

"You don't really believe that, Raven." Brand took her shoulders, but she shook her head, not answering. Firmly he turned her to face him, making a slow, thorough study of her. "Do you make a habit of condemning children for their parents' mistakes?"

"No, but I..."

"You don't have the right to do it to yourself."

She shut her eyes on a sigh. "I know, I know that, but..."

"There're no buts on this one, Raven." His fingers tightened until she opened her eyes again. "You know who you are."

There was only the sound of the sea and the rain and fire. "I wanted you," she managed in a trembling voice, "when you held me, touched me. You were the first man I'd ever wanted." She swallowed, and again he felt the shudder course through her. "Then I'd remember all those cramped little rooms, all those men with my mother...." She broke off and would have turned away again if his hands hadn't held her still.

Brand removed his hands from her arms, then slowly, his eyes still on hers, he used them to frame her face. "Sleeping with a stranger is different from making love with someone you care for."

Raven moistened her lips. "Yes, I know that, but..."

"Do you?" The question stopped her. She could do no more than let out a shaky breath. "Let me show you, Raven."

Her eyes were trapped by his. She knew he would release her if she so much as shook her head. Fear was tiny pinpoints along her skin. Need was a growing warmth in her blood. She lifted her hands to his wrists. "Yes."

Again Brand gently brushed the hair away from her cheeks. When her face was framed by his hands alone, he lowered his head and kissed her eyes closed. He could feel her trembling in his arms. Her hands still held his wrists, and her fingers tightened when he brought his mouth to hers. His was patient, waiting until her lips softened and parted.

The kisses grew deeper, but slowly, now moister until she swayed against him. His fingers caressed, his mouth roamed. Firelight flickered over them in reds and golds, casting its own shadows. Raven could feel the heat from it through the silk she wore, but it was the glow inside of her which built and flamed hot.

Brand lowered his hands to her shoulders, gently massaging as he teased her lower lip with his teeth. Raven felt the gown slip down over her breasts, then cling briefly to her hips before it drifted to the floor. She started to protest, but he deepened the kiss. The thought spiraled away. Down the curve of her back, over the slight flare of her hips, he ran his hands. Then he picked her up in his arms. With her mind spinning, she sank into the mattress. When Brand joined her, the touch of his naked body against hers jolted her, bringing on a fresh surge of doubts and fears.

"Brandon, please, I..." The words were muffled, then died inside his mouth.

Easily, his hands caressed her, stroking without hurry. Somewhere in the back of her mind she knew he held himself under tight control. But her mind had relaxed, and her limbs were heavy. His mouth wandered to her throat, tasting, giving pleasure, arousing by slow, irresistible degrees. He worked her nipple with his thumb, and she moaned and moved against him. Brand allowed his mouth to journey downward, laying light, feathering kisses over the curve of her breast. Lightly, very lightly, he ran his tongue over the tip. Raven felt the heat between her thighs, and tangling her fingers in his hair, pressed him closer. She arched and shuddered not from fear but from passion.

Heat unlike anything she had ever known or imagined was building inside her. She was still aware of the flicker of the fire and candlelight on her closed lids, of the soft brush of linen sheets against her back, of the faint, pleasant smell of woodsmoke. But these sensations were dim, while her being seemed focused on the liquefying touch of his tongue over her skin, the feathery brush of his fingers on her thighs. Over the hiss of rain and fire, she heard him murmur her name, heard her own soft, mindless response.

Her breath quickened, and her mouth grew hungry.

Suddenly desperate, she drew his face back to hers. She wrapped her arms around him tightly as the pressure of the kiss pushed her head deep into the pillow. Brand lay across her, flesh to flesh, so that her breasts yielded to his chest. Raven could feel the light mat of his hair against her skin.

His hand lay on her stomach and drifted down as she moved under him. There was a flash of panic as he slid between her thighs, then her breath caught in a heady rush of pleasure. He was still patient, his fingers gentle and unhurried as they gradually increased her rhythm.

For Raven, there was no world beyond the firelit room, beyond the four-poster bed. His mouth took hers, his tongue probing deeply, then moving to her ear, her throat, her neck and back to her lips. All the while, his hands and fingers were taking her past all thought, past all reason.

Then he was on top of her, and she opened for him, ready to give, to receive. She was too steeped in wonder to comprehend his strict, unwavering control. She knew only that she wanted him and urged him to take her. There was a swift flash of pain, dulled by a pleasure too acute to be measured. She cried out, but the sound was muffled against his mouth, then all was lost on wave after wave of delight.

Chapter 11

With her head in the curve of Brand's shoulder, Raven watched the fire. Her hand lay over his heart. She could feel its quick, steady rhythm under her palm.

The room was quiet, and outside, the rain had slackened to a murmur. Raven knew she would remember this moment every time she lay listening to rain against windows. Brand's arm was under her, curled over her back with his hand loosely holding her arm. Since he had rolled from her and drawn her against his side, he had been silent. Raven thought he slept and was content to lie with him, watching the fire and listening to the rain. She shifted her head, wanting to look at him and found he wasn't asleep. She could see the sheen of his eyes as he stared at the ceiling. Raven lifted a hand to his cheek.

"I thought you were asleep."

Brand caught her hand and pressed it to his lips. "No, I…" Looking down at her, he broke off, then slowly brushed a tear from her lash with his thumb. "I hurt you."

"No." Raven shook her head. For a moment she buried her face in the curve of his neck, where she could feel his warmth, smell his scent. "Oh, no, you didn't hurt me. You made me feel wonderful. I feel…free." She looked up at him again and smiled. "Does that sound foolish?"

"No." Brand ran his fingers through the length of her hair, pushing it back when it would have hidden her face from him. Her skin was flushed. In her eyes he could see the reflected flames from the fire. "You're so beautiful."

She smiled again and kissed him. "I've always thought the same about you."

He laughed, drawing her closer. "Have you?"

She lay half across him, heated flesh to heated flesh. "Yes, I always thought you'd make a remarkably lovely girl, and I see by your sister's picture that I was right."

He lifted a brow. "Strange, I never realized the direction of your thoughts. Perhaps it's best I didn't."

Raven gave one of her low, rich chuckles and pressed her lips against the column of his throat. She loved the way his tones could become suddenly suavely British. "I'm sure you make a much better man."

"That's comforting," he said dryly as he began to stroke her back, "under the circumstances." His fingers lingered at her hip to caress.

"I'm sure I like you much better this way." Raven kissed the side of his throat again, working her way to his ear. Under her breast she felt the sudden jump and scramble of his heartbeat. "Brandon..." She sighed, nuzzling his ear. "You're so good to me, so kind, so gentle."

She heard him groan before he rolled over, reversing their positions. His eyes were heated and intense and very green, reminding her of the moment he had held her like this on the plane. Now again her pulse began to hammer, but not with fear.

"Love isn't always kind, Raven," he said roughly. "It isn't always gentle."

His mouth came down on hers crushingly, urgently, as all the restraints he had put on himself snapped. There was no patience in him now, only passion. Where before he had taken her up calmly, easily, now he took her plummeting at a desperate velocity. Her mouth felt bruised and tender from his, yet she learned hunger incited hunger. Raven wanted more, and still more, so she caught him closer.

Demanding, possessing, he took his hands over her. "So long," she heard him mutter. "I've wanted you for so long." Then his teeth found the sensitive area of her neck, and she heard nothing. She plunged toward the heat and the dark.

Brand felt her give and respond and demand. He

was nearly wild with need. He wanted to touch all of her, taste all of her. He was as desperate as a starving man and as ruthless. Where before, responding to her innocence, he had been cautious, now he took what he had wanted for too many years. She was his as he had dreamed she would be: soft and yielding, then soft and hungry beneath him.

He could hear her moan, feel the bite of her fingernails in his shoulders as he took his mouth down the curve of her breast. The skin of her stomach was smooth and quivered under his tongue. He slipped a hand between her thighs, and she strained against him so that he knew she was as desperate as he. Yet he wouldn't take her, not yet. He felt an impossible greed. His tongue moved to follow the path of his hands. All the years he'd wanted her, all the frustrated passion, burst out, catching them both in the explosion. Not knowing the paths, Raven went where he led her and learned that desire was deeper, stronger, than anything she had known possible.

He was pulling her down—down until the heat was too intense to bear. But she wanted more. His hands were rough, bruising her skin. But she craved no gentleness. She was steeped in passion too deep for escape. She called out for him, desperately, mindlessly, for him to take her. She knew there couldn't be more; they'd gone past all the rules. Pleasure could not be sharper; passion could not be darker than it was at that moment.

Then he was inside her, and everything that had gone before paled against the color and the heat.

His mouth was buried at her neck. From far off he heard her gasps for breath merge with his own. They moved together like lightning, so that he could no longer think. There was only Raven. All passion intensified, concentrated, until he thought he would go mad from it. The pain of it shot through him, then flowed from him, leaving him weak.

They lay still, with Brand over her, his face buried in her hair. His breathing was ragged, and he gave no thought to his weight as he relaxed completely. Beneath him Raven shuddered again and again with the release of passion. She gripped his shoulders tightly, not wanting him to move, not wanting to relinquish the unity. If he had shown her the tenderness and compassion of loving the first time, now he had shown her darker secrets.

A log fell in the grate, scattering sparks against the screen. Brand lifted his head and looked down at her. His eyes were heavy, still smoldering, as they lowered to her swollen mouth. He placed a soft kiss on them, then, shifting his weight, prepared to rise.

"No, don't go." Raven took his arm, sitting up as he did.

"Only to bank the fire."

Bringing her knees to her chest, Raven watched as Brand stacked the fire for the night. The light danced over his skin as she stared, entranced. The ripple of muscles was surprising in one so lean. She saw them

in his shoulders, his back, his thighs. The passion in
the cool, easygoing man was just as surprising, but
she knew the feel of it now, just as she knew the feel
of the muscles. He turned and looked at her with the
fire leaping at his back. They studied each other, both
dazed by what had passed between them. Then he
shook his head.

"My God, Raven, I want you again."

She held her arms out to him.

There was a brilliant ribbon of sunlight across Raven's eyes. It was a warm, red haze. She allowed her
lids to open slowly before turning to Brand.

He slept still, his breathing deep and even. She had
to suppress the urge to brush his hair away from his
face because she didn't want to wake him. Not yet.
For the first time in her life she woke to look at her
lover's face. She felt a warm, settled satisfaction.

He *is* beautiful, she thought, remembering how he
had been faintly distressed to hear her say so the night
before. *And I love him.* Raven almost said the words
aloud as she let herself think them. I've always loved
him, right from the beginning, all through the years in
between—and even more now that we're together. But
no mistakes this time. She closed her eyes tight on the
sudden fear that he could walk out of her life again.
No demands, no pressures. We'll just be together;
that's all I need.

She dropped her eyes to his mouth. It had been
tender in the night, she remembered, then hungry, al-

most brutal. She hadn't realized how badly he had
wanted her, or she him, until the barriers had shattered. *Five years, five empty years!* Raven pushed the
thought away. There was no yesterday, no tomorrow;
only the present.

Suddenly she smiled, thinking of the enormous
breakfasts he habitually ate. She would usually stum-
ble into the kitchen for coffee as he was cleaning off
a plate. Cooking wasn't her best thing, she mused, but
it would be fun to surprise him. His arm was tossed
around her waist, holding her against him so that their
bodies had warmed each other even in sleep. Carefully
Raven slipped out from under it. Padding to the closet,
she found a robe, then left Brand sleeping to go downstairs.

The kitchen was washed in sunlight. Raven went
straight to the percolator. First things first, she decided. Strangely, she was wide-awake, there was none
of the drowsy fogginess she habitually used coffee to
chase away. She felt vital, full of energy, very much
the way she felt when finishing a live concert, she
realized as she scooped out coffee. Perhaps there was
a parallel. Raven fit the lid on the pot, then plugged
it in. She had always felt that performing for an audience was a bit like making love: sharing yourself,
opening your emotions, pulling down the barriers.
That's what she had done with Brand. The thought
made her smile, and she was singing as she rummaged
about for a frying pan.

Upstairs, Brand stirred, reached for her and found

her gone. He opened his eyes to see that the bed beside him was empty. Quickly he pushed himself up
and scanned the room. The fire was still burning. It
had been late when he had added the last logs. The
drapes were open to the full strength of the sun. It
spilled across the bed and onto the floor. Raven's
nightgown lay where it had fallen the night before.

Not a dream, he told himself, tugging a hand
through his hair. They'd been together last night,
again and again until every ounce of energy had been
drained. Then they had slept, still holding each other,
still clinging. His eyes drifted to the empty pillow beside him again. *But where—where the devil is she
now?* Feeling a quick flutter of panic, he rose, tugged
on his jeans and went to find her.

Before Brand reached the bottom of the stairs, her
voice drifted to him.

Every morning when I wake,
I'll see your eyes.
And there'll only be the love we make,
No more good-byes.

He recognized the song as the one he had teased
her about weeks before when they had sat in his car
in the hills above Los Angeles. The knot in his stomach untied itself. He walked down the hall, listening
to the husky, morning quality of her voice, then
paused in the doorway to watch her.

Her movements suited the song she sang: cheerful,

happy. The kitchen was filled with morning noises and scents. There was the popping rhythm of the percolator as the coffee bubbled on the burner, the hiss and sizzle of the fat sausage she had frying in a cast-iron skillet, the clatter of crockery as she searched for a platter. Her hair was streaming down her back, still tumbled from the night, while the short terry robe she wore rode high up on her thighs as she stretched to reach the top shelf of a cupboard.

Raven stopped singing for a moment to swear good-naturedly about her lack of height. After managing to get a grip on the platter, she lowered her heels back to the floor and turned. She gave a gasp when she spotted Brand, dropped the fork she held and just managed to save the platter from following it.

"Brandon!" Raven circled her throat with her hand a moment and took a deep breath. "You scared me! I didn't hear you come down."

Brand didn't answer her smile. He didn't move but only looked at her. "I love you, Raven."

Her eyes widened, and her lips trembled open, then shut again. The words, she reminded herself, mean so many different things. It was important not to take a simple statement and deepen its meaning. Raven kept her voice calm as she stooped to pick up the fork. "I love you, too, Brandon."

He frowned at the top of her head, then at her back as she turned away to the sink. She turned on the tap to rinse off the fork. "You sound like my sister. I've already two of those; I don't need another."

Raven took her time. She turned off the tap, composed her face into a smile, then turned. "I don't think of you as a brother, Brandon." The tension at the back of her neck made it difficult to move calmly back to the cupboard for cups and saucers. "It isn't easy for me to tell you how I feel. I needed your support, your compassion. You helped me last night more than I can say."

"Now you make me sound like a bloody doctor. I said I love you, Raven." There was a snap of anger in the words this time. When Raven turned back to him, her eyes were eloquent.

"Brandon, you don't have to feel obligated..." She broke off as his eyes flared. Storming into the room, he flicked off the gas under the smoking sausage, then yanked the percolator cord from the wall. Coffee continued to pop for a few moments, then subsided weakly.

"Don't tell me what I have to do!" he shouted. "I know what I have to do." He grabbed her by the shoulders and shook her. "I *have* to love you. It's not an obligation, it's a fact, it's a demand, it's a terror."

"Brandon..."

"Shut up," he commanded. He pulled her close, trapping the dishes she held between them before he kissed her. She tasted the desperation, the temper. "Don't tell me you love me in that calm, steady voice." Brand lifted his head only to change the angle of the kiss. His mouth was hard and insistent before it parted from hers. "I need more than that from you,

Raven, much more than that.'' His eyes blazed green into hers. "I'll have more, damn it!''

"Brandon.'' She was breathless, dizzy, then laughing. This was no dream. "The cup's digging a permanent hole in my chest. Please, let me put the dishes down.'' He said something fierce about the dishes, but she managed to pull away from him enough to put them on the counter. "Oh, Brandon!'' Immediately Raven threw her arms around his neck. "You have more; you have everything. I was afraid—and a fool to be afraid—to tell you how much I love you.'' She placed her hands on his cheeks, holding his face away from her so that he could read what was in her eyes. "I love you, Brandon.''

Quick and urgent, their lips came together. They clung still when he swept her up in his arms. "You'll have to do without your coffee for a while,'' he told her as she pressed a kiss to the curve of his neck. She only murmured an assent as he began to carry her down the hall.

"Too far,'' she whispered.

"Mmm?''

"The bedroom's much too far away.''

Brand turned his head to grin at her. "Too far,'' he agreed, taking a sharp right into the music room. "Entirely too far.'' They sank together on a sofa. "How's this?'' He slipped his hands beneath the robe to feel her skin.

"We've always worked well together here.'' Raven laughed into his eyes, running her fingers along the muscles of his shoulders. It was real, she thought triumphantly, kissing him again.

"The secret," Brand decided, then dug his teeth playfully into her neck, "is a strong melody."

"It's nothing without the proper lyric."

"Music doesn't always need words." He switched to the other side of her neck as his hand roamed to her breast.

"No," she agreed, finding that her own hands refused to be still. They journeyed down his back and up again. "But harmony—two strong notes coming together and giving a bit to each other."

"Melding," he murmured. "I'm big on melding." He loosened the belt of her robe.

"Oh, Brandon!" she exclaimed suddenly, remembering. "Mrs. Pengalley…she'll be here soon."

"This should certainly clinch her opinion of show people," he decided as his mouth found her breast.

"Oh, no, Brandon, stop!" She laughed and moaned and struggled.

"Can't," he said reasonably, trailing his lips back up to her throat. "Savage lust," he explained and bit her ear. "Uncontrollable. Besides," he said as he kissed her, then moved to her other ear, "it's Sunday, her day off."

"It is?" Raven's mind was too clouded to recall trivial things like days of the week. "Savage lust?" she repeated as he pushed the robe from her shoulders. "Really?"

"Absolutely. Shall I show you?"

"Oh, yes," she whispered and brought his mouth back to hers. "Please do."

A long time later Raven sat on the hearth rug and watched Brand stir up the fire. She had reheated the coffee and brought it in along with the sausages. Brand had pulled a sweater on with his jeans, but she still wore the short, terry robe. Holding a coffee cup in both hands, she yawned and thought that she had never felt so relaxed. She felt like a cat sitting in her square of sunlight, watching Brand fix a log onto snapping flames. He turned to find her smiling at him.

"What are you thinking?" He stretched out on the floor beside her.

"How happy I am." She handed him his coffee, leaning over to kiss him as he took it. It all seemed so simple, so right.

"How happy?" he demanded. He smiled at her over the rim of the cup.

"Oh, somewhere between ecstatic and delirious, I think." She sought his hand with hers. Their fingers linked. "Bordering on rapturous."

"Just bordering on?" Brand asked with a sigh. "Well, we'll work on it." He shook his head, then kissed her hand. "Do you know you nearly drove me mad in this room yesterday?"

"Yesterday?" Raven tossed her hair back over her shoulder with a jerk of her head. "What are you talking about?"

"I don't suppose you'll ever realize just how arousing your voice is," he mused as he sipped his coffee and studied her face. "That might be part of the reason—that touch of innocence with a hell-smoked voice."

"I like that." Raven reached behind her to set down her empty cup. The movement loosened the tie of her robe, leaving it open to brush the curve of her breasts. "Do you want one of these sausages? They're probably awful."

Brand lifted his eyes from the smooth expanse of flesh that the shift of material had revealed. He shook his head again and laughed. "You make them sound irresistible."

"A starving man can't be picky," she pointed out. Raven plucked one with her fingers and handed it over. "They're probably greasy."

He lifted a brow at this but took a bite. "Aren't you going to have one?"

"No. I know better than to eat my own cooking." She handed him a napkin.

"We could go out to eat."

"Use your imagination," she suggested, resting her hands on her knees. "Pretend you've already eaten. It always works for me."

"My imagination isn't as good as yours." Brand finished off the sausage. "Maybe if you tell me what I've had."

"An enormous heap of scrambled eggs," she decided, narrowing her eyes. "Five or six, at least. You really should watch your cholesterol. And three pieces of toast with that dreadful marmalade you pile on."

"You haven't tried it," he reminded her.

"I imagined I did," she explained patiently. "You also had five slices of bacon." She put a bit of censure in her voice, and he grinned.

"I've a healthy morning appetite."

"I don't see how you could eat another bite after all that. Coffee?" Raven reached for the pot.

"No, I imagine I've had enough."

She laughed and leaning over, linked her arms around his neck. "Did I really drive you mad, Brandon?" She found the taste of her own power delicious and sweet.

"Yes." He rubbed her nose with his. "First it was all but impossible to simply be in the same room with you, wanting you as I did. Then that song." He gave a quiet laugh, then drew back to look at her. "Music doesn't always soothe the savage beast. And then that damn album jacket. I had to be furious, or I'd have thrown you down on the rug then and there."

He saw puzzlement, then comprehension, dawn in her eyes. "Is that why you…" She stopped, and the smile grew slowly. Raven tilted her head and ran the tip of her tongue over her teeth. "I suppose that now that you've had your way with me, I won't drive you mad anymore."

"That's right." He kissed her lightly. "I can take you or leave you." Brand set down his empty cup, then ruffled her hair, amused by her wry expression. "It's noon," he said with a glance at the clock. "We'd best get to it if we're going to get any work

done today. That novelty number we were toying
with, the one for the second female lead—I'd an idea
for that.''

''Really?'' Raven unhooked her hands from behind
his neck. ''What sort of idea?''

''We might bounce up the beat, a bit of early forties
jive tempo, you know. It'd be a good contrast to the
rest of the score.''

''*Hmmm,* could be a good dance number.'' Raven
slipped her hands under his sweater and ran them up
his naked chest. She smiled gently at the look of surprise that flickered in his eyes. ''We need a good
dance number there.''

''That's what I was thinking,'' Brand murmured.
The move had surprised him, and the light touch of
her fingers sent a dull thud of desire hammering in his
stomach. He reached for her, but she rose and moved
to the piano.

''Like this, then?'' Raven played a few bars of the
melody they had worked with, using the tempo he had
suggested. ''A little boogie-woogie?''

''Yes.'' He forced his attention to the bouncing,
repetitive beat but found his blood beating with it.
''That's the idea.''

She looked back over her shoulder and smiled at
him. ''Then all we need are the lyrics.'' She experimented a moment longer, then went to the coffeepot.
''Cute and catchy.'' Raven drank, smiling down at
Brand. ''With a chorus.''

''Any ideas?''

"Yes." She set down the cup. "I have some ideas." Raven sat down beside him, facing him, and thoughtfully brushed the hair back from his forehead. "If they're going to cast Carly, as it appears they're going to do, we need something to suit that baby-doll voice of hers. Her songs should be a direct foil for Lauren's." She pressed her lips lightly to his ear. "Of course, the chorus could carry the meat of it." Again she slipped a hand under his sweater, letting her fingertips toy with the soft mat of hair on his chest. She slid her eyes up to his. "What do you think?"

Brand took her arm and pulled her against him, but she turned her head so that the kiss only brushed her cheek. "Raven," he said after a laughing moan. But when she trailed her finger down to his stomach, she felt him suck in air. Again he moaned her name and crushed her against him.

Raven tilted her head back for the kiss. It was deep and desperate, but when he would have urged her down, she shifted so that her body covered his. She buried her mouth at his neck and felt the pulse hammering against her lips. Her hands were still under his sweater so that she was aware of the heating of his skin. He tugged at her robe, but she only pressed harder against him, lodging the fabric between them. She nipped at the cord of his neck.

"Raven." His voice was low and husky. "For God's sake, let me touch you."

"Am I driving you mad, Brandon?" she murmured, nearly delirious with her own power. Before he could answer, she brought her lips to his and took her tongue deep into his mouth. Slowly she hiked up his sweater, feeling the shudders of his skin as she worked it over his chest and shoulders. Even as she tossed it aside, Raven began journeying down his chest, using her lips and tongue to taste him.

It was a new sensation for her: the knowledge that he was as vulnerable to her as she was to him. There was harmony between them and the mutual need to make the music real and full. Before, he had guided her, but now she was ready to experiment with her own skill. She wanted to toy with tempos, to take the lead. She wanted to flow *pianissimo,* savoring each touch, each taste. Now it was her turn to teach him as he had taught her.

His skin was hot under her tongue. He was moving beneath her, but the first wave of desperation had passed into a drugged pleasure. Her fingers weren't shy but rather sought curiously, stroking over him to find what excited, what pleased. His taste was something she knew now she would starve without. She could feel his fingers in her hair tightening as his passion built. As she had the night before, she sensed his control, but now the challenge of breaking it excited her.

His stomach was taut and tightened further when she glided over it. She heard his breathing catch. Finding the snap to his jeans, she undid it, then began to tug them down over his hips. The rhythm was gathering speed.

Then her mouth was on his, ripping them both far beyond the gentle pace she had initiated. She was suddenly starving, trembling with the need. Pushing herself up, Raven let the robe fall from her shoulders. Her hair tumbled forward to drape her breasts.

"Touch me." Her eyes were heavy but locked in his. "Touch me now."

Brand's fingers tangled in her hair as they sought her flesh. When she would have swayed back down to him, he held her upright, wanting to watch the pleasure and passion on her face. Her eyes were blurred with it. The need built fast and was soon too great.

"Raven." There was desperate demand in his voice as he took her hips.

She let him guide her, then gave a sharp gasp of pleasure. Their bodies fused in a soaring rhythm, completely tuned to each other. Raven shuddered from the impact. Then, drained, she lowered herself until she lay prone on him. He brought his arms around her to hold her close as the two of them flowed from passion to contentment.

Tangled with him, fresh from loving in a room quiet and warm, Raven gave a long, contented sigh. "Brandon," she murmured, just wanting to hear the sound of his name.

"Hmm?" He stroked her hair, seemingly lost somewhere in a world between sleep and wakefulness.

"I never knew it could be like this."

"Neither did I."

Raven shifted until she could look at his face. "But

you've been with so many women.'' She curled up at his side, preparing to rest her head in the curve of his shoulder.

Brand rose on his elbow, then tilted her face up to his. He studied her softly flushed cheeks, the swollen mouth and drowsy eyes. ''I've never been in love with my lover before,'' he told he quietly.

For a moment there was silence. Then she smiled. ''I'm glad. I suppose I've never been sure of that until now.''

''Be sure of it.'' He kissed her, hard and quick and possessively.

She settled against him again but shivered, then laughed. ''A few moments ago I'd have sworn I'd never be cold again.''

Grinning, Brand reached for her robe. ''I seriously doubt we'll get any work done unless you get dressed. In fact, I'd suggest unattractive clothes.''

After tugging her arms through the sleeves, Raven put her hands on his shoulders. Her eyes were light and full of mischief. ''Do I distract you, Brandon?''

''You might put it that way.''

''I'll probably be tempted to try all the time, now that I know I can.'' Raven kissed him, then gave a quick shrug. ''I won't be able to help myself.''

''I'll hold you to that.'' Brand lifted a brow. ''Would you like to start now?''

She gave his hair a sharp tug. ''I don't think that's very flattering. I'm going to go see about those unattractive clothes.''

"Later," he said, pulling her back when she started to rise.

Raven laughed again, amazed with what she saw in his eyes. "Brandon, really!"

"Later," he said again and pressed her back gently to the floor.

Chapter 12

Summer came to Cornwall in stages. Cool mornings turned to warm afternoons that had bees humming outside the front windows. The stinging chill of the nights mellowed. The first scent of honeysuckle teased the air. Then the roses, lush wild roses, began to bloom. And all through the weeks the countryside blossomed, Raven felt that she, too, was blooming. She was loved.

Throughout her life, if anyone had asked her what one thing she wanted most, Raven would have answered, "To be loved." She had starved for it as a child, had hungered as an adolescent when she had been shuffled from town to town, never given the opportunity to form lasting friendships and affections. It was this need, in part, that had made her so successful as a performer. Raven was willing to let the audience love her. She never felt herself beyond their reach when she stood in the spotlight. And they knew it. The love she had gained from her audiences had filled an enormous need. It had filled her but had not satisfied her as much, she discovered, as Brand's love.

As the weeks passed, she forgot the demands and responsibilities of the performer and became more and more in tune with the woman. She had always known herself; it had been important early that she grasp an identity. But for the first time in her life Raven focused on her womanhood. She explored it, discovered it, enjoyed it.

Brand was demanding as a lover, not only in the physical sense but in an emotional one as well. He wanted her body, her heart, her thoughts, with no reservations. His need for an absolute commitment was the only shadow in the summery passing of days. Raven found it impossible not to hold parts of herself in reserve. She'd been hurt and knew how devastating pain could be when you loved without guard. Her mother had broken her heart too many times to count, with always a promise of happiness after the severest blow. Raven had learned to cope with that, to guard against it to some extent.

She had loved Brand before, naively perhaps, but totally. When he had walked out of her life, Raven had thought she would never be whole again. For five years she had insulated herself against the men who had touched her life. They could be friends—loving friends—but never lovers. The wounds had healed, but

the scar had been a constant reminder to be careful.
She had promised herself that no man would ever hurt
her as Brand Carstairs had. And Raven discovered the
vow she had made still held true. He was the only
man who would ever have the power to hurt her. That
realization was enough to both exhilarate and frighten.

There was no doubt that he had awakened her physically. Her fears had been swept away by the tides of
love. Raven found that in this aspect of their relationship she could indeed give herself to Brand unreserv-
edly. Knowing she could arouse him strengthened her
growing confidence as a woman. She learned her pas-
sions were as strong and sensitive as his. She had kept
them restricted far too long. If Brand could heat her
blood with a look, Raven was aware he was just as
susceptible to her. There was nothing of the cool, British reserve in his lovemaking; she thought of him as
all Irish then, stormy and passionate.

One morning he woke her at dawn by strewing the
bed with wild rosebuds. The following evening he surprised her with iced champagne while she bathed in
the ancient footed tub. At night he could be brutally
passionate, waking and taking her with a desperate
urgency that allowed no time for surprise, protest or
response. At times he appeared deliriously happy; at
others she would catch him studying her with an odd,
searching expression.

Raven loved him, but she could not yet bring herself to trust him completely. They both knew it, and
they both avoided speaking of it.

* * *

Seated next to Brand at the piano, Raven experimented with chords for the opening bars of a duet. "I really think a minor mode with a raised seventh." She frowned thoughtfully. "I imagine a lot of strings here, a big orchestration of violins and cellos." She played more, hearing the imagined arrangement rather than the solitary piano. "What do you think?" Raven turned her head to find Brand looking down at her.

"Go ahead," he suggested, drawing on a cigarette. "Play the lot."

She began, only to have him interrupt during a bridge. "No." He shook his head. "That part doesn't fit."

"That was your part," she reminded him with a grin.

"Genius is obliged to correct itself," he returned, and Raven gave an unladylike snort. He looked down his very straight British nose. "Had you a comment, then?"

"Who, me? I never interrupt genius."

"Wise," he said and turned back to spread his own fingers over the keys. "Like this." Brand played the same melody from the beginning, only altering a few notes on the bridge section.

"Did you change something?"

"I realize your inferior ear might not detect the subtlety," he began. She jammed her elbow into his ribs. "Well said," he murmured, rubbing the spot. "Shall we try again?"

"I love it when you're dignified, Brandon."

"Really?" He lifted an inquiring brow. "Now, where was I?"

"You were about to demonstrate the first movement from Tchaikovsky's Second Symphony."

"Ah." Nodding, Brand turned back to the keys. He ran through the difficult movement with a fluid skill that had Raven shaking her head.

"Show-off," she accused when he finished with a flourish.

"You're just jealous."

With a sigh she lifted her shoulders. "Unfortunately, you're right."

Brand laughed and put his hand palm to palm with hers. "I have the advantage in spread."

Raven studied her small, narrow-boned hand. "It's a good thing I didn't want to be a concert pianist."

"Beautiful hands," Brand told her, making one of his sudden and completely natural romantic gestures by lifting her fingers to his lips. "I'm quite helplessly in love with them."

"Brandon." Disarmed, Raven could only look at him. A tremble of warmth shot up her spine.

"They always smell of that lotion you have in the little white pot on the dresser."

"I didn't think you'd notice something like that." She shivered in response when his lips brushed the inside of her wrist.

"There's nothing about you I don't notice." He kissed her other wrist. "You like your bath too hot, and you leave your shoes in the most unexpected places. And you always keep time with your left foot." Brand looked back up at her, keeping one hand entwined with hers while he reached up with the other to brush the hair from her shoulder. "And when I touch you like this, your eyes go to smoke." He ran a fingertip gently over the point of her breast and watched her irises darken and cloud. Very slowly he leaned over and touched his lips to hers. Lazily he ran his finger back and forth until her nipple was taut and straining against the fabric of her blouse.

Her mouth was soft and opened willingly. Raven tilted her head back, inviting him to take more. Currents of pleasure were already racing along her skin. Brand drew her closer, one hand lingering at her breast.

"I can feel your bones melt," he murmured. His mouth grew hungrier, his hand more insistent. "It drives me crazy." His fingers drifted from her breast to the top button of her blouse. Even as he loosened it, the phone shrilled from the table across the room. He swore, and Raven gave a laugh and hugged him.

"Never mind, love," she said on a deep breath. "I'll remind you where you left off this time, too." Slipping out of his arms, she crossed the room to answer. "Hello."

"Hello, I'd like to speak with Brandon Carstairs, please," a voice said.

Raven smiled at the musical lilt in the voice and wondered vaguely how one of Brand's fans had gotten access to his number. "Mr. Carstairs is quite busy at the moment." She grinned over at him and got both

a grin and a nod of approval before he crossed to her.
He began to distract her by kissing her neck.

"Would you ask him to call his mother when he's
free?"

"I beg your pardon?" Raven stifled a giggle and
tried to struggle out of Brand's arms.

"His mother, dear," the voice repeated. "Ask him
to call his mother when he has a minute, won't you?
He has the number."

"Oh, please, Mrs. Carstairs, wait! I'm sorry."
Wide-eyed, she looked up at Brand. "Brandon's right
here. Your mother," Raven said in a horrified whisper
that had him grinning again. Still holding her firmly
to his side, he accepted the receiver.

"Hullo, Mum." Brand kissed the top of Raven's
head, then chuckled. "Yes, I was busy. I was kissing
a beautiful woman I'm madly in love with." The color
rising in Raven's cheeks had him laughing. "No, no,
it's all right, love, I intend to get back to it. How are
you? And the rest?"

Raven nudged herself free of Brand's arm. "I'll
make some tea," she said quietly, then slipped from
the room.

Mrs. Pengalley had left the kitchen spotlessly clean,
and Raven spent some time puttering around it aim-
lessly while the kettle heated on the stove. She found
herself suddenly hungry, then remembered that she
and Brand had worked straight through lunch. She got
out the bread, deciding to make buttered toast fingers
to serve with the tea.

Afternoon tea was one of Brand's rituals, and

Raven had grown fond of it. She enjoyed the late afternoon breaks in front of the fireplace with tea and biscuits or scones or buttered toast. They could be any two people then, Raven mused, two people sitting in front of a fireplace having unimportant conversations. The kettle sang out, and she moved to switch off the flame.

Raven went about the mechanical domestic tasks of brewing tea and buttering toast, but her thoughts kept drifting back to Brand. There had been such effortless affection in his voice when he had spoken to his mother, such relaxed love. And Raven had felt a swift flash of envy. It was something she had experienced throughout childhood and adolescence, but she hadn't expected to feel it again. Raven reminded herself she was twenty-five and no longer a child.

The chores soothed her. She loaded the tray and started back down the hall with her feelings more settled. When she heard Brand's voice, she hesitated, not wanting to interrupt his conversation. But the weight of the tray outbalanced her sense of propriety.

He was sunk into one of the chairs by the fire when Raven entered. With a smile he gestured her over so that she crossed the room and set the tray on the table beside him. "I will, Mum, perhaps next month. Give everyone my love." He paused and smiled again, taking Raven's hand. "She's got big gray eyes, the same color as the dove Shawn kept in the coop on the roof. Yes, I'll tell her. Bye, Mum. I love you."

Hanging up, Brand glanced at the ladened tea tray, then up at Raven. "You've been busy."

She crouched down and began pouring. "I discovered I was starving." She watched with the usual shake of her head as he added milk to his tea. That was one English habit Raven knew she would never comprehend. She took her own plain.

"My mother says to tell you you've a lovely voice over the phone." Brand picked up a toast finger and bit into it.

"You didn't have to tell her you'd been kissing me," Raven mumbled, faintly embarrassed. Brand laughed, and she glared at him.

"Mum knows I have a habit of kissing women," he explained gravely. "She probably knows I've occasionally done a bit more than that, but we haven't discussed that particular aspect of my life for some time." He took another bite of toast, studying Raven's face. "She wants to meet you. If the score keeps going along at this pace, I thought we might drive up to London next month."

"I'm not used to families, Brandon," she said. Raven reached for her cup, but he placed his hand over hers, waiting until she looked back up at him.

"They're easy people, Raven. They're important to me. You're important to me. I want them to know you."

She felt her stomach tighten, and lowered her eyes.

"Raven." Brand gave a short, exasperated sigh. "When are you going to talk to me?"

She couldn't pretend not to understand him. She could only shake her head and avoid the subject a little while longer. The time when they would have to return to California and face reality would come soon enough. "Please, tell me about your family. It might help me get used to being confronted with all of them if I know a bit more than I've read in the gossip columns." Raven smiled. Her eyes asked him to smile back and not to probe. Not yet.

Brand struggled with a sense of frustration but gave in. He could give her a little more time. "I'm the oldest of five." He gestured toward the mantel. "Michael's the distinguished-looking one with the pretty blond wife. He's a solicitor." Brand smiled, remembering the pleasure it had given him to send his brother to a good university. He'd been the first Carstairs to receive that sort of education. "There was nothing distinguished about him at all as a boy," Brand remarked. "He liked to give anyone within reach a bloody nose."

"Sounds like a good lawyer," Raven observed dryly. "Please go on."

"Alison's next. She graduated from Oxford at the top of her class." He watched Raven glance up at the photo of the fragile, lovely blonde. "An amazing brain," Brand continued, smiling. "She does something incomprehensible with computers and has a particular fondness for rowdy rugby matches. That's where she met her husband."

Raven shook her head, trying to imagine the delicate-looking woman shouting at rugby games or programming sophisticated computers. "I suppose your other brother's a physicist."

"No, Shawn's a veterinarian." Affection slipped into Brand's voice.

"Your favorite?"

He tilted his head as he reached for more tea. "If one has a favorite among brothers and sisters, I suppose so. He's simply one of the nicest people I know. He's incapable of hurting anyone. As a boy he was the one who always found the bird with the broken wing or the dog with a sore paw. You know the type."

Raven didn't, but she murmured something and continued to sip at her tea. Brand's family was beginning to fascinate her. Somehow, she had thought that people raised in the same house under the same circumstances would be more the same. These people seemed remarkably diverse. "And your other sister?"

"Moray." He grinned. "She's in school yet, claims she's going into finance or drama. Or perhaps," he added, "anthropology. She's undecided."

"How old is she?"

"Eighteen. She thinks your records are smashing, by the way, and had them all the last time I was home."

"I believe I'll like her," Raven decided. She let her gaze sweep the mantel again. "Your parents must be very proud of all of you. What does your father do?"

"He's a carpenter." Brand wondered if she was aware of the wistful look in her eyes. "He still works six days a week, even though he knows money isn't a problem anymore. He has a great deal of pride." He paused a moment, stirring his tea, his eyes on Raven. "Mum still hangs sheets out on a line, even though I bought her a perfectly good dryer ten years ago. That's the sort of people they are.''

"You're very lucky," Raven told him and rose to wander about the room.

"Yes, I know that." Brand watched her move around the room with her quick, nervous stride. "Though I doubt I thought a great deal about it while I was growing up. It's very easy to take it all for granted. It must have been very difficult for you.''

Raven lifted her shoulders, then let them fall. "I survived." Walking to the window, she looked out on the cliffs and the sea. "Let's go for a walk, Brandon. It's so lovely out.''

He rose and walked to her. Taking her by the shoulders, Brand turned her around to face him. "There's more to life than surviving, Raven.''

"I survived intact," she told him. "Not everyone does.''

"Raven, I know you call home twice a week, but you never tell me anything about it." He gave her a quick, caring shake. "Talk to me.''

"Not about that, not now, not here." She slipped her arms around him and pressed her cheek to his chest. "I don't want anything to touch us here—nothing from the past, nothing from tomorrow. Oh, there's so much ugliness, Brandon, so many responsibilities. I want time. Is that so wrong?" She held him tighter, suddenly possessive. "Can't this be our fantasy, Brandon? That there isn't anybody but us? Just for a little while.''

She heard him sigh as his lips brushed the crown

of her head. "For a little while, Raven. But fantasies have to end, and I want the reality, too."

Raven lifted her face, then framed his with her hands. "Like Joe in the script," she reflected and smiled. "He finds his reality in the end, doesn't he?"

"Yes." Brand bent to kiss her and found himself lingering over it longer than he had intended. "Proving dreams come true," he murmured.

"But I'm not a dream, Brandon." She took both of his hands in hers while her eyes smiled at him. "And you've already brought me to life."

"And without magic."

Raven lifted a brow. "That depends on your point of view," she countered. "I still feel the magic." Slowly she lifted his hand to the neckline of her blouse. "I think you were here when we left off."

"So I was." He loosened the next button, watching her face. "What about that walk?"

"Walk? In all that rain?" Raven glanced over to the sun-filled window. "No." Shaking her head, she looked back at Brand. "I think we'd better stay inside until it blows over."

He ran his finger down to the next button, smiling at her while he toyed with it. "You're probably right."

Chapter 13

Mrs. Pengalley made it a point to clean the music room first whenever Raven and Brand left her alone in the house. It was here they spent all their time working—if what show people did could be considered work. She had her own opinion on that. She gathered up the cups, as she always did, and sniffed them. Tea. Now and again she had sniffed wine and occasionally some bourbon, but she was forced to admit that Mr. Carstairs didn't seem to live up to the reputation of heavy drinking that show people had. Mrs. Pengalley was the smallest bit disappointed.

They lived quietly, too. She had been sure when Brand had notified her to expect him to be in residence for three months that he would have plans to entertain. Mrs. Pengalley knew what sort of entertainment show business people went in for. She had waited for the fancy cars to start arriving, the fancy people in their outrageous clothes. She had told Mr. Pengalley it was just a matter of time.

But no one had come, no one at all. There had been no disgraceful parties to clean up after. There had only been Mr. Carstairs and the young girl with the big gray eyes who sang as pretty as you please. But of course, Mrs. Pengalley reminded herself, she was in *that* business, too.

Mrs. Pengalley walked over to shake the wrinkles from the drapes at the side window. From there she could see Raven and Brand walking along the cliffs. Always in each other's pockets, she mused and sniffed to prevent herself from smiling at them. She snapped the drape back into place and began dusting off the furniture.

And how was a body supposed to give anything a proper dusting, she wanted to know, when they were always leaving their papers with the chicken scratchings on them all over everywhere? Picking up a piece of staff paper, Mrs. Pengalley scowled down at the lines and notes. She couldn't make head nor tail out of the notations; she scanned the words instead.

Loving you is no dream/I need you here to hold on to/Wanting you is everything/Come back to me.

She clucked her tongue and set the paper back down. Fine song, that one, she thought, resuming her dusting. Doesn't even rhyme.

Outside, the wind from the sea was strong, and

Brand slipped his arm around Raven's shoulders. Turning her swiftly to face him, he bent her backward and gave her a long, lingering kiss. She gripped his shoulders for balance, then stared at him when his mouth lifted.

"What," she began and let out a shaky breath, "was that for?"

"For Mrs. Pengalley," he answered easily. "She's peeking out the music room window."

"Brandon, you're terrible." His mouth came down to hers again. Her halfhearted protest turned into total response. With a quiet sound of pleasure, Brand deepened the kiss and dragged her closer to him. Raven could feel the heat of the sun on her skin even as the sea breeze cooled it. The wind brought them the scent of honeysuckle and roses.

"That," he murmured as his mouth brushed over her cheeks, "was for me."

"Have any other friends?" Raven asked.

Laughing, Brand gave her a quick hug and released her. "I suppose we've given her enough to cluck her tongue over today."

"So that's what you want me for." Raven tossed her head. "Shock value."

"Among other things."

They wandered to the sea wall, for some moments looking out in comfortable silence. Raven liked the cliffs with their harsh faces and sheer, dizzying drop. She liked the constant, boiling noise of the sea, the screaming of the gulls.

The score was all but completed, with only a few minor loose ends and a bit of polishing to be done. Copies of completed numbers had been sent back to California. Raven knew they were drawing out a job that could be finished quickly. She had her own reasons for procrastinating, though she wasn't wholly certain of Brand's. She didn't want to break the spell.

Raven wasn't sure precisely what Brand wanted from her because she hadn't permitted him to tell her yet. There were things, she knew, that had to be settled between them—things that could be avoided for the time being while they both simply let themselves be consumed by love. But the time would come when they would have to deal with the everyday business of living.

Would their work be a problem? That was one of the questions Raven refused to ask herself. Or if she asked it, she refused to answer. Commitments went with their profession, time-consuming commitments that made it difficult to establish any sort of a normal life. And there was so little privacy. Every detail of their relationship would be explored in the press. There would be pictures and stories, true and fabricated. The worst kind, Raven mused, were those with a bit of both. All of this, she realized, could be handled with hard work and determination if the love was strong enough. She had no doubt theirs was, but she had other doubts.

Would she ever be able to rid herself of the nagging fear that he might leave her again? The memory of the hurt kept her from giving herself to Brand completely. And her feelings of responsibility to her mother created yet another barrier. This was something she had always refused to share with anyone. She couldn't even bring herself to share it with the person she cared for most in the world. Years before, she had made a decision to control her own life, promising herself she would never depend too heavily on anything or anyone. Too often she had watched her mother relinquish control and lose.

If she could have found a way, Raven would have prolonged the summer. But more and more, the knowledge that the idyll was nearly at an end intruded into her thoughts. The prelude to fantasy was over. She hoped the fantasy would become a reality.

Brand watched Raven's face as she leaned her elbows on the rough stone wall and looked out to sea. There was a faraway look in her eyes that bothered him. He wanted to reach her, but their time alone together was slipping by rapidly. A cloud slid across the sun for a moment, and the light shifted and dimmed. He heard Raven sigh.

"What are you thinking?" he demanded, catching her flying hair in his hand.

"That of all the places I've ever been, this is the best." Raven tilted her head to smile up at him but didn't alter her position against the wall. "Julie and I took a break in Monaco once, and I was sure it was the most beautiful spot on earth. Now I know it's the second."

"I knew you'd love it if I could ever get you here," Brand mused, still toying with the ends of her hair. "I had some bad moments thinking you'd refuse. I'm not at all sure I could have come up with an alternate plan."

"Plan?" Raven's forehead puckered over the word. "I don't know what you mean. What plan?"

"To get you here, where we could be alone."

Raven straightened away from the wall but continued looking out to sea. "I thought we came here to write a score."

"Yes." Brand watched the flight of a bird as it swooped down over the waves. "The timing of that was rather handy."

"Handy?" Raven felt the knot start in her stomach. The clouds shifted over the sun again.

"I doubt you'd have agreed to work with me again if the project hadn't been so tempting," he said. Brand frowned up at a passing cloud. "You certainly wouldn't have agreed to live with me."

"So you dangled the score in front of my nose like a meaty bone?"

"Of course not. I wanted to work with you on the project the moment it was offered to me. It was all just a matter of timing, really."

"Timing and planning," she said softly. "Like a chess game. Julie's right; I've never been any good at strategy." Raven turned away, but Brand caught her arm before she could retreat.

"Raven?"

"How could you?" She whirled back to face him. Her eyes were dark and hot, her cheeks flushed with fury. Brand narrowed his eyes and studied her.

"How could I what?" he asked coolly, releasing her arm.

"How could you use the score to trick me into coming here?" She dragged at her hair as the wind blew it into her face.

"I'd have used anything to get you back," Brand said. "And I didn't trick you, Raven. I told you nothing but the truth."

"Part of the truth," she continued.

"Perhaps," he agreed. "We're both rather good at that, aren't we?" He didn't touch her, but the look he gave her became more direct. "Why are you angry? Because I love you or because I made you realize you love me?"

"Nobody *makes* me do anything!" She balled her hands into fists as she whirled away. "Oh, I detest being maneuvered. I run my own life, make my own decisions."

"I don't believe I've made any for you."

"No, you just led me gently along by the nose until I *chose* what was best for myself." Raven turned back again, and now her voice was low and vibrant with anger. "Why couldn't you have been honest with me?"

"You wouldn't have let me anywhere near you if I'd been completely honest. I had experience with you before, remember?"

Raven's eyes blazed. "Don't tell me what I would've done, Brandon. You're not inside my head."

"No, you've never let me in there." He pulled out a cigarette, cupped his hands around a match and lit it. Before speaking, he took a long, contemplative drag. "We'll say I wasn't in the mood to be taking chances, then. Will that suit you?"

His cool, careless tone fanned her fury. "You had no right!" she tossed at him. "You had no right to arrange my life this way. Who said I had to play by your rules, Brandon? When did you decide I was incapable of planning for myself?"

"If you'd like to be treated as a rational adult, perhaps you should behave as one," he suggested in a deceptively mild tone. "At the moment I'd say you're being remarkably childish. I didn't bring you here under false pretenses, Raven. There was a score to be written, and this was a quiet place to do it. It was also a place I felt you'd have the chance to get used to being with me again. I wanted you back."

"*You* felt. *You* wanted!" Raven tossed back her hair. "How incredibly selfish! What about *my* feelings? Do you think you can just pop in and out of my life at your convenience?"

"As I remember, I was pushed out."

"You left me!" The tears came from nowhere and blinded her. "Nothing's ever hurt me like that before. Nothing!" Tears of hurt sprang to her eyes. "I'll be damned if you'll do it to me again. You went away without a word!''

''You mightn't have liked the words I wanted to say.'' Brand tossed the stub of his cigarette over the wall. ''You weren't the only one who was hurt that night. How the hell else could I be rational unless I put some distance between us? I couldn't have given you the time you seemed to need if I'd stayed anywhere near you.''

''Time?'' Raven repeated as thoughts trembled and raced through her mind. ''You gave me time?''

''You were a child when I left,'' he said shortly. ''I'd hoped you'd be a woman when I came back.''

''You had hoped...'' Her voice trailed off into an astonished whisper. ''Are you telling me you stayed away, giving me a chance to—to grow up?''

''I didn't see I had any choice.'' Brand dug his hands into his pockets as his brows came together.

''Didn't you?'' She remembered her despair at his going, the emptiness of the years. ''And of course, why should you have given me one? You simply took it upon yourself to decide for me.''

''It wasn't a matter of deciding.'' He turned away from her, knowing he was losing his grip on his temper. ''It was a matter of keeping sane. I simply couldn't stay near you and not have you.''

''So you stayed away for five years, then suddenly reappeared, using my music as an excuse to lure me into bed. You didn't give a damn about the quality of

Fantasy. You just used it—and the talent and sweat of the performers—for your own selfish ends.''

''That,'' he said in a deadly calm voice, ''is beyond contempt.'' Turning, he walked away. Within moments Raven heard the roar of an engine over the sound of the sea.

She stood, watching the car speed down the lane. If she had meant to deal a savage blow, she had succeeded. The shock of her own words burned in her throat. She shut her eyes tightly.

Even with her eyes closed, she could see clearly the look of fury on Brand's face before he had walked away. Raven ran a shaking hand through her hair. Her head was throbbing with the aftereffects of temper. Slowly she opened her eyes and stared out at the choppy green sea.

Everything we've had these past weeks was all part of some master plan, she thought. Even as she stood, the anger drained out of her, leaving only the weight of unhappiness.

She resented the fact that Brand had secretly placed a hand on the reins of her life, resented that he had offered her the biggest opportunity in her career as a step in drawing her to him. And yet… Raven shook her head in frustration. Confused and miserable, she turned to walk back to the house.

Mrs. Pengalley met her at the music room door. ''There's a call for you, miss, from California.'' She had watched the argument from the window with a healthy curiosity. Now, however, the look in the gray eyes set her maternal instincts quivering. She repressed an urge to smooth down Raven's hair. "I'll make you some tea," she said.

Raven walked to the phone and lifted the receiver. "Yes, hello."

"Raven, it's Julie."

"Julie." Raven sank down in a chair. She blinked back fresh tears at the sound of the familiar voice. "Back from the isles of Greece?"

"I've been back for a couple weeks, Raven."

Of course. She should have known that. "Yes, all right. What's happened?"

"Karter contacted me because he wasn't able to reach you this morning. Some trouble on the line or something."

"Has she left again?" Raven's voice was dull.

"Apparently she left last night. She didn't go very far." Hearing the hesitation in Julie's voice, Raven felt the usual tired acceptance sharpen into apprehension.

"Julie?" Words dried up, and she waited.

"There was an accident, Raven. You'd better come home."

Raven closed her eyes. "Is she dead?"

"No, but it's not good, Raven. I hate having to tell you over the phone this way. The housekeeper said Brand wasn't there."

"No." Raven opened her eyes and looked vaguely around the room. "No, Brandon isn't here." She managed to snap herself back. "How bad, Julie? Is she in the hospital?"

Julie hesitated again, then spoke quietly. "She's not going to make it, Raven. I'm sorry. Karter says hours at best."

"Oh, God." Raven had lived with the fear all her life, yet it still came as a shock. She looked around the room again a little desperately, trying to orient herself.

"I know there's no good way to tell you this, Raven, but I wish I could find a better one."

"What?" She brought herself back again with an enormous effort. "No, I'm all right. I'll leave right away."

"Shall I meet you and Brand at the airport?"

The question drifted through Raven's mind. "No. No, I'll go straight to the hospital. Where is she?"

"St. Catherine's, intensive care."

"Tell Dr. Karter I'll be there as soon as I can. Julie…"

"Yes?"

"Stay with her."

"Of course I will. I'll be here."

Raven hung up and sat staring at the silent phone.

Mrs. Pengalley came back into the room carrying a cup of tea. She took one look at Raven's white face and set it aside. Without speaking, she went to the liquor cabinet and took out the brandy. After pouring out two fingers, she pressed the snifter on Raven.

"Here now, miss, you drink this." The Cornish burr was brisk.

Raven's eyes shifted to her. "What?"

"Drink up, there's a girl."

She obeyed as Mrs. Pengalley lifted the glass to her lips. Instantly Raven sucked in her breath at the unexpected strength of the liquor. She took another sip, then let out a shaky sigh.

"Thank you." She lifted her eyes to Mrs. Pengalley again. "That's better."

"Brandy has its uses," the housekeeper said righteously.

Raven rose, trying to put her thoughts in order. There were things to be done and no time to do them. "Mrs. Pengalley, I have to go back to America right away. Could you pack some things for me while I call the airport?"

"Aye." She studied Raven shrewdly. "He's gone off to cool his heels, you know. They all do that. But he'll be back soon enough."

Realizing Mrs. Pengalley spoke of Brand, Raven dragged a hand through her hair. "I'm not altogether certain of that. If Brandon's not back by the time I have to go to the airport, would you ask Mr. Pengalley to drive me? I know it's an inconvenience, but it's terribly important."

"If that's what you want." Mrs. Pengalley sniffed. Young people, she thought, always flying off the handle. "I'll pack your things, then."

"Thank you." Raven glanced around the music room, then picked up the phone.

An hour later she hesitated at the foot of the stairs. Everything seemed to have happened at once. She willed Brand to return, but there was no sign of his car in the driveway. Raven struggled over writing a note but could think of nothing to say on paper that could make up for the words she had thrown at him. And how could she say in a few brief lines that her mother was dying and she had to go to her?

Yet there wasn't time to wait until he returned. She knew she couldn't risk it. Frantically she pulled a note pad from her purse. "Brandon," she wrote quickly, "I had to go. I'm needed at home. Please, forgive me. I love you, Raven."

Dashing back into the music room, she propped the note against the sheet of staff paper on top of the pile on the piano. Then, hurrying from the room, she grabbed her suitcases and ran outside. Mr. Pengalley was waiting in his serviceable sedan to drive her to the airport.

Chapter 14

Five days passed before Raven began thinking clearly again. Karter had been right about there only being a matter of hours. Raven had had to deal not only with grief but also with an unreasonable guilt that she hadn't been in time. The demand of details saved her from giving into the urge to sink into self-pity and self-rebuke. She wondered once, during those first crushing hours, if that was why people tied so many traditions and complications to death: to keep from falling into total despair.

She was grateful that Karter handled the police himself in a way that ensured the details would be kept out of the papers.

After the first busy days there was nothing left but to accept that the woman she had loved and despised was gone. There was no more she could do. The disease had beaten them, just as surely as if it had been a cancer. Gradually she began to accept her mother's death as the result of a long, debilitating illness. She didn't cry, knowing she had already mourned, knowing it was time to put away the unhappiness. She had never had control of her mother's life; she needed the strength to maintain control of her own.

A dozen times during those days Raven phoned the house in Cornwall. There was never an answer. She could almost hear the hollow, echoing sounds of the ring through the empty rooms. More than once she considered simply getting on a plane and going back, but she always pushed the thought aside. He wouldn't be there waiting for her.

Where could he be? she wondered again and again. *Where would he have gone? He hasn't forgiven me.* And worse, she thought again and again, *he'll never forgive me.*

After hanging up the phone a last time, Raven looked at herself in her bedroom mirror. She was pale. The color that had drained from her face five days ago in Cornwall had never completely returned. There was too much of a helpless look about her. Raven shook her head and grabbed her blusher. Borrowed color, she decided, was better than none at all. She had to start somewhere.

Yes, she thought again, still holding the sable brush against her cheek. I've got to start somewhere. Turning away from the mirror, Raven again picked up the phone.

Thirty minutes later she came downstairs wearing a black silk dress. She had twisted her hair up and was setting a plain, stiff-brimmed black hat over it as she stepped into the hall.

"Raven?" Julie came out of the office. "Are you going out?"

"Yes, if I can find that little envelope bag and my car keys. I think they're inside it." She was already poking into the hall closet.

"Are you all right?"

Raven drew her head from the closet and met Julie's look. "I'm better," she answered, knowing Julie wouldn't be satisfied with a clichéd reply. "The lecture you gave me after the funeral, about not blaming myself? I'm trying to put it into practice."

"It wasn't a lecture," Julie countered. "It was simply a statement of facts. You did everything you could do to help your mother; you couldn't have done any more."

Raven sighed before she could stop herself. "I did everything I knew how to do, and I suppose that's the same thing." She shook off the mood as she shut the closet door. "I *am* better, Julie, and I'm going to be fine." She smiled, then, glimpsing a movement, looked beyond Julie's shoulder. Wayne stepped out of the office. "Hello, Wayne, I didn't know you were here."

He moved past Julie. "Well, I can definitely approve of that dress," he greeted her.

"And so you should," Raven returned dryly. "You charged me enough for it."

"Don't be a philistine, darling. Art has no price."
He flicked a finger over the shoulder of the dress.
"Where are you off to?"

"Alphonso's. I'm meeting Henderson for lunch."

Wayne touched Raven's cheek with a fingertip. "A
bit heavy on the blush," he commented.

"I'm tired of looking pale. Don't fuss." She placed
a hand on each of his cheeks, urging him to bend so
that she could kiss him. "You've been a rock, Wayne.
I haven't told you how much I appreciate your being
here the last few days."

"I needed to escape from the office."

"I adore you." She lowered her hands to meet his
arms and squeezed briefly. "Now, stop worrying
about me." Raven shot a look past his shoulder to
Julie. "You, too. I'm meeting Henderson to talk over
plans for a new tour."

"New tour?" Julie frowned. "Raven, you've been
working nonstop for over six months. The album, the
tour, the score." She paused. "After all of this you
need a break."

"After all this the thing I need least is a break,"
Raven corrected. "I want to work."

"Then take a sabbatical," Julie insisted. "A few
months back you were talking about finding a moun-
tain cabin in Colorado, remember?"

"Yes." Raven smiled and shook her head. "I was
going to write and be rustic, wasn't I? Get away from
the glitter-glamour and into the woods." Raven
grinned, recalling the conversation. "You said some-

thing about not being interested in anything more rustic than a margarita at poolside.''

Julie lifted a thin, arched brow. "I've changed my mind. I'm going shopping for hiking boots.''

Wayne's comment was a dubious *"hmmm."*

Raven smiled. "You're sweet,'' she said to Julie as she kissed her cheek. "But it isn't necessary. I need to do something that takes energy, physical energy. I'm going to talk to Henderson about a tour of Australia. My records do very well there.''

"If you'd just talk to Brand…'' Julie began, but Raven cut her off.

"I've tried to reach him; I can't.'' There was something final and flat in the statement. "Obviously he doesn't want to talk to me. I'm not at all sure I blame him.''

"He's in love with you,'' Wayne said from behind her. Raven turned and met the look. "A few thousand people saw the sparks flying the night of your concert in New York.''

"Yes, he loves me, and I love him. It doesn't seem to be enough, and I can't quite figure out why. No, please.'' She took his hand, pressing it between both of hers. "I have to get my mind off it all for a while. I feel as if I had been having a lovely picnic and got caught in a landslide. The bruises are still a bit sore. I could use some good news,'' she added, glancing from one of them to the other, "if the two of you are ever going to decide to tell me.''

Raven watched as Wayne and Julie exchanged glances. She grinned, enjoying what she saw. "I've been noticing a few sparks myself. Isn't this a rather sudden situation?''

"Very," Wayne agreed, smiling at Julie over Raven's head. "It's only been going on for about six years."

"Six years!" Raven's brows shot up in amazement.

"I didn't choose to be one of a horde," Wayne said mildly, lighting one of his elegant cigarettes.

"And I always thought he was in love with you," Julie stated, letting her gaze drift from Raven to Wayne.

"With *me?*" Raven laughed spontaneously for the first time in days.

"I fail to see the humour in that," Wayne remarked from behind a nimbus of smoke. "I'm considered by many to be rather attractive."

"Oh, you are," she agreed, then giggled and kissed his cheek. "Madly so. But I can't believe anyone could think you were in love with me. You've always dated those rather alarmingly beautiful models with their sculpted faces and long legs."

"I don't think we need bring all that up at the moment," Wayne retorted.

"It's all right." Julie smiled sweetly and tucked her hair behind her ear. "I haven't any problem with Wayne's checkered past."

"When did all this happen, please?" Amused, Raven cut into their exchange. "I turn my back for a few weeks, and I find my two best friends making calf's eyes at each other."

"I've never made calf's eyes at anyone," Wayne

remonstrated, horrified. "Smoldering glances, perhaps." He lifted his rakishly scarred brow.

"When?" Raven repeated.

"I looked up from my deck chair the first morning out on the cruise," Julie began, "and who do you suppose is sauntering toward me in a perfectly cut Mediterranean white suit?"

"Really?" Raven eyed Wayne dubiously. "I'm not certain whether I'm surprised or impressed."

"It seemed like a good opportunity," he explained, tapping his expensive ashes into a nearby dish, "if I could corner her before she charmed some shipping tycoon or handy sailor."

"I believe I charmed a shipping tycoon a few years ago," Julie remarked lazily. "And as to the sailor…"

"Nevertheless," Wayne went on, shooting her a glance. "I decided a cruise was a very good place to begin winning her over. It was," he remarked, "remarkably simple."

"Oh?" Julie's left brow arched. "Really?"

Wayne tapped out his cigarette, then moved over to gather her in his arms. "A piece of cake," he added carelessly. "Of course, women habitually find me irresistible."

"It would be safer if they stopped doing so. I might be tempted to wring their necks," Julie cooed, winding her arms around his neck.

"The woman's going to be a trial to live with." Wayne kissed her as though he'd decided to make the best of it.

"I can see you two are going to be perfectly miserable together. I'm so sorry." Walking over, Raven slipped an arm around each of them. "You will let me give you the wedding?" she began, then stopped. "That is, are you having a wedding?"

"Absolutely," Wayne told her. "We don't trust each other enough for anything less encumbering." He gave Julie a flashing grin that inexplicably made Raven want to weep.

Raven hugged them both again fiercely. "I needed to hear something like this right now. I'm going to leave you alone. I imagine you can entertain yourselves while I'm gone. Can I tell Henderson?" she asked. "Or is it a secret?"

"You can tell him," Julie said, watching as Raven adjusted her hat in the hall mirror. "We're planning on taking the plunge next week."

Raven's eyes darted up to Julie's in the mirror. "My, you two move fast, don't you?"

"When it's right, it's right."

Raven smiled in quick agreement. "Yes, I suppose it is. There's probably champagne in the refrigerator, isn't there, Julie?" She turned away from the mirror. "We can have a celebration drink when I get back. I'll just be a couple of hours."

"Raven." Julie stopped her as she headed for the door. Raven looked curiously over her shoulder. "Your purse." Smiling, Julie retrieved it from a nearby table. "You won't forget to eat, will you?" she demanded as she placed it in Raven's hand.

"I won't forget to eat," Raven assured her, then dashed through the door.

Within the hour Raven was seated in the glassed-in terrace room of Alphonso's toying with a plate of scampi. There were at least a dozen people patronizing the restaurant whom she knew personally. A series of greetings had been exchanged before she had been able to tuck herself into a corner table.

The room was an elaborate jungle, with exotic plants and flowers growing everywhere. The sun shining through the glass and greenery gave the terrace a warmth and glow. The floor was a cool ceramic tile, and there was a constant trickle of water from a fountain at the far end of the room. Raven enjoyed the casual elegance, the wicker accessories and the pungent aromas of food and flowers that filled the place. Now, however, she gave little attention to the terrace room as she spoke with her agent.

Henderson was a big, burly man whom Raven had always thought resembled a logjammer rather than the smooth, savvy agent he was. He had a light red thatch of hair that curled thinly on top of his head and bright merry blue eyes that she knew could sharpen to a sword's point. There was a friendly smattering of freckles over his broad, flat-featured face.

He could smile and look genial and none too bright. It was one of his best weapons. Raven knew Henderson was as sharp as they came, and when necessary, he could be hard as nails. He was fond of her, not only because she made him so rich, but because she never resented having done so. He couldn't say the same about all of his clients.

Now Henderson allowed Raven to ramble on about

ideas for a new tour, Australia, New Zealand, pro-
motion for the new album that was already shooting
up the charts a week after its release. He ate his veal
steadily, washing it down with heavy red wine while
Raven talked and sipped occasionally from her glass
of white wine.

He noticed she made no mention of the *Fantasy*
score or of her time in Cornwall. The last progress
report he had received from her had indicated the project was all but completed. The conversations he had
had with Jarett had been enthusiastic. Lauren Chase
had approved each one of her numbers, and the choreography had begun. The score seemed to be falling
into place without a hitch.

So Henderson had been surprised when Raven had
returned alone so abruptly from Cornwall. He had expected her to phone him when the score was completed, then to take the week or two she had indicated
she and Brand wanted to relax and do nothing. But
here she was, back early and without Brand.

She chattered nervously, darting from one topic to
another. Henderson didn't interrupt, only now and
again making some noncommittal sounds as he at-
tended to his meal. Raven talked nonstop for fifteen
minutes, then began to wind down. Henderson waited,
then took a long swallow of wine.

"Well, now," he said, patting his lips with a white
linen napkin. "I don't imagine there should be any
problem setting up an Australian tour." His voice
suited his looks.

"Good." Raven pushed the scampi around on her

plate. She realized she had talked herself out. Spearing a bit of shrimp, she ate absently.

"While it's being set up, you could take yourself a nice little vacation somewhere."

Raven's brows rose. "No, I thought you could book me on the talk-show circuit, dig up some guest shots here and there."

"Could do that, too," he said genially. "After you take a few weeks off."

"I want gigs, not a few weeks off." Her brows lowered suspiciously. "Have you been talking to Julie?"

He looked surprised. "No, about what?"

"Nothing." Raven shook her head, then smiled. "Gigs, Henderson."

"You've lost weight, you know," he pointed out and shoveled in some more veal. "It shows in your face. Eat."

Raven gave an exasperated sigh and applied herself to her lunch. "Why does everyone treat me like a dimwitted child?" she mumbled, swallowing shrimp. "I'm going to start being temperamental and hard to get along with until I get some star treatment." Henderson said something quick and rude between mouthfuls which she ignored. "What about Jerry Michaels? Didn't I hear he was lining up a variety special for the fall? You could get me on that."

"Simplest thing in the world," Henderson agreed. "He'd be thrilled to have you."

"Well?"

"Well what?"

"Henderson." Resolutely, Raven pushed her plate aside. "Are you going to book me on the Jerry Michaels show?"

"No." He poured more wine into his glass. The sun shot through it, casting a red shadow on the tablecloth.

"Why?" Annoyance crept into Raven's tone.

"It's not for you." Henderson lifted a hand, palm up, as she began to argue. "I know who's producing the show, Raven. It's not for you."

She subsided a bit huffily, but she subsided. His instincts were the best in the field. "All right, forget the Michaels gig. What, then?"

"Want some dessert?"

"No, just coffee."

He signaled the waiter, then, after ordering blueberry cheesecake for himself and coffee for both of them, he settled back in his chair. "What about *Fantasy?*"

Raven twirled her wineglass between her fingers. "It's finished," she said flatly.

"And?"

"And?" she repeated, looking up. His merry blue eyes were narrowed. "It's finished," she said again. "Or essentially finished. I can't foresee any problem with the final details. Brandon or his agent will get in touch with you if there are, I'm sure."

"Jarett will probably need the two of you off and on during the filming," Henderson said mildly. "I wouldn't consider myself finished with it for a while yet."

Raven frowned into the pale golden liquid in her glass. "Yes, you're right, of course. I hadn't thought about it. Well..." She shook her head and pushed the wine away. "I'll deal with that when the times comes."

"How'd it go?"

She looked at Henderson levelly, but her thoughts drifted. "We wrote some of the best music either one of us has ever done. That I'm sure of. We work remarkably well together. I was surprised."

"You didn't think you would?" Henderson eyed the blueberry cheesecake the waiter set in front of him.

"No, I didn't think we would. Thank you," this to the waiter before she looked at Henderson again. "But everything else apart, we did work well together."

"You'd worked well together before," he pointed out. "'Clouds and Rain.'" He saw her frown but continued smoothly. "Did you know sales on that have picked up again after your New York concert? You got yourself a lot of free press, too."

"Yes," Raven mumbled into her coffee. "I'm sure we did."

"I've had a lot of questions thrown at me during the last weeks," he continued blandly, even when her eyes lifted and narrowed. "From the inside," he said with a smile, "as well as the press. I was at a nice little soiree just last week. You and Brand were the main topic of conversation."

"As I said, we work well together." Raven set down her cup. "Brandon was right; we are good for each other artistically."

"And personally?" Henderson took a generous bite of cheesecake.

"Well." Raven lifted a brow. "You certainly get to the point."

"That's all right, you don't have to answer me." He swallowed the cake, then broke off another piece. "You can tell *him*."

"Who?"

"Brand," Henderson answered easily and added cream to his coffee. "He just walked in."

Raven whirled around in her chair. Instantly her eyes locked on Brand's. With the contact came a wild, swift surge of joy. Her first instinct was to spring from the table and run to him. Indeed, she had pushed the chair back, preparing to do so, when the expression on his face cut through her initial spring of delight. It was ice-cold fury. Raven sat where she was, watching as he weaved his way through the crowded restaurant toward her. There were casual greetings along the way which he ignored. Raven heard the room fall silent.

He reached her without speaking once or taking his eyes from her. Raven's desire to hold out a hand to him was also overcome. She thought he might strike it away. The look in his eyes had her blood beating uneasily. Henderson might not have been sitting two feet away.

"Let's go."

"Go?" Raven repeated dumbly.

"Now." Brand took her hand and yanked her to her feet. She might have winced at the unexpected pressure if she hadn't been so shocked by it.

"Brandon…"

"Now," he repeated. He began to walk away, dragging her behind him. Raven could feel the eyes following them. Shock, delight, anxiety all faded into temper.

"Let go of me!" she demanded in a harsh undertone. "What's the matter with you? You can't drag me around like this." She bumped into a lunching comedian, then skirted around him with a mumbled apology as Brand continued to stalk away with her hand in his. "Brandon, stop this! I will not be dragged out of a public restaurant."

He halted then and turned so that their faces were very close. "Would you prefer that I say what I have to say to you here and now?" His voice was clear and cool in the dead silence of the room. It was very easy to see the violence of temper just beneath the surface. Raven could feel it in the grip of his hand on hers. They were spotlighted again, she thought fleetingly, but hardly in the manner in which they had been in New York. She took a deep breath.

"No." Raven struggled for dignity and kept her voice lowered. "But there isn't any need to make a scene, Brandon."

"Oh, I'm in the mood for a scene, Raven," he tossed back in fluid British tones that carried well. "I'm in the mood for a bloody beaut of a scene."

Before she could comment, Brand turned away again and propelled her out of the restaurant. There was a Mercedes at the curb directly outside. He shoved her inside it, slamming the door behind her.

Raven straightened in the seat, whipping her head around as he opened the other door. "Oh, you're going to get one," she promised and ripped off her hat to throw it furiously into the back seat. "How *dare* you…"

"Shut up. I mean it." Brand turned to her as she started to speak again. "Just shut up until we get where we're going, otherwise I might be tempted to strangle you here and be done with it."

He shot away from the curb, and Raven flopped back against her seat. I'll shut up, all right, she thought on wave after wave of anger. I'll shut up. It'll give me time to think through exactly what I have to say.

Chapter 15

By the time Brand stopped the car in front of the Bel-Air, Raven felt she had her speech well in order. As he climbed out of his side, she climbed out of hers, then turned to face him on the sidewalk. But before she could speak, he had her arm in a tight grip and was pulling her toward the entrance.

"I told you not to drag me."

"And I told you to shut up." He brushed past the doorman and into the lobby. Raven was forced into an undignified half-trot in order to keep up with his long-legged stride.

"I will *not* be spoken to like that," she fumed and gave her arm an unsuccessful jerk. "I will *not* be carted through a hotel lobby like a piece of baggage."

"I'm tired of playing it your way." Brand turned,

grabbing both of her shoulders and dragging her against him. His fingers bit into her skin and shocked her into silence. "My game now, my rules."

His mouth came down hard on hers. It was a kiss of rage. His teeth scraped across her lips, forcing them open so that he could plunder and seek. He held her bruisingly close, as if daring her to struggle.

When Brand pulled away, he stared at her for a long, silent moment, then swore quickly, fiercely. Turning, he pulled her to the elevators.

Though she was no longer certain if it was fear or anger, Raven was trembling with emotion as they took the silent ride up. Brand could feel the throbbing pulse as he held her arm. He swore again, pungently, but she didn't glance at him. As the doors slid open, he pulled her into the hall and toward the penthouse.

There were no words exchanged between them as he slid the key into the lock. He released her arm as he pushed the door open. Without protest, Raven walked inside. She moved to the center of the room.

The suite was elegant, even lush, in a dignified, old-fashioned style with a small bricked fireplace and a good, thick carpet. Behind her the door slammed—a final sound—and she heard Brand toss the key with a faint metallic jingle onto a table. Raven drew a breath and turned around.

"Brandon…"

"No, I'll do the talking first." He crossed to her, his eyes locked on hers. "My rules, remember?"

"Yes." She lifted her chin. Her arm throbbed

faintly where his fingers had dug into it. "I remember."

"First rule, no more bits and pieces. I won't have you closing parts of yourself off from me anymore." They were standing close. Now that the first dazed shock and surprise were passing, Raven noticed signs of strain and fatigue on his face. His words were spilling out so quickly, she couldn't interrupt. "You did the same thing to me five years ago, but then we weren't lovers. You were always holding out, never willing to trust."

"No." She shook her head, scrambling for some defense. "No, that's not true."

"Yes, it's true," he countered and took her by the shoulders again. "Did you tell me about your mother all those years ago? Or how you felt, what you were going through? Did you bring me into your life enough to let me help you, or at least comfort you?"

This was not what she had expected from him. Raven could only press her hand to her temple and shake her head again. "No, it wasn't something…"

"Wasn't something you wanted to share with me." He dropped her arms and stepped away from her. "Yes, I know." His voice was low and furious again as he pulled out a cigarette. He knew he had to do something with his hands or he'd hurt her again. He watched as she unconsciously nursed her arm where he had gripped her. "And this time, Raven, would you have told me anything about it if it hadn't been for the nightmare? If you hadn't been half asleep and frightened, would you have told me, trusted me?''

"I don't know." She made a small sound of confusion. "My mother had nothing to do with you."

Brand hurled the cigarette away before he lit it. "How can you say that to me? How can you stand there and say that to me?" He took a step toward her, then checked himself and stalked to the bar. "Damn you, Raven," he said under his breath. He poured bourbon and drank. "Maybe I should have stayed away," he managed in a calmer tone. "You'd already tossed me out of your life five years ago."

"*I* tossed you out?" This time her voice rose. "You walked out on me. You left me flat because I wouldn't be your lover." Raven walked over to the bar and leaned her palms on it. "You walked out of my house and out of my life, and the only word I had from you was what I read in the paper. It didn't take you long to find other women—several other women."

"I found as many as I could," Brand agreed and drank again. "As quickly as I could. I used women, booze, gambling—anything—to try to get you out of my system." He studied the dregs of liquor in his glass and added thoughtfully, "It didn't work." He set the glass down and looked at her again. "Which is why I knew I had to be patient with you."

Raven's eyes were still dark with hurt. "Don't talk to me about tossing you out."

"That's exactly what you did." Brand grabbed her wrist as she turned to swirl away from him. He held her still, the narrow, mahogany bar between them. "We were alone, remember? Julie was away for a few days."

Raven kept her eyes level. "I remember perfectly."

"Do you?" He arched a brow. Both his eyes and voice were cool again. "There might be a few things you don't remember. When I came to the house that night I was going to ask you to marry me."

Raven could feel every thought, every emotion, pour out of her body. She could only stare at him.

"Surprised?" Brand released her wrist and again reached in his pocket for a cigarette. "Apparently we have two differing perspectives on that night. I *loved* you." The words were an accusation that kept her speechless. "And God help me, all those weeks we were together I was faithful to you. I never touched another woman." He lit the cigarette, and as the end flared, Raven heard him say softly, "I nearly went mad."

"You never told me." Her voice was weak and shaken. Her eyes were huge gray orbs. "You never once said you loved me."

"You kept backing off," he retorted. "And I knew you were innocent and afraid, though I didn't know why." He gave her a long, steady look. "It would have made quite a lot of difference if I had, but you didn't trust me."

"Oh, Brandon."

"That night," he went on, "you were so warm, and the house was so quiet. I could feel how much you wanted me. It drove me crazy. Good God, I was trying to be gentle, patient, when the need for you was all but destroying me." He ran a tense hand through his hair. "And you were giving, melting, everywhere I touched you. And then—then you were struggling like some terrified child, pushing at me as if I'd tried to kill you, telling me not to touch you. You said you couldn't bear to have me touch you."

He looked back at her, but his eyes were no longer cool. "You're the only woman who's ever been able to hurt me like that."

"Brandon." Raven shut her eyes. "I was only twenty, and there were so many things…"

"Yes, I know now; I didn't know then." His tone was flat. "Though there really weren't so many changes this time around." Raven opened her eyes and started to speak, but he shook his head. "No, not yet. I've not finished. I stayed away to give you time, as I told you before. I didn't see any other way. I could hardly stay, kicking my heels in L.A., waiting for you to make up your mind. I didn't know how long I'd stay away, but during those five years I concentrated on my career. So did you."

Brand paused, spreading his long, elegant hands on the surface of the bar. "Looking back, I suppose that's all for the best. You needed to establish yourself, and I had a surge of productivity. When I started reading about you regularly in the gossip columns I knew it was time to come back." He watched her mouth fall open at that, and her eyes heat. "Get as mad as you damn well like when I've finished," he said shortly. "But don't interrupt."

Raven turned away to search for control. "All right, go on," she managed and faced him again.

"I came to the States without any real plan, except to see you. The solid idea fell into my lap by way of *Fantasy* when I was in New York. I used the score to get you back," he said simply and without apology. "When I stood up in that recording booth watching you again, I knew I'd have used anything, but the score did nicely." He pushed his empty glass aside with his fingertip. "I wasn't lying about wanting to work with you again for professional reasons or about feeling you were particularly right for *Fantasy*. But I would have if it had been necessary. So perhaps you weren't so far wrong about what you said on the cliffs that day." He moved from the bar to the window. "Of course, there was a bit more to it in my mind than merely getting you to bed."

Raven felt her throat burn. "Brandon." She swallowed and shut her eyes. "I've never been more ashamed of anything in my life than what I said to you. Anger is hardly an excuse, but I'd hoped—I'd hoped you'd forgive me."

Brand turned his head and studied her a moment. "Perhaps if you hadn't left, it would have been easier."

"I had to. I told you in the note…"

"What note?" His voice sharpened as he turned to face her.

"The note." Raven was uncertain whether to step forward or back. "I left it on the piano with the music."

"I didn't see any note. I didn't see anything but that you were gone." He let out a long breath. "I dumped all the music into a briefcase. I didn't notice a note."

"Julie called only a little while after you'd left to tell me about the accident."

His eyes shot back to hers again. "What accident?"

Raven stared at him.

"Your mother?" he said, reading it in her eyes.

"Yes. She'd had an accident. I had to get back right away."

He jammed his hands into his pockets. "Why didn't you wait for me?"

"I wanted to; I couldn't." Raven laced her fingers together to prevent her hands from fluttering. "Dr. Karter said it would only be a matter of hours. As it was…" She paused and turned away. "I was too late, anyway."

Brand felt the anger drain from him. "I'm sorry. I didn't know."

Raven didn't know why the simple, quiet statement should bring on the tears she hadn't shed before. They blinded her eyes and clogged her throat so that speech was impossible.

"I went a bit crazy when I got back to the house and found you'd packed and gone." Brand spoke wearily now. "I don't know exactly what I did at first;

afterwards I got roaring drunk. The next morning I dumped all the music together, packed some things and took off for the States.

"I stopped off for a couple of days in New York, trying to sort things out. It seems I spend a great deal of time running after you. It's difficult on the pride. In New York I came up with a dozen very logical, very valid reasons why I should go back to England and forget you. But there was one very small, very basic point I couldn't argue aside." He looked at her again. Her back was to him, her head bent so that with her hair pulled up he could see the slender length of her neck. "I love you, Raven."

"Brandon." Raven turned her tear-drenched face toward him. She blinked at the prisms of light that blinded her, then shook her head quickly when she saw him make a move to come to her. "No, please don't. I won't be able to talk if you touch me." She drew in a deep breath, brushing the tears away with her fingertips. "I've been very wrong; I have to tell you."

He stood away from her, though impatience was beginning to simmer through him again. "I had my say," he agreed. "I suppose you should have yours."

"All those years ago," she began. "All those years ago there were things I couldn't say, things I couldn't even understand because I was so—dazzled by everything. My career, the fame, the money, the perpetual spotlight." The words came quickly, and her voice grew stronger with them. "Everything happened at once; there didn't seem to be any time to get used to it all. Suddenly I was in love with Brandon Carstairs.'' She laughed and brushed at fresh tears. ''*The* Brandon Carstairs. You have to understand, one minute you were an image, a name on a record, and the next you were a man, and I loved you.''

Raven moistened her lips, moving to stare from the window as Brand had. ''And my mother—my mother was my responsibility, Brandon. I've felt that always, and it isn't something that can be changed overnight. You were the genuine knight on a charger. I couldn't—wouldn't talk to you about that part of my life. I was afraid, and I was never sure of you. You never told me you loved me, Brandon.''

''I was terrified of you,'' he murmured, ''of what I was feeling for you. You were the first.'' He shrugged. ''But you were always pulling back from me. Always putting up No Trespassing signs whenever I started to get close.''

''You always seemed to want so much.'' She hugged her arms. ''Even this time, in Cornwall, when we were so close. It didn't seem to be enough. I always felt you were waiting for more.''

''You still put up the signs, Raven.'' She turned, and his eyes locked on hers. ''Your body isn't enough. That isn't what I waited five years for.''

''Love should be enough,'' she tossed back, suddenly angry and confused.

''No.'' Brand shook his head, cutting her off. ''It isn't enough. I want a great deal more than that.'' He waited a moment, watching the range of expressions on her face. "I want your trust, without conditions, without exceptions. I want a commitment, a total one. It's all or nothing this time, Raven."

She backed away. "You can't own me, Brandon."

A quick flash of fury shot into his eyes. "Damn it, I don't want to own you, but I want you to belong to me. Don't you know there's a difference?"

Raven stared at him for a full minute. She dropped her arms, no longer cold. The tension that had begun to creep up the back of her neck vanished. "I didn't," she said softly. "I should have."

Slowly she crossed to him. She was vividly aware of every detail of his face: the dark, expressive brows drawn together now with thought, the blue-green eyes steady but with the spark of temper, the faint touch of mauve beneath them that told her he'd lost sleep. It came to her then that she loved him more as a woman than she had as a girl. A woman could love without fear, without restrictions. Raven lifted her fingertip to his cheek as if to smooth away the tension.

Then they were locked in each other's arms, mouth to mouth. His hands went to her hair, scattering pins until it tumbled free around them. He murmured something she had no need to understand, then plunged deep again into her mouth. Hurriedly, impatiently, they began to undress each other. No words were needed. They sought only touch, to give, to fulfill.

His fingers fumbled with the zipper of her dress,

making him swear and her laugh breathlessly until he pulled her with him to the rug. Then, somehow, they were flesh to flesh. Raven could feel the shudders racing through him to match her own as they touched. His mouth was no more greedy than hers, his hands no less demanding. Their fire blazed clean and bright. Need erupted in them both so that she pulled him to her, desperate to have him, frantic to give.

Raw pleasure shot through her, rocking her again and again as she moved with him. His face was buried in her hair, his body damp to her touch. Air was forcing its way from her lungs in moans and gasps as they took each other higher and faster. Then the urgency passed, and a sweetness took its place.

Time lost all meaning as they lay together. Neither moved nor spoke. Tensions and angers, ecstasies and desperations, had all passed. All that was left was a soft contentment. She could feel his breath move lightly against her neck.

"Brandon," Raven murmured, letting her lips brush his skin.

"*Hmm?*"

"I think I still had something to say, but it's slipped my mind." She gave a low laugh.

Brand lifted his head and grinned. "Maybe it'll come back to you. Probably wasn't important."

"You're right, I'm sure." She smiled, touching his cheek. "It had something to do with loving you beyond sanity or some such thing and wanting more than anything in the world to belong to you. Nothing important.''

Brand lowered his mouth to hers and nipped at her still tender lip. ''You were distracted,'' he mused, seeking her breast with his fingertip.

Raven ran her hands down his back. ''I was in a bit of a hurry.''

''This time...'' He began to taste her neck and shoulder. ''This time we'll slow down the tempo. A bit more orchestration, don't you think?'' His fingers slid gently and teasingly over the point of her breast.

''Yes, quite a bit more orchestration. Brandon...'' Her words were lost on a sound of pleasure as his tongue found her ear. ''Once more, with feeling,'' she whispered.

* * * * *

TREASURES LOST,
TREASURES FOUND

To Dixie Browning,
the true lady of the island.

Chapter 1

He had believed in it. Edwin J. Hardesty hadn't been the kind of man who had fantasies or followed dreams, but sometime during his quiet, literary life he had looked for a pot of gold. From the information in the reams of notes, the careful charts and the dog-eared research books, he thought he'd found it.

In the panelled study, a single light shot a beam across a durable oak desk. The light fell over a hand—narrow, slender, without the affectation of rings or polish. Yet even bare, it remained an essentially feminine hand, the kind that could be pictured holding a porcelain cup or waving a feather fan. It was a surprisingly elegant hand for a woman who didn't consider herself elegant, delicate or particularly feminine. Kathleen Hardesty was, as her father had been, and as he'd directed her to be, a dedicated educator.

Minds were her concern—the expanding and the fulfilling of them. This included her own as well as every one of her students'. For as long as she could remember, her father had impressed upon her the importance of education. He'd stressed the priority of it over every other aspect of life. Education was the cohesiveness that held civilization together. She grew up surrounded by the dusty smell of books and the quiet, placid tone of patient instruction.

She'd been expected to excel in school, and she had. She'd been expected to follow her father's path into education. At twenty-eight, Kate was just finishing her first year at Yale as an assistant professor of English literature.

In the dim light of the quiet study, she looked the part. Her light brown hair was tidily secured at the nape of her neck with all the pins neatly tucked in. Her practical tortoiseshell reading glasses seemed dark against her milk-pale complexion. Her high cheekbones gave her face an almost haughty look that was often dispelled by her warm, doe-brown eyes.

Though her jacket was draped over the back of her chair, the white blouse she wore was still crisp. Her cuffs were turned back to reveal delicate wrists and a slim Swiss watch on her left arm. Her earrings were tasteful gold studs given to Kate by her father on her twenty-first birthday, the only truly personal gift she could ever remember receiving from him.

Seven long years later, one short week after her father's funeral, Kate sat at his desk. The room still carried the scent of his cologne and a hint of the pipe tobacco he'd only smoked in that room.

She'd finally found the courage to go through his papers.

She hadn't known he was ill. In his early sixties, Hardesty had looked robust and strong. He hadn't told his daughter about his visits to the doctor, his check-ups, ECG results or the little pills he carried with him everywhere. She'd found his pills in his inside pocket after his fatal heart attack. Kate hadn't known his heart was weak because Hardesty never shared his short-comings with anyone. She hadn't known about the charts and research papers in his desk; he'd never shared his dreams either.

Now that she was aware of both, Kate wasn't cer-tain she ever really knew the man who'd raised her. The memory of her mother was dim; that was to be expected after more than twenty years. Her father had been alive just a week before.

Leaning back for a moment, she pushed her glasses up and rubbed the bridge of her nose between her thumb and forefinger. She tried, with only the desk lamp between herself and the dark, to think of her father in precise terms.

Physically, he'd been a tall, big man with a full head of steel-gray hair and a patient face. He had fa-vored dark suits and white shirts. The only vanity she could remember had been his weekly manicures. But it wasn't a physical picture Kate struggled with now. As a father…

He was never unkind. In all her memories, Kate couldn't remember her father ever raising his voice to her, ever striking her. He never had to, she thought with a sigh. All he had to do was express disappointment, disapproval, and that was enough.

He had been brilliant, tireless, dedicated. But all of that had been directed toward his vocation. As a father, Kate reflected... He'd never been unkind. That was all that would come to her, and because of it she felt a fresh wave of guilt and grief.

She hadn't disappointed him, that much she could cling to. He had told her so himself, in just those words, when she was accepted by the English Department at Yale. Nor had he expected her ever to disappoint him. Kate knew, though it had never been discussed, that her father wanted her to become head of the English Department within ten years. That had been the extent of his dream for her.

Had he ever realized just how much she'd loved him? She wondered as she shut her eyes, tired now from the hours of reading her father's handwriting. Had he ever known just how desperately she'd wanted to please him? If he'd just once said he was proud...

In the end, she hadn't had those few intense last moments with her father one reads about in books or sees in the movies. When she'd arrived at the hospital, he was already gone. There'd been no time for words. No time for tears.

Now she was on her own in the tidy Cape Cod house she'd shared with him for so long. The housekeeper would still come on Wednesday mornings, and the gardener would come on Saturdays to cut the grass. She alone would have to deal with the paperwork, the sorting, the shifting, the clearing out.

That could be done. Kate leaned back farther in her father's worn leather chair. It could be done because all of those things were practical matters. She dealt easily with the practical. But what about these papers she'd found? What would she do about the carefully drawn charts, the notebooks filled with information, directions, history, theory? In part, because she was raised to be logical, she considered filing them neatly away.

But there was another part, the part that enabled one to lose oneself in fantasies, in dreams, in the "perhapses" of life. This was the part that allowed Kate to lose herself totally in the possibilities of the written word, in the wonders of a book. The papers on her father's desk beckoned her.

He'd believed in it. She bent over the papers again. He'd believed in it or he never would have wasted his time documenting, searching, theorizing. She would never be able to discuss it with him. Yet, in a way, wasn't he telling her about it through his words?

Treasure. Sunken treasure. The stuff of fiction and Hollywood movies. Judging by the stack of papers and notebooks on his desk, Hardesty must have spent months, perhaps years, compiling information on the location of an English merchant ship lost off the coast of North Carolina two centuries before.

It brought Kate an immediate picture of Edward Teach—Blackbeard, the bloodthirsty pirate with the crazed superstitions and reign of terror. The stuff of romances, she thought. Of romance...

Ocracoke Island. The memory was sharp, sweet and painful. Kate had blocked out everything that had happened that summer four years before. Everything and everyone. Now, if she was to make a rational decision about what was to be done, she had to think of those long, lazy months on the remote Outer Banks of North Carolina.

She'd begun work on her doctorate. It had been a surprise when her father had announced that he planned to spend the summer on Ocracoke and invited her to accompany him. Of course, she'd gone, taking her portable typewriter, boxes of books, reams of paper. She hadn't expected to be seduced by white sand beaches and the call of gulls. She hadn't expected to fall desperately and insensibly in love.

Insensibly, Kate repeated to herself, as if in defense. She'd have to remember that was the most apt adjective. There'd been nothing sensible about her feelings for Ky Silver.

Even the name, she mused, was unique, unconventional, flashy. They'd been as suitable for each other as a peacock and a wren. Yet that hadn't stopped her from losing her head, her heart and her innocence during that balmy, magic summer.

She could still see him at the helm of the boat her father had rented, steering into the wind, laughing, dark hair flowing wildly. She could still remember that heady, weightless feeling when they'd gone scuba diving in the warm coastal waters. Kate had been too caught up in what was happening to herself to think about her father's sudden interest in boating and diving.

She'd been too swept away by her own feelings of astonishment that a man like Ky Silver should be attracted to someone like her to notice her father's preoccupation with currents and tides. There'd been too much excitement for her to realize that her father never bothered with fishing rods like the other vacationers.

But now her youthful fancies were behind her, Kate told herself. Now, she could clearly remember how many hours her father had closeted himself in his hotel room, reading book after book that he brought with him from the mainland library. He'd been researching even then. She was sure he'd continued that research in the following summers when she had refused to go back. Refused to go back, Kate remembered, because of Ky Silver.

Ky had asked her to believe in fairy tales. He asked her to give him the impossible. When she refused, frightened, he shrugged and walked away without a second look. She had never gone back to the white sand and gulls since then.

Kate looked down again at her father's papers. She had to go back now—go back and finish what her father had started. Perhaps, more than the house, the trust fund, the antique jewelry that had been her mother's, this was her father's legacy to her. If she filed those papers neatly away, they'd haunt her for the rest of her life.

She had to go back, Kate reaffirmed as she took off her glasses and folded them neatly on the blotter. And it was Ky Silver she'd have to go to. Her father's aspirations had drawn her away from Ky once; now, four years later, they were drawing her back.

But Dr. Kathleen Hardesty knew the difference between fairy tales and reality. Reaching in her father's desk drawer, she drew out a sheet of thick creamy stationery and began to write.

Ky let the wind buffet him as he opened the throttle. He liked speed in much the same way he liked a lazy afternoon in the hammock. They were two of the things that made life worthwhile. He was used to the smell of salt spray, but he still inhaled deeply. He was well accustomed to the vibration of the deck under his feet, but he still felt it. He wasn't a man to let anything go unnoticed or unappreciated.

He grew up in this quiet, remote little coastal town, and though he'd traveled and intended to travel more, he didn't plan to live anywhere else. It suited him— the freedom of the sea, and the coziness of a small community.

He didn't resent the tourists because he knew they helped keep the village alive, but he preferred the island in winter. Then the storms blew wild and cold, and only the hearty would brave the ferry across Hatteras Inlet.

He fished, but unlike the majority of his neighbors, he rarely sold what he caught. What he pulled out of the sea, he ate. He dove, occasionally collecting shells, but again, this was for his own pleasure. Often he took tourists out on his boat to fish or to scuba dive, because there were times he enjoyed the company. But there were afternoons, like this sparkling one, when he simply wanted the sea to himself.

He had always been restless. His mother had said that he came into the world two weeks early because he grew impatient waiting. Ky turned thirty-two that spring, but was far from settled. He knew what he wanted—to live as he chose. The trouble was that he wasn't certain just what he wanted to choose.

At the moment, he chose the open sky and the endless sea. There were other moments when he knew that that wouldn't be enough.

But the sun was hot, the breeze cool and the shoreline was drawing near. The boat's motor was purring smoothly and in the small cooler was a tidy catch of fish he'd cook up for his supper that night. On a crystal, sparkling afternoon, perhaps it was enough.

From the shore he looked like a pirate might if there were pirates in the twentieth century. His hair was long enough to curl over his ears and well over the collar of a shirt had he worn one. It was black, a rich, true black that might have come from his Arapaho or Sicilian blood. His eyes were the deep, dark green of the sea on a cloudy day. His skin was bronzed from years in the sun, taut from the years of swimming and pulling in nets. His bone structure was also part of his heritage, sculpted, hard, defined.

When he smiled as he did now, racing the wind to shore, his face took on that reckless freedom women found irresistible. When he didn't smile, his eyes could turn as cold as a lion's before a leap. He discovered long ago that women found that equally irresistible.

Ky drew back on the throttle so that the boat slowed, rocked, then glided into its slip in Silver Lake Harbor. With the quick, efficient movements of one born to the sea, he leaped onto the dock to secure the lines.

"Catch anything?"

Ky straightened and turned. He smiled, but absently, as one does at a brother seen almost every day of one's life. "Enough. Things slow at the Roost?"

Marsh smiled, and there was a brief flicker of family resemblance, but his eyes were a calm light brown and his hair was carefully styled. "Worried about your investment?"

Ky gave a half-shrug. "With you running things?"

Marsh didn't comment. They knew each other as intimately as men ever know each other. One was restless, the other calm. The opposition never seemed to matter. "Linda wants you to come up for dinner. She worries about you."

She would, Ky thought, amused. His sister-in-law

loved to mother and fuss, even though she was five years younger than Ky. That was one of the reasons the restaurant she ran with Marsh was such a success—that, plus Marsh's business sense and the hefty investment and shrewd renovations Ky had made. Ky left the managing up to his brother and his sister-in-law. He didn't mind owning a restaurant, even keeping half an eye on the profit and loss, but he certainly had no interest in running one.

After the lines were secure, he wiped his palms down the hips of his cut-offs. "What's the special tonight?"

Marsh dipped his hands into his front pockets and rocked back on his heels. "Bluefish."

Grinning, Ky tossed back the lid of his cooler revealing his catch. "Tell Linda not to worry. I'll eat."

"That's not going to satisfy her." Marsh glanced at his brother as Ky looked out to sea. "She thinks you're alone too much."

"You're only alone too much if you don't like being alone." Ky glanced back over his shoulder. He didn't want to debate now, when the exhilaration of the speed and the sea were still upon him. But he'd never been a man to placate. "Maybe you two should think about having another baby, then Linda would be too busy to worry about big brothers."

"Give me a break. Hope's only eighteen months old."

"You've got to add nine to that," Ky reminded him carelessly. He was fond of his niece, despite—no, because she was a demon. "Anyway, it looks like the family lineage is in your hands."

"Yeah." Marsh shifted his feet, cleared his throat and fell silent. It was a habit he'd carried since childhood, one that could annoy or amuse Ky depending on his mood. At the moment, it was only mildly distracting.

Something was in the air. He could smell it, but he couldn't quite identify it. A storm brewing, he wondered? One of those hot, patient storms that seemed capable of brewing for weeks. He was certain he could smell it.

"Why don't you tell me what else is on your mind?" Ky suggested. "I want to get back to the house and clean these."

"You had a letter. It was put in our box by mistake."

It was a common enough occurrence, but by his brother's expression Ky knew there was more. His sense of an impending storm grew sharper. Saying nothing, he held out his hand.

"Ky…" Marsh began. There was nothing he could say, just as there'd been nothing to say four years before. Reaching in his back pocket, he drew out the letter.

The envelope was made from heavy cream-colored paper. Ky didn't have to look at the return address. The handwriting and the memories it brought leaped out at him. For a moment, he felt his breath catch in his lungs as it might if someone had caught him with a blow to the solar plexus. Deliberately, he expelled it. "Thanks," he said, as if it meant nothing. He stuck the letter in his pocket before he picked up his cooler and gear.

"Ky—" Again Marsh broke off. His brother had turned his head, and the cool, half-impatient stare said very clearly—back off. "If you change your mind about dinner," Marsh said.

"I'll let you know." Ky went down the length of the dock without looking back.

He was grateful he hadn't bothered to bring his car down to the harbor. He needed to walk. He needed the fresh air and the exercise to keep his mind clear while he remembered what he didn't want to remember. What he never really forgot.

Kate. Four years ago she'd walked out of his life with the same sort of cool precision with which she'd walked into it. She had reminded him of a Victorian doll—a little prim, a little aloof. He'd never had much patience with neatly folded hands or haughty manners, yet almost from the first instant he'd wanted her.

At first, he thought it was the fact that she was so different. A challenge—something for Ky Silver to conquer. He enjoyed teaching her to dive, and watching the precise step-by-step way she learned. It hadn't been any hardship to look at her in a snug scuba suit, although she didn't have voluptuous curves. She had a trim, neat, almost boylike figure and what seemed like yards of thick, soft hair.

He could still remember the first time she took it

down from its pristine knot. It left him breathless, hurting, fascinated. Ky would have touched it— touched her then and there if her father hadn't been standing beside her. But if a man was clever, if a man was determined, he could find a way to be alone with a woman.

Ky had found ways. Kate had taken to diving as though she'd been born to it. While her father had buried himself in his books, Ky had taken Kate out on the water—under the water, to the silent, dreamlike world that had attracted her just as it had always attracted him.

He could remember the first time he kissed her. They had been wet and cool from a dive, standing on the deck of his boat. He was able to see the lighthouse behind her and the vague line of the coast. Her hair had flowed down her back, sleek from the water, dripping with it. He'd reached out and gathered it in his hand.

"What are you doing?"

Four years later, he could hear that low, cultured, eastern voice, the curiosity in it. It took no effort for him to see the curiosity that had been in her eyes.

"I'm going to kiss you."

The curiosity had remained in her eyes, fascinating him. "Why?"

"Because I want to."

It was as simple as that for him. He wanted to. Her body had stiffened as he'd drawn her against him. When her lips parted in protest, he closed his over them. In the time it takes a heart to beat, the rigidity had melted from her body. She'd kissed him with all the young, stored-up passion that had been in her— passion mixed with innocence. He was experienced enough to recognize her innocence, and that too had fascinated him. Ky had, foolishly, youthfully and completely, fallen in love.

Kate had remained an enigma to him, though they shared impassioned hours of laughter and long, lazy talks. He admired her thirst for learning and she had a predilection for putting knowledge into neat slots that baffled him. She was enthusiastic about diving, but it hadn't been enough for her simply to be able to swim freely underwater, taking her air from tanks. She had to know how the tanks worked, why they were fashioned a certain way. Ky watched her absorb what he told her, and knew she'd retain it.

They had taken walks along the shoreline at night and she had recited poetry from memory. Beautiful words, Byron, Shelley, Keats. And he, who'd never been overly impressed by such things, had eaten it up because her voice had made the words somehow personal. Then she'd begin to talk about syntax, iambic pentameters, and Ky would find new ways to divert her.

For three months, he did little but think of her. For the first time, Ky had considered changing his lifestyle. His little cottage near the beach needed work. It needed furniture. Kate would need more than milk crates and the hammock that had been his style. Because he'd been young and had never been in love before, Ky had taken his own plans for granted.

She'd walked out on him. She'd had her own plans, and he hadn't been part of them.

Her father came back to the island the following summer, and every summer thereafter. Kate never came back. Ky knew she had completed her doctorate and was teaching in a prestigious ivy league school where her father was all but a cornerstone. She had what she wanted. So, he told himself as he swung open the screen door of his cottage, did he. He went where he wanted, when he wanted. He called his own shots. His responsibilities extended only as far as he chose to extend them. To his way of thinking, that itself was a mark of success.

Setting the cooler on the kitchen floor, Ky opened the refrigerator. He twisted the top off a beer and drank half of it in one icy cold swallow. It washed some of the bitterness out of his mouth.

Calm now, and curious, he pulled the letter out of his pocket. Ripping it open, he drew out the single neatly written sheet.

Dear Ky,
You may or may not be aware that my father suffered a fatal heart attack two weeks ago. It was very sudden, and I'm currently trying to tie up the many details this involves.

In going through my father's papers, I find that he had again made arrangements to come to the island this summer, and engage your services. I now find it necessary to take his place. For reasons which I'd rather explain in person, I need your help. You have my father's deposit. When I arrive in Ocracoke on the fifteenth, we can discuss terms.

If possible, contact me at the hotel, or leave a message. I hope we'll be able to come to a mutually agreeable arrangement. Please give my best to Marsh. Perhaps I'll see him during my stay.

Best,
Kathleen Hardesty

So the old man was dead. Ky set down the letter and lifted his beer again. He couldn't say he'd had any liking for Edwin Hardesty. Kate's father had been a stringent, humorless man. Still, he hadn't disliked him. Ky had, in an odd way, gotten used to his company over the last few summers. But this summer, it would be Kate.

Ky glanced at the letter again, then jogged his memory until he remembered the date. Two days, he mused. She'd be there in two days…to discuss terms. A smile played around the corners of his mouth but it didn't have anything to do with humor. They'd discuss terms, he agreed silently as he scanned Kate's letter again.

She wanted to take her father's place. Ky wondered if she'd realized, when she wrote that, just how ironic it was. Kathleen Hardesty had been obediently dogging her father's footsteps all her life. Why should that change after his death?

Had she changed? Ky wondered briefly. Would that fascinating aura of innocence and aloofness still cling to her? Or perhaps that had faded with the years. Would that rather sweet primness have developed into a rigidity? He'd see for himself in a couple of days, he realized, but tossed the letter onto the counter rather than into the trash.

So, she wanted to engage his services, he mused. Leaning both hands on either side of the sink, he looked out the window in the direction of the water he could smell, but not quite see. She wanted a business arrangement—the rental of his boat, his gear and his time. He felt the bitterness well up and swallowed it as cleanly as he had the beer. She'd have her business arrangement. And she'd pay. He'd see to that.

Ky left the kitchen with his catch still in the cooler. The appetite he'd worked up with salt spray and speed had vanished.

Kate pulled her car onto the ferry to Ocracoke and set the brake. The morning was cool and very clear. Even so, she was tempted to simply lean her head back and close her eyes. She wasn't certain what impulse had pushed her to drive from Connecticut rather than fly, but now that she'd all but reached her destination, she was too weary to analyze.

In the bucket seat beside her was her briefcase, and

inside, all the papers she'd collected from her father's desk. Perhaps once she was in the hotel on the island, she could go through them again, understand them better. Perhaps the feeling that she was doing the right thing would come back. Over the last few days she'd lost that sense.

The closer she came to the island, the more she began to think she was making a mistake. Not to the island, Kate corrected ruthlessly—the closer she came to Ky. It was a fact, and Kate knew it was imperative to face facts so that they could be dealt with logically.

She had a little time left, a little time to calm the feelings that had somehow gotten stirred up during the drive south. It was foolish, and somehow it helped Kate to remind herself of that. She wasn't a woman returning to a lover, but a woman hoping to engage a diver in a very specific venture. Past personal feelings wouldn't enter into it because they were just that. Past.

The Kate Hardesty who'd arrived on Ocracoke four years ago had little to do with the Doctor Kathleen Hardesty who was going there now. She wasn't young, inexperienced or impressionable. Those reckless, wild traits of Ky's wouldn't appeal to her now. They wouldn't frighten her. They would be, if Ky agreed to her terms, business partners.

Kate felt the ferry move beneath her as she stared through the windshield. Yes, she thought, unless Ky had changed a great deal, the prospect of diving for treasure would appeal to his sense of adventure.

She knew enough about diving in the technical

sense to be sure she'd find no one better equipped for the job. It was always advisable to have the best. More relaxed and less weary, Kate stepped out of her car to stand at the rail. From there she could watch the gulls swoop and the tiny uninhabited islands pass by. She felt a sense of homecoming, but pushed it away. Connecticut was home. Once Kate did what she came for, she'd go back.

The water swirled behind the boat. She couldn't hear it over the motor, but looking down she could watch the wake. One island was nearly imperceptible under a flock of big, brown pelicans. It made her smile, pleased to see the odd, awkward-looking birds again. They passed the long spit of land, where fishermen parked trucks and tried their luck, near the point where bay met sea. She could watch the waves crash and foam where there was no shore, just a turbulent marriage of waters. That was something she hadn't forgotten, though she hadn't seen it since she left the island. Nor had she forgotten just how treacherous the current was along that verge.

Excitement. She breathed deeply before she turned back to her car. The treacherous was always exciting.

When the ferry docked, she had only a short wait before she could drive her car onto the narrow blacktop. The trip to town wouldn't take long, and it wasn't possible to lose your way if you stayed on the one long road. The sea battered on one side, the sound flowed smoothly on the other—both were deep blue in the late morning light.

Her nerves were gone, at least that's what she told herself. It had just been a case of last minute jitters— very normal. She was prepared to see Ky again, speak to him, work with him if they could agree on the terms.

With the windows down, the soft moist air blew around her. It was soothing. She'd almost forgotten just how soothing air could be, or the sound of water lapping constantly against sand. It was right to come. When she saw the first faded buildings of the village, she felt a wave of relief. She was here. There was no turning back now.

The hotel where she had stayed that summer with her father was on the sound side of the island. It was small and quiet. If the service was a bit slow by northern standards, the view made up for it.

Kate pulled up in front and turned off the ignition. Self-satisfaction made her sigh. She'd taken the first step and was completely prepared for the next.

Then as she stepped out of the car, she saw him. For an instant, the confident professor of English literature vanished. She was only a woman, vulnerable to her own emotions.

Oh God, he hasn't changed. Not at all. As Ky came closer, she could remember every kiss, every murmur, every crazed storm of their loving. The breeze blew his hair back from his face so that every familiar angle and plane was clear to her. With the sun warm on her skin, bright in her eyes, she felt the years spin back, then forward again. He hadn't changed.

He hadn't expected to see her yet. Somehow he thought she'd arrive that afternoon. Yet he found it necessary to go by the Roost that morning knowing the restaurant was directly across from the hotel where she'd be staying.

She was here, looking neat and a bit too thin in her tailored slacks and blouse. Her hair was pinned up so that the soft femininity of her neck and throat were revealed. Her eyes seemed too dark against her pale skin—skin Ky knew would turn golden slowly under the summer sun.

She looked the same. Soft, prim, calm. Lovely. He ignored the thud in the pit of his stomach as he stepped in front of her. He looked her up and down with the arrogance that was so much a part of him. Then he grinned because he had an overwhelming urge to strangle her.

"Kate. Looks like my timing's good."

She was almost certain she couldn't speak and was therefore determined to speak calmly. "Ky, it's nice to see you again."

"Is it?"

Ignoring the sarcasm, Kate walked around to her trunk and released it. "I'd like to get together with you as soon as possible. There are some things I want to show you, and some business I'd like to discuss."

"Sure, always open for business."

He watched her pull two cases from her trunk, but didn't offer to help. He saw there was no ring on her hand—but it wouldn't have mattered.

"Perhaps we can meet this afternoon then, after I've settled in." The sooner the better, she told herself. They would establish the purpose, the ground rules and the payment. "We could have lunch in the hotel."

"No, thanks," he said easily, leaning against the side of her car while she set her cases down. "You want me, you know where to find me. It's a small island."

With his hands in the pockets of his jeans, he walked away from her. Though she didn't want to, Kate remembered that the last time he'd walked away, they'd stood in almost the same spot.

Picking up her cases, she headed for the hotel, perhaps a bit too quickly.

Chapter 2

She knew where to find him. If the island had been double in size, she'd still have known where to find him. Kate acknowledged that Ky hadn't changed. That meant if he wasn't out on his boat, he would be at home, in the small, slightly dilapidated cottage he owned near the beach. Because she felt it would be a strategic error to go after him too soon, she dawdled over her unpacking.

But there were memories even here, where she'd spent one giddy, whirlwind night of love with Ky. It had been the only time they were able to sleep together through the night, embracing each other in the crisp hotel sheets until the first light of dawn crept around the edges of the window shades. She remembered how reckless she'd felt during those few stolen hours, and how dull the morning had seemed because it brought them to an end.

Now she could look out the same window she had stood by then, staring out in the same direction she'd stared out then when she watched Ky walk away. She remembered the sky had been streaked with a rose color before it had brightened to a pure, pale blue.

Then, with her skin still warm from her lover's touch and her mind glazed with lack of sleep and passion, Kate had believed such things could go on forever. But of course they couldn't. She had seen that only weeks later. Passion and reckless nights of loving had to give way to responsibilities, obligations.

Staring out the same window, in the same direction, Kate could feel the sense of loss she'd felt that long ago dawn without the underlying hope that they'd be together again. And again.

They wouldn't be together again, and there'd been no one else since that one heady summer. She had her career, her vocation, her books. She had had her taste of passion.

Turning away, she busied herself by rearranging everything she'd just arranged in her drawers and closet. When she decided she'd stalled in her hotel room long enough, Kate started out. She didn't take her car. She walked, just as she always walked to Ky's home.

She told herself she was over the shock of seeing him again. It was only natural that there be some strain, some discomfort. She was honest enough to admit that it would have been easier if there'd been only strain and discomfort, and not that one sharp quiver of pleasure. Kate acknowledged it, now that it had passed.

No, Ky Silver hadn't changed, she reminded herself. He was still arrogant, self-absorbed and cocky. Those traits might have appealed to her once, but she'd been very young. If she were wise, she could use those same traits to persuade Ky to help her. Yes, those traits, she thought, and the tempting offer of a treasure hunt. Even at her most pessimistic, she couldn't believe Ky would refuse. It was his nature to take chances.

This time she'd be in charge. Kate drew in a deep breath of warm air that tasted of sea. Somehow she felt it would steady her. Ky was going to find she was no longer naive, or susceptible to a few careless words of affection.

With her briefcase in hand, Kate walked through the village. This too was the same, she thought. She was glad of it. The simplicity and solitude still appealed to her. She enjoyed the dozens of little shops, the restaurants and small inns tucked here and there, all somehow using the harbor as a central point, the lighthouse as a landmark. The villagers still made the most of their notorious one-time resident and permanent ghost, Blackbeard. His name or face was lavishly displayed on store signs.

She passed the harbor, unconsciously scanning for Ky's boat. It was there, in the same slip he'd always used—clean lines, scrubbed deck, shining hardware.

The flying bridge gleamed in the afternoon light and looked the same as she remembered. Reckless, challenging. The paint was fresh and there was no film of salt spray on the bridge windows. However careless Ky had been about his own appearance or his home, he'd always pampered his boat.

The *Vortex*. Kate studied the flamboyant lettering on the stern. He could pamper, she thought again, but he also expected a lot in return. She knew the speed he could urge out of the second-hand cabin cruiser he'd lovingly reconstructed himself. Nothing could block the image of the days she'd stood beside him at the helm. The wind had whipped her hair as he'd laughed and pushed for speed, and more speed. Her heart thudded, her pulse raced until she was certain nothing and no one could catch them. She'd been afraid, of him, of the rush of wind—but she'd stayed with both. In the end, she'd left both.

He enjoyed the demanding, the thrilling, the frightening. Kate gripped the handle of her briefcase tighter. Isn't that why she came to him? There were dozens of other experienced divers, many, many other experts on the coastal waters of the Outer Banks. There was only one Ky Silver.

"Kate? Kate Hardesty?"

At the sound of her name, Kate turned and felt the years tumble back again. "Linda!" This time there was no restraint. With an openness she showed to very few, Kate embraced the woman who dashed up to her, "It's wonderful to see you." With a laugh, she drew

Linda away to study her. The same chestnut hair cut short and pert, the same frank, brown eyes. It seemed very little had changed on the island. "You look wonderful."

"When I looked out the window and saw you, I could hardly believe it. Kate, you've barely changed at all." With her usual candor and lack of pretention, Linda took a quick, thorough survey. It was quick only because she did things quickly, but it wasn't subtle. "You're too thin," she decided. "But that might be jealousy."

"You still look like a college freshman," Kate returned. "That is jealousy."

As swiftly as the laugh had come, Linda sobered. "I'm sorry about your father, Kate. These past weeks must've been difficult for you."

Kate heard the sincerity, but she'd already tied up her grief and stored it away. "Ky told you?"

"Ky never tells me anything," Linda said with a sniff. In an unconscious move, she glanced in the direction of his boat. It was in its slip and Kate had been walking north—in the direction of Ky's cottage. There could be only one place she could have been going. "Marsh did. How long are you going to stay?"

"I'm not sure yet." She felt the weight of her briefcase. Dreams held the same weight as responsibilities. "There are some things I have to do."

"One of the things you have to do is have dinner at the Roost tonight. It's the restaurant right across from your hotel."

Kate looked back at the rough wooden sign. "Yes, I noticed it. Is it new?"

Linda glanced over her shoulder with a self-satisfied nod. "By Ocracoke standards. We run it."

"We?"

"Marsh and I." With a beaming smile, Linda held out her left hand. "We've been married for three years." Then she rolled her eyes in a habit Kate remembered. "It only took me fifteen years to convince him he couldn't live without me."

"I'm happy for you." She was, and if she felt a pang, she ignored it. "Married and running a restaurant. My father never filled me in on island gossip."

"We have a daughter too. Hope. She's a year and a half old and a terror. For some reason, she takes after Ky." Linda sobered again, laying a hand lightly on Kate's arm. "You're going to see him now." It wasn't a question; she didn't bother to disguise it as one.

"Yes." Keep it casual, Kate ordered herself. Don't let the questions and concern in Linda's eyes weaken you. There were ties between Linda and Ky, not only newly formed family ones, but the older tie of the island. "My father was working on something. I need Ky's help with it."

Linda studied Kate's calm face. "You know what you're doing?"

"Yes." She didn't show a flicker of unease. Her stomach slowly wrapped itself in knots. "I know what I'm doing."

"Okay." Accepting Kate's answer, but not satisfied, Linda dropped her hand. "Please come by—the restaurant or the house. We live just down the road from Ky. Marsh'll want to see you, and I'd like to show off Hope—and our menu," she added with a grin. "Both are outstanding."

"Of course I'll come by." On impulse, she took both of Linda's hands. "It's really good to see you again. I know I didn't keep in touch, but—"

"I understand." Linda gave her hands a quick squeeze. "That was yesterday. I've got to get back, the lunch crowd's pretty heavy during the season." She let out a little sigh, wondering if Kate was as calm as she seemed. And if Ky were as big a fool as ever. "Good luck," she murmured, then dashed across the street again.

"Thanks," Kate said under her breath. She was going to need it.

The walk was as beautiful as she remembered. She passed the little shops with their display windows showing handmade crafts or antiques. She passed the blue and white clapboard houses and the neat little streets on the outskirts of town with their bleached green lawns and leafy trees.

A dog raced back and forth on the length of his chain as she wandered by, barking at her as if he knew he was supposed to but didn't have much interest in it. She could see the tower of the white lighthouse. There'd been a keeper there once, but those days were over. Then she was on the narrow path that led to Ky's cottage.

Her palms were damp. She cursed herself. If she had to remember, she'd remember later, when she was alone. When she was safe.

The path was as it had been, just wide enough for a car, sparsely graveled, lined with bushes that always grew out a bit too far. The bushes and trees had always had a wild, overgrown look that suited the spot. That suited him.

Ky had told her he didn't care much for visitors. If he wanted company, all he had to do was go into town where he knew everyone. That was typical of Ky Silver, Kate mused. If I want you, I'll let you know. Otherwise, back off.

He'd wanted her once.... Nervous, Kate shifted the briefcase to her other hand. Whatever he wanted now, he'd have to hear her out. She needed him for what he was best at—diving and taking chances.

When the house came into view, she stopped, staring. It was still small, still primitive. But it no longer looked as though it would keel over on its side in a brisk wind.

The roof had been redone. Obviously Ky wouldn't need to set out pots and pans during a rain any longer. The porch he'd once talked vaguely about building now ran the length of the front, sturdy and wide. The screen door that had once been patched in a half a dozen places had been replaced by a new one. Yet nothing looked new, she observed. It just looked right.

The cedar had weathered to silver, the windows were untrimmed but gleaming. There was, much to her surprise, a spill of impatiens in a long wooden planter.

She'd been wrong, Kate decided as she walked closer. Ky Silver had changed. Precisely how, and precisely how much, she had yet to find out.

She was nearly to the first step when she heard sounds coming from the rear of the house. There was a shed back there, she remembered, full of boards and tools and salvage. Grateful that she didn't have to meet him in the house, Kate walked around the side to the tiny backyard. She could hear the sea and knew it was less than a two-minute walk through high grass and sand dunes.

Did he still go down there in the evenings? she wondered. Just to look, he'd said. Just to smell. Sometimes he'd pick up driftwood or shells or whatever small treasures the sea gave up to the sand. Once he'd given her a small smooth shell that fit into the palm of her hand—very white with a delicate pink center. A woman with her first gift of diamonds could not have been more thrilled.

Shaking the memories away, she went into the shed. It was as tall as the cottage and half as wide. The last time she'd been there, it'd been crowded with planks and boards and boxes of hardware. Now she saw the hull of a boat. At a worktable with his back to her, Ky sanded the mast.

"You've built it." The words came out before she could stop them, full of astonished pleasure. How many times had he told her about the boat he'd build one day? It had seemed to Kate it had been his only concrete ambition. Mahogany on oak, he'd said. A seventeen-foot sloop that would cut through the water like a dream. He'd have bronze fastenings and teak on the deck. One day he'd sail the inner coastal waters from Ocracoke to New England. He'd described the boat so minutely that she'd seen it then just as clearly as she saw it now.

"I told you I would." Ky turned away from the mast and faced her. She, in the doorway, had the sun at her back. He was half in shadow.

"Yes." Feeling foolish, Kate tightened her grip on the briefcase. "You did."

"But you didn't believe me." Ky tossed aside the sandpaper. Did she have to look so neat and cool, and impossibly lovely? A trickle of sweat ran down his back. "You always had a problem seeing beyond the moment."

Reckless, impatient, compelling. Would he always bring those words to her mind? "You always had a problem dealing with the moment," she said.

His brow lifted, whether in surprise or derision she couldn't be sure. "Then it might be said *we* always had a problem." He walked to her, so that the sun slanting through the small windows fell over him, then behind him. "But it didn't always seem to matter." To satisfy himself that he still could, Ky reached out and touched her face. She didn't move, and her skin was as soft and cool as he remembered. "You look tired Kate."

The muscles in her stomach quivered, but not her voice. "It was a long trip."

His thumb brushed along her cheekbone. "You need some sun."

This time she backed away. "I intend to get some."

"So I gathered from your letter." Pleased that she'd retreated first, Ky leaned against the open door. "You wrote that you wanted to talk to me in person. You're here. Why don't you tell me what you want?"

The cocky grin might have made her melt once. Now it stiffened her spine. "My father was researching a project. I intend to finish it."

"So?"

"I need your help."

Ky laughed and stepped past her into the sunlight. He needed the air, the distance. He needed to touch her again. "From your tone, there's nothing you hate more than asking me for it."

"No." She stood firm, feeling suddenly strong and bitter. "Nothing."

There was no humor in his eyes as he faced her again. The expression in them was cold and flat. She'd seen it before. "Then let's understand each other before we start. You left the island and me, and took what I wanted."

He couldn't make her cringe now as he once had with only that look. "What happened four years ago has nothing to do with today."

"The hell it doesn't." He came toward her again so that she took an involuntary step backward. "Still afraid of me?" he asked softly.

As it had a moment ago, the question turned the fear to anger. "No," she told him, and meant it. "I'm not afraid of you, Ky. I've no intention of discussing the past, but I will agree that I left the island and you. I'm here now on business. I'd like you to hear me out. If you're interested, we'll discuss terms, nothing else."

"I'm not one of your students, professor." The drawl crept into his voice, as it did when he let it. "Don't instruct."

She curled her fingers tighter around the handle of her briefcase. "In business, there are always ground rules."

"Nobody agreed to let you make them."

"I made a mistake," Kate said quietly as she fought for control. "I'll find someone else."

She'd taken only two steps away when Ky grabbed her arm. "No, you won't." The stormy look in his eyes made her throat dry. She knew what he meant. She'd never find anyone else that could make her feel as he made her feel, or want as he made her want. Deliberately, Kate removed his hand from her arm.

"I came here on business. I've no intention of fighting with you over something that doesn't exist any longer."

"We'll see about that." How long could he hold on? Ky wondered. It hurt just to look at her and to feel her withdrawing with every second that went by. "But for now, why don't you tell me what you have in that businesslike briefcase, professor."

Kate took a deep breath. She should have known it wouldn't be easy. Nothing was ever easy with Ky. "Charts," she said precisely. "Notebooks full of research, maps, carefully documented facts and precise theories. In my opinion, my father was very close to pinpointing the exact location of the *Liberty*, an English merchant vessel that sank, stores intact, off the North Carolina coast two hundred and fifty years ago."

He listened without a comment or a change of expression from beginning to end. When she finished, Ky studied her face for one long moment. "Come inside," he said and turned toward the house. "Show me what you've got."

His arrogance made her want to turn away and go back to town exactly as she'd come. There were other divers, others who knew the coast and the waters as well as Ky did. Kate forced herself to calm down, forced herself to think. There were others, but if it was a choice between the devil she knew and the unknown, she had no choice. Kate followed him into the house.

This, too, had changed. The kitchen she remembered had had a paint splattered floor, with the only usable counter space being a tottering picnic table. The floor had been stripped and varnished, the cabinets redone, and scrubbed butcher block counters lined the sink. He had put in a skylight so that the sun spilled down over the picnic table, now re-worked and re-painted, with benches along either side.

"Did you do all of this yourself?"

"Yeah. Surprised?"

So he didn't want to make polite conversation. Kate set her briefcase on the table. "Yes. You always seemed content that the walls were about to cave in on you."

"I was content with a lot of things, once. Want a beer?"

"No." Kate sat down and drew the first of her father's notebooks out of her briefcase. "You'll want to read these. It would be unnecessary and time-consuming for you to read every page, but if you'd look over the ones I've marked, I think you'll have enough to go by."

"All right." Ky turned from the refrigerator, beer in hand. He sat, watching her over the rim as he took the first swallow, then he opened the notebook.

Edwin Hardesty's handwriting was very clear and precise. He wrote down his facts in didactic, unromantic terms. What could have been exciting was as dry as a thesis, but it was accurate. Ky had no doubt of that.

The *Liberty* had been lost, with its stores of sugar, tea, silks, wine and other imports for the colonies. Hardesty had listed the manifest down to the last piece of hardtack. When it had left England, the ship had also been carrying gold. Twenty-five thousand in coins of the realm. Ky glanced up from the notebook to see Kate watching him.

"Interesting," he said simply, and turned to the next page she marked.

There'd been only three survivors who'd washed up on the island. One of the crew had described the storm that had sunk the *Liberty*, giving details on the height of the waves, the splintering wood, the water gushing into the hole. It was a grim, grisly story which Hardesty had recounted in his pragmatic style, complete with footnotes. The crewman had also given the last known location of the ship before it had gone down. Ky didn't require Hardesty's calculations to figure the ship had sunk two-and-a-half miles off the coast of Ocracoke.

Going from one notebook to another, Ky read through Hardesty's well drafted theories, his clear to-the-point documentations, corroborated and recorroborated. He scanned the charts, then studied them with more care. He remembered the man's avid interest in diving, which had always seemed inconsistent with his precise lifestyle.

So he'd been looking for gold, Ky mused. All these years the man had been digging in books and looking for gold. If it had been anyone else, Ky might have dismissed it as another fable. Little towns along the coast were full of stories about buried treasure. Edward Teach had used the shallow waters of the inlets to frustrate and outwit the crown until his last battle off the shores of Ocracoke. That alone kept the dreams of finding sunken treasures alive.

But it was Doctor Edwin J. Hardesty, Yale professor, an unimaginative, humorless man who didn't believe there was time to be wasted on the frivolous, who'd written these notebooks.

Ky might still have dismissed it, but Kate was sitting across from him. He had enough adventurous blood in him to believe in destinies.

Setting the last notebook aside, he picked up his beer again. "So, you want to treasure hunt."

She ignored the humor in his voice. With her hands folded on the table, she leaned forward. "I intend to follow through with what my father was working on."

"Do you believe it?"

Did she? Kate opened her mouth and closed it again. She had no idea. "I don't believe that all of my father's time and research should go for nothing. I want to try. As it happens, I need you to help me do it. You'll be compensated."

"Will I?" He studied the liquid left in the beer bottle with a half smile. "Will I indeed?"

"I need you, your boat and your equipment for a month, maybe two. I can't dive alone because I just don't know the waters well enough to risk it, and I don't have the time to waste. I have to be back in Connecticut by the end of August."

"To get more chalk dust under your fingernails."

She sat back slowly. "You have no right to criticize my profession."

"I'm sure the chalk's very exclusive at Yale," Ky commented. "So you're giving yourself six weeks or so to find a pot of gold."

"If my father's calculations are viable, it won't take that long."

"If," Ky repeated. Setting down his bottle, he leaned forward. "I've got no timetable. You want six weeks of my time, you can have it. For a price."

"Which is?"

"A hundred dollars a day and fifty percent of whatever we find."

Kate gave him a cool look as she slipped the notebooks back into her briefcase. "Whatever I was four years ago, Ky, I'm not a fool now. A hundred dollars a day is outrageous when we're dealing with monthly rates. And fifty percent is out of the question." It gave her a certain satisfaction to bargain with him. This made it business, pure and simple. "I'll give you fifty dollars a day and ten percent."

With the maddening half grin on his face he swirled the beer in the bottle. "I don't turn my boat on for fifty a day."

She tilted her head a bit to study him. Something tore inside him. She'd often done that whenever he said something she wanted to think over. "You're more mercenary than you once were."

"We've all got to make a living, professor." Didn't she feel anything? he thought furiously. Wasn't she suffering just a little, being in the house where they'd made love their first and last time? "You want a service,'' he said quietly, ''you pay for it. Nothing's free. Seventy-five a day and twenty-five percent. We'll say it's for old-times' sake.''

''No, we'll say it's for business' sake.'' She made herself extend her hand, but when his closed over it, she regretted the gesture. It was callused, hard, strong. Kate knew how his hand felt skimming over her skin, driving her to desperation, soothing, teasing, seducing.

''We have a deal.'' Ky thought he could see a flash of remembrance in her eyes. He kept her hand in his knowing she didn't welcome his touch. Because she didn't. ''There's no guarantee you'll find your treasure.''

''That's understood.''

''Fine. I'll deduct your father's deposit from the total.''

''All right.'' With her free hand, she clutched at her briefcase. ''When do we start?''

''Meet me at the harbor at eight tomorrow.'' Deliberately, he placed his other free hand over hers on the leather case. ''Leave this with me. I want to look over the papers some more.''

''There's no need for you to have them,'' Kate began, but his hands tightened on hers.

''If you don't trust me with them, you take them along.'' His voice was very smooth and very quiet. At its most dangerous. ''And find yourself another diver.''

Their gazes locked. Her hands were trapped and so

was she. Kate knew there would be sacrifices she'd have to make. "I'll meet you at eight."

"Fine." He released her hands and sat back. "Nice doing business with you, Kate."

Dismissed, she rose. Just how much had she sacrificed already? she wondered. "Goodbye."

He lifted and drained his half-finished beer when the screen shut behind her. Then he made himself sit there until he was certain that when he rose and walked to the window she'd be out of sight. He made himself sit there until the air flowing through the screens had carried her scent away.

Sunken ships and deep-sea treasure. It would have excited him, captured his imagination, enthusiasm and interest if he hadn't had an overwhelming urge to just get in his boat and head toward the horizon. He hadn't believed she could still affect him that way, that much, that completely. He'd forgotten that just being within touching distance of her tied his stomach in knots.

He'd never gotten over her. No matter what he filled his life with over the past four years, he'd never gotten over the slim, intellectual woman with the haughty face and doe's eyes.

Ky sat, staring at the briefcase with her initials stamped discreetly near the handle. He'd never expected her to come back, but he'd just discovered he'd never accepted the fact that she'd left him. Somehow, he'd managed to deceive himself through the years. Now, seeing her again, he knew it had just been a matter of pure survival and nothing to do with truth.

He'd had to go on, to pretend that that part of his life was behind him, or he would have gone mad.

She was back now, but she hadn't come back to him. A business arrangement. Ky ran his hand over the smooth leather of the case. She simply wanted the best diver she knew and was willing to pay for him. Fee for services, nothing more, nothing less. The past meant little or nothing to her.

Fury grew until his knuckles whitened around the bottle. He'd give her what she paid for, he promised himself. And maybe a bit extra.

This time when she went away, he wouldn't be left feeling like an inadequate fool. She'd be the one who would have to go on pretending for the rest of her life. This time when she went away, he'd be done with her. God, he'd have to be.

Rising quickly, he went out to the shed. If he stayed inside, he'd give in to the need to get very, very drunk.

Chapter 3

Kate had the water in the tub so hot that the mirror over the white pedestal sink was fogged. Oil floated on the surface, subtly fragrant and soothing. She'd lost track of how long she lay there—soaking, recharging. The next irrevocable step had been taken. She'd survived. Somehow during her discussion with Ky in his kitchen she had fought back the memories of laughter and passion. She couldn't count how many meals they'd shared there, cooking their catch, sipping wine.

Somehow during the walk back to her hotel, she'd overcome the need to weep. Tomorrow would be just a little easier. Tomorrow, and every day that followed. She had to believe it.

His animosity would help. His derision toward her kept Kate from romanticizing what she had to tell herself had never been more than a youthful summer fling. Perspective. She'd always been able to stand back and align everything in its proper perspective.

Perhaps her feelings for Ky weren't as dead as she had hoped or pretended they were. But her emotions were tinged with bitterness. Only a fool asked for more sorrow. Only a romantic believed that bitterness could ever be sweet. It had been a long time since Kate had been a romantic fool. Even so, they would work together because both had an interest in what might be lying on the sea floor.

Think of it. Two hundred and fifty years. Kate closed her eyes and let her mind drift. The silks and sugar would be gone, but would they find brass fittings deep in corrosion after two-and-a-half centuries? The hull would be covered with fungus and barnacles, but how much of the oak would still be intact? Might the log have been secured in a waterproof hold and still be legible? It could be donated to a museum in her father's name. It would be something—the last something she could do for him. Perhaps then she'd be able to lay all her ambiguous feelings to rest.

The gold, Kate thought as she rose from the tub, the gold would survive. She wasn't immune to the lure of it. Yet she knew it would be the hunt that would be exciting, and somehow fulfilling. If she found it…

What would she do? Kate wondered. She dropped the hotel towel over the rod before she wrapped herself in her robe. Behind her, the mirror was still fogged with steam from the water that drained slowly from the tub. Would she put her share tidily in some conservative investments? Would she take a leisurely trip to the Greek islands to see what Byron had seen and fallen in love with there? With a laugh, Kate walked through to the other room to pick up her brush. Strange, she hadn't thought beyond the search yet. Perhaps that was for the best, it wasn't wise to plan too far ahead.

You always had a problem seeing beyond the moment.

Damn him! With a sudden fury, Kate slammed the brush onto the dresser. She'd seen beyond the moment. She'd seen that he'd offered her no more than a tentative affair in a run-down beach shack. No guarantees, no commitment, no future. She only thanked God she'd had enough of her senses left to understand it and to walk away from what was essentially nothing at all. She'd never let Ky know just how horribly it had hurt to walk away from nothing at all.

Her father had been right to quietly point out the weaknesses in Ky, and her obligation to herself and her chosen profession. Ky's lack of ambition, his careless attitude toward the future weren't qualities, but flaws. She'd had a responsibility, and by accepting it had given herself independence and satisfaction.

Calmer, she picked up her brush again. She was dwelling on the past too much. It was time to stop. With the deft movements of habit, she secured her hair into a sleek twist. From this time on, she'd think only of what was to come, not what had, or might have been.

She needed to get out.

With panic just under the surface, Kate pulled a dress out of her closet. It no longer mattered that she was tired, that all she really wanted to do was to crawl into bed and let her mind and body rest. Nerves wouldn't permit it. She'd go across the street, have a drink with Linda and Marsh. She'd see their baby, have a long, extravagant dinner. When she came back to the hotel, alone, she'd make certain she'd be too tired for dreams.

Tomorrow, she had work to do.

Because she dressed quickly, Kate arrived at the Roost just past six. What she saw, she immediately approved of. It wasn't elegant, but it was comfortable. It didn't have the dimly lit, cathedral feel of so many of the restaurants she'd dined in with her father, with colleagues, back in Connecticut. It was relaxed, welcoming, cozy.

There were paintings of ships and boats along the stuccoed walls, of armadas and cutters. Throughout the dining room was other sailing paraphernalia—a ship's compass with its brass gleaming, a colorful spinnaker draped behind the bar with the stools in front of it shaped like wooden kegs. There was a crow's nest spearing toward the ceiling with ferns spilling out and down the mast.

The room was already half full of couples and families, the bulk of whom Kate identified as tourists. She could hear the comforting sound of cutlery scraping lightly over plates. There was the smell of good food and the hum of mixed conversations.

Comfortable, she thought again, but definitely well organized. Waiters and waitresses in sailor's denims moved smoothly, making every second count without looking rushed. The window opened out to a full evening view of Silver Lake Harbor. Kate turned her back on it because she knew her gaze would fall on the *Vortex* or its empty slip.

Tomorrow was soon enough for that. She wanted one night without memories.

"Kate."

She felt the hands on her shoulders and recognized the voice. There was a smile on her face when she turned around. "Marsh, I'm so glad to see you."

In his quiet way, he studied her, measured her and saw both the strain and the relief. In the same way, he'd had a crush on her that had faded into admiration and respect before the end of that one summer. "Beautiful as ever. Linda said you were, but it's nice to see for myself."

She laughed, because he'd always been able to make her feel as though life could be honed down to the most simple of terms. She'd never questioned why that trait had made her relax with Marsh and tingle with Ky.

"Several congratulations are in order, I hear. On your marriage, your daughter and your business."

"I'll take them all. How about the best table in the house?"

"No less than I expected." She linked her arm through his. "Your life agrees with you," she decided as he led her to a table by the window. "You look happy."

"Look and am." He lifted a hand to brush hers. "We were sorry to hear about your father, Kate."

"I know. Thank you."

Marsh sat across from her and fixed her with eyes so much calmer, so much softer than his brother's. She'd always wondered why the man with the dreamer's eyes had been so practical while Ky had been the real dreamer. "It's tragic, but I can't say I'm sorry it brought you back to the island. We've missed you." He paused, just long enough for effect. "All of us."

Kate picked up the square carmine-colored napkin and ran it through her hands. "Things change," she said deliberately. "You and Linda are certainly proof of that. When I left, you thought she was a bit of a nuisance."

"That hasn't changed," he claimed and grinned. He glanced up at the young, pony-tailed waitress. "This is Cindy, she'll take good care of you, Miss Hardesty—" He looked back at Kate with a grin. "I guess I should say Dr. Hardesty."

"Miss'll do," Kate told him. "I've taken the summer off."

"Miss Hardesty's a guest, a special one," he added,

giving the waitress a smile. "How about a drink before you order? Or a bottle of wine?"

"Piesporter," the reply came from a deep, masculine voice.

Kate's fingers tightened on the linen, but she forced herself to look up calmly to meet Ky's amused eyes.

"The professor has a fondness for it."

"Yes, Mr. Silver."

Before Kate could agree or disagree, the waitress had dashed off.

"Well, Ky," Marsh commented easily. "You have a way of making the help come to attention."

With a shrug, Ky leaned against his brother's chair. If the three of them felt the air was suddenly tighter, each concealed it in their own way. "I had an urge for scampi."

"I can recommend it," Marsh told Kate. "Linda and the chef debated the recipe, then babied it until they reached perfection."

Kate smiled at Marsh as though there were no dark, brooding man looking down at her. "I'll try it. Are you going to join me?"

"I wish I could. Linda had to run home and deal with some crisis—Hope has a way of creating them and browbeating the babysitter—but I'll try to get back for coffee. Enjoy your dinner." Rising, he sent his brother a cool, knowing look, then walked away.

"Marsh never completely got over that first case of adulation," Ky commented, then took his brother's seat without invitation.

"Marsh has always been a good friend." Kate draped the napkin over her lap with great care. "Though I realize this is your brother's restaurant, Ky, I'm sure you don't want my company for dinner any more than I want yours."

"That's where you're wrong." He sent a quick, dashing smile at the waitress as she brought the wine. He didn't bother to correct Kate's assumption on the Roost's ownership. Kate sat stone-faced, her manners too good to allow her to argue, while Cindy opened the bottle and poured the first sip for Ky to taste.

"It's fine," he told her. "I'll pour." Taking the bottle, he filled Kate's glass to within half an inch of the rim. "Since we've both chosen the Roost tonight, why don't we have a little test?"

Kate lifted her glass and sipped. The wine was cool and dry. She remembered the first bottle they'd shared—sitting on the floor of his cottage the night she gave him her innocence. Deliberately, she took another swallow. "What kind of test?"

"We can see if the two of us can share a civilized meal in public. That was something we never got around to before."

Kate frowned as he lifted his glass. She'd never seen Ky drink from a wineglass. The few times they had indulged in wine, it had been drunk out of one of the half a dozen water glasses he'd owned. The stem-ware seemed too delicate for his hand, the wine too mellow for the look in his eye.

No, they'd never eaten dinner in public before. Her

father would have exuded disapproval for socializing with someone he'd considered an employee. Kate had known it, and hadn't risked it.

Things were different now, she told herself as she lifted her own glass. In a sense, Ky was now her employee. She could make her own judgments. Recklessly, she toasted him. "To a profitable arrangement then."

"I couldn't have said it better myself." He touched the rim of his glass to hers, but his gaze was direct and uncomfortable. "Blue suits you," he said, referring to her dress, but not taking his eyes off hers. "The deep midnight blue that makes your skin look like something that should be tasted very, very carefully."

She stared at him, stunned at how easily his voice could take on that low, intimate tone that had always made the blood rush out of her brain. He'd always been able to make words seem something dark and secret. That had been one of his greatest skills, one she had never been prepared for. She was no more prepared for it now.

"Would you care to order now?" The waitress stopped beside the table, cheerful, eager to please.

Ky smiled when Kate remained silent. "We're having scampi. The house dressing on the salads will be fine." He leaned back, glass in hand, still smiling. But the smile on his lips didn't connect with his eyes. "You're not drinking your wine. Maybe I should've asked if your taste has changed over the years."

"It's fine." Deliberately she sipped, then kept the glass in her hand as though it would anchor her. "Marsh looks well," she commented. "I was happy to hear about him and Linda. I always pictured them together."

"Did you?" Ky lifted his glass toward the lowering evening light slanting through the window. He watched the colors spear through the wine and glass and onto Kate's hand. "He didn't. But then…" Shifting his gaze, he met her eyes again. "Marsh always took more time to make up his mind than me."

"Recklessness," she continued as she struggled just to breathe evenly, "was always more your style than your brother's."

"But you didn't come to my brother with your charts and notes, did you?"

"No." With an effort she kept her voice and her eyes level. "I didn't. Perhaps I decided a certain amount of recklessness had its uses."

"Find me useful, do you, Kate?"

The waitress served the salads but didn't speak this time. She saw the look in Ky's eyes.

So had Kate. "When I'm having a job done, I've found that it saves a considerable amount of time and trouble to find the most suitable person." With forced calm, she set down her wine and picked up her fork. "I wouldn't have come back to Ocracoke for any other reason." She tilted her head, surprised by the quick surge of challenge that rushed through her.

"Things will be simpler for both of us if that's clear up front."

Anger moved through him, but he controlled it. If they were playing word games, he had to keep his wits. She'd always been clever, but now it appeared the cleverness was glossed over with sophistication. He remembered the innocent, curious Kate with a pang. "As I recall, you were always one for complicating rather than simplifying. I had to explain the purpose, history and mechanics of every piece of equipment before you'd take the first dive."

"That's called caution, not complication."

"You'd know more about caution than I would. Some people spend half their lives testing the wind." He drank deeply of wine. "I'd rather ride with it."

"Yes." This time it was she who smiled with her lips only. "I remember very well. No plans, no ties, tomorrow the wind might change."

"If you're anchored in one spot too long, you can become like those trees out there." He gestured out the window where a line of sparse junipers bent away from the sea. "Stunted."

"Yet you're still here, where you were born, where you grew up."

Slowly Ky poured her more wine. "The island's too isolated, the life a bit too basic for some. I prefer it to those structured little communities with their parties and country clubs."

Kate looked like she belonged in such a place, Ky thought as he fought against the frustrated desire that ebbed and flowed inside him. She belonged in an elegant silk suit, holding a Dresden cup and discussing an obscure eighteenth-century English poet. Was that why she could still make him feel rough and awkward and too full of longings?

If they could be swept back in time, he'd have stolen her, taken her out to open sea and kept her there. They would have traveled from port to exotic port. If having her meant he could never go home again, then he'd have sailed until his time was up. But he would have had her. Ky's fingers tightened around his glass. By God, he would have had her.

The main course was slipped in front of him discreetly. Ky brought himself back to the moment. It wasn't the eighteenth century, but today. Still, she had brought him the past with the papers and maps. Perhaps they'd both find more than they'd bargained for.

"I looked over the things you left with me."

"Oh?" She felt a quick tingle of excitement but speared the first delicate shrimp as though it were all that concerned her.

"Your father's research is very thorough."

"Of course."

Ky let out a quick laugh. "Of course," he repeated, toasting her. "In any case, I think he might have been on the right track. You do realize that the section he narrowed it down to goes into a dangerous area."

Her brows drew together, but she continued to eat. "Sharks?"

"Sharks are a little difficult to confine to an area,"

he said easily. "A lot of people forget that the war came this close in the forties. There are still mines all along the coast of the Outer Banks. If we're going down to the bottom, it'd be smart to keep that in mind."

"I've no intention of being careless."

"No, but sometimes people look so far ahead they don't see what's under their feet."

Though he'd eaten barely half of his meal, Ky picked up his wine again. How could he eat when his whole system was aware of her? He couldn't stop himself from wondering what it would be like to pull those confining pins out of her hair as he'd done so often in the past. He couldn't prevent the memory from springing up about what it had been like to bundle her into his arms and just hold her there with her body fitting so neatly against his. He could picture those long, serious looks she'd give him just before passion would start to take over, then the freedom he could feel racing through her in those last heady moments of love-making.

How could it have been so right once and so wrong now? Wouldn't her body still fit against his? Wouldn't her hair flow through his hands as it fell—that quiet brown that took on such fascinating lights in the sun. She'd always murmur his name after passion was spent, as if the sound alone sustained her. He wanted to hear her say it, just once more, soft and breathless while they were tangled together, bodies still warm and pulsing. He wasn't sure he could resist it.

Absently Ky signaled for coffee. Perhaps he didn't want to resist it. He needed her. He'd forgotten just how sharp and sure a need could be. Perhaps he'd take her. He didn't believe she was indifferent to him— certain things never fade completely. In his own time, in his own way, he'd take what he once had from her. And pray it would be enough this time.

When he looked back at her, Kate felt the warning signals shiver through her. Ky was a difficult man to understand. She knew only that he'd come to some decision and that it involved her. Grateful for the warming effects of the coffee, she drank. She was in charge this time, she reminded herself, every step of the way and she'd make him aware of it. There was no time like the present to begin.

"I'll be at the harbor at eight," she said briskly. "I'll require tanks of course, but I brought my own wet suit. I'd appreciate it if you'd have my briefcase and its contents on board. I believe we'd be wise to spend between six and eight hours out a day."

"Have you kept up with your diving?"

"I know what to do."

"I'd be the last to argue that you had the best teacher." He tilted his cup back in a quick, impatient gesture Kate found typical of him. "But if you're rusty, we'll take it slow for a day or two."

"I'm a perfectly competent diver."

"I want more than competence in a partner."

He saw the flare in her eyes and his need sharpened. It was a rare and arousing thing to watch her controlled and reasonable temperament heat up. "We're not partners. You're working for me."

"A matter of viewpoint," Ky said easily. He rose, deliberately blocking her in. "We'll be putting in a full day tomorrow, so you'd better go catch up on all the sleep you've been missing lately."

"I don't need you to worry about my health, Ky."

"I worry about my own," he said curtly. "You don't go under with me unless you're rested and alert. You come to the harbor in the morning with shadows under your eyes, you won't make the first dive." Furiously she squashed the urge to argue with the reasonable. "If you're sluggish, you make mistakes," Ky said briefly. "A mistake you make can cost me. That logical enough for you, professor?"

"It's perfectly clear." Bracing herself for the brush of bodies, Kate rose. But bracing herself didn't stop the jolt, not for either of them.

"I'll walk you back."

"It's not necessary."

His hand curled over her wrist, strong and stubborn. "It's civilized," he said lazily. "You were always big on being civilized."

Until you'd touch me, she thought. No, she wouldn't remember that, not if she wanted to sleep tonight. Kate merely inclined her head in cool agreement. "I want to thank Marsh."

"You can thank him tomorrow." Ky dropped the waitress's tip on the table. "He's busy."

She started to protest, then saw Marsh disappear

into what must have been the kitchen. "All right." Kate moved by him and out into the balmy evening air.

The sun was low, though it wouldn't set for nearly an hour. The clouds to the west were just touched with mauve and rose. When she stepped outside, Kate decided there were more people in the restaurant than there were on the streets.

A charter fishing boat glided into the harbor. Some of the tourists would be staying on the island, others would be riding back across Hatteras Inlet on one of the last ferries of the day.

She'd like to go out on the water now, while the light was softening and the breeze was quiet. Now, she thought, while others were coming in and the sea would stretch for mile after endless empty mile.

Shaking off the mood, she headed for the hotel. What she needed wasn't a sunset sail but a good solid night's sleep. Daydreaming was foolish, and tomorrow too important.

The same hotel. Ky glanced up at her window. He already knew she had the same room. He'd walked her there before, but then she'd have had her arm through his in that sweet way she had of joining them together. She'd have looked up and laughed at him over something that had happened that day. And she'd have kissed him, warm, long and lingeringly before the door would close behind her.

Because her thoughts had run the same gamut, Kate turned to him while they were still outside the hotel.

"Thank you, Ky." She made a business out of shifting her purse strap on her arm. "There's no need for you to go any further out of your way."

"No, there isn't." He'd have something to take home with him that night, he thought with sudden, fierce impatience. And he'd leave her something to take up to the room where they'd had one long, glorious night. "But then we've always looked at needs from different angles." He cupped his hand around the back of her neck, holding firm as he felt her stiffen.

"Don't." She didn't back away. Kate told herself she didn't back away because to do so would make her seem vulnerable. And she was, feeling those long hard fingers play against her skin again.

"I think this is something you owe me," he told her in a voice so quiet it shivered on the air. "Maybe something I owe myself."

He wasn't gentle. That was deliberate. Somewhere inside him was a need to punish for what hadn't been—or perhaps what had. The mouth he crushed on hers hungered, the arms he wrapped around her demanded. If she'd forgotten, he thought grimly, this would remind her. And remind her.

With her arms trapped between them, he could feel her hands ball into tight fists. Let her hate him, loathe him. He'd rather that than cool politeness.

But God she was sweet. Sweet and as delicate as one of the frothy waves that lapped and spread along the shoreline. Dimly, distantly, he knew he could drown in her without a murmur or complaint.

She wanted it to be different. Oh, how she wanted it to be different so that she'd feel nothing. But she felt everything.

The hard, impatient mouth that had always thrilled and bemused her—it was the same. The lean restless body that fit so unerringly against her—no different. The scent that clung to him, sea and salt—hadn't changed. Always when he kissed her, there'd been the sounds of water or wind or gulls. That, too, remained constant. Behind them boats rocked gently in their slips, water against wood. A gull resting on pilings let out a long, lonely call. The light dimmed as the sun dropped closer to the sea. The flood of past feelings rose up to merge and mingle with the moment.

She didn't resist him. Kate had told herself she wouldn't give him the satisfaction of a struggle. But the command to her brain not to respond was lost in the thin clouds of dusk. She gave because she had to. She took because she had no choice.

His tongue played over hers and her fists uncurled until Kate's palms rested against his chest. So warm, so hard, so familiar. He kissed as he always had, with complete concentration, no inhibitions and little patience.

Time tumbled back and she was young and in love and foolish. Why, she wondered while her head swam, should that make her want to weep?

He had to let her go or he'd beg. Ky could feel it

rising in him. He wasn't fool enough to plead for what was already gone. He wasn't strong enough to accept that he had to let go again. The tug-of-war going on inside him was fierce enough to make him moan. On the sound he pulled away from her, frustrated, infuriated, bewitched.

Taking a moment, he stared down at her. Her look was the same, he realized—that half surprised, half speculative look she'd given him after their first kiss. It disoriented him. Whatever he'd sought to prove, Ky knew now he'd only proven that he was still as much enchanted with her as he'd ever been. He bit back an oath, instead, giving her a half-salute as he walked away.

"Get eight hours of sleep," he ordered without turning around.

Chapter 4

Some mornings the sun seemed to rise more slowly than others, as if nature wanted to show off her particular majesty just a bit longer. When she'd gone to bed, Kate had left her shades up knowing that the morning light would awaken her before the travel alarm beside her bed rang.

She took the dawn as a gift to herself, something individual and personal. Standing at the window, she watched it bloom. The first quiet breeze of morning drifted through the screen to run over her hair and face, through the thin material of her nightshirt, cool and promising. While she stood, Kate absorbed the colors, the light and the silent thunder of day breaking over water.

The lazy contemplation was far different from her

structured routine of the past months and years. Mornings had been a time to dress, a time to run over her schedule and notes for the day's classes over two cups of coffee and a quick breakfast. She never had time to give herself the dawn, so she took it now.

She slept better than she'd expected, lulled by the quiet, exhausted by the days of traveling and the strain on her emotions. There'd been no dreams to haunt her from the time she'd turned back the sheets until the first light had fallen over her face. Then she rose quickly. There'd be no dreams now.

Kate let the morning wash over her with all its new promises, its beginnings. Today was the start. Everything, from the moment she'd taken out her father's papers until she'd seen Ky again, had been a prelude. Even the brief, torrid embrace of the night before had been no more than a ghost of the past. Today was the real beginning.

She dressed and went out into the morning.

Breakfast was impossible. The excitement she'd so meticulously held off was beginning to strain for freedom. The feeling that what she was doing was right was back with her. Whatever it took, whatever it cost her, she'd look for the gold her father had dreamed of. She'd follow his directions. If she found nothing, she'd have looked anyway.

In looking, Kate had come to believe she'd lay all her personal ghosts to rest.

Ky's kiss. It had been aching, disturbing as it had always been. She'd been absorbed, just as she'd always been. Though she knew she had to face both Ky and the past, she hadn't known it would be so frighteningly easy to go back—back to that dark, dreamy world where only he had taken her.

Now that she knew, now that she'd faced even that, Kate had to prepare to fight the wind.

He'd never forgiven her, she realized, for saying no. For bruising his pride. She'd gone back to her world when he'd asked her to stay in his. Asked her to stay, Kate remembered, without offering anything, not even a promise. If he'd given her that, no matter how casual or airy the promise might have been, she wouldn't have gone. She wondered if he knew that.

Perhaps he thought if he could make her lose herself to him again, the scales would be even. She wouldn't lose. Kate stuck her hands into the pockets of her brief pleated shorts. No, she didn't intend to lose. If he had pressed her last night, if he'd known just how weakened she'd been by that one kiss...

But he wouldn't know, she told herself. She wouldn't weaken again. For the summer, she'd make the treasure her goal and her one ambition. She wouldn't leave the island empty-handed this time.

He was already on board the *Vortex*. Kate could see him stowing gear, his hair tousled by the breeze that flowed in from the sea. With only cut-offs and a sleeveless T-shirt between him and the sun she could see the muscles coil and relax, the skin gleam.

Magnificent. She felt the dull ache deep in her stomach and tried to rationalize it away. After all, a

well-honed masculine build should make a woman respond. It was natural. One could even call it imper-
sonal, Kate decided. As she started down the dock she
wished she could believe it.

He didn't see her. A fishing boat already well out
on the water had caught his attention. For a moment,
she stopped, just watching him. Why was it she could
always sense the restlessness in him? There was
movement in him even when he was still, sound even
when he was silent. What was it he saw when he
looked out over the sea? Challenge? Romance?

He was a man who always seemed poised for action, for doing. Yet he could sit quietly and watch the
waves as if there were nothing more important than
that endless battle between earth and water.

Just now he stood on the deck of his boat, hands
on hips, watching the tubby fishing vessel putt toward
the horizon. It was something he'd seen countless
times, yet he stopped to take it in again. Kate looked
where Ky looked and wished she could see what he
was seeing.

Quietly she went forward, her deck shoes making
no sound, but he turned, eyes still intense. "You're
early," he said, and with no more greeting reached
out a hand to help her on board.

"I thought you might be as anxious to start as I
am."

Palm met palm, rough against smooth. Both of them
broke contact as soon as possible.

"It should be an easy ride." He looked back to sea,

toward the boat, but this time he didn't focus on it. ''The wind's coming in from the north, no more than ten knots.''

''Good.'' Though it wouldn't have mattered to her nor, she thought, to him, if the wind had been twice as fast. This was the morning to begin.

She could sense the impatience in him, the desire to be gone and doing. Wanting to make things as simple as possible Kate helped Ky cast off, then walked to the stern. That would keep the maximum distance between them. They didn't speak. The engine roared to life, shattering the calm. Smoothly, Ky maneuvered the small cruiser out of the harbor, setting up a small wake that caused the water to lap against pilings. He kept the same steady even speed while they sailed through the shallows of Ocracoke Inlet. Looking back, Kate watched the distance between the boat and the village grow.

The dreamy quality remained. The last thing she saw was a child walking down a pier with a rod cocked rakishly over his shoulder. Then she turned her face to the sea.

Warm wind, glaring sun. Excitement. Kate hadn't been sure the feelings would be the same. But when she closed her eyes, letting the dull red light glow behind her lids, the salty mist touch her face, she knew this was a love that had remained constant, one that had waited for her.

Sitting perfectly still, she could feel Ky increase the speed until the boat was eating its way through the water as sleekly as a cat moves through the jungle. With her eyes closed, she enjoyed the movement, the speed, the sun. This was a thrill that had never faded. Tasting it again, she understood that it never would.

She'd been right, Kate realized, the hunt would be much more exciting than the final goal. The hunt, and no matter how cautious she was, the man at the helm.

He'd told himself he wouldn't look back at her. But he had to—just once. Eyes closed, a smile playing around her mouth, hair dancing around her face where the wind nudged it from the pins. It brought back a flash of memory—to the first time he'd seen her like that and realized he had to have her. She looked calm, totally at peace. He felt there was a war raging inside him that he had no control over.

Even when he turned back to sea again Ky could see her, leaning back against the stern, absorbing what wind and water offered. In defense, he tried to picture her in a classroom, patiently explaining the intricacies of *Don Juan* or *Henry IV*. It didn't help. He could only imagine her sitting behind him, soaking up sun and wind as if she'd been starved for it.

Perhaps she had been. Though she didn't know what direction Ky's thoughts had taken, Kate realized she'd never been further away from the classroom or the demands she placed on herself there than she was at this moment. She was part teacher, there was no question of that, but she was also, no matter how she'd tried to banish it, part dreamer.

With the sun and the wind on her skin, she was too

exhilarated to be frightened by the knowledge, too content to worry. It was a wild, free sensation to experience again something known, loved, then lost.

Perhaps... Perhaps it was too much like the one frenzied kiss she'd shared with Ky the night before, but she needed it. It might be a foolish need, even a dangerous one. Just once, only this once, she told herself, she wouldn't question it.

Steady, strong, she opened her eyes again. Now she could watch the sun toss its diamonds on the surface of the water. They rippled, enticing, enchanting. The fishing boat Ky had watched move away from the island before them was anchored, casting its nets. A purse seiner, she remembered. Ky had explained the wide, weighted net to her once and how it was often used to haul in menhaden.

She wondered why he'd never chosen that life, where he could work and live on the water day after day. But not alone, she recalled with a ghost of a smile. Fishermen were their own community, on the sea and off it. It wasn't often Ky chose to share himself or his time with anyone. There were times, like this one, when she understood that perfectly.

Whether it was the freedom or the strength that was in her, Kate approached him without nerves. "It's as beautiful as I remember."

He dreaded having her stand beside him again. Now, however, he discovered the tension at the base of his neck had eased. "It doesn't change much." Together they watched the gulls swoop around the fishing boat, hoping for easy pickings. "Fishing's been good this year."

"Have you been doing much?"

"Off and on."

"Clamming?"

He had to smile when he remembered how she'd looked, jeans rolled up to her knees, bare feet full of sand as he'd taught her how to dig. "Yeah."

She, too, remembered, but her only memories were of warm days, warm nights. "I've often wondered what it's like on the island in winter."

"Quiet."

She took the single careless answer with a nod. "I've often wondered why you preferred that."

He turned to her, measuring. "Have you?"

Perhaps that had been a mistake. Since it had already been made, Kate shrugged. "It would be foolish of me to say I hadn't thought of the island or you at all during the last four years. You've always made me curious."

He laughed. It was so typical of her to put things that way. "Because all your tidy questions weren't answered. You think too much like a teacher, Kate."

"Isn't life a multiple choice?" she countered. "Maybe two or three answers would fit, but only one's ultimately right."

"No, only one's ultimately wrong." He saw her eyes take on that thoughtful, considering expression. She was, he knew, weighing the pros and cons of his statement. Whether she agreed or not, she'd consider all the angles. "You haven't changed either," he murmured.

"I thought the same of you. We're both wrong. Neither of us have stayed the same. That's as it should be." Kate looked away from him, further east, then gave a quick cry of pleasure. "Oh, look!" Without thinking, she put her hand on his arm, slender fingers gripping taut muscle. "Dolphins."

She watched them, a dozen, perhaps more, leap and dive in their musical pattern. Pleasure was touched with envy. To move like that, she thought, from water to air and back to water again. It was a freedom that might drive a man mad with the glory of it. But what a madness...

"Fantastic, isn't it?" she murmured. "To be part of the air and the sea. I'd nearly forgotten."

"How much?" Ky studied her profile until he could have etched the shape of it on the wind. "How much have you nearly forgotten?"

Kate turned her head, only then realizing just how close they stood. Unconsciously, she'd moved nearer to him when she'd seen the dolphins. Now she could see nothing but his face, inches from hers, feel nothing but the warm skin beneath her hand. His question, the depth of it, seemed to echo off the surface of the water to haunt her.

She stepped back. The drop before her was very deep and torn with rip tides. "All that was necessary," she said simply. "I'd like to look over my father's charts. Did you bring them on board?"

"Your briefcase is in the cabin." His hands gripped the wheel tightly, as though he were fighting against a storm. Perhaps he was. "You should be able to find your way below."

Without answering, Kate walked around him to the short steep steps that led belowdecks.

There were two narrow bunks with the spreads taut enough to bounce a coin if one was dropped. The galley just beyond would have all the essentials, she knew, in small, efficient scale. Everything would be in its place, as tidy as a monk's cell.

Kate could remember lying with Ky on one of the pristine bunks, flushed with passion while the boat swayed gently in the current and the music from his radio played jazz.

She gripped the leather of her case as if the pain in her fingers would help fight off the memories. To fight everything off entirely was too much to expect, but the intensity eased. Carefully she unfolded one of her father's charts and spread it on the bunk.

Like everything her father had done, the chart was precise and without frills. Though it had certainly not been his field, Hardesty had drawn a chart any sailor would have trusted.

It showed the coast of North Caroline, Pamlico Sound and the Outer Banks, from Manteo to Cape Lookout. As well as the lines of latitude and longitude, the chart also had the thin crisscrossing lines that marked depth.

Seventy-six degrees north by thirty-five degrees

east. From the markings, that was the area her father had decided the *Liberty* had gone down. That was southeast of Ocracoke by no more than a few miles. And the depth…Yes, she decided as she frowned over the chart, the depth would still be considered shallow diving. She and Ky would have the relative freedom of wet suits and tanks rather than the leaded boots and helmets required for deep-sea explorations.

X marks the spot she thought, a bit giddy, but made herself fold the chart with the same care she'd used to open it. She felt the boat slow then heard the re-sounding silence when the engines shut off. A fresh tremor of anticipation went through her as she climbed the steps into the sunlight again.

Ky was already checking the tanks though she knew he would have gone over all the equipment thoroughly before setting out. "We'll go down here," he said as he rose from his crouched position. "We're about half a mile from the last place your father went in last summer."

In one easy motion he pulled off his shirt. Kate knew he was self aware, but he'd never been self-conscious. Ky had already stripped down to brief bikini trunks before she turned away for her own gear.

If her heart was pounding, it was possible to tell herself it was in anticipation of the dive. If her throat was dry, she could almost believe it was nerves at the thought of giving herself to the sea again. His body was hard and brown and lean, but she was only concerned with his skill and his knowledge. And he, she told herself, was only concerned with his fee and his twenty-five percent of the find.

She wore a snug tank suit under her shorts that clung to subtle curves and revealed long, slender legs that Ky knew were soft as water, strong as a runner's. He began to pull on the thin rubber wet suit. They were here to look for gold, to find a treasure that had been lost. Some treasures, he knew, could never be recovered.

As he thought of it, Ky glanced up to see Kate draw the pins from her hair. It fell, soft and slow, over, then past her shoulders. If she'd shot a dart into his chest, she couldn't have pierced his heart more accurately. Swearing under his breath, Ky lifted the first set of tanks.

"We'll go down for an hour today."

"But—"

"An hour's more than enough," he interrupted without sparing her a glance. "You haven't worn tanks in four years."

Kate slipped into the set he offered her, securing the straps until they were snug, but not tight. "I didn't tell you that."

"No, but you'd sure as hell have told me if you had." The corner of his mouth lifted when she remained silent. After attaching his own tanks, Ky climbed over the side onto the ladder. She could either argue, he figured, or she could follow.

To clear his mask, he spat into it, rubbed, then reached down to rinse in salt water. Pulling it over his eyes and nose, Ky dropped into the sea. It took less than ten seconds before Kate plunged into the water beside him. He paused a moment, to make certain she didn't flounder or forget to breathe, then he headed for greater depth.

No, she wouldn't forget to breathe, but the first breath was almost a sigh as her body submerged. It was as thrilling to her as it had been the first time, this incredible ability to stay beneath the ocean's surface and breathe air.

Kate looked up to see the sun spearing through the water, and held out a hand to watch the watery light play on her skin. She could have stayed there, she realized, just reveling in it. But with a curl of her body and a kick, she followed Ky into depth and dimness.

Ky saw a school of menhaden and wondered if they'd end up in the net of the fishing boat he'd watched that morning. When the fish swerved in a mass and rushed past him, he turned to Kate again. She'd been right when she'd told him she knew what to do. She swam as cleanly and as competently as ever.

He expected her to ask him how he intended to look for the *Liberty*, what plan he'd outlined. When she hadn't, Ky had figured it was for one of two reasons. Either she didn't want to have any in-depth conversation with him at the moment, or she'd already reasoned it out for herself. It seemed more likely to be the latter, as her mind was also as clean and competent as ever.

The most logical method of searching seemed to be
a semi-circular route around Hardesty's previous
dives. Slowly and methodically, they would widen the
circle. If Hardesty had been right, they'd find the *Liberty* eventually. If he'd been wrong…they'd have
spent the summer treasure hunting.

Though the tanks on her back reminded Kate not
to take the weightless freedom for granted, she
thought she could stay down forever. She wanted to
touch—the water, the sea grass, the soft, sandy bottom. Reaching out toward a school of bluefish she
watched them scatter defensively then regroup. She
knew there were times when, as a diver moved
through the dim, liquid world, he could forget the need
for the sun. Perhaps Ky had been right in limiting the
dive. She had to be careful not to take what she found
again for granted.

The flattened disklike shape caught Ky's attention.
Automatically, he reached for Kate's arm to stop her
forward progress. The stingray that scuttled along the
bottom looking for tasty crustaceans might be amusing
to watch, but it was deadly. He gauged this one to be
as long as he was tall with a tail as sharp and cruel
as a razor. They'd give it a wide berth.

Seeing the ray reminded Kate that the sea wasn't
all beauty and dreams. It was also pain and death.
Even as she watched, the stingray struck out with its
whiplike tail and caught a small, hapless bluefish.
Once, then twice. It was nature, it was life. But she

turned away. Through the protective masks, her eyes met Ky's.

She expected to see derision for an obvious weakness, or worse, amusement. She saw neither. His eyes were gentle, as they were very rarely. Lifting a hand, he ran his knuckles down her cheek, as he'd done years before when he'd chosen to offer comfort or affection. She felt the warmth, it reflected in her eyes. Then, as quickly as the moment had come, it was over. Turning, Ky swam away, gesturing for her to follow.

He couldn't afford to be distracted by those glimpses of vulnerability, those flashes of sweetness. They had already done him in once. Top priority was the job they'd set out to do. Whatever other plans he had, Ky intended to be in full control. When the time was right, he'd have his fill of Kate. That he promised himself. He'd take exactly what he felt she owed him. But she wouldn't touch his emotions again. When he took her to bed, it would be with cold calculation.

That was something else he promised himself.

Though they found no sign of the *Liberty*, Ky saw wreckage from other ships—pieces of metal, rusted, covered with barnacles. They might have been from a sub or a battleship from World War II. The sea absorbed what remained in her.

He was tempted to swim farther out, but knew it would take twenty minutes to return to the boat. Circling around, he headed back, overlapping, double-checking the area they'd just covered.

Not quite a needle in a haystack, Ky mused, but

close. Two centuries of storms and currents and sea quakes. Even if they had the exact location where the *Liberty* had sunk, rather than the last known location, it took calculation and guesswork, then luck to narrow the field down to a radius of twenty miles.

Ky believed in luck much the same way he imagined Hardesty had believed in calculation. Perhaps with a mixture of the two, he and Kate would find what was left of the *Liberty*.

Glancing over, he watched Kate gliding beside him. She was looking everywhere at once, but Ky didn't think her mind was on treasure or sunken ships. She was, as she'd been that summer before, completely enchanted with the sea and the life it held. He wondered if she still remembered all the information she'd demanded of him before the first dive. What about the physiological adjustments to the body? How was the CO_2 absorbed? What about the change in external pressure?

Ky felt a flash of humor as they started to ascend. He was dead sure Kate remembered every answer he'd given her, right down to the decimal point in pounds of pressure per square inch.

The sun caught her as she rose toward the surface, slowly. It shone around and through her hair, giving her an ethereal appearance as she swam straight up, legs kicking gently, face tilted toward sun and surface. If there were mermaids, Ky knew they'd look as she did—slim, long, with pale loose hair free in the water. A man could only hold on to a mermaid if he accepted the world she lived in as his own. Reaching out, he caught the tip of her hair in his fingers just before they broke the surface together.

Kate came up laughing, letting her mouthpiece fall and pushing her mask up. "Oh, it's wonderful! Just as I remembered." Treading water, she laughed again and Ky realized it was a sound he hadn't heard in four years. But he remembered it exactly.

"You looked like you wanted to play more than you wanted to look for sunken ships." He grinned at her, enjoying her pleasure and the ease of a smile he'd never expected to see again.

"I did." Almost reluctant, she reached out for the ladder to climb on board. "I never expected to find anything the first time down, and it was so wonderful just to dive again." She stripped off her tanks then checked the valves herself before she set them down. "Whenever I go down I begin to believe I don't need the sun anymore. Then when I come up it's warmer and brighter than I remember."

With the adrenaline still flowing, she peeled off her flippers, then her mask, to stand, face lifted toward the sun. "There's nothing else exactly like it."

"Skin diving." Ky tugged down the zipper of his wet suit. "I tried some in Tahiti last year. It's incredible being in that clear water with no equipment but a mask and flippers, and your own lungs."

"Tahiti?" Surprised and interested, Kate looked back as Ky stripped off the wet suit. "You went there?"

"Couple of weeks late last year." He dropped the wet suit in the big plastic can he used for storing equipment before rinsing.

"Because of your affection for islands?"

"And grass skirts."

The laughter bubbled out again. "I'm sure you'd look great in one."

He'd forgotten just how quick she could be when she relaxed. Because the gesture appealed, Ky reached over and gave her hair a quick tug. "I wish I'd taken snapshots." Turning, he jogged down the steps into the cabin.

"Too busy ogling the natives to put them on film for posterity?" Kate called out as she dropped down on the narrow bench on the starboard side.

"Something like that. And of course trying to pretend I didn't notice the natives ogling me."

She grinned. "People in grass skirts," she began then let out a muffled shout as he tossed a peach in her direction. Catching it cleanly, Kate smiled at him before she bit into the fruit.

"Still have good reflexes," Ky commented as he came up the last step.

"Especially when I'm hungry." She touched her tongue to her palm where juice dribbled. "I couldn't eat this morning, I was too keyed up."

He held out one of two bottles of cold soda he'd taken from the refrigerator. "About the dive?"

"That and…" Kate broke off, surprised that she was talking to him as if it had been four years before.

"And?" Ky prompted. Though his tone was casual, his gaze had sharpened.

Aware of it, Kate rose, turning away to look back over the stern. She saw nothing there but sky and water. "It was the morning," she murmured. "The way the sun came up over the water. All that color." She shook her head and water dripped from the ends of her hair onto the deck. "I haven't watched a sunrise in a very long time."

Making himself relax again, Ky leaned back, biting into his own peach as he watched her. "Why?"

"No time. No need."

"Do they both mean the same thing to you?"

Restless, she moved her shoulders. "When your life revolves around schedules and classes, I suppose one equals the other."

"That's what you want? A daily timetable?"

Kate looked back over her shoulder, meeting his eyes levelly. How could they ever understand each other? she wondered. Her world was as foreign to him as his to her. "It's what I've chosen."

"One of your multiple choices of life?" Ky countered, giving a short laugh before he tilted his bottle back again.

"Maybe, or maybe some parts of life only have one choice." She turned completely around, determined not to lose the euphoria that had come to her with the dive. "Tell me about Tahiti, Ky. What's it like?"

"Soft air, soft water. Blue, green, white. Those are

the colors that come to mind, then outrageous splashes of red and orange and yellow.''

"Like a Gauguin painting."

The length of the deck separated them. Perhaps that made it easier for him to smile. "I suppose, but I don't think he'd have appreciated all the hotels and resorts. It isn't an island that's been left to itself."

"Things rarely are."

"Whether they should be or not."

Something in the way he said it, in the way he looked at her, made Kate think he wasn't speaking of an island now, but of something more personal. She drank, cooling her throat, moistening her lips. "Did you scuba?"

"Some. Shells and coral so thick I could've filled a boat with them if I'd wanted. Fish that looked like they should've been in an aquarium. And sharks." He remembered one that had nearly caught him half a mile out. Remembering made him grin. "The waters off Tahiti are anything but boring."

Kate recognized the look, the recklessness that would always surface just under his skill. Perhaps he didn't look for trouble, but she thought he'd rarely sidestep it. No, she doubted they'd ever fully understand each other, if they had a lifetime.

"Did you bring back a shark's tooth necklace?"

"I gave it to Hope." He grinned again. "Linda won't let her have it yet."

"I should think not. Does it feel odd, being an uncle?"

"No. She looks like me."

"Ah, the male ego."

Ky shrugged, aware that he had a healthy share and was comfortable with it. "I get a kick out of watching her run Marsh and Linda in circles. There's not much entertainment on the island."

She tried to imagine Ky being entertained by something as tame as a baby girl. She failed. "It's strange," Kate said after a moment. "Coming back to find Marsh and Linda married and parents. When I left Marsh treated Linda like his little sister."

"Didn't your father keep you up on progress on the island?"

The smile left her eyes. "No."

Ky lifted a brow. "Did you ask?"

"No."

He tossed his empty bottle into a small barrel. "He hadn't told you anything about the ship either, about why he kept coming back to the island year after year."

She tossed her drying hair back from her face. It hadn't been put in the tone of a question. Still, she answered because it was simpler that way. "No, he never mentioned the *Liberty* to me."

"That doesn't bother you?"

The ache came, but she pushed it aside. "Why should it?" she countered. "He was entitled to his own life, his privacy."

"But you weren't."

She felt the chill come and go. Crossing the deck,

Kate dropped her bottle beside Ky's before reaching for her shirt. "I don't know what you mean."

"You know exactly what I mean." He closed his hand over hers before she could pull the shirt on. Because it would've been cowardly to do otherwise, she lifted her head and faced him. "You know," he said again, quietly. "You just aren't ready to say it out loud yet."

"Leave it alone, Ky." Her voice trembled, and though it infuriated her, she couldn't prevent it. "Just leave it."

He wanted to shake her, to make her admit, so that he could hear, that she'd left him because her father had preferred it. He wanted her to say, perhaps sob, that she hadn't had the strength to stand up to the man who had shaped and molded her life to suit his values and wants.

With an effort, he relaxed his fingers. As he had before, Ky turned away with something like a shrug. "For now," he said easily as he went back to the helm. "Summer's just beginning." He started the engine before turning around for one last look. "We both know what can happen during a summer."

Chapter 5

"The first thing you have to understand about Hope," Linda began, steadying a vase the toddler had jostled, "is that she has a mind of her own."

Kate watched the chubby black-haired Hope climb onto a wing-backed chair to examine herself in an ornamental mirror. In the fifteen minutes Kate had been in Linda's home, Hope hadn't been still a moment. She was quick, surprisingly agile, with a look in her eyes that made Kate believe she knew exactly what she wanted and intended to get it, one way or the other. Ky had been right. His niece looked like him, in more ways than one.

"I can see that. Where do you find the energy to run a restaurant, keep a home and manage a fireball?"

"Vitamins," Linda sighed. "Lots and lots of vitamins. Hope, don't put your fingers on the glass."

"Hope!" the toddler cried out, making faces at herself in the mirror. "Pretty, pretty, pretty."

"The Silver ego," Linda commented. "It never tarnishes."

With a chuckle, Kate watched Hope crawl backwards out of the chair, land on her diaper-padded bottom and begin to systematically destroy the tower of blocks she'd built a short time before. "Well, she is pretty. It only shows she's smart enough to know it."

"It's hard for me to argue that point, except when she's spread toothpaste all over the bathroom floor." With a contented sigh, Linda sat back on the couch. She enjoyed having Monday afternoons off to play with Hope and catch up on the dozens of things that went by the wayside when the restaurant demanded her time. "You've been here over a week now, and this is the first time we've been able to talk."

Kate bent over to ruffle Hope's hair. "You're a busy woman."

"So are you."

Kate heard the question, not so subtly submerged in the statement, and smiled. "You know I didn't come back to the island to fish and wade, Linda."

"All right, all right, the heck with being tactful." With a mother's skill, she kept her antenna honed on her active toddler and leaned toward Kate. "What *are* you and Ky doing out on his boat every day?"

With Linda, evasions were neither necessary nor advisable. "Looking for treasure," Kate said simply.

"Oh." Expressing only mild surprise, Linda saved

a budding African violet from her daughter's curious fingers. "Blackbeard's treasure." She handed Hope a rubber duck in lieu of the plant. "My grandfather still tells stories about it. Pieces of eight, a king's ransom and bottles of rum. I always figured that it was buried on land."

Amused at the way Linda could handle the toddler without breaking rhythm, Kate shook her head. "No, not Blackbeard's."

There were dozens of theories and myths about where the infamous pirate had hidden his booty, and fantastic speculation on just how rich the trove was. Kate had never considered them any more than stories. Yet she supposed, in her own way, she was following a similar fantasy.

"My father'd been researching the whereabouts of an English merchant ship that sank off the coast here in the eighteenth century."

"Your father?" Instantly Linda's attention sharpened. She couldn't conceive of the Edwin Hardesty she remembered from summers past as a treasure searcher. "That's why he kept coming to the island every summer? I could never figure out why..." She broke off, grimaced, then plunged ahead. "I'm sorry, Kate, but he never seemed the type to take up scuba diving as a hobby, and I never once saw him with a fish. He certainly managed to keep what he was doing a secret."

"Yes, even from me."

"You didn't know?" Linda glanced over idly as

Hope began to beat on a plastic bucket with a wooden puzzle piece.

"Not until I went through his papers a few weeks ago. I decided to follow through on what he'd started."

"And you came to Ky."

"I came to Ky." Kate smoothed the material of her thin summer skirt over her knees. "I needed a boat, a diver, preferably an islander. He's the best."

Linda's attention shifted from her daughter to Kate. There was simple understanding there, but it didn't completely mask impatience. "Is that the only reason you came to Ky?"

Needs rose up to taunt her. Memories washed up in one warm wave. "Yes, that's the only reason."

Linda wondered why Kate should want her to believe what Kate didn't believe herself. "What if I told you he's never forgotten you?"

Kate shook her head quickly, almost frantically. "Don't."

"I love him." Linda rose to distract Hope who'd discovered tossing blocks was more interesting than stacking them. "Even though he's a frustrating, difficult man. He's Marsh's brother." She set Hope in front of a small army of stuffed animals before she turned and smiled. "He's my brother. And you were the first mainlander I was ever really close to. It's hard for me to be objective."

It was tempting to pour out her heart, her doubts. Too tempting. "I appreciate that, Linda. Believe me, what was between Ky and me was over a long time ago. Lives change.''

Making a neutral sound, Linda sat again. There were some people you didn't press. Ky and Kate were both the same in that area, however diverse they were otherwise. ''All right. You know what I've been doing the past four years.'' She sent a long-suffering look in Hope's direction. ''Tell me what your life's been like.''

''Quieter.''

Linda laughed. ''A small border war would be quieter than life in this house.''

''Earning my doctorate as early as I did took a lot of concentrated effort.'' She'd needed that one goal to keep herself level, to keep herself...calm. ''When you're teaching as well it doesn't leave much time for anything else.'' Shrugging, she rose. It sounded so staid, she realized. So dull. She'd wanted to learn, she'd wanted to teach, but in and of itself, it sounded hollow.

There were toys spread all over the living room, tiny pieces of childhood. A tie was tossed carelessly over the back of a chair next to a table where Linda had dropped her purse. Small pieces of a marriage. Family. She wondered, with a panic that came and went quickly, how she would ever survive the empty house back in Connecticut.

''This past year at Yale has been fascinating and difficult.'' Was she defending or explaining? Kate wondered impatiently. ''Strange, even though my father taught, I didn't realize that being a teacher is just as hard and demanding as being a student.''

"Harder," Linda declared after a moment. "You have to have the answers."

"Yes." Kate crouched down to look at Hope's collection of stuffed animals. "I suppose that's part of the appeal, though. The challenge of either knowing the answer or reasoning it out, then watching it sink in."

"Hoping it sinks in?" Linda ventured.

Kate laughed again. "Yes, I suppose that's it. When it does, that's the most rewarding aspect. Being a mother can't be that much different. You're teaching every day."

"Or trying to," Linda said dryly.

"The same thing."

"You're happy?"

Hope squeezed a bright pink dragon then held it out for Kate. Was she happy? Kate wondered as she obliged by cuddling the dragon in turn. She'd been aiming for achievement, she supposed, not happiness. Her father had never asked that very simple, very basic question. She'd never taken the time to ask herself. "I want to teach," she answered at length. "I'd be unhappy if I couldn't."

"That's a roundabout way of answering without answering at all."

"Sometimes there isn't any yes or no."

"Ky!" Hope shouted so that Kate jolted, whipping her head around to the front door.

"No." Linda noted the reaction, but said nothing. "She means the dragon. He gave it to her, so it's Ky."

"Oh." She wanted to swear but managed to smile as she handed the baby back her treasured dragon. It wasn't reasonable that just his name should make her hands unsteady, her pulse unsteady, her thoughts unsteady. "He wouldn't pick the usual, would he?" she asked carelessly as she rose.

"No." She gave Kate a very direct, very level look. "His tastes have always run to the unique."

Amusement helped to relax her. Kate's brow rose as she met the look. "You don't give up, do you?"

"Not on something I believe in." A trace of stubbornness came through. The stubbornness, Kate mused, that had kept her determinedly waiting for Marsh to fall in love with her. "I believe in you and Ky," Linda continued. "You two can make a mess of it for as long as you want, but I'll still believe in you."

"You haven't changed," Kate said on a sigh. "I came back to find you a wife, a mother, and the owner of a restaurant, but you haven't changed at all."

"Being a wife and mother only makes me more certain that what I believe is right." She had her share of arrogance, too, and used it. "We don't own the restaurant," she added as an afterthought.

"No?" Surprised, Kate looked up again. "But I thought you said the Roost was yours and Marsh's."

"We run it," Linda corrected. "And we do have a twenty percent interest." Sitting back, she gave Kate a pleased smile. There was nothing she liked better than to drop small bombs in calm water and watch the ripples. "Ky owns the Roost."

"Ky?" Kate couldn't have disguised the astonishment if she'd tried. The Ky Silver she thought she knew hadn't owned anything but a boat and a shaky beach cottage. He hadn't wanted to. Buying a restaurant, even a small one on a remote island took more than capital. It took ambition.

"Apparently he didn't bother to mention it."

"No." He'd had several opportunities, Kate recalled, the night they'd had dinner. "No, he didn't. It doesn't seem characteristic," she murmured. "I can picture him buying another boat, a bigger boat or a faster boat, but I can't imagine him buying a restaurant."

"I guess it surprised everyone except Marsh—but then Marsh knows Ky better than anyone. A couple of weeks before we were married, Ky told us he'd bought the place and intended to remodel. Marsh was ferrying over to Hatteras every day to work, I was helping out in my aunt's craft shop during the season. When Ky asked if we wanted to buy in for twenty percent and take over as managers, we jumped at it." She smiled, pleased, and perhaps relieved. "It wasn't a mistake for any of us."

Kate remembered the homey atmosphere, the excellent sea food, the fast service. No, it hadn't been a mistake, but Ky... "I just can't picture Ky in business, not on land anyway."

"Ky knows the island," Linda said simply. "And he knows what he wants. To my way of thinking, he just doesn't always know how to get it."

Kate was going to avoid that area of speculation. "I'm going to take a walk down to the beach," she decided. "Would you like to come?"

"I'd love to, but—" With a gesture of her hand Linda indicated why Hope had been quiet for the last few minutes. With her arm hooked around her dragon, she was sprawled over the rest of the animals, sound asleep.

"It's either stop or go with her, isn't it?" Kate observed with a laugh.

"The nice thing is that when she stops, so can I." Expertly Linda gathered up Hope, cradling her daughter on her shoulder. "Have a nice walk, and stop into the Roost tonight if you have the chance."

"I will." Kate touched Hope's head, the thick, dark, disordered hair that was so much like her uncle's. "She's beautiful, Linda. You're very lucky."

"I know. It's something I don't ever forget."

Kate let herself out of the house and walked along the quiet street. Clouds were low, making the light gloomy, but the rain held off. She could taste it in the breeze, the clean freshness of it, mixed with the faintest hint of the sea. It was in that direction she walked.

On an island, she'd discovered, you were much more drawn to the water than to the land. It was the one thing she'd understood completely about Ky, the one thing she'd never questioned.

It had been easier to avoid going to the beach in Connecticut, though she'd always loved the rocky, windy New England coast. She'd been able to resist it, knowing what memories it would bring back. Pain. Kate had learned there were ways of avoiding pain. But here, knowing you could reach the edge of land by walking in any direction, she couldn't resist. It might have been wiser to walk to the sound, or the inlet. She walked to the sea.

It was warm enough that she needed no more than the sheer skirt and blouse, breezy enough so that the material fluttered around her. She saw two men, caps low over foreheads, their rods secured in the sand, talking together while they sat on buckets and waited for a strike. Their voices didn't carry above the roar and thunder of surf, but she knew their conversation would deal with bait and lures and yesterday's catch. She wouldn't disturb them, nor they her. It was the way of the islander to be friendly enough, but not intrusive.

The water was as gray as the sky, but she didn't mind. Kate had learned not just to accept its moods but to appreciate the contrasts of each one. When the sea was like this, brooding, with threats of violence on the surface, that meant a storm. She found it appealed to a restlessness in herself she rarely acknowledged.

Whitecaps tossed with systematic fever. The spray

rose high and wide. The cry of gulls didn't seem lonely or plaintive now, but challenging. No, a gray gloomy sky meeting a gray sea was anything but dull. It teamed with energy. It boiled with life.

The wind tugged at her hair, loosening pins. She didn't notice. Standing just away from the edge of the surf, Kate faced wind and sea with her eyes wide. She had to think about what she'd just discovered about Ky. Perhaps what she had been determined not to discover about herself.

Thinking there, alone in the gray threatening light before a storm, was what Kate felt she needed. The constant wind blowing in from the east would keep her head clear. Maybe the smells and sounds of the sea would remind her of what she'd had and rejected, and what she'd chosen to have.

Once she'd had a powerful force that had held her swirling, breathless. That force was Ky, a man who could pull on your emotions, your senses, by simply being. The recklessness had attracted her once, the tough arrogance combined with unexpected gentleness. What she saw as his irresponsibility had disturbed her. Kate sensed that he was a man who would drift through life when she'd been taught from birth to seek out a goal and work for it to the exclusion of all else. It was that very different outlook on life that set them poles apart.

Perhaps he had decided to take on some responsibility in his life with the restaurant, Kate decided. If he had she was glad of it. But it couldn't make any difference. They were still poles apart.

She chose the calm, the ordered. Success was satisfaction in itself when success came from something loved. Teaching was vital to her, not just a job, not even a profession. The giving of knowledge fed her. Perhaps for a moment in Linda's cozy, cluttered home it hadn't seemed like enough. Not quite enough. Still, Kate knew if you wished for too much, you often received nothing at all.

With the wind whipping at her face she watched the rain begin far out to sea in a dark curtain. If the past had been a treasure she'd lost, no chart could take her back. In her life, she'd been taught only one direction.

Ky never questioned his impulses to walk on the beach. He was a man who was comfortable with his own mood swings, so comfortable, he rarely noticed them. He hadn't deliberately decided to stop work on his boat at a certain time. He simply felt the temptation of sea and storm and surrendered to it.

Ky watched the seas as he made his way up and over the hill of sand. He could have found his way without faltering in the dark, with no moon. He'd stood on shore and watched the rain at sea before, but repetition didn't lessen the pleasure. The wind would bring it to the island, but there was still time to seek shelter if shelter were desired. More often than not, Ky would let the rain flow over him while the waves rose and fell wildly.

He'd seen his share of tropical storms and hurricanes. While he might find them exhilarating, he appreciated the relative peace of a summer rain. Today he was grateful for it. It had given him a day away from Kate.

They had somehow reached a shaky, tense coexistence that made it possible for them to be together day after day in a relatively small space. The tension was making him nervy; nervy enough to make a mistake when no diver could afford to make one.

Seeing her, being with her, knowing she'd withdrawn from him as a person was infinitely more difficult than being apart from her. To Kate, he was only a means to an end, a tool she used in the same way he imagined she used a textbook. If that was a bitter pill, he felt he had only himself to blame. He'd accepted her terms. Now all he had to do was live with them.

He hadn't heard her laugh again since the first dive. He missed that, Ky discovered, every bit as much as he missed the taste of her lips, the feel of her in his arms. She wouldn't give him any of it willingly, and he'd nearly convinced himself he didn't want her any other way.

But at night, alone, with the sound of the surf in his head, he wasn't sure he'd survive another hour. Yet he had to. It was the fierce drive for survival that had gotten him through the last years. Her rejection had eaten away at him, then it had pushed him to prove something to himself. Kate had been the reason for his risking every penny he'd had to buy the Roost. He'd needed something tangible. The Roost had given him that, in much the same way the charter boat he'd recently bought gave him a sense of worth he once thought was unnecessary.

So he owned a restaurant that made a profit, and a boat that was beginning to justify his investment. It had given his innate love of risk an outlet. It wasn't money that mattered, but the dealing, the speculation, the possibilities. A search for sunken treasure wasn't much different.

What was she looking for really? Ky wondered. Was the gold her objective? Was she simply looking for an unusual way to spend her holiday? Was she still trying to give her father the blind devotion he'd expected all her life? Was it the hunt? Watching the wall of rain move slowly closer, Ky found of all the possibilities he wanted it to be the last.

With perhaps a hundred yards between them, both Kate and Ky looked out to the sea and the rain without being aware of each other. He thought of her and she of him, but the rain crept closer and time slipped by. The wind grew bolder. Both of them could admit to the restlessness that churned inside them, but neither could acknowledge simple loneliness.

Then they turned to walk back up the dunes and saw each other.

Kate wondered how long he'd been there, and how, when she could feel the waves of tension and need, she hadn't known the moment he'd stepped onto the beach. Her mind, her body—always so calm and co-operative—sprang to fevered life when she saw him. Kate knew she couldn't fight that, only the outcome. Still she wanted him. She told herself that just wanting was asking for disaster, but that didn't stop the need. If she ran from him now she'd admit defeat. Instead Kate took the first step across the sand toward him.

The thin white cotton of her skirt flapped around her, billowing, then clinging to the slender body he already knew. Her skin seemed very pale, her eyes very dark. Again Ky thought of mermaids, of illusions and of foolish dreams.

"You always liked the beach before a storm," Kate said when she reached him. She couldn't smile though she told herself she would. She wanted, though she told herself she wouldn't.

"It won't be much longer." He hooked his thumbs into the front pockets of his jeans. "If you didn't bring your car, you're going to get wet."

"I was visiting Linda." Kate turned her head to look back at the rain. No, it wouldn't be much longer. "It doesn't matter," she murmured. "Storms like this are over just as quickly as they begin." Storms like this, she thought, and like others. "I met Hope. You were right."

"About what?"

"She looks like you." This time she did manage to smile, though the tension was balled at the base of her neck. "Did you know she named a doll after you?"

"A dragon's not a doll," Ky corrected. His lips

curved. He could resist a great deal, be apathetic about
a great deal more, but he found it virtually impossible
to do either when it came to his niece. "She's a great
kid. Hell of a sailor."

"You take her out on your boat?"

He heard the astonishment and shrugged it away.
"Why not? She likes the water."

"I just can't picture you..." Breaking off, Kate
turned back to the sea again. No, she couldn't picture
him entertaining a child with toy dragons and boat
rides, just as she couldn't picture him in the business
world with ledgers and accountants. "You surprise
me," she said a bit more casually. "About a lot of
things."

He wanted to reach out and touch her hair, wrap
those loose blowing ends around his finger. He kept
his hands in his pockets. "Such as?"

"Linda told me you own the Roost."

He didn't have to see her face to know it would
hold that thoughtful, considering expression. "That's
right, or most of it anyway."

"You didn't mention it when we were having dinner there."

"Why should I?" She didn't have to see him to
know he shrugged. "Most people don't care who
owns a place as long as the food's good and the service is quick."

"I guess I'm not most people." She said it quietly,
so quietly the words barely carried over the sound of
the waves. Even so, Ky tensed.

"Why would it matter to you?"

Before she could think, she turned back, her eyes full of emotion. "Because it all matters. The whys, the hows. Because so much has changed and so much is the same. Because I want…" Breaking off, she took a step back. The look in her eyes turned to panic just before she started to dash away.

"What?" Ky demanded, grabbing her arm. "What do you want?"

"I don't know!" she shouted, unaware that it was the first time she'd done so in years. "I don't know what I want. I don't understand why I don't."

"Forget about understanding." He pulled her closer, holding her tighter when she resisted—or tried to. "Forget everything that's not here and now." The nights of restlessness and frustration already had his mercurial temperament on edge. Seeing her when he hadn't expected to made his emotions teeter. "You walked away from me once, but I won't crawl for you again. And you," he added with his eyes suddenly dark, his face suddenly close, "you damn well won't walk away as easy this time, Kate. Not this time."

With his arms wrapped around her he held her against him. His lips hovered above hers, threatening, promising. She couldn't tell. She didn't care. It was their taste she wanted, their pressure, no matter how harsh, how demanding. No matter what the consequence. Intellect and emotion might battle, and the battle might be eternal. Yet as she stood there crushed against him, feeling the wind whip at both of them, she already knew what the inevitable outcome would be.

"Tell me what you want, Kate." His voice was low, but as demanding as a shout. "Tell me what you want—now."

Now, she thought. If there could only be just now. She started to shake her head, but his breath feathered over her skin. That alone made future and past fade into insignificance.

"You," she heard herself murmur. "Just you." Reaching up she drew his face down to hers.

A wild passionate wind, a thunderous surf, the threat of rain just moments away. She felt his body— hard and confident against hers. She tasted his lips— soft, urgent. Over the thunder in her head and the thunder to the east, she heard her own moan. She wanted, as long as the moment lasted.

His tongue tempted; she surrendered to it. He dove deep and took all, then more. It might never be enough. With no hesitation, Kate met demand with demand, heat with heat. While mouth sought mouth, her hands roamed his face, teaching what she hadn't forgotten, reacquainting her with the familiar.

His skin was rough with a day's beard, the angle of cheek and jaw, hard and defined. As her fingers inched up she felt the soft brush of his hair blown by the wind. The contrast made her tremble before she dove her fingers deeper.

She could make him blind and deaf with needs. Knowing it, Ky couldn't stop it. The way she touched him, so sure, so sweet while her mouth was molten fire. Desire boiled in him, rising so quickly he was weak with it before his mind accepted what his body couldn't deny. He held her closer, hard against soft, rough against smooth, flame against flame.

Through the thin barrier of her blouse he felt her flesh warm to his touch. He knew the skin here would be delicate, as fragile as the underside of a rose. The scent would be as sweet, the taste as honeyed. Memories, the moment, the dream of more, all these combined to make him half mad. He knew what it would be like to have her, and knowing alone aroused. He felt her now, and feeling made him irrational.

He wanted to take her right there, next to the sea, while the sky opened up and poured over them.

"I want you." With his face buried against her neck he searched for all the places he remembered. "You know how much. You always knew."

"Yes." Her head was spinning. Every touch, every taste added speed to the whirl. Whatever doubts she'd had, Kate had never doubted the want. She hadn't always understood it, the intensity of it, but she'd never doubted it. It was pulling at her now—his, hers—the mutual, mindless passion they'd always been able to ignite in one another. She knew where it would lead— to dark, secret places full of sound and velocity. Not the eye of the hurricane, never the calm with him, but full fury from beginning to end. She knew where it would lead, and knew there'd be glory and freedom. But Ky had spoken no less than the truth when he'd said she wouldn't walk away so easily this time. It was that truth that made her reach for reason, when it would have been so simple to reach for madness.

"We can't." Breathless, she tried to turn in his arms. "Ky, *I* can't." This time when she took his face in her hands it was to draw it away from hers. "This isn't right for me."

Fury mixed with passion. It showed in his eyes, in the press of his fingers on her arms. "It's right for you. It's never been anything but right for you."

"No." She had to deny it, she had to mean it, because he was so persuasive. "No, it's not. I've always been attracted to you. It'd be ridiculous for me to try to pretend otherwise, but this isn't what I want for myself."

His fingers tightened. If they brought her pain neither of them acknowledged it. "I told you to tell me what you wanted. You did."

As he spoke the sky opened, just as he'd imagined. Rain swept in from the sea, tasting of salt, the damp wind and mystery. Instantly drenched, they stood just as they were, close, distant, with his hands firm on her arms and hers light on his face. She felt the water wash over her body, watched it run over his. It stirred her. She couldn't say why, she wouldn't give in to it.

"At that moment I did want you, I can't deny it."

"And now?" he demanded.

"I'm going back to the village."

"Damn it, Kate, what else do you want?"

She stared at him through the rain. His eyes were

dark, stormy as the sea that raged behind him. Somehow he was more difficult to resist when he was like this, volatile, on edge, not quite controlled. She felt desire knot in her stomach, and swim in her head. That was all, Kate told herself. That was all it had ever been. Desire without understanding. Passion without future. Emotion without reason.

"Nothing you can give me," she whispered, knowing she'd have to dig for the strength to walk away, dig for it even to take the first step. "Nothing we can give to each other." Dropping her hands she stepped back. "I'm going back."

"You'll come back to me," Ky said as she took the first steps from him. "And if you don't," he added in a tone that made her hesitate, "it won't make any difference. We'll finish what's been started again."

She shivered, but continued to walk. Finish what's been started again. That was what she most feared.

Chapter 6

The storm passed. In the morning the sea was calm and blue, sprinkled with diamonds of sunlight from a sky where all clouds had been whisked away. It was true that rain freshened things—the air, grass, even the wood and stone of buildings.

The day was perfect, the wind calm. Kate's nerves rolled and jumped.

She'd committed herself to the project. It was her agreement with Ky that forced her to go to the harbor as she'd been doing every other morning. It made her climb on deck when she wanted nothing more than to pack and leave the island the way she'd come. If Ky could complete the agreement after what had passed between them on the beach, so could she.

Perhaps he sensed the fatigue she was feeling, but

he made no comment on it. They spoke only when necessary as he headed out to open sea. Ky stood at the helm, Kate at the stern. Still, even the roar of the engine didn't disguise the strained silence. Ky checked the boat's compass, then cut the engines. Silence continued, thunderously.

With the deck separating them, each began to don their equipment—wet suits, the weight belts that would give them neutral buoyancy in the water, headlamps to light the sea's dimness, masks for sight. Ky checked his depth gauge and compass on his right wrist, then the luminous dial of the watch on his left while Kate attached the scabbard for her diver's knife onto her leg just below the knee.

Without speaking, they checked the valves and gaskets on the tanks, then strapped them on, securing buckles. As was his habit, Ky went into the water first, waiting until Kate joined him. Together they jackknifed below the surface.

The familiar euphoria reached out for her. Each time she dived, Kate expected the underwater world to become more commonplace. Each time it was still magic. She acknowledged what made it possible for her to join creatures of the sea—the regulator with its mouthpiece and hose that brought her air from the tanks on her back, the mask that gave her visibility. She knew the importance of every gauge. She acknowledged the technology, then put it in the practical side of her brain while she simply enjoyed.

They swam deeper, keeping in constant visual contact. Kate knew Ky often dived alone, and that doing so was always a risk. She also knew that no matter how much anger and resentment he felt toward her, she could trust him with her life.

She relied on Ky's instincts as much as his ability. It was his expertise that guided her now, perhaps more than her father's careful research and calculations. They were combing the very edge of the territory her father had mapped out, but Kate felt no discouragement. If she hadn't trusted Ky's skill and instincts, she would never have come back to Ocracoke.

They were going deeper now than they had on their other dives. Kate equalized by letting a tiny bit of air into her suit. Feeling the "squeeze" on her eardrums at the change in pressure, she relieved it carefully. A damaged eardrum could mean weeks without being able to dive.

When Ky signaled for her to switch on her head lamp she obeyed without question. Excitement began to rise.

The sunlight was fathoms above them. The world here never saw it. Sea grass swayed in the current. Now and then a fish, curious and brave enough, would swim along beside them only to vanish in the blink of an eye at a sudden movement.

Ky swam smoothly through the water, using his feet to propel him at a steady pace. Their lamps cut through the murk, surprising more fish, illuminating rock formations that had existed under the sea for centuries. Kate discovered shapes and faces in them.

No, she could never dive alone, Kate decided as Ky slowed his pace to keep rhythm with her more meandering one. It was so easy for her to lose her sense of time and direction. Air came into her lungs with a simple drawing of breath as long as the tanks held oxygen, but the gauges on her wrist only worked if she remembered to look at them.

Even mortality could be forgotten in enchantment. And enchantment could too easily lead to a mistake. It was a lesson she knew, but one that could slip away from her. The timelessness, the freedom was seductive. The feeling was somehow as sensual as the timeless freedom felt in a lover's arms. Kate knew this pleasure could be as dangerous as a lover, but found it as difficult to resist.

There was so much to see, to touch. Crustaceans of different shapes, sizes and hues. They were alive here in their own milieu, so different from when they washed up helplessly on the beach for children to collect in buckets. Fish swam in and out of waving grass that would be limp and lifeless on land. Unlike dolphins or man, some creatures would never know the thrill of both air and water.

Her beam passed over another formation, crusted with barnacles and sea life. She nearly passed it, but curiosity made her turn back so that the light skimmed over it a second time. Odd, she thought, how structured some of the shapes could be. It almost looked like…

Hesitating, using her arms to reverse her progress,

Kate turned in the water to play her light over the shape from end to end. Excitement rose so quickly she grabbed Ky's arm in a grip strong enough to make him stop to search for a defect in her equipment. With a shake of her head Kate warded him off, then pointed.

When their twin lights illuminated the form on the ocean floor, Kate nearly shouted with the discovery. It wasn't a shelf of rock. The closer they swam toward it the more apparent that became. Though it was heavily corroded and covered with crustaceans, the shape of the cannon remained recognizable.

Ky swam around the barrel. When he removed his knife and struck the cannon with the hilt the metallic sound rang out strangely. Kate was certain she'd never heard anything more musical. Her laughter came out in a string of bubbles that made Ky look in her direction and grin.

They'd found a corroded cannon, he thought, and she was as thrilled as if they'd found a chest full of doubloons. And he understood it. They'd found something perhaps no one had seen for two centuries. That in itself was a treasure.

With a movement of his hand he indicated for her to follow, then they began to swim slowly east. If they'd found a cannon, it was likely they'd find more.

Reluctant to leave her initial discovery, Kate swam with him, looking back as often as she looked ahead. She hadn't realized the excitement would be this intense. How could she explain what it felt like to discover something that had lain untouched on the sea floor for more than two centuries? Who would understand more clearly, she wondered, her colleagues at Yale or Ky? Somehow she felt her colleagues would understand intellectually, but they would never understand the exhilaration. Intellectual pleasure didn't make you giddy enough to want to turn somersaults.

How would her father have felt if he'd found it? She wished she knew. She wished she could have given him that one instant of exultation, perhaps shared it with him as they'd so rarely shared anything. He'd only known the planning, the theorizing, the bookwork. With one long look at that ancient weapon, she'd known so much more.

When Ky stopped and touched her shoulders, her emotions were as mixed as her thoughts. If she could have spoken she'd have told him to hold her, though she wouldn't have known why. She was thrilled, yet running through the joy was a thin shaft of sorrow— for what was lost, she thought. For what she'd never be able to find again.

Perhaps he knew something of what moved her. They couldn't communicate with words, but he touched her cheek—just a brush of his finger over her skin. It was more comforting to her than a dozen soft speeches.

She understood then that she'd never stopped loving him. No matter how many years, how many miles had separated them, what life she had she'd left with him. The time in between had been little more than existence. It was possible to live with emptiness, even to be content with it until you had that heady taste of life again.

She might have panicked. She might have run if she hadn't been trapped there, fathoms deep in the midst of a discovery. Instead she accepted the knowledge, hoping that time would tell her what to do.

He wanted to ask her what was going through her mind. Her eyes were full of so many emotions. Words would have to wait. Their time in the sea was almost up. He touched her face again and waited for the smile. When she gave it to him, Ky pointed at something behind her that he had just noticed moments before.

An oaken plank, old, splintered and bumpy with parasites. For the second time Ky removed his knife and began to pry the board from its bed. Silt floated up thinly, cutting visibility before it settled again. Replacing his knife, Ky gave the thumbs-up signal that meant they'd surface. Kate shook her head indicating that they should continue to search, but Ky merely pointed to his watch, then again to the surface.

Frustrated with the technology that allowed her to dive, but also forced her to seek air again, Kate nodded.

They swam west, back toward the boat. When she passed the cannon again, Kate felt a quick thrill of pride. She'd found it. And the discoveries were only beginning.

The moment her head was above water, she started

to laugh. "We found it!" She grabbed the ladder with one hand as Ky began to climb up, placing his find and his tanks on the deck first. "I can't believe it, after hardly more than a week. It's incredible, that cannon lying down there all these years." Water ran down her face but she didn't notice. "We have to find the hull, Ky." Impatient, she released her tanks and handed them up to him before she climbed aboard.

"The chances are good—eventually."

"Eventually?" Kate tossed her wet hair out of her eyes. "We found this in less than a week." She indicated the board on the deck. She crouched over it, just wanting to touch. "We found the *Liberty*."

"We found a wreck," he corrected. "It doesn't have to be the *Liberty*."

"It is," she said with a determination that caused his brow to lift. "We found the cannon and this just on the edge of the area my father had charted. It all fits too well."

"Regardless of what wreck it is, it's undocumented. You'll get your name in the books, professor."

Annoyed she rose. They stood facing each other on either side of the plank they'd lifted out of the sea. "I don't care about having my name in the books."

"Your father's name then." He unzipped his wet suit to let his skin dry.

She remembered her feelings after spotting the cannon, how Ky had seemed to understand them. Could they only be kind to each other, only be close to each other, fathoms under the surface? "Is there something wrong with that?"

"Only if it's an obsession. You always had a problem with your father."

"Because he didn't approve of you?" she shot back.

His eyes took on that eerily calm, almost flat expression that meant his anger was lethal. "Because it mattered too much to you what he approved of."

That stung. The truth often did. "I came here to finish my father's project," she said evenly. "I made that clear from the beginning. You're still getting your fee."

"You're still following directions. His directions." Before she could retort, he turned toward the cabin. "We'll eat and rest before we go back under."

With an effort, she held on to her temper. She wanted to dive again, badly. She wanted to find more. Not for her father's approval, Kate thought fiercely. Certainly not for Ky's. She wanted this for herself. Pulling down the zipper of her wet suit, she went down the cabin steps.

She'd eat because strength and energy were vital to a diver. She'd rest for the same reason. Then, she determined, she'd go back to the wreck and find proof that it was the *Liberty*.

Calmer, she watched Ky go through a small cupboard. "Peanut butter?" she asked when she saw the jar he pulled out.

"Protein."

Her laugh helped her to relax again. "Do you still eat it with bananas?"

"It's still good for you."

Though she wrinkled her nose at the combination, she reminded herself that beggars couldn't be choosers. "When we find the treasure," she said recklessly, "I'll buy you a bottle of champagne."

Their fingers brushed as he handed her the first sandwich. "I'll hold you to it." He picked up his own sandwich and a quart of milk. "Let's eat on deck."

He wasn't certain if he wanted the sun or the space, but it wasn't any easier to be with her in that tiny cabin than it had been the first time, or the last. Taking her assent for granted, Ky went up the stairs again, without looking back. Kate followed.

"It might be good for you," Kate commented as she took the first bite, "but it still tastes like something you give five-year-olds when they scrape their knees."

"Five-year-olds require a lot of protein."

Giving up, Kate sat cross-legged on the deck. The sun was bright, the movement of the boat gentle. She wouldn't let his digs get to her, nor would she dig back. They were in this together, she reminded herself. Tension and sniping wouldn't help them find what they sought.

"It's the *Liberty*, Ky," she murmured, looking at the plank again. "I know it is."

"It's possible." He stretched out with his back against the port side. "But there are a lot of wrecks, unidentified and otherwise, all through these waters. Diamond Shoals is a graveyard.''

''Diamond Shoals is fifty miles north.''

''And the entire coastline along these barrier islands is full of littoral currents, rip currents and shifting sand ridges. Two hundred years ago they didn't have modern navigational devices. Hell, they didn't even have the lighthouses until the nineteenth century. I couldn't even give you an educated guess as to how many ships went down from the time Columbus set out until World War II.''

Kate took another bite. ''We're only concerned with one ship.''

''Finding one's no big problem,'' he returned. ''Finding a specific one's something else. Last year, after a couple of hurricanes breezed through, they found wrecks uncovered on the beach on Hatteras. There are plenty of houses on the island that were built from pieces of wreckage like that.'' He pointed to the plank with the remains of his sandwich.

Kate frowned at the board again. ''It could be the *Liberty* just as easily as it couldn't.''

''All right.'' Appreciating her stubbornness, Ky grinned. ''But whatever it is, there might be treasure. Anything lost for more than two hundred years is pretty much finders keepers.''

She didn't want to say that it wasn't any treasure she wanted. Just the *Liberty*'s. From what he said before, Kate was aware he already understood that. It was simply different for him. She took a long drink of cold milk. "What do you plan to do with your share?"

With his eyes half closed, he shrugged. He could do as he pleased now, a cache of gold wouldn't change that. "Buy another boat, I imagine."

"With what two-hundred-year-old gold would be worth today, you'd be able to buy a hell of a boat."

He grinned, but kept his eyes shaded. "I intend to. What about you?"

"I'm not sure." She wished she had some tangible goal for the money, something exciting, even fanciful. It just didn't seem possible to think beyond the hunt yet. "I thought I might travel a bit."

"Where?"

"Greece maybe. The islands."

"Alone?"

The food and the motion of the boat lulled her. She made a neutral sound as she shut her eyes.

"Isn't there some dedicated teacher you'd take with you? Someone you could discuss the Trojan War with?"

"Mmm, I don't want to go to Greece with a dedicated teacher."

"Someone else?"

"There's no one."

Sitting on the deck with her face lifted, her hair blowing, she looked like a finely crafted piece of porcelain. Something a man might look at, admire, but not touch. When her eyes were open, hot, her skin flushed with passion, he burned for her. When she was like this, calm, distant, he ached. He let the needs run through him because he knew there was no stopping them.

"Why?"

"Hmm?"

"Why isn't there anyone?"

Lazily she opened her eyes. "Anyone?"

"Why don't you have a lover?"

The sleepy haze cleared from her eyes instantly. He saw her fingers tense on the dark blue material that stretched snugly over her knees. "It's none of your business whether I do or not."

"You've just told me you don't."

"I told you there's no one I'd travel with," she corrected, but when she started to rise, he put a hand on her shoulder.

"It's the same thing."

"No, it's not, but it's still none of your business, Ky, any more than your personal life is mine."

"I've had women," he said easily. "But I haven't had a lover since you left the island."

She felt the pain and the pleasure sweep up through her. It was dangerous to dwell on the sensation. As dangerous as it was to lose yourself deep under the ocean. "Don't." She lifted her hand to remove his from her shoulder. "This isn't good for either of us."

"Why?" His fingers linked with hers. "We want each other. We both know the rules this time around."

Rules. No commitment, no promises. Yes, she understood them this time, but like mortality during a dive, they could easily be forgotten. Even now, with his eyes on hers, her fingers caught in his, the structure of those rules became dimmer and dimmer. He would hurt her again. There was never any question of that. Somehow, in the last twenty-four hours, it had become a matter of *how* she would deal with the pain, not *if.*

"Ky, I'm not ready." Her voice was low, not pleading, but plainly vulnerable. Though she wasn't aware of it, there was no defense she could put to better use.

He drew her up so that they were both standing, touching only hand to hand. Though she was tall, her slimness made her appear utterly fragile. It was that and the way she looked at him, with her head tilted back so their eyes could meet, that prevented him from taking what he was determined to have, without questions, without her willingness. Ruthlessly, that was how he told himself he wanted to take her, even though he knew he couldn't.

"I'm not a patient man."

"No."

He nodded, then released her hand while he still could. "Remember it," he warned before he turned to go to the helm. "We'll take the boat east, over the wreck and dive again."

An hour later they found a piece of rigging, broken and corroded, less than three yards from the cannon. By hand signals, Ky indicated that they'd start a stockpile of the salvage. Later they'd come back with the means of bringing it up. There were more planks, some too big for a man to carry up, some small enough for Kate to hold in one hand.

When she found a pottery bowl, miraculously unbroken, she realized just what an archaeologist must feel after hours of digging when he unearths a fragment of another era. Here it was, cupped in her hand, a simple bowl, covered with silt, covered with age. Someone had eaten from it once, a seaman, relaxing briefly below deck, perhaps on his first voyage across the Atlantic to the New World. His last journey in any event, Kate mused as she turned the bowl over in her hand.

The rigging, the cannon, the planks equaled ship. The bowl equaled man.

Though she put the bowl with the other pieces of their find, she intended to take it up with her on this dive. Whatever other artifacts they found could go to a museum, but the first, she'd keep.

They found pieces of glass that might have come from bottles that held whiskey, chunks of crockery that hadn't survived intact like the bowl. Bits of cups, bowls, plates littered the sea floor.

The galley, she decided. They must have found the galley. Over the years, the water pressure would have simply disintegrated the ship until it was all pieces spread on and under the floor of the ocean. It would, in essence, have become part of the sea, a home for the creatures and plant life that dwelt there.

But they'd found the galley. If they could find

something, just one thing with the ship's name inscribed on it, they'd be certain.

Diligently, using her knife as a digging tool, Kate worked at the floor of the sea. It wasn't a practical way to search, but she saw no harm in trying her luck. They'd found crockery, glass, the unbroken bowl. Even as she glanced up she saw Ky examining what might have been half a dinner plate.

When she unearthed a long wooden ladle, Kate found that her excitement increased. They *had* found the galley, and in time, she'd prove to Ky that they'd found the *Liberty*.

Engrossed in her find, she turned to signal to Ky and moved directly into the path of a stingray.

He saw it. Ky was no more than a yard from Kate when the movement of the ray unearthing itself from its layer of sand and silt had caught his eye. His movement was pure reflex, done without thought or plan. He was quick. But even as he grabbed Kate's hand to swing her back behind him, out of range, the wicked, saw-toothed tail lashed out.

Her scream was muffled by the water, but the sound went through Ky just as surely as the stingray's poison went through Kate. Her body went stiff against his, rigid in pain and shock. The ladle she'd found floated down, out of her grip, until it landed silently on the bottom.

He knew what to do. No rational diver goes down unless he has a knowledge of how to handle an emergency. Still Ky felt a moment of panic. This wasn't just another diver, it was Kate. Before his mind could clear, her stiffened body went limp against him. Then he acted.

Cool, almost mechanically, he tilted her head back with the chin carry to keep her air passage open. He held her securely, pressing his chest into her tanks, keeping his hand against her ribcage. It ran through his mind that it was best she'd fainted. Unconscious she wouldn't struggle as she might had she been awake and in pain. It was best she'd fainted because he couldn't bear to think of her in pain. He kicked off for the surface.

On the rise he squeezed her, hard, forcing expanding air out of her lungs. There was always the risk of embolism. They were going up faster than safety allowed. Even while he ventilated his own lungs, Ky kept a lookout. She would bleed, and blood brought sharks.

The minute they surfaced, Ky released her weight belt. Supporting her with his arm wrapped around her, his hand grasping the ladder, Ky unhooked his tanks, slipped them over the side of the boat, then removed Kate's. Her face was waxy, but as he pulled the mask from her face she moaned. With that slight sound of life some of the blood came back to his own body. With her draped limply over his shoulder, he climbed the ladder onto the *Vortex*.

He laid her down on the deck, and with hands that didn't hesitate, began to pull the wet suit from her. She moaned again when he drew the snug material over the wound just above her ankle, but she didn't reach the surface of consciousness. Grimly, Ky examined the laceration the ray had caused. Even through the protection of her suit, the tail had penetrated deep into her skin. If Ky had only been quicker...

Cursing himself, Ky hurried to the cabin for the first aid kit.

As consciousness began to return, Kate felt the ache swimming up from her ankle to her head. Spears of pain shot through her, sharp enough to make her gasp and struggle, as if she could move away from it and find ease again.

"Try to lie still."

The voice was gentle and calm. Kate balled her hands into fists and obeyed it. Opening her eyes, she stared up at the pure blue sky. Her mind whirled with confusion, but she stared at the sky as though it were the only tangible thing in her life. If she concentrated, she could rise above the hurt. The ladle. Opening her hand she found it empty, she'd lost the ladle. For some reason it seemed vital that she have it.

"We found the galley." Her voice was hoarse with anguish, but her one hand remained open and limp. "I found a ladle. They'd have used it for spooning soup into that bowl. The bowl—it wasn't even broken. Ky..." Her voice weakened with a new flood of sensation as memory began to return. "It was a stingray. I wasn't watching for it, it just seemed to be there. Am I going to die?"

"No!" His answer was sharp, almost angry. Bending over her, he placed both hands on her shoulders so that she'd look directly into his face. He had to be sure she understood everything he said. "It was a stingray," he confirmed, not adding that it had been a good ten feet long. "Part of the spine's broken off, lodged just above your ankle."

He watched her eyes cloud further, part pain, part fear. His hands tightened on her shoulders. "It's not in deep. I can get it out, but it'll hurt like hell."

She knew what he was saying. She could stay as she was until he got her back to the doctor on the island, or she could trust him to treat her now. Though her lips trembled, she kept her eyes on his and spoke clearly.

"Do it now."

"Okay." He continued to stare at her, into the eyes that were glazed with shock. "Hang on. Don't try to be brave. Scream as much as you want but try not to move. I'll be quick." Bending farther, he kissed her hard. "I promise."

Kate nodded, then concentrating on the feeling of his lips against hers, shut her eyes. He was quick. Within seconds she felt the hurt rip through her, over the threshold she thought she could bear and beyond.... She pulled in air to scream, but went back under the surface into liquid dimness.

Ky let the blood flow freely onto the deck for a moment, knowing it would wash away some of the poison. His hands had been rock steady when he'd pulled the spine from her flesh. His mind had been cold. Now with her blood on his hands, they began to shake. Ignoring them, and the icy fear of seeing Kate's smooth skin ripped and raw, Ky washed the wound, cleansed it, bound it. Within the hour, he'd have her to a doctor.

With unsteady fingers, he checked the pulse at the base of her neck. It wasn't strong, but it was steady. Lifting an eyelid with his thumb, he checked her pupils. He didn't believe she was in shock, she'd simply escaped from the pain. He thanked God for that.

On a long breath he let his forehead rest against hers, only for a moment. He prayed that she'd remain unconscious until she was safely under a doctor's care.

He didn't take the time to wash her blood from his hands before he took the helm. Ky whipped the boat around in a quick circle and headed full throttle back to Ocracoke.

Chapter 7

As she started to float toward consciousness, Kate focused, drifted, then focused again. She saw the whirl of a white ceiling rather than the pure blue arc of sky. Even when the mist returned she remembered the hurt and thrashed out against it. She couldn't face it a second time. Yet she found as she rose closer to the surface that she didn't have the will to fight against it. That brought fear. If she'd had the strength, she might have wept.

Then she felt a cool hand on her cheek. Ky's voice pierced the last layers of fog, low and gentle. "Take it easy, Kate. You're all right now. It's all over."

Though her breath hitched as she inhaled, Kate opened her eyes. The pain didn't come. All she felt was his hand on her cheek, all she saw was his face.

"Ky." When she said his name, Kate reached for his hand, the one solid thing she was sure of. Her own voice frightened her. It was hardly more than a wisp of air.

"You're going to be fine. The doctor took care of you." As he spoke, Ky rubbed his thumb over her knuckles, establishing a point of concentration, and kept his other hand lightly on her cheek, knowing that contact was important. He'd nearly gone mad waiting for her to open her eyes again. "Dr. Bailey, you remember. You met him before."

It seemed vital that she should remember so she forced her mind to search back. She had a vague picture of a tough, weathered old man who looked more suited to the sea than the examining room. "Yes. He likes…likes ale and flounder."

He might have laughed at her memory if her voice had been stronger. "You're going to be fine, but he wants you to rest for a few more days."

"I feel…strange." She lifted a hand to her own head as if to assure herself it was still there.

"You're on medication, that's why you're groggy. Understand?"

"Yes." Slowly she turned her head and focused on her surroundings. The walls were a warm ivory, not the sterile white of a hospital. The dark oak trim gleamed dully. On the hardwood floor lay a single rug, its muted Indian design fading with age. It was the only thing Kate recognized. The last time she'd been in Ky's bedroom only half the dry wall had been in place and one of the windows had had a long thin crack in the bottom pane. "Not the hospital," she managed.

"No." He stroked her head, needing to touch as much as to check for her fever that had finally broken near dawn. "It was easier to bring you here after Bailey took care of you. You didn't need a hospital, but neither of us liked the idea of your being in a hotel right now."

"Your house," she murmured, struggling to concentrate her strength. "This is your bedroom, I remember the rug."

They'd made love on it once. That's what Ky remembered. With an effort, he kept his hands light. "Are you hungry?"

"I don't know." Basically, she felt nothing. When she tried to sit up, the drug spun in her head, making both the room and reality reel away. That would have to stop, Kate decided while she waited for the dizziness to pass. She'd rather have some pain than that helpless, weighted sensation.

Without fuss, Ky moved the pillows and shifted her to a sitting position. "The doctor said you should eat when you woke up. Just some soup." Rising he looked down on her, in much the same way, Kate thought, as he'd looked at a cracked mast he was considering mending. "I'll fix it. Don't get up," he added as he walked to the door. "You're not strong enough yet."

As he went into the hall he began to swear in a low steady stream.

Of course she wasn't strong enough, he thought with a last vicious curse. She was pale enough to fade into the sheets she lay on. No resistance, that's what Bailey had said. Not enough food, not enough sleep, too much strain. If he could do nothing else, Ky determined as he pulled open a kitchen cupboard, he could do something about that. She was going to eat, and lie flat on her back until the doctor said otherwise.

He'd known she was weak, that was the worst of it. Ky dumped the contents of a can into a pot then hurled the empty container into the trash. He'd seen the strain on her face, the shadows under her eyes, he'd heard the traces of fatigue come and go in her voice, but he'd been too wrapped up in his own needs to do anything about it.

With a flick of the wrist, he turned on the burner under the soup, then the burner under the coffee. God, he needed coffee. For a moment he simply stood with his fingers pressed against his eyes waiting for his system to settle.

He couldn't remember ever spending a more frantic twenty-four hours. Even after the doctor had checked and treated her, even when Ky had brought her home and she'd been fathoms deep under the drug, his nerves hadn't eased. He'd been terrified to leave the room for more than five minutes at a time. The fever had raged through her, though she'd been unaware.

Most of the night he'd sat beside her, bathing away
the sweat and talking to her, though she couldn't hear.
Through the night he'd existed on coffee and
nerves. With a half-laugh he reached for a cup. It
looked like that wasn't going to change for a while
yet.

He knew he still wanted her, knew he still felt
something for her, under the bitterness and anger. But
until he'd seen her lying unconscious on the deck of
his boat, with her blood on his hands, he hadn't realized that he still loved her.

He'd known what to do about the want, even the
bitterness, but now, faced with love, Ky hadn't a clue.
It didn't seem possible for him to love someone so
frail, so calm, so…different than he. Yet the emotion
he'd once felt for her had grown and ripened into
something so solid he couldn't see any way around it.
For now, he'd concentrate on getting her on her feet
again. He poured the soup into a bowl and carried it
upstairs.

It would have been an easy matter to close her eyes
and slide under again. Too easy. Willing herself to
stay awake, Kate concentrated on Ky's room. There
were a number of changes here as well, she mused.
He'd trimmed the windows in oak, giving them a wide
sill where he'd scattered the best of his shells. A piece
of satiny driftwood stood, beautiful as a piece of
sculpture. There was a paneled closet door with a fac-
eted glass knob where there'd once been a rod, a

round-backed rattan chair where there'd been packing crates.

Only the bed was the same, she mused. The wide four-poster had been his mother's. She knew he'd given the rest of his family's furniture to Marsh. Ky had told her once he'd felt no need or desire for it, but he kept the bed. He was born there, unexpectedly, during a night in which the island had been racked by a storm.

And they'd made love there, Kate remembered as she ran her fingers over the sheets. The first time, and the last.

Stopping the movement of her fingers, she looked over as Ky came back into the room. Memories had to be pushed aside. "You've done a lot of work in here."

"A bit." He set the tray over her lap as he sat on the edge of the bed.

As the scent of the soup reached her, Kate shut her eyes. Just the aroma seemed to be enough. "It smells wonderful."

"The smell won't put any meat on you."

She smiled, and opened her eyes again. Then before she'd realized it, Ky had spoon-fed her the first bite. "It tastes wonderful too." Though she reached for the spoon, he dipped it into the bowl himself then held it to her lips. "I can do it," she began, then was forced to swallow more broth.

"Just eat." Fighting off waves of emotion he spoke briskly. "You look like hell."

"I'm sure I do," she said easily. "Most people don't look their best a couple of hours after being stung by a stingray."

"Twenty-four," Ky corrected as he fed her another spoon of soup.

"Twenty-four what?"

"Hours." Ky slipped in another spoonful when her eyes widened.

"I've been unconscious for twenty-four hours?" She looked to the window and the sunlight as if she could find some means of disproving it.

"You slipped in and out quite a bit before Bailey gave you the shot. He said you probably wouldn't remember." Thank God, Ky added silently. Whenever she'd fought her way back to consciousness, she'd been in agony. He could still hear her moans, feel the way she'd clutched him. He never knew a person could suffer physically for another's pain the way he'd suffered for hers. Even now it made his muscles clench.

"That must've been some shot he gave me."

"He gave you what you needed." His eyes met hers. For the first time Kate saw the fatigue in them, and the anger.

"You've been up all night," she murmured. "Haven't you had any rest at all?"

"You needed to be watched," he said briefly. "Bailey wanted you to stay under, so you'd sleep through the worst of the pain, and so you'd just sleep period." His voice changed as he lost control over the anger.

He couldn't prevent the edge of accusation from showing, partly for her, partly for himself. "The wound wasn't that bad, do you understand? But you weren't in any shape to handle it. Bailey said you've been well on the way to working yourself into exhaustion."

"That's ridiculous. I don't—"

Ky swore at her, filling her mouth with more soup. "Don't tell me it's ridiculous. I had to listen to him. I had to look at you. You don't eat, you don't sleep, you're going to fall down on your face."

There was too much of the drug in her system to allow her temper to bite. Instead of annoyance, her words came out like a sigh. "I didn't fall on my face."

"Only a matter of time." Fury was coming too quickly. Though his fingers tightened on the spoon, Ky held it back. "I don't care how much you want to find the treasure, you can't enjoy it if you're flat on your back."

The soup was warming her. As much as her pride urged her to refuse, her system craved the food. "I won't be," she told him, not even aware that her words were beginning to slur. "We'll dive again tomorrow, and I'll prove it's the *Liberty*."

He started to swear at her, but one look at the heavy eyes and the pale cheeks had him swallowing the words. "Sure." He spooned in more soup knowing she'd be asleep again within moments.

"I'll give the ladle and the rigging and the rest to a museum." Her eyes closed. "For my father."

Ky set the tray on the floor. "Yes, I know."

"It was important to him. I need...I just need to give him something." Her eyes fluttered open briefly. "I didn't know he was ill. He never told me about his heart, about the pills. If I'd known..."

"You couldn't have done any more than you did." His voice was gentle again as he shifted the pillows down.

"I loved him."

"I know you did."

"I could never seem to make the people I love understand what I need. I don't know why."

"Rest now. When you're well, we'll find the treasure."

She felt herself sinking into warmth, softness, the dark. "Ky." Kate reached out and felt his fingers wrap around hers. With her eyes closed, it was all the reality she needed.

"I'll stay," he murmured, brushing the hair from her cheek. "Just rest."

"All those years..." He could feel her fingers relaxing in his as she slipped deeper. "I never forgot you. I never stopped wanting you. Not ever..."

He stared down at her as she slept. Her face was utterly peaceful, pale as marble, soft as silk. Unable to resist, he lifted her fingers to his own cheek, just to feel her flesh against his. He wouldn't think about what she'd said now. He couldn't. The strain of the last day had taken a toll on him as well. If he didn't get some rest, he wouldn't be able to care for her when she woke again.

Rising, Ky pulled down the shades, and took off his shirt. Then he lay down next to Kate in the big four-poster bed and slept for the first time in thirty-six hours.

The pain was a dull, consistent throb, not the silvery sharp flash she remembered, but a gnawing ache that wouldn't pass. When it woke her, Kate lay still, trying to orient herself. Her mind was clearer now. She was grateful for that, even though with the drug out of her system she was well aware of the wound. It was dark, but the moonlight slipped around the edges of the shades Ky had drawn. She was grateful for that too. It seemed she'd been a prisoner of the dark for too long.

It was night. She prayed it was only hours after she'd last awoken, not another full day later. She didn't want that quick panic at the thought of losing time again. Because she needed to be certain she was in control this time, she went over everything she remembered.

The pottery bowl, the ladle, then the stingray. She closed her eyes a moment, knowing it would be a very long time before she forgot what it had felt like to be struck with that whiplike tail. She remembered waking up on the deck of the *Vortex*, the pure blue sky overhead, and the strong, calm way Ky had spoken to her before he'd pulled out the spine. That pain, the horror of that one instant was very clear. Then, there was nothing else.

She remembered nothing of the journey back to the island, or of Dr. Bailey's ministrations or of being transported to Ky's home. Her next clear image was of waking in his bedroom, of dark oak trim on the windows, wide sills with shells set on them.

He'd fed her soup—yes, that was clear, but then things started to become hazy again. She knew he'd been angry, though she couldn't remember why. At the moment, it was more important to her that she could put events in some sort of sequence.

As she lay in the dark, fully awake and finally aware, she heard the sound of quiet, steady breathing beside her. Turning her head, Kate saw Ky beside her, hardly more than a silhouette with the moonlight just touching the skin of his chest so that she could see it rise and fall.

He'd said he would stay, she remembered. And he'd been tired. Abruptly Kate remembered there'd been fatigue in his eyes as well as temper. He'd been caring for her.

A mellow warmth moved through her, one she hadn't felt in a very long time. He had taken care of her, and though it had made him angry, he'd done it. And he'd stayed. Reaching out, she touched his cheek.

Though the gesture was whisper light, Ky awoke immediately. His sleep had been little more than a half doze so that he could recharge his system yet be aware of any sign that Kate needed attention. Sitting up, he shook his head to clear it.

He looked like a boy caught napping. For some reason the gesture moved Kate unbearably. "I didn't mean to wake you," she murmured.

He reached for the lamp beside the bed and turned it on low. Though his body revolted against the interruption, his mind was fully awake. "Pain?"

"No."

He studied her face carefully. The glazed look from the drug had left her eyes, but the color hadn't returned. "Kate."

"All right. Some."

"Bailey left some pills."

As he started to rise, Kate reached for him again. "No, I don't want anything. It makes me groggy."

"It takes away the pain."

"Not now, Ky, please. I promise I'll tell you if it gets bad."

Because her voice was close to desperate he made himself content with that. At the moment, she looked too fragile to argue with. "Are you hungry?"

She smiled, shaking her head. "No. It must be the middle of the night. I was only trying to orient myself." She touched him again, in gratitude, in comfort. "You should sleep."

"I've had enough. Anyway, you're the patient."

Automatically, he put his hand to her forehead to check for fever. Touched, Kate laid hers over it. She felt the quick reflexive tensing of his fingers.

"Thank you." When he would have removed his hand, she linked her fingers with his. "You've been taking good care of me."

"You needed it," he said simply and much too swiftly. He couldn't allow her to stir him now, not when they were in that big, soft bed surrounded by memories.

"You haven't left me since it happened."

"I had no place to go."

His answer made her smile. Kate reached up her free hand to touch his cheek. There had been changes, she thought, many changes. But so many things had stayed the same. "You were angry with me."

"You haven't been taking care of yourself." He told himself he should move away from the bed, from Kate, from everything that weakened him there.

He stayed, leaning over her, one hand caught in hers. Her eyes were dark, soft in the dim light, full of the sweetness and innocence he remembered. He wanted to hold her until there was no more pain for either of them, but he knew, if he pressed his body against hers now, he wouldn't stop. Again he started to move, pulling away the hand that held hers. Again Kate stopped him.

"I would've died if you hadn't gotten me up."

"That's why it's smarter to dive with a partner."

"I might still have died if you hadn't done everything you did."

He shrugged this off, too aware that the fingers on his face were stroking lightly, something she had done in the past. Sometimes before they'd made love, and often afterward, when they'd talked in quiet voices, she'd stroke his face, tracing the shape of it as though she'd needed to memorize it. Perhaps she, too, sometimes awoke in the middle of the night and remembered too much.

Unable to bear it, Ky put his hand around her wrist and drew it away. "The wound wasn't that bad," he said simply.

"I've never seen a stingray that large." She shivered and his hand tightened on her wrist.

"Don't think about it now. It's over."

Was it? she wondered as she lifted her head and looked into his eyes. Was anything ever really over? For four years she'd told herself there were joys and pains that could be forgotten, absorbed into the routine that was life as it had to be lived. Now, she was no longer sure. She needed to be. More than anything else, she needed to be sure.

"Hold me," she murmured.

Was she trying to make him crazy? Ky wondered. Did she want him to cross the border, that edge he was trying so desperately to avoid? It took most of the strength he had left just to keep his voice even. "Kate, you need to sleep now. In the morning—"

"I don't want to think about the morning," she murmured. "Only now. And now I need you to hold me." Before he could refuse, she slipped her arms around his waist and rested her head on his shoulder.

She felt his hesitation, but not his one vivid flash

of longing before his arms came around her. On a long
breath Kate closed her eyes. Too much time had
passed since she'd had this, the gentleness, the sweetness she'd experienced only with Ky. No one else had
ever held her with such kindness, such simple compassion. Somehow, she never found it odd that a man
could be so reckless and arrogant, yet kind and com-
passionate at the same time.

Perhaps she'd been attracted to the recklessness, but
it had been the kindness she had fallen in love with.
Until now, in the quiet of the deep night, she hadn't
understood. Until now, in the security of his arms, she
hadn't accepted what she wanted.

Life as it had to be lived, she thought again. Was
taking what she so desperately needed part of that?

She was so slender, so soft beneath the thin nightshirt. Her hair lay over his skin, loose and free, its
color muted in the dim light. He could feel her palms
against his back, those elegant hands that had always
made him think more of an artist than a teacher. Her
breathing was quiet, serene, as he knew it was when
she slept. The light scent of woman clung to the material of the nightshirt.

Holding her didn't bring the pain he'd expected but
a contentment he'd been aching for without realizing
it. The tension in his muscles eased, the knot in his
stomach vanished. With his eyes closed, he rested his
cheek on her hair. It seemed like a lifetime since he'd
known the pleasure of quiet satisfaction. She'd asked

him to hold her, but had she known he needed to be held just as badly?

Kate felt him relax degree by degree and wondered if it had been she who'd caused the tension in him, and she who'd ultimately released it. Had she hurt him more than she'd realized? Had he cared more than she'd dared to believe? Or was it simply that the physical need never completely faded? It didn't matter, not tonight.

Ky was right. She knew the rules this time around. She wouldn't expect more than he offered. Whatever he offered was much, much more than she'd had in the long, dry years without him. In turn, she could give what she ached to give. Her love.

"It's the same for me as it always was," she murmured. Then, tilting her head back, she looked at him. Her hair streamed down her back, her eyes were wide and honest. He felt the need slam into him like a fist.

"Kate—"

"I never expected to feel the same way when I came back," she interrupted. "I don't think I'd have come. I wouldn't have had the courage."

"Kate, you're not well." He said it very slowly, as if he had to explain to them both. "You've lost blood, had a fever. It's taken a lot out of you. It'd be best, I think, if you tried to sleep now."

She felt no fever now. She felt cool and light and full of needs. "That day on the beach during the storm, you said I'd come to you." Kate brought her hands up his back until they reached his shoulders.

"Even then I knew you were right. I'm coming to you now. Make love with me, Ky, here, in the bed where you loved me that first time."

And the last, he remembered, fighting back a torrent of desire. "You're not well," he managed a second time.

"Well enough to know what I want." She brushed her lips over his chin where his beard grew rough with neglect. So long…that was all that would come clearly to her. It had been so long. Too long. "Well enough to know what I need. It's always been you." Her fingers tightened on his shoulders, her lips inches from his. "It's only been you."

Perhaps moving away from her was the answer. But some answers were impossible. "Tomorrow you may be sorry."

She smiled in her calm, quiet way that always moved him. "Then we'll have tonight."

He couldn't resist her. The warmth. He didn't want to hurt her. The softness. The need building inside him threatened to send them both raging even though he knew she was still weak, still fragile. He remembered how it had been the first time, when she'd been innocent. He'd been so careful, though he had never felt the need to care before, and hadn't since. Remembering that, he laid her back.

"We'll have tonight," he repeated and touched his lips to hers.

Sweet, fresh, clean. Those words went through his head, those sensations went through his system as her lips parted for his. So he lingered over her kiss, enjoying with tenderness what he'd once promised himself to take ruthlessly. His mouth caressed, without haste, without pressure. Tasting, just tasting, while the hunger grew.

Her hands reached for his face, fingers stroking, the rough, the smooth. She could hear her own heart beat in her head, feel the slow, easy pleasure that came in liquid waves. He murmured to her, lovely, quiet words that made her thrill when she felt them formed against her mouth. With his tongue he teased hers in long, lazy sweeps until she felt her mind cloud as it had under the drug. Then when she felt the first twinge of desperation, he kissed her with an absorbed patience that left her weak.

He felt it—that initial change from equality to submission that had always excited him. The aggression would come later, knocking the breath from him, taking him to the edge. He knew that too. But for the moment, she was soft, yielding.

He slid his hands over the nightshirt, stroking, lingering. The material between his flesh and hers teased them both. She moved to his rhythm, glorying in the steady loss of control. He took her deeper with a touch, still deeper with a taste. She dove, knowing the full pleasure of ultimate trust. Wherever he took her, she wanted to go.

With a whispering movement he took his hand over the slender curve of her breast. She was soft, the material smooth, making her hardening nipple a sensuous contrast. He loitered there while her breathing grew unsteady, reveling in the changes of her body. Lingering over each separate button of her nightshirt, Ky unfastened them, then slowly parted the material, as if he were unveiling a priceless treasure.

He'd never forgotten how lovely she was, how exciting delicacy could be. Now that he had her again, he allowed himself the time to look, to touch carefully, all the while watching the contact of his lean tanned hand against her pale skin. With tenderness he felt seldom and demonstrated rarely, he lowered his mouth, letting his lips follow the progress his fingers had already begun.

She was coming to life under him. Kate felt her blood begin to boil as though it had lain dormant in her veins for years. She felt her heart begin to thump as though it had been frozen in ice until that moment. She heard her name as only he said it. As only he could.

Sensations? Could there be so many of them? Could she have known them all once, experienced them all once, then lived without them? A whisper, a sigh, the brush of a fingertip along her skin. The scent of a man touched by the sea, the taste of her lover lingering yet on her lips. The glow of soft lights against closed lids. Time faded. No yesterday. No tomorrow.

She could feel the slick material of the nightshirt slide away, then the warm, smooth sheets beneath her back. The skim of his tongue along her ribcage incited a thrill that began in her core and exploded inside her head.

She remembered the dawn breaking slowly over the sea. Now she knew the same magnificence inside her own body. Light and warmth spread through her, gradually, patiently, until she was glowing with a new beginning.

He hadn't known he could hold such raging desire in check and still feel such complete pleasure, such whirling excitement. He was aware of every heightening degree of passion that worked through her. He understood the changing, rippling thrill she felt if he used more pressure here, a longer taste there. It brought him a wild sense of power, made only more acute by the knowledge that he must harness it. She was fluid. She was silk. And then with a suddenness that sent him reeling, she was fire.

Her body arched on the first tumultuous crest. It ripped through her like a madness. Greedy, ravenous for more, she began to demand what he'd only hinted at. Her hands ran over him, nearly destroying his control in a matter of seconds. Her mouth was hot, hungry, and sought his with an urgency he couldn't resist. Then she rained kisses over his face, down his throat until he gripped the sheets with his hands for fear of crushing her too tightly and bruising her skin.

She touched him with those slender, elegant fingers so that the blood rushed fast and furious into his head. "You make me crazy," he murmured.

"Yes." She could do no more than whisper, but her eyes opened. "Yes."

"I want to watch you go up," he said softly as he slid into her. "I want to see what making love with me does to you."

She arched again, the moan inching out of her as she experienced a second wild peak. He saw her eyes darken, cloud as he took her slowly, steadily toward the verge between passion and madness. He watched the color come into her cheeks, saw her lips tremble as she spoke his name. Her hands gripped his shoulders, but neither of them knew her short tapered nails dug into his skin.

They moved together, neither able to lead, both able to follow. As pleasure built, he never took his eyes from her face.

All sensation focused into one. They were only one. With a freedom that reaches perfection only rarely, they gave perfection to each other.

Chapter 8

She was sleeping soundly when Ky woke. Ky observed a hint of color in her cheeks and was determined to see that it stayed there. The touch of his hand to her hair was gentle but proprietary. Her skin was cool and dry, her breathing quiet but steady.

What she'd given him the night before had been offered with complete freedom, without shadows of the past, with none of the bitter taste of regret. It was something else he intended to keep constant.

No, he wasn't going to allow her to withdraw from him again. Not an inch. He'd lost her four years ago, or perhaps he'd never really had her—not in the way he'd believed, not in the way he'd taken for granted. But this time, Ky determined, it would be different.

In his own way, he needed to take care of her. Her

fragility drew that from him. In another way, he needed a partner on equal terms. Her strength offered him that. For reasons he never completely understood, Kate was exactly what he'd always wanted.

Clumsiness, arrogance, inexperience, or perhaps a combination of all three made him lose her once. Now that he had a second chance, he was going to make sure it worked. With a little more time, he might figure out how.

Rising, he dressed in the shaded light of the bedroom, then left her to sleep.

When she woke slowly, Kate was reluctant to surface from the simple pleasure of a dream. The room was dim, her mind was hazy with sleep and fantasy. The throb in her leg came as a surprise. How could there be pain when everything was so perfect? With a sigh, she reached for Ky and found the bed empty.

The haze vanished immediately, as did all traces of sleep and the pretty edge of fantasy. Kate sat up, and though the movement jolted the pain in her leg, she stared at the empty space beside her.

Had that been a dream as well? she wondered. Tentatively, she reached out and found the sheets cool. All a fantasy brought on by medication and confusion? Unsure, unsteady, she pushed the hair away from her face. Was it possible that she'd imagined it all—the gentleness, the sweetness, the passion?

She'd needed Ky. That hadn't been a dream. Even now she could feel the dull ache in her stomach that came from need. Had the need caused her to fantasize all that strange, stirring beauty during the night? The bed beside her was empty, the sheets cool. She was alone.

The pleasure she awoke with drained, leaving her empty, leaving her grateful for the pain that was her only grip on reality. She wanted to weep, but found she hadn't the energy for tears.

"So you're up."

Ky's voice made her whip her head around. Her nerves were strung tight. He walked into the bedroom carrying a tray, wearing an easy smile.

"That saves me from having to wake you up to get some food into you." Before he approached the bed, he went to both windows and drew up the shades. Light poured into the room and the warm breeze that had been trapped behind the shades rushed in to ruffle the sheets. Feeling it, she had to control a shudder. "How'd you sleep?"

"Fine." The awkwardness was unexpected. Kate folded her hands and sat perfectly still. "I want to thank you for everything you've done."

"You've already thanked me once. It wasn't necessary then or now." Because her tone had put him on guard, Ky stopped next to the bed to take a good long look at her. "You're hurting."

"It's not bad."

"This time you take a pill." After setting the tray on her lap, he walked to the dresser and picked up a small bottle. "No arguments," he said, anticipating her refusal.

"Ky, it's really not bad." When had he offered her a pill before? The struggle to remember brought only more frustration. "There's barely any pain."

"Any pain's too much." He sat on the bed, and putting the pill into her palm curled her hand over it with his own. "When it's you."

With her fingers curled warmly under his, she knew. Elation came so quietly she was afraid to move and chase it away. "I didn't dream it, did I?" she whispered.

"Dream what?" He kissed the back of her hand before he handed her the glass of juice.

"Last night. When I woke up, I was afraid it had all been a dream."

He smiled and, bending, touched his lips to hers. "If it was, I had the same dream." He kissed her again, with humor in his eyes. "It was wonderful."

"Then it doesn't matter whether it was a dream or not."

"Oh no, I prefer reality."

With a laugh, she started to drop the pill on the tray, but he stopped her. "Ky—"

"You're hurting," he said again. "I can see it in your eyes. Your medication wore off hours ago, Kate."

"And kept me unconscious for an entire day."

"This is mild, just to take the edge off. Listen—" His hand tightened on hers. "I had to watch you in agony."

"Ky, don't."

"No, you'll do it for me if not for yourself. I had to watch you bleed and faint and drift in and out of consciousness." He ran his hand down her hair, then cupped her face so she'd look directly into his eyes. "I can't tell you what it did to me because I don't know how to describe it. I know I can't watch you in pain any more."

In silence, she took the pill and drained the glass of juice. For him, as he said, not for herself. When she swallowed the medication, Ky tugged at her hair. "It hardly has more punch than an aspirin, Kate. Bailey said he'd give you something stronger if you needed it, but he'd rather you go with this."

"It'll be fine. It's really more uncomfortable than painful." It wasn't quite the truth, nor did he believe her, but they both let it lie for the moment. Each of them moved cautiously, afraid to spoil what might have begun to bloom again. Kate glanced down at the empty juice glass. The cold, fresh flavor still lingered on her tongue. "Did Dr. Bailey say when I could dive again?"

"Dive?" Ky's brows rose as he uncovered the plate of bacon, eggs and toast. "Kate, you're not even getting up out of bed for the rest of the week."

"Out of bed?" she repeated. "A week?" She ignored the overloaded plate of food as she gaped at him. "Ky, I was stung by a stingray, not attacked by a shark."

"You were stung by a stingray," he agreed. "And your system was so depleted Bailey almost sent you to a hospital. I realize things might've been rough on you since your father died, but you haven't helped anything by not taking care of yourself."

It was the first time he'd mentioned her father's death, and Kate noted he still expressed no sympathy. "Doctors tend to fuss," she began.

"Bailey doesn't," he interrupted. The anger came back and ran along the edge of his words. "He's a tough, cynical old goat, but he knows his business. He told me that you'd apparently worked yourself right to the edge of exhaustion, that your resistance was nil, and that you were a good ten pounds underweight." He held out the fork. "We're going to do something about that, professor. Starting now."

Kate looked down at what had to be four large eggs, scrambled, six slices of bacon and four pieces of toast. "I can see you intend to," she murmured.

"I'm not having you sick." He took her hand again and his grip was firm. "I'm going to take care of you, Kate, whether you like it or not."

She looked back at him in her calm, considering way. "I don't know if I do like it," she decided. "But I suppose we'll both find out."

Ky dipped the fork into the eggs. "Eat."

A smile played at the corners of her mouth. She'd never been pampered in her life and thought it might be entirely too easy to get used to it. "All right, but this time I'll feed myself."

She already knew she'd never finish the entire meal, but for his sake, and the sake of peace, she determined to deal with half of it. That had been precisely his strategy. If he'd have brought her a smaller portion, she'd have eaten half of that, and have eaten less. He knew her better than either one of them fully realized.

"You're still a wonderful cook," she commented, breaking a piece of bacon in half. "Much better than I."

"If you're good, I might broil up some flounder tonight."

She remembered just how exquisitely he prepared fish. "How good?"

"As good as it takes." He accepted the slice of toast she offered him but dumped on a generous slab of jam. "Maybe I'll beg some of the hot fudge cake from the Roost."

"Looks like I'll have to be on my best behavior."

"That's the idea."

"Ky…" She was already beginning to poke at her eggs. Had eating always been quite such an effort? "About last night, what happened—"

"Should never have stopped," he finished.

Her lashes swept up, and her eyes were quiet and candid. "I'm not sure."

"I am," he countered. Taking her face in his hands, he kissed her, softly, with only a hint of passion. But the hint was a promise of much more. "Let it be enough for now, Kate. If it has to get complicated, let's wait until other things are a little more settled."

Complicated. Were commitments complicated, the future, promises? She looked down at her plate knowing she simply didn't have the strength to ask or to answer. Not now. "In a way I feel as though I'm slipping back—to that summer four years ago. And yet…"

"It's like a step forward."

Kate looked at him again, but this time reached out. He'd always understood. Though he said little, though his way was sometimes rough, he'd always understood. "Yes. Either way it's a little unnerving."

"I've never liked smooth water. You get a better ride with a few waves."

"Perhaps." She shook her head. Slipping back, stepping forward, it hardly mattered. Either way, she was moving toward him. "Ky, I can't eat any more."

"I figured." Easily, he picked up an extra fork from the tray and began eating the cooling eggs himself. "It's still probably more than you eat for breakfast in a week."

"Probably," she agreed in a murmur, realizing just how well he'd maneuvered her. Kate lay back against the propped-up pillows, annoyed that she was growing sleepy again. No more medication, she decided silently as Ky polished off their joint breakfast. If she could just avoid that, and go out for a little while, she'd be fine. The trick would be to convince Ky.

Kate looked toward the window, and the sunshine. "I don't want to lose a week's time going over the wreck."

He didn't have to follow the direction of her gaze to follow the direction of her thoughts. "I'll be going down," he said easily. "Tomorrow, the next day anyway." Sooner, he thought to himself, depending on how Kate mended.

"Alone?"

He caught the tone as he bit into the last piece of bacon. "I've gone down alone before."

She would have protested, stating how dangerous it was, if she'd believed it would have done any good. Ky did a great deal alone because that was how he preferred it. Instead, Kate chose another route.

"We're looking for the *Liberty* together, Ky. It isn't a one-man operation."

He sent her a long, quiet look before he picked up the coffee she hadn't touched. "Afraid I'll take off with the treasure?"

"Of course not." She wouldn't allow her emotions to get in the way. "If I hadn't trusted your integrity," she said evenly, "I wouldn't have shown you the chart in the first place."

"Fair enough," he allowed with a nod. "So if I continue to dive while you're recuperating, we won't lose time."

"I don't want to lose you either." It was out before she could stop it. Swearing lightly, Kate looked toward the window again. The sky was the pale blue sometimes seen on summer mornings.

Ky merely sat for a moment while the pleasure of her words rippled through him. "You'd worry about me?"

Angry, Kate turned back. He looked so smug, so

infuriatingly content. "No, I wouldn't worry. God usually makes a point of looking after fools."

Grinning, he set the tray on the floor beside the bed. "Maybe I'd like you to worry, a little."

"Sorry I can't oblige you."

"Your voice gets very prim when you're annoyed," he commented. "I like it."

"I'm not prim."

He ran a hand down her loosened hair. No, she looked anything but prim at the moment. Soft and feminine, but not prim. "Your voice is. Like one of those pretty, lacy ladies who used to sit in parlors eating finger sandwiches."

She pushed his hand aside. He wouldn't get around her with charm. "Perhaps I should shout instead."

"Like that too, but more…" He kissed one cheek, then the other. "I like to see you smile at me. The way you smile at nobody else."

Her skin was already beginning to warm. No, he might not get around her with charm, but…he'd distract her from her point if she wasn't careful. "I'd be bored, that's all. If I have to sit here, hour after hour with nothing to do."

"I've got lots of books." He slipped her nightshirt down her shoulder then kissed her bare skin with the lightest of touches. "Probably lay my hands on some crossword puzzles, too."

"Thanks a lot."

"There's a copy of Byron downstairs."

Despite her determination not to, Kate looked toward him again. "Byron?"

"I bought it after you left. The words are wonderful." He had the three buttons undone with such quick expertise, she never noticed. "But I could always hear the way you'd say them. I remember one night on the beach, when the moon was full on the water. I don't remember the name of the poem, but I remember how it started, and how it sounded when you said it. 'It is the hour'," he began, then smiled at her.

"'It is the hour'," Kate continued, "'when from the boughs the nightingale is heard/It is the hour when lovers' vows seem sweet in every whisper'd word/ And gentle winds, and waters near make music to the lonely ear'…" She trailed off, remembering even the scent of that night. "You were never very interested in Byron's technique."

"No matter how hard you tried to explain it to me."

Yes, he was distracting her. Kate was already finding it difficult to remember what point she'd been trying to make. "He was one of the leading poets of his day."

"Hmm." Ky caught the lobe of her ear between his teeth.

"He had a fascination for war and conflict, and yet he had more love affairs in his poems than Shelley or Keats."

"How about out of his poems?"

"There too." She closed her eyes as his tongue began to do outrageous things to her nervous system.

"He used humor, satire as well as a pure lyrical style. If he'd ever completed *Don Juan*…" She trailed off with a sigh that edged toward a moan.

"Did I interrupt you?" Ky brushed his fingers down her thigh. "I really love to hear you lecture."

"Yes."

"Good." He traced her lips with his tongue. "I just thought maybe I could give you something to do for a while." He skimmed his hand over her hip then up to the side of her breast. "So you won't be bored by staying in bed. Want to tell me more about Byron?"

With a long quiet breath, she wound her arms around his neck. The point she'd been trying to make didn't seem important any longer. "No, but I might like staying in bed after all, even without the crossword puzzles."

"You'll relax." He said it softly, but the command was unmistakable. She might have argued, but the kiss was long and lingering, leaving her slow and helplessly yielding.

"I don't have a choice," she murmured. "Between the medication and you."

"That's the idea." He'd love her, Ky thought, but so gently she'd have nothing to do but feel. Then she'd sleep. "There are things I want from you." He lifted his head until their eyes met. "Things I need from you."

"You never tell me what they are."

"Maybe not." He laid his forehead on hers. Maybe he just didn't know how to tell her. Or how to ask.

"For now, what I want is to see you well." Again he lifted his head, and his eyes focused on hers. "I'm not an unselfish man, Kate. I want that just as much for myself as I want it for you. I fully intended to have you back in my bed, but I didn't want it for you. I fully intended to have you back in my bed, but I didn't care to have you unconscious here first."

"Whatever you intended, I make my own choices." Her hands slid up his shoulders to touch his face. "I chose to make love with you then. I choose to make love with you now."

He laughed and pressed her palm to his lips. "Professor, you think I'd have given you a choice? Maybe we don't know each other as well as we should at this point, but you should know that much."

Thoughtfully, she ran her thumb down his cheekbone. It was hard, elegantly defined. Somehow it suited him in the same way the unshaven face suited him. But did she? Kate wondered. Were they, despite all their differences, right for each other?

It seemed when they were like this, there was no question of suitability, no question of what was right or wrong. Each completed the other. Yet there had to be more. No matter how much each of them denied it on the surface, there had to be more. And ultimately, there had to be a choice.

"When you take what isn't offered freely, you have nothing." She felt the rough scrape of his unshaven face on her palm and the thrill went through her system. "If I give, you have whatever you need without asking."

"Do I?" he murmured before he touched his lips to hers again. "And you? What do you have?"

She closed her eyes as her body drifted on a calm, quiet plane of pleasure. "What I need."

For how long? The question ran through his mind, prodding against his contentment. But he didn't ask. There'd be a time, he knew, for more questions, for the hundreds of demands he wanted to make. For ultimatums. Now she was sleepy, relaxed in the way he wanted her to be.

With no more words he let her body drift, stroking gently, letting her system steep in the pleasure he could give. With no one else could he remember asking so little for himself and receiving so much. She was the hinge that could open or close the door on the better part of him.

He listened to her sigh as he touched her. The second was a kind of pure contentment that mirrored his own feelings. It seemed neither of them required any more.

Kate knew it shouldn't be so simple. It had never been simple with anyone else, so that in the end she'd never given herself to anyone else. Only with Ky had she ever known that full excitement that left her free. Only with Ky had she ever known the pure ease that felt so right.

They'd been apart four years, yet if it had been forty, she would have recognized his touch in an instant. That touch was all she needed to make her want him.

She remembered the demands and fire that had always been threaded through their lovemaking before. It had been the excitement she'd craved even while it had baffled her. Now there was patience touched with a consideration she didn't know he was capable of.

Perhaps if she hadn't loved him already, she would have fallen in love at that moment when the sun filtered through the windows and his hands were on her skin. She wanted to give him the fire, but his hands kept it banked. She wanted to meet any demands, but he made none. Instead, she floated on the clouds he brought to her.

Though the heat smoldered inside him, she kept him sane. Just by her pliancy. Though passion began to take over, she kept him calm. Just by her serenity. He'd never looked for serenity in his life. It had simply come to him, as Kate had. He'd never understood what it meant to be calm, but he had known the emptiness and the chaos of living without it.

Without urgency or force, he slipped inside her. Slowly, with a sweetness that made her weak, he gave her the ultimate gift. Passion, fulfillment, with the softer emotions covering a need that seemed insatiable.

Then she slept, and he left her to her dreams.

When she awoke again, Kate wasn't groggy, but weak. Even as sleep cleared, a sense of helpless an-

noyance went though her. It was midafternoon. She
didn't need a clock, the angle of the sunlight that
slanted through the window across from the bed told
her what time it was. More hours had been lost without her knowledge. And where was Ky?

Kate groped for her nightshirt and slipped into it.
If he followed his pattern, he'd be popping through
the door with a loaded lunch tray and a pill. Not this
time, Kate determined as she eased herself out of bed.
Nothing else was going into her system that made her
lose time.

But as she stood, the dregs of the medication swam
in her head. Reflexively, she nearly sat again before
she stopped herself. Infuriated, she gripped the bedpost, breathed deeply then put her weight on her in-
jured foot. It took the pain to clear her head.

Pain had its uses, she thought grimly. After she'd
given the hurt a moment to subside, it eased into a
throb. That could be tolerated, she told herself and
walked to the mirror over Ky's dresser.

She didn't like what she saw. Her hair was listless,
her face washed-out and her eyes dull. Swearing, she
put her hands to her cheeks and rubbed as though she
could force color into them. What she needed, Kate
decided, was a hot shower, a shampoo and some fresh
air. Regardless of what Ky thought, she was going to
have them.

Taking a deep breath, she headed for the door. Even
as she reached for the knob, it opened.

"What're you doing up?"

Though they were precisely the words she'd expected, Kate had expected them from Ky, not Linda. "I was just—"

"Do you want Ky to skin me alive?" Linda demanded, backing Kate toward the bed with a tray of steaming soup in her hand. "Listen, you're supposed to rest and eat, then eat and rest. Orders."

Realizing abruptly that she was retreating, Kate held her ground. "Whose?"

"Ky's. And," she continued before Kate could retort, "Dr. Bailey's."

"I don't have to take orders from either of them."

"Maybe you don't," Linda agreed dryly. "But I don't argue with a man who's protecting his woman, or with the man who poked a needle into my bottom when I was three. Both of them can be nasty. Now lie down."

"Linda…" Though she knew the sigh sounded long suffering, Kate couldn't prevent it. "I've a cut on my leg. I've been in bed for something like forty-eight hours straight. If I don't have a shower and a breath of air soon, I'm going to go crazy."

A smile tugged at Linda's mouth that she partially concealed by nibbling on her lower lip. "A bit grumpy, are we?"

"I can be more than a bit." This time the sigh was simply bad tempered. "Look at me!" Kate demanded, tugging on her hair. "I feel as though I've just crawled out from under a rock."

"Okay. I know how I felt after I'd delivered Hope.

After I'd had my cuddle with her I wanted a shower and shampoo so bad I was close to tears.'' She set the tray on the table beside the bed. ''You can have ten minutes in the shower, then you can eat while I change your bandage. But Ky made me swear I'd make you eat every bite.'' She put her hands on her hips. ''So that's the deal.''

''He's overreacting,'' Kate began. ''It's absurd. I don't need to be babied this way.''

''Tell me that when you don't look like I could blow you over. Now come on, I'll give you a hand in the shower.''

''No, damn it, I'm perfectly capable of taking a shower by myself.'' Ignoring the pain in her leg, she stormed out of the room, slamming the door at her back. Linda swallowed a laugh and sat down on the bed to wait.

Fifteen minutes later, refreshed and thoroughly ashamed of herself, Kate came back in. Wrapped in Ky's robe, she rubbed a towel over her hair. ''Linda—''

''Don't apologize. If I'd been stuck in bed for two days, I'd snap at the first person who gave me trouble. Besides—'' Linda knew how to play her cards ''—if you're really sorry you'll eat all your soup, so Ky won't yell at me.''

''All right.'' Resigned, Kate sat back in the bed and took the tray on her lap. She swallowed the first bite of soup and stifled her objection as Linda began to fiddle with her bandage. ''It's wonderful.''

"The seafood chowder's one of our specialties. Oh, honey." Linda's eyes darkened with concern after she removed the gauze. "This must've hurt like hell. No wonder Ky's been frantic."

Drumming up her courage, Kate leaned over enough to look at the wound. There was no inflammation as she'd feared, no puffiness. Though the slice was six inches in length, it was clean. Her stomach muscles unknotted. "It's not so bad," she murmured. "There's no infection."

"Look, I've been caught by a stingray, a small one. I probably had a cut half an inch across and I cried like a baby. Don't tell me it's not so bad."

"Well, I slept through most of it." She winced, then deliberately relaxed her muscles.

Linda narrowed her eyes as she studied Kate's face. "Ky said you should have a pill if there was any pain when you woke."

"If you want to do me a favor, you can dump them out." Calmly, Kate ate another spoonful of soup. "I really hate to argue with him, or with you, but I'm not taking any more pills and losing any more time. I appreciate the fact that he wants to pamper me. It's unexpectedly sweet, but I can only take it so far."

"He's worried about you. He feels responsible."

"For my carelessness?" With a shake of her head, Kate concentrated on finishing the soup. "It was an accident, and if there's blame, it's mine. I was so wrapped up in looking for salvage I didn't take basic precautions. I practically bumped into the ray." With an effort, she controlled a shudder. "Ky acted much more quickly than I. He'd already started to pull me out of range. If he hadn't, things would have been much more serious."

"He loves you."

Kate's fingers tightened on the spoon. With exaggerated care, she set it back on the tray. "Linda, there's a vast difference between concern, attraction, even affection and love."

Linda simply nodded in agreement. "Yes. I said Ky loves you."

She managed to smile and pick up the tea that had been cooling beside the soup. *"You* said," Kate returned simply. *"Ky* hasn't."

"Well neither did Marsh until I was ready to strangle him, but that didn't stop me."

"I'm not you." Kate lay back against the pillows, grateful that most of the weakness and the weariness had passed. "And Ky isn't Marsh."

Impatient, Linda rose and swirled around the room. "People who complicate simple things make me so mad!"

Smiling, Kate sipped her tea. "Others simplify the complicated."

With a sniff, Linda turned back. "I've known Ky Silver all my life. I watched him bounce around from one cute girl to the next, then one attractive woman to another until I lost count. Then you came along." Stopping, she leaned against the bedpost. "It was as if someone had hit him over the head with a blunt instrument. You dazed him, Kate, almost from the first minute. You fascinated him.''

"Dazing, fascinating.'' Kate shrugged while she tried to ignore the ache in her heart. "Flattering, I suppose, but neither of those things equals love.''

The stubborn line came and went between Linda's brows. "I don't believe love comes in an instant, it grows. If you could have seen the way Ky was after you left four years ago, you'd know—''

"Don't tell me about four years ago,'' Kate interrupted. "What happened four years ago is over. Ky and I are two different people today, with different expectations. This time...'' She took a deep breath. "This time when it ends, I won't be hurt because I know the limits.''

"You've just gotten back together and you're already talking about endings and limitations!'' Dragging a hand through her hair, Linda came forward to sit on the edge of the bed. "What's wrong with you? Don't you know how to wish anymore? How to dream?''

"I was never very good at either. Linda...'' She hesitated, wanting to choose her phrasing carefully. "I don't want to expect any more from Ky than what he can easily give. After August, I know we'll each go back to our separate worlds—there's no bridge between them. Maybe I was meant to come back so we could make up for whatever pain we caused each other before. This time I want to leave still being friends. He's...'' She hesitated again because this phrasing was even more important. "He's always been a very important part of my life."

Linda waited a moment, then narrowed her eyes. "That's about the dumbest thing I've ever heard."

Despite herself, Kate laughed. "Linda—"

Holding up her hands, she shook her head and cut Kate off. "No, I can't talk about it anymore, I get too mad and I'm supposed to be taking care of you." She let out her breath on a huff as she removed Kate's tray. "I just can't understand how anyone so smart could be so stupid, but the more I think about it the more I can see that you and Ky deserve each other."

"That sounds more like an insult than a compliment."

"It was."

Kate pushed her tongue against her teeth to hold back a smile. "I see."

"Don't look so smug just because you've made me so angry I don't want to talk about it anymore." She drew her shoulders back. "I might just give Ky a piece of my mind when he gets home."

"That's his problem," Kate said cheerfully. "Where'd he go?"

"Diving."

Amusement faded. "Alone?"

"There's no use worrying about it." Linda spoke briskly as she cursed herself for not thinking of a simple lie. "He dives alone ninety percent of the time."

"I know." But Kate folded her hands, preparing to worry until he returned.

Chapter 9

"I'm going with you."

The sunlight was strong, the scent of the ocean pure. Through the screen the sound of gulls from a quarter of a mile away could be heard clearly. Ky turned from the stove where he poured the last cup of coffee and eyed Kate as she stood in the doorway.

She'd pinned her hair up and had dressed in thin cotton pants and a shirt, both of which were baggy and cool. It occured to him that she looked more like a student than a college professor.

He knew enough of women and their illusions to see that she'd added color to her cheeks. She hadn't needed blusher the evening before when he'd returned from the wreck. Then she had been angry, and passionate. He nearly smiled as he lifted his cup.

"You wasted your time getting dressed," he said easily. "You're going back to bed."

Kate disliked stubborn people, people who demanded their own way flatly and unreasonably. At that moment, she decided they were *both* stubborn. "No." On the surface she remained as calm as he was while she walked into the kitchen. "I'm going with you."

Unlike Kate, Ky never minded a good argument. Preparing for one, he leaned back against the stove. "I don't take down a diver against doctor's orders."

She'd expected that. With a shrug, she opened the refrigerator and took out a bottle of juice. She knew she was being bad tempered, and though it was completely out of character, she was enjoying the experience. The simple truth was that she had to do something or go mad.

As far as she could remember, she'd never spent two more listless days. She had to move, think, feel the sun. It might have been satisfying to stomp her feet and demand, but, she thought, fruitless. If she had to compromise to get her way, then compromise she would.

"I can rent a boat and equipment and go down on my own." With the glass in hand, she turned, challenging. "You can't stop me."

"Try me."

It was said simply, quietly, but she'd seen the flare of anger in his eyes. Better, she thought. Much better. "I've a right to do precisely as I choose. We both know it." Perhaps her leg was uncomfortable, but as to the rest of her body, it was charged up and ready to move. Nor was there anything wrong with her mind. Kate had plotted her strategy very well. After all, she thought grimly, there'd certainly been enough time to think it through.

"We both know you're not in any shape to dive." His first urge was to carry her back to bed, his second to shake her until she rattled. Ky did neither, only drank his coffee and watched her over the rim. A power struggle wasn't something he'd expected, but he wouldn't back away from it. "You're not stupid, Kate. You know you can't go down yet, and you know I won't let you."

"I've rested for two days. I feel fine." As she walked toward him she was pleased to see him frown. He understood she had a mind of her own, and that he had to deal with it. The truth was, she was stronger than either of them had expected her to be. "As far as diving goes, I'm willing to leave that to you for the next couple of days, but..." She paused, wanting to be certain he knew she was negotiating, not conceding. "I'm going out on the *Vortex* with you. And I'm going out this morning."

He lifted a brow. She'd never intended to dive, but she'd used it as a pressure point to get what she wanted. He couldn't blame her. Ky remembered recovering from a broken leg when he was fourteen. The pain was vague in his mind now, but the boredom was still perfectly clear. "You'll lie down in the cabin when you're told."

She smiled and shook her head. "I'll lie down in the cabin if I need to."

He took her chin in his hand and squeezed. "Damn right you will. Okay, let's go. I want an early start."

Once he was resigned, Ky moved quickly. She could either keep up, or be left behind. Within minutes he parked his car near his slip at Silver Lake Harbor and was boarding the *Vortex*. Content, Kate took a seat beside him at the helm and prepared to enjoy the sun and the wind. Already she felt the energy begin to churn.

"I've done a chart of the wreck as of yesterday's dive," he told her as he maneuvered out of the harbor.

"A chart?" Automatically she pushed at her hair as she turned toward him. "You didn't show me."

"Because you were asleep when I finished it."

"I've been asleep ninety percent of the time," she mumbled.

As he headed out to sea, Ky laid a hand on her shoulder. "You look better, Kate, no shadows. No strain. That's more important."

For a moment, just a moment, she pressed her cheek against his hand. Few women could resist such soft concern, and yet…she didn't want his concern to cloud their reason for being together. Concern could turn to pity. She needed him to see her as a partner, as equal. As long as she was his lover, it was vital that they meet on the same ground. Then when she left… When she left there'd be no regrets.

"I don't need to be pampered anymore, Ky."

His shoulders moved as he glanced at the compass. "I enjoyed it."

She was resisting being cared for. He understood it, appreciated it and regretted it. There had been something appealing about seeing to her needs, about having her depend on him. He didn't know how to tell her he wanted her to be well and strong just as much as he wanted her to turn to him in times of need.

Somehow, he felt their time together had been too short for him to speak. He didn't deal well with caution. As a diver, he knew its importance, but as a man... As a man he fretted to go with his instincts, with his impulses.

His fingers brushed her neck briefly before he turned to the wheel. He'd already decided he'd have to approach his relationship with Kate as he'd approach a very deep, very dangerous dive—with an eye on currents, pressure and the unexpected.

"That chart's in the cabin," he told her as he cut the engine. "You might want to look it over while I'm down."

She agreed with a nod, but the restlessness was already on her as Ky began to don his equipment. She didn't want to make an issue of his diving alone. He wouldn't listen to her in any case; if anything came of it, it would only be an argument. In silence she watched him check his tanks. He'd be down for an hour. Kate was already marking time.

"There are cold drinks in the galley." He adjusted

the strap of his mask before climbing over the side. "Don't sit in the sun too long."

"Be careful," she blurted out before she could stop herself.

Ky grinned, then was gone with a quiet splash.

Though she ran over to the side, Kate was too late to watch him dive. For a long time after, she simply leaned over the boat, staring at the water's surface. She imagined Ky going deeper, deeper, adjusting his pressure, moving out with power until he'd reached the bottom and the wreck.

He'd brought back the bowl and ladle the evening before. They sat on the dresser in his bedroom while the broken rigging and pieces of crockery were stored downstairs. Thus far he'd done no more than gather what they'd already found together, but today, Kate thought with a twinge of impatience, he'd extend the search. Whatever he found, he'd find alone.

She turned away from the water, frustrated that she was excluded. It occurred to her that all her life she'd been an onlooker, someone who analyzed and explained the action rather than causing it. This search had been her first opportunity to change that, and now she was back to square one.

Stuffing her hands in her pockets, Kate looked up at the sky. There were clouds to the west, but they were thin and white. Harmless. She felt too much like that herself at the moment—something unsubstantial. Sighing, she went below deck. There was nothing to do now but wait.

Ky found two more cannons and sent up buoys to mark their position. It would be possible, if he didn't find something more concrete, to salvage the cannons and have them dated by an expert. Though he swam from end to end, searching carefully, he knew it was unlikely he'd find a date stamp through the layers of corrosion. But in time… Satisfied, he swam north.

If he accomplished nothing else on this dive, he wanted to establish the size of the site. With luck it would be fairly small, perhaps no bigger than a football field. However, there was always the chance that the wreckage could be scattered over several square miles. Before they brought in a salvage ship, he wanted to take a great deal of care with the preliminary work.

They would need tools. A metal detector would be invaluable. Thus far, they'd done no more than find a wreck, no matter how certain Kate was that it was the *Liberty*. For the moment he had no way to determine the origin of the ship, he had to find cargo. Once he'd found that, perhaps treasure would follow.

Once he'd found the treasure… Would she leave? Would she take her share of the gold and the artifacts and drive home?

Not if he could help it, Ky determined as he shone his headlamp over the sea floor. When the search was over and they'd salvaged what could be salvaged from the sea, it would be time to salvage what they'd once had—what had perhaps never truly been lost. If they could find what had been buried for centuries, they could find what had been buried for four years.

He couldn't find much without tools. Most of the ship—or what remained of it—was buried under silt. On another dive, he'd use the prop-wash, the excavation device he'd constructed in his shop. With that he could blow away inches of sediment at a time—a slow but safe way to uncover artifacts. But someone would have to stay on board to run it.

He thought of Kate and rejected the idea immediately. Though he had no doubt she could handle the technical aspect—it would only have to be explained to her once—she'd never go for it. Ky began to think it was time they enlisted Marsh.

He knew his air time was almost up and he'd have to surface for fresh tanks. Still, he lingered near the bottom, searching, prodding. He wanted to take something up for Kate, something tangible that would put the enthusiasm back in her eyes.

It took him more than half of his allotted time to find it, but when Ky held the unbroken bottle in his hand, he knew Kate's reaction would be worth the effort. It was a common bottle, not priceless crystal, but he could see no mold marks, which meant it had been hand blown. Crust was weathered over it in layers, but Ky took the time to carefully chip some away, from the bottom only. If the date wasn't on the bottom, he'd need the crust to have the bottle dated. Already he was thinking of the Corning Glass Museum and their rate of success.

Then he saw the date, and with a satisfied grin placed the find in the goodie bag on his belt. With his air supply running short, he started toward the surface.

His hour was up. Or so nearly up, Kate thought, that he should have surfaced already if he'd allowed himself any safety factor. She paced from port to starboard and back again. Would he always risk his own welfare to the limit?

She'd long since given up sitting quietly in the cabin, going over the makeshift chart Ky had begun. She'd found a book on shipwrecks that Ky had obviously purchased recently, and though it had also been among her father's research books, she'd skimmed through it again.

It gave a detailed guide to identifying and excavating a wreck, listed common mistakes and hazards. She found it difficult to read about hazards while Ky was alone beneath the surface. Still, even the simple language of the book couldn't disguise the adventure. For perhaps half the time Ky had been gone, she'd lost herself in it. Spanish galleons, Dutch merchant ships, English frigates.

She'd found the list of wrecks off North Carolina alone extensive. But these, she'd thought, had already been located, documented. The adventure there was over. One day, because of the chain her father had started and she'd continued, the *Liberty* would be among them.

Fretfully, Kate waited for Ky to surface. She thought of her father. He'd pored over this same book

as well—planning, calculating. Yet his calculations
hadn't taken him beyond the initial stage. If he'd
shared his goal with her, would he have taken her on
his summer quests? She'd never know, because she'd
never been given the choice.

She was making her own choices now, Kate mused.
Her first had been to return to Ocracoke, accepting the
consequences. Her next had been to give herself to Ky
without conditions. Her last, she thought as she stared
down at the quiet water, would be to leave him again.
Yet, in reality, perhaps she'd still been given no
choice. It was all a matter of currents. She could only
swim against them for so long.

Relief washed over her when she spotted the flow
of bubbles. Ky grabbed the bottom rung of the ladder
as he pushed up his mask. "Waiting for me?"

Relief mixed with annoyance for the time she'd
spent worrying about him. "You cut it close."

"Yeah, a little." He passed up his tanks. "I had to
stop and get you a present."

"It's not a joke, Ky." Kate watched him come over
the side, agile, lean and energetic. "You'd be furious
with me if I'd cut my time that close."

"Leave it up to Linda to fuss," he advised as he
pulled down the zipper of his wet suit. "She was born
that way." Then he grabbed her, crushing her against
him so that she felt the excitement he'd brought up
with him. His mouth closed over hers, tasting of salt
from the sea. Because he was wet, her clothes clung
to him, binding them together for the brief instant he

held her. But when he would have released her, she held fast, drawing the kiss out into something that warmed his cool skin.

"I worry about you, Ky." For one last moment, she held on fiercely. "Damn it, is that what you want to hear?"

"No." He took her face in his hands and shook his head. "No."

Kate broke away, afraid she'd say too much, afraid she'd say things neither of them were ready to hear. She knew the rules this time. She groped for something calm, something simple. "I suppose I got a bit frantic waiting up here. It's different when you're down."

"Yeah." What did she want from him? he wondered. Why was it that every time she started to show her concern for him, she clammed up? "I've got some more things to add to the chart."

"I saw the buoys you sent up." Kate moistened her lips and relaxed, muscle by muscle.

"Two more cannons. From the size of them, I'd say she was a fairly small ship. It's unlikely she was constructed for battle."

"She was a merchant ship."

"Maybe. I'm going to take the metal detector down and see what I come up with. From the stuff we've found, I don't think she's buried too deep."

Kate nodded. Delve into business, keep the personal aspect light. "I'd like to send off a piece of the planking and some of the glass to be analyzed. I think we'll have more luck with the glass, but it doesn't hurt to cover all the angles.''

"No, it doesn't. Don't you want your present?''

At ease again, she smiled. "I thought you were joking. Did you bring me a shell?''

"I thought you'd like this better.'' Reaching into his bag, Ky brought out the bottle. "It's too bad it's not still corked. We could've had wine with peanut butter.''

"Oh, Ky, it's not damaged!'' Thrilled, she reached out for it, but he pulled it back out of reach and grinned.

"Bottoms up,'' he told her and turned the bottle upside down.

Kate stared at the smeared bottom of the bottle. "Oh, God,'' she whispered. "It's dated. 1749.'' Gingerly, she took the bottle in both hands. "The year before the *Liberty* sank.''

"It's another ship, maybe,'' Ky reminded her. "But it does narrow down the time element.''

"Over two hundred years,'' she murmured. "Glass, it's so breakable, so vulnerable, and yet it survived two centuries.'' Her eyes lit with enthusiasm as she looked back at him. "Ky, we should be able to find out where the bottle was made.''

"Probably, but most glass bottles found on wrecks from the seventeenth and eighteenth century were manufactured in England anyway. It wouldn't prove the ship was English.''

She let out a huff of breath, but her energy hadn't dimmed. "You've been doing your research."

"I don't go into any project until I know the angles." Ky knelt down to check the fresh tanks.

"You're going back down now?"

"I want to get as much mapped out as I can before we start dealing with too much equipment."

She'd done enough homework herself to know that the most common mistake of the modern day salvor was in failing to map out a site. Yet she couldn't stem her impatience. It seemed so time-consuming when they could be concentrating on getting under the layers of silt.

It seemed to her that she and Ky had changed positions somehow. She'd always been the cautious one, proceeding step by logical step, while he'd taken the risks. Struggling with the impotence of having to wait and watch, she stood back while he strapped on the fresh tanks. As she watched, Ky picked up a brass rod.

"What's that for?"

"It's the base for this." He held out a device that resembled a compass. "It's called an azimuth circle. It's a cheap, effective way to map out the site. I drive this into the approximate center of the wreck so that it becomes the datum point, align the circle with the magnetic north, then I use a length of chain to measure the distance to the cannons, or whatever I need to map. After I get it set, I'll be back up for the metal detector."

Frustration built again. He was doing all the work while she simply stood still. "Ky, I feel fine. I could help if—"

"No." He didn't bother to argue or list reasons. He simply went over the side and under.

It was midafternoon when they started back. Ky spent the last hour at sea adding to the chart, putting in the information he'd gathered that day. He'd brought more up in his goodie bag—a tankard, spoons and forks that might have been made of iron. It seemed they had indeed found the galley. Kate decided she'd begin a detailed list of their finds that evening. If it was all she could do at the moment, she'd do it with pleasure.

Her mood had lifted a bit since she'd caught three good-sized bluefish while Ky had been down at the wreck the second time. No matter how much Ky argued, she fully intended to cook them herself and eat them sitting at the table, not lying in bed.

"Pretty pleased with yourself aren't you?"

She gave him a cool smile. They were cruising back toward Silver Lake harbor and though she felt a weariness, it was a pleasant feeling, not the dragging fatigue of the past days. "Three bluefish in that amount of time's a very respectable haul."

"No argument there. Especially since I intend to eat half of them."

"I'm going to grill them."

"Are you?"

She met his lifted brow with a neutral look. "I caught, I cook."

Ky kept the boat at an even speed as he studied her. She looked a bit tired, but he thought he could convince her to take a nap if he claimed he wanted one himself. She was healing quickly. And she was right. He couldn't pamper her. "I could probably bring myself to start the charcoal for you."

"Fair enough. I'll even let you clean them."

He laughed at the bland tone and ruffled her hair until the pins fell out.

"Ky!" Automatically, Kate reached up to repair the damage.

"Wear it up in the school room," he advised, tossing some of the pins overboard. "I find it difficult to resist you when your hair's down and just a bit mussed."

"Is that so?" She debated being annoyed, then decided there were more productive ways to pass the time. Kate let the wind toss her hair as she moved closer to him so that their bodies touched. She smiled at the quick look of surprise in his eyes as she slipped both hands under his T-shirt. "Why don't you turn off the engine and show me what happens when you stop resisting?"

For all her generosity and freedom in lovemaking, she'd never been the initiator. Ky found himself both baffled and aroused as she smiled up at him, her hands stroking slowly over his chest. "You know what happens when I stop resisting," he murmured.

She gave a low, quiet laugh. "Refresh my memory." Without waiting for an answer, she drew back on the throttle herself until the boat was simply idling. "You didn't make love with me last night." Her hands slid around and up his back.

"You were sleeping." She was seducing him in the middle of the afternoon, in the middle of the ocean. He found he wanted to savor the new experience as much as he wanted to bring it to fruition.

"I'm not sleeping now." Rising on her toes, she brushed her lips over his, lightly, temptingly. She felt his heartbeat race against her body and reveled in a sense of power she'd never explored. "Or perhaps you're in a hurry to get back, and uh, clean fish."

She was taunting him. Why had he never seen the witch in her before? Ky felt his stomach knot with need, but when he drew her closer, she resisted. Just slightly. Just enough to torment. "If I make love with you now, I won't be gentle."

She kept her lips inches from his. "Is that a warning?" she whispered. "Or a promise?"

He felt the first tremor move through him and was astonished. Not even for her had he ever trembled. Not even for her. The need grew, stretching restlessly, recklessly. "I'm not sure you know what you're doing, Kate."

Nor did she, but she smiled because it no longer mattered. Only the outcome mattered. "Come down to the cabin with me and we'll both find out." She slipped away from him and without a word disappeared below deck.

His hand wasn't steady when he reached for the key to turn off the engines. He needed a moment, perhaps a bit more, to regain the control he'd held so carefully since they'd become lovers again. Even since he'd had her blood on his hands, he had a tremendous fear of hurting her. Since he'd had a taste of her again, he had an equal fear of driving her away. Caution was a strain, but he'd kept it in focus with sheer will. As Ky started down the steps, he told himself he'd continue to be cautious.

She'd unbuttoned her blouse but hadn't removed it. When he came into the narrow cabin with her, Kate smiled. She was afraid, though she hardly knew why. But over the fear was a heady sense of power and strength that fought for full release. She wanted to take him to the edge, to push him to the limits of passion. At that moment, she was certain she could.

When he came no closer to her, Kate stepped forward and pulled his shirt over his head. "Your skin's gold," she murmured. "It's always excited me." Taking her pleasure slowly, she ran her hands up his sides, feeling the quiver she caused. "You've always excited me."

Her hands were steady, her pulse throbbed as she unsnapped his cut-offs. With her eyes on his, she slowly, slowly, undressed him. "No one's ever made me want the way you make me want."

He had to stop her and take control again. She

couldn't know the effect of those long, fragile fingers when they brushed easily over his skin, or how her calm eyes made him rage inside.

"Kate…" He took her hands in his and bent to kiss her. But she turned her head, meeting his neck with warm lips that sent a spear of fire up his spine.

Then her body was pressed against his, flesh meeting flesh where her blouse parted. Her mouth trailed over his chest, her hands down his back to his hips. He felt the fury of desire whip through him as though it had sharp, hungry teeth.

So he forgot control, gentleness, vulnerability. She drove him to forget. She intended to.

They were tangled on the narrow bunk, her blouse halfway down her back and parted so that her breasts pushed into his chest, driving him mad with their firm, subtle curves. She nipped at his lips, demanding, pushing for more, still more. Waves of passion overtook them.

His need was incendiary. She was like a flame, impossible to hold, searing here, singeing there until his body was burning with needs and fierce fantasies.

Her hands were swift, sending sharp gasping pleasure everywhere at once until he wasn't sure he could take it anymore. Yet he no longer thought of stopping her. Less of stopping himself.

His hands gripped her with an urgency that made her moan from the sheer strength in them. She wanted his strength now—mindless strength that would carry them both to a place they'd never gone before. And she was leading. The knowledge made her laugh aloud as she tasted his skin, his lips, his tongue.

She slid down his body, feeling each jolt of pleasure as it shot through him. There could be no slow, lingering loving now. They'd pushed each other beyond reason. The air here was dark and thin and whirling with sound. Kate drank it in.

When he found her moist, hot and ready she let him take her over peak after shuddering peak, knowing as he drove her, she drove him. Her body was filled with sensations that came and went like comets, slipped away and burst on her again, and again. Through the thunder in her head she heard herself say his name, clear and quick.

On the sound, she took him into her and welcomed the madness.

Chapter 10

She was wrong.

Kate had thought she'd be ready, even anxious to dive again. There hadn't been a day during her recuperation that she hadn't thought of going down. Every time Ky had brought back an artifact, she was thrilled with the discovery and frustrated with her own lack of participation. Like a schoolgirl approaching summer, she'd begun to count the days.

Now, a week after the accident, Kate stood on the deck of the *Vortex* with her mouth dry and her hands trembling as she pulled on her wet suit. She could only be grateful that Ky was already over the side, hooking up his home-rigged prop-wash to the boat's propeller. Drafted to the crew, Marsh stood at the stern watching his brother. With Linda's eager support, he'd agreed to give Ky a few hours a day of his precious free time while he was needed.

Kate took the moment she had alone to gather her thoughts and her nerve.

It was only natural to be anxious about diving after the experience she'd had. Kate told herself that was logical. But it didn't stop her hands from trembling as she zipped up her suit. She could equate it with falling off a horse and having to mount again. It was psychological. But it didn't ease the painful tension in her stomach.

Trembling hands and nerves. With or without them she told herself as she hooked on her weight belt, she was going down. Nothing, not even her own fears, was going to stop her from finishing what she'd begun.

"He's got it," Marsh called out when Ky signaled him.

"I'll be ready." Kate picked up the cloth bag she'd use to bring up small artifacts. With luck, and if the prop-wash did its job, she knew they'd soon need more sophisticated methods to bring up the salvage.

"Kate."

She didn't look up, but continued to hook on the goodie bag. "Yes?"

"You know it's only natural that you'd be nervous going down." Marsh touched a hand to her shoulder, but she busied herself by strapping on her diving knife. "If you want a little more time, I'll work with Ky and you can run the wash."

"No." She said it too quickly, then cursed herself. "It's all right, Marsh." With forced calm she hung the underwater camera she'd purchased only the day before around her neck. "I have to take the first dive sometime."

"It doesn't have to be now."

She smiled at him again thinking how calm, how steady he appeared when compared to Ky. This was the sort of man it would have made sense for her to be attracted to. Confused emotions made no sense. "Yes, it does. Please." She put her hand on his arm before he could speak again. "Don't say anything to Ky."

Did she think he'd have to? Marsh wondered as he inclined his head in agreement. Unless he was way off the mark, Marsh was certain Ky knew every expression, every gesture, every intonation of her voice.

"Let's run it a couple of minutes at full throttle." Ky climbed over the side, dripping and eager. "With the depth and the size of the prop, we're going to have to test the effect. There might not be enough power to do us any good."

In agreement, Marsh went to the helm. "Are you thinking about using an air lift?"

Ky's only answer was a noncommital grunt. He had thought of it. The metal tube with its stream of compressed air was a quick, efficient way to excavate on silty bottoms. They might get away with the use of a small air lift, if it became necessary. But perhaps the prop-wash would do the job well enough. Either way, he was thinking more seriously about a bigger ship, with more sophisticated equipment and more power. As he saw it, it all depended on what they found today.

He picked up one last piece of equipment—a small powerful spear gun. He'd take no more chances with Kate.

"Okay, slow it down to the minimum," he ordered. "And keep it there. Once Kate and I are down, we don't want the prop-wash shooting cannonballs around."

Kate stopped the deep breathing she was using to ease tension. Her voice was cool and steady. "Would it have that kind of power?"

"Not at this speed." Ky adjusted his mask then took her hand. "Ready?"

"Yes."

Then he kissed her, hard. "You've got guts, professor," he murmured. His eyes were dark, intense as they passed over her face. "It's one of the sexiest things about you." With this he was over the side.

He knew. Kate gave a quiet unsteady sigh as she started down the ladder. He knew she was afraid, and that had been his way of giving her support. She looked up once and saw Marsh. He lifted his hand in salute. Throat dry, nerves jumping, Kate let the sea take her.

She felt a moment's panic, a complete disorientation the moment she was submerged. It ran through her head that down here, she was helpless. The deeper she went, the more vulnerable she became. Choking for air, she kicked back toward the surface and the light.

Then Ky had her hands, holding her to him, holding her under. His grip was firm, stilling the first panic. Feeling the wild race of her pulse, he held on during her first resistance.

Then he touched her cheek, waiting until she'd calmed enough to look at him. In his eyes she saw strength and challenge. Pride alone forced her to fight her way beyond the fear and meet him, equal to equal.

When she'd regulated her breathing, accepting that her air came through the tanks on her back, he kissed the back of her hand. Kate felt the tension give. She wouldn't be helpless, she reminded herself. She'd be careful.

With a nod, she pointed down, indicating she was ready to dive. Keeping hands linked, they started toward the bottom.

The whirlpool action created by the wash of the prop had already blasted away some of the sediment. At first glance Ky could see that if the wreck was buried under more than a few feet, they'd need something stronger than his home-made apparatus and single prop engine. But for now, it would do. Patience, which came to him only with deliberate effort, was more important at this stage than speed. With the wreck, he thought, and—he glanced over at the woman beside him—with a great deal more. He had to take care not to hurry.

It was still working, blowing away some of the overburden at a rate Ky figured would equal an inch per minute. He and Kate alone couldn't deal with any more speed. He watched the swirl of water and sediment while she swam a few feet away to catalog one of the cannons on film. When she came closer, he grinned as she placed the camera in front of her face again. She was relaxed, her initial fear forgotten. He could see it simply in the way she moved. Then she let the camera fall so they could begin the search again.

Kate saw something solid wash away from the hole being created by the whirl of water. Grabbing it up, she found herself holding a candlestick. In her excitement, she turned it over and over in her hand.

Silver? she wondered with a rush of adrenaline. Had they found their first real treasure? It was black with oxidation, so it was impossible to be certain what it was made of. Still, it thrilled her. After days and days of only waiting, she was again pursuing the dream.

When she looked up, Ky was already gathering the uncovered items and laying them in the mesh basket. There were more candleholders, more tableware, but not the plain unglazed pottery they'd found before. Kate's pulse began to drum with excitement while she meticulously snapped pictures. They'd be able to find a hallmark, she was certain of it. Then they'd know if they had indeed found a British ship. Ordinary seamen didn't use silver, or even pewter table service.

They'd uncovered more than the galley now. And they were just beginning.

When Ky found the first piece of porcelain he signaled to her. True, the vase—if that's what it once had been—had suffered under the water pressure and the years. It was broken so that only half of the shell remained, but so did the manufacturer's mark.

When Kate read it, she gripped Ky's arm. *Whieldon.* English. The master potter who'd trained the likes of Wedgwood. Kate cupped the broken fragment in her hands as though it were alive. When she lifted her eyes to Ky's they were filled with triumph.

Fretting against her inability to speak, Kate pointed to the mark again. Ky merely nodded and indicated the basket. Though she was loath to part with it, Kate found herself even more eager to discover more. She settled the porcelain in the mesh. When she swam back, Ky's hands were filled with other pieces. Some were hardly more than shards, others were identifiable as pieces left from bowls or lids.

No, it didn't prove it was a merchant ship, Kate told herself as she gathered what she could herself. So far, it only proved that the officers and perhaps some passengers had eaten elegantly on their way to the New World. English officers, she reminded herself. In her mind they'd taken the identification that far.

The force of the wash sent an object shooting up. Ky reached out for it and found a crusted, filthy pot he guessed would have been used for tea or coffee. Perhaps it was cracked under the layers, but it held together in his hands. He tapped on his tank to get Kate's attention.

She knew it was priceless the moment she saw it. Stemming impatience, she signaled for Ky to hold it out as she lifted the camera again. Obliging, he crossed his legs like a genie and posed.

It made her giggle. They'd perhaps just found something worth thousands of dollars, but he could still act silly. Nothing was too serious for Ky. As she brought him into frame, Kate felt the same foolish pleasure. She'd known the hunt would be exciting, perhaps rewarding, but she'd never known it would be fun. She swam forward and reached for the vase herself.

Running her fingers over it, she could detect some kind of design under the crust. Not ordinary pottery, she was sure. Not utility-ware. She held something elegant, something well crafted.

He understood its worth as well as she. Taking it from her, Ky indicated they would bring it and the rest of the morning's salvage to the surface. Pointing to his watch he showed her that their tanks were running low.

She didn't argue. They'd come back. The *Liberty* would wait for them. Each took a handle of the mesh basket and swam leisurely toward the surface.

"Do you know how I feel?" Kate demanded the moment she could speak.

"Yes." Ky gripped the ladder with one hand and

waited for her to unstrap her tanks and slip them over onto the deck. "I know just how you feel."

"The teapot." Breathing fast, she hauled herself up the ladder. "Ky, it's priceless. It's like finding a perfectly formed rose inside a mass of briars." Before he could answer, she was laughing and calling out to Marsh. "It's fabulous! Absolutely fabulous."

Marsh cut the engine then walked over to help them. "You two work fast." Bending he touched a tentative finger to the pot. "God, it's all in one piece."

"We'll be able to date it as soon as it's cleaned. But look." Kate drew out the broken vase. "This is the mark of an English potter. English," she repeated, turning to Ky. "He trained Wedgwood, and Wedgwood didn't begin manufacturing until the 1760s, so—"

"So this piece more than likely came from the era we're looking for," Ky finished. "*Liberty* or not," he continued, crouching down beside her. "It looks like you've found yourself an eighteenth-century wreck that's probably of English origin and certainly hasn't been recorded before." He took one of her hands between both of his. "Your father would've been proud of you."

Stunned, she stared at him. Emotions raced through her with such velocity she had no way of controlling or channeling them. The hand holding the broken vase began to tremble. Quickly, she set it down in the basket again and rose.

"I'm going below," she managed and fled.

Proud of her. Kate put a hand over her mouth as she stumbled into the cabin. His pride, his love. Wasn't it all she'd really ever wanted from her father? Was it possible she could only gain it after his death?

She drank in deep gulps of air and struggled to level her emotions. No, she wanted to find the *Liberty*, she wanted to bring her father's dream to reality, have his name on a plaque in a museum with the artifacts they'd found. She owed him that. But she'd promised herself she'd find the *Liberty* for herself as well. For herself.

It was her choice, her first real decision to come in from the sidelines and act on her own. For herself, Kate thought again as she brought the first surge of emotion under control.

"Kate?"

She turned, and though she thought she was perfectly calm, Ky could see the turmoil in her eyes. Unsure how to handle it, he spoke practically.

"You'd better get out of that suit."

"But we're going back down."

"Not today." To prove his point he began to strip out of his own suit just as Marsh started the engines.

Automatically, she balanced herself as the boat turned. "Ky, we've got two more sets of tanks. There's no reason for us to go back when we're just getting started."

"Your first dive took most of the strength you've built up. If you want to dive tomorrow, you've got to take it slow today."

Her anger erupted so quickly, it left them both astonished. "The hell with that!" she exploded. "I'm sick to death of being treated as if I don't know my own limitations or my own mind and body."

Ky walked into the galley and picked up a can of beer. With a flick of his wrist, air hissed out. "I don't know what you're talking about."

"I lay in bed for the better part of a week because of pressure from you and Linda and anyone else who came around me. I'm not tolerating this any longer."

With one hand, he pushed dripping hair from his forehead as he lifted the can. "You're tolerating exactly what's necessary until I say differently."

"You say?" she tossed back. Cheeks flaming, she strode over to him. "I don't have to do what you say, or what anyone says. Not anymore. It's about time you remember just who's in charge of this salvage operation."

His eyes narrowed. "In charge?"

"I hired you. Seventy-five a day and twenty-five percent. Those were the terms. There was nothing in there about you running my life."

He abruptly went still. For a moment, all that could be heard over the engines was her angry breathing. Dollars and percents, he thought with a deadly sort of calm. Just dollars and percents. "So that's what it comes down to?"

Too overwrought to see beyond her own anger, she continued to lash out. "We made an agreement. I fully intend to see that you get everything we arranged, but

I won't have you telling me when I can go down. I won't have you judging when I'm well and when I'm not. I'm sick to death of being dictated to. And I won't be—not by you, not by anyone. Not any longer.''

The metal of the can gave under his fingers. "Fine. You do exactly what you want, professor. But while you're about it, get yourself another diver. I'll send you a bill.'' Ky went up the cabin steps the way he came down. Quickly and without a sound.

With her hands gripped together, Kate sat down on the bunk and waited until she heard the engines stop again. She refused to think. Thinking hurt. She refused to feel. There was too much to feel. When she was certain she was in control, she stood up and went up on deck.

Everything was exactly as she'd left it—the wire basket filled with bits of porcelain and tableware, her nearly depleted tanks. Ky was gone. Marsh walked over from the stern where he'd been waiting for her.

"You're going to need a hand with these.''

Kate nodded and pulled a thigh length T-shirt over her tank suit. "Yes. I want to take everything back to my room at the hotel. I have to arrange for shipping.''

"Okay.'' But instead of reaching down for the basket, he took her arm. "Kate, I don't like to give advice.''

"Good.'' Then she swore at her own rudeness. "I'm sorry, Marsh. I'm feeling a little rough at the moment.''

"I can see that, and I know things aren't always

smooth for you and Ky. Look, he has a habit of closing himself up, of not saying everything that's on his
mind. Or worse," Marsh added. "Of saying the first
thing that comes to mind."

"He's perfectly free to do so. I came here for the
specific purpose of finding and excavating the *Liberty*.
If Ky and I can't deal together on a business level, I
have to do without his help."

"Listen, he has a few blind spots."

"Marsh, you're his brother. Your allegiance is with
him as it should be."

"I care about both of you."

She took a deep breath, refusing to let the emotion
surface and carry her with it. "I appreciate that. The
best thing you can do for me now, perhaps for both
of us, is to tell me where I can rent a boat and some
equipment. I'm going back out this afternoon."

"Kate."

"I'm going back out this afternoon," she repeated.
"With or without your help."

Resigned, Marsh picked up the mesh basket. "All
right, you can use mine."

It took the rest of the morning for Kate to arrange
everything, including the resolution of a lengthy argument with Marsh. She refused to let him come with
her, ending by saying she'd simply rent a boat and do
without his assistance altogether. In the end, she stood
at the helm of his boat alone and headed out to sea.

She craved the solitude. Almost in defiance, she

pushed the throttle forward. If it was defiance, she didn't care, any more than she cared whom she was defying. It was vital to do this one act for herself.

She refused to think about Ky, about why she'd exploded at him. If her words had been harsh, they'd also been necessary. She comforted herself with that. For too long, for a lifetime, she'd been influenced by someone else's opinion, someone else's expectations.

Mechanically, she stopped the engines and put on her equipment, checking and rechecking as she went. She'd never gone down alone before. Even that seemed suddenly a vital thing to do.

With a last look at her compass, she took the mesh basket over the side.

As she went deep, a thrill went through her. She was alone. In acres and acres of sea, she was alone. The water parted for her like silk. She was in control, and her destiny was her own.

She didn't rush. Kate found she wanted that euphoric feeling of being isolated under the sea where only curious fish bothered to give her a passing glance. Ultimately, her only responsibility here was to herself. Briefly, she closed her eyes and floated. At last, only to herself.

When she reached the site, she felt a new surge of pride. This was something she'd done without her father. She wouldn't think of the whys or the hows now, but simply the triumph. For two centuries, it had waited. And now, *she'd* found it. She circled the hole the prop-wash had created and began to fan using her hand.

Her first find was a dinner plate with a flamboyant floral pattern around the rim. She found one, then half a dozen, two of which were intact. On the back was the mark of an English potter. There were cups as well, dainty, exquisite English china that might have graced the table of a wealthy colonist, might have become a beloved heirloom, if nature hadn't interfered. Now they looked like something out of a horror show— crusted, misshapen with sea life. They couldn't have been more beautiful to her.

As she continued to fan, Kate nearly missed what appeared to be a dark sea shell. On closer examination she saw it was a silver coin. She couldn't make out the currency, but knew it didn't matter. It could just as easily be Spanish, as she'd read that Spanish currency had been used by all European nations with settlements in the New World.

The point was, it was a coin. The first coin. Though it was silver, not gold, and unidentifiable at the moment, she'd found it by herself.

Kate started to slip it into her goodie bag when her arm was jerked back.

The thrill of fear went wildly from her toes to her throat. The spear gun was on board the *Vortex*. She had no weapon. Before she could do more than turn in defense, she was caught by the shoulders with Ky's furious hands.

Terror died, but the anger in his eyes only incited

her own. Damn him for frightening her, for interfering. Shaking him away, Kate signaled for him to leave. With one arm, he encircled her waist and started for the surface.

Only once did she even come close to breaking away from him. Ky simply banded his arm around her again, more tightly, until she had a choice between submitting or cutting off her own air.

When they broke the surface, Kate drew in breath to shout, but even in this, she was out-maneuvered.

"Idiot!" he shouted at her, dragging her to the ladder. "One day off your back and you jump into forty feet of water by yourself. I don't know why in hell I ever thought you had any brains."

Breathless, she heaved her tanks over the side. When she was on solid ground again, she intended to have her say. For now, she'd let him have his.

"I take my eyes off you for a couple hours and you go off half-cocked. If I'd murdered Marsh, it would have been on your head."

To her further fury, Kate saw that she'd boarded the *Vortex*. Marsh's boat was nowhere in sight.

"Where's the *Gull*?" she demanded.

"Marsh had the sense to tell me what you were doing." The words came out like bullets as he stripped his gear. "I didn't kill him because I needed him to come out with me and take the *Gull* back." He stood in front of her, dripping, and as furious as she'd ever seen him. "Don't you have any more sense than to dive out here alone?"

She tossed her head back. "Don't you?"

Infuriated, he grabbed her and started to peel the wet suit from her himself. "We're not talking about me, damn it. I've been diving since I was six. I know the currents."

"*I* know the currents."

"And I haven't been flat on my back for a week."

"I was flat on my back for a week because you were overreacting." She struggled away from him, and because the wet suit was already down to her waist, peeled it off. "You've no right to tell me when and where I can dive, Ky. Superior strength gives you no right to drag me up when I'm in the middle of salvaging."

"The hell with what I have a right to do." Grabbing her again, he shook her with more violence than he'd ever shown her. A dozen things might have happened to her in the thirty minutes she'd been down. A dozen things he knew too well. "I make my own rights. You're not going down alone if I have to chain you up to stop it."

"You told me to get another diver," she said between her teeth. "Until I do, I dive alone."

"You threw that damn business arrangement in my face. Percentages. Lousy percentages and a daily rate. Do you know how that made me feel?"

"No!" she shouted, pushing him away. "No, I don't know how that made you feel. I don't know how anything makes you feel. You don't tell me." Dragging both hands through her dripping hair she walked away. "We agreed to the terms. That's all I know."

"That was before."

"Before what?" she demanded. Tears brimmed for no reason she could name, but she blinked them back again. "Before I slept with you?"

"Damn it, Kate." He was across the deck, backing her into the rail before she could take a breath. "Are you trying to get at me for something I did or didn't do four years ago? I don't even know what it is. I don't know what you want from me or what you don't want and I'm sick of trying to outguess you."

"I don't want to be pushed into a corner," she told him fiercely. "That's what I don't want. I don't want to be expected to fall in passively with someone else's plans for me. That's what I don't want. I don't want it assumed that I simply don't have any personal goals or wishes of my own. Or any basic competence of my own. *That's* what I don't want!"

"Fine." They were both losing control, but he no longer gave a damn. Ky ripped off his wet suit and tossed it aside. "You just remember something, lady. I don't expect of you and I don't assume. Once maybe, but not anymore. There was only one person who ever pushed you into a corner and it wasn't me." He hurled his mask across the deck where it bounced and smacked into the side. "I'm the one who let you go."

She stiffened. Even with the distance between them

he could see her eyes frost over. "I won't discuss my father with you."

"You caught on real quick though, didn't you?"

"You resented him. You—"

"I?" Ky interrupted. "Maybe you better look at yourself, Kate."

"I loved him," she said passionately. "All my life I tried to show him. You don't understand."

"How do you know that I don't understand?" he exploded. "Don't you know I can see what you're feeling every time we find something down there? Do you think I'm so blind I don't see that you're hurting because *you* found it, not him? Don't you think it tears me apart to see that you punish yourself for not being what you think he wanted you to be? And I'm tired," he continued as her breath started to hitch. "Damn tired of being compared to and measured by a man you loved without ever being close to him."

"I don't." She covered her face, hating the weakness but powerless against it. "I don't do that. I only want…"

"What?" he demanded. "What do you want?"

"I didn't cry when he died," she said into her hands. "I didn't cry, not even at the funeral. I owed him tears, Ky. I owed him something."

"You don't owe him anything you didn't already give him over and over again." Frustrated, he dragged a hand through his hair before he went to her. "Kate." Because words seemed useless, he simply gathered her close.

"I didn't cry."

"Cry now," he murmured. He pressed his lips to the top of her head. "Cry now."

So she did, desperately, for what she'd never been able to quite touch, for what she'd never been able to quite hold. She'd ached for love, for the simple companionship of understanding. She wept because it was too late for that now from her father. She wept because she wasn't certain she could ask for love again from anyone else.

Ky held her, lowering her onto the bench as he cradled her in his lap. He couldn't offer her words of comfort. They were the most difficult words for him to come by. He could only offer her a place to weep, and silence.

As the tears began to pass, she kept her face against his shoulder. There was such simplicity there, though it came from a man of complications. Such gentleness, though it sprang from a restless nature. "I couldn't mourn for him before," she murmured. "I'm not sure why."

"You don't have to cry to mourn."

"Maybe not," she said wearily. "I don't know. But it's true, what you said. I've wanted to do all this for him because he'll never have the chance to finish what he started. I don't know if you can understand, but I feel if I do this I'll have done everything I could. For him, and for myself."

"Kate." Ky tipped back her head so he could see

her face. Her eyes were puffy, rimmed with red. "I don't have to understand. I just have to love you."

He felt her stiffen in his arms and immediately cursed himself. Why was it he never said things to her the way they should be said? Sweetly, calmly, softly. She was a woman who needed soft words, and he was a man who always struggled with them.

She didn't move, and for a long, long moment, they stayed precisely as they were.

"Do you?" she managed after a moment.

"Do I what?"

Would he make her drag it from him? "Love me?"

"Kate." Frustrated, he drew away from her. "I don't know how else to show you. You want bouquets of flowers, bottles of French champagne, poems? Damn it, I'm not made that way."

"I want a straight answer."

He let out a short breath. Sometimes her very calmness drove him to distraction. "I've always loved you. I've never stopped."

That went through her, sharp, hot, with a mixture of pain and pleasure she wasn't quite sure how to deal with. Slowly, she rose out of his arms, and walking across the deck, looked out to sea. The buoys that marked the site bobbed gently. Why were there no buoys in life to show you the way?

"You never told me."

"Look, I can't even count the number of women I've said it to." When she turned back with her brow raised, he rose, uncomfortable. "It was easy to say it to them because it didn't mean anything. It's a hell of a lot harder to get the words out when you mean them, and when you're afraid someone's going to back away from you the minute you do.''

"I wouldn't have done that.''

"You backed away, you went away for four years, when I asked you to stay.''

"You asked me to stay,'' she reminded him. "You asked me not to go back to Connecticut, but to move in with you. Just like that. No promises, no commitment, no sign that you had any intention of building a life with me. I had responsibilities.''

"To do what your father wanted you to do.''

She swallowed that. It was true in its way. "All right, yes. But you never said you loved me.''

He came closer. "I'm telling you now.''

She nodded, but her heart was in her throat. "And I'm not backing away. I'm just not sure I can take the next step. I'm not sure you can either.''

"You want a promise.''

She shook her head, not certain what she'd do if indeed he gave her one. "I want time, for both of us. It seems we both have a lot of thinking to do.''

"Kate.'' Impatient, he came to her, taking her hands. They trembled. "Some things you don't have to think about. Some things you can think about too much.''

"You've lived your life a certain way a long time, and I mine,'' she said quickly. "Ky, I've just begun to change—to feel the change. I don't want to make a mistake, not with you. It's too important. With time—''

''We've lost four years,'' he interrupted. He needed to resolve something, he discovered, and quickly. ''I can't wait any longer to hear it if it's inside you.''

Kate let out the breath she'd been holding. If he could ask, she could give. It would be enough. ''I love you, Ky. I never stopped either. I never told you when I should have.''

He felt the weight drain from his body as he cupped her face. ''You're telling me now.''

It was enough.

Chapter 11

Love. Kate had read hundreds of poems about that one phenomenon. She'd read, analyzed and taught from countless novels where love was the catalyst to all action, all emotion. With her students, she'd dissected innumerable lines from books, plays and verse that all led back to that one word.

Now, for perhaps the first time in her life, it was offered to her. She found it had more power than could possibly be taught. She found she didn't understand it.

Ky hadn't Byron's way with words, or Keat's romantic phrasing. What he'd said, he'd said simply. It meant everything. She still didn't understand it.

She could, in her own way, understand her feelings. She'd loved Ky for years, since that first revelation

one summer when she'd come to know what it meant
to want to fully share oneself with another.

But what, she wondered, did Ky find in her to love?
It wasn't modesty that caused her to ask herself this
question, but the basic practicality she'd grown up
with. Where there was an effect, there was a cause.
Where there was reaction, there was action. The world
ran on this principle. She'd won Ky's love—but how?

Kate had no insecurity about her own intelligence.
Perhaps, if anything, she overrated her mind, and it
was this that caused her to underrate her other attri-
butes.

He was a man of action, of restless and mercurial
nature. She, on the other hand, considered herself almost blandly level. While she thrived on routine, Ky
thrived on the unexpected. Why should he love her?
Yet he did.

If she accepted that, it was vital to come to a resolution. Love led to commitment. It was there that she
found the wall solid, without footholds.

He lived on a remote island because he was basically a loner, because he preferred moving at his own
pace, in his own time. She was a teacher who lived
by a day-to-day schedule. Without the satisfaction of
giving knowledge, she'd stagnate. In the structured
routine of a college town, Ky would go mad.

Because she could find no compromise, Kate opted
to do what she'd decided to do in the beginning. She'd
ride with the current until the summer was over. Perhaps by then, an answer would come.

They spoke no more of percentages. Kate quietly dropped the notion of keeping her hotel room. These, she told herself, were small matters when so much more hung in the balance during her second summer with Ky.

The days went quickly with her and Ky working together with the prop-wash or by hand. Slowly, painstakingly, they uncovered more salvage. The candlesticks had turned out to be pewter, but the coin had been Spanish silver. Its date had been 1748.

In the next two-week period, they uncovered much more—a heavy intricately carved silver platter, more china and porcelain, and in another area dozens of nails and tools.

Kate documented each find on film, for practical and personal reasons. She needed the neat, orderly way of keeping track of the salvage. She wanted to be able to look back on those pictures and remember how she felt when Ky held up a crusted teacup or an oxidized tankard. She'd be able to look and remember how he'd played an outstanding game with a large lazy bluefish. And lost.

More than once Ky had suggested the use of a larger ship equipped for salvage. They discussed it, and its advantages, but they never acted on it. Somehow, they both felt they wanted to move slowly, working basically with their own hands until there came a time when they had to make a decision.

The cannons and the heavier pieces of ship's planking couldn't be brought up without help, so these they left to the sea for the time being. They continued to use tanks, rather than changing to a surface-supplied source of air, so they had to surface and change gear every hour or so. A diving rig would have saved time—but that wasn't their goal.

Their methods weren't efficient by professional salvor standards, but they had an unspoken agreement. Stretch time. Make it last.

The nights they spent together in the big four-poster, talking of the day's finds, or of tomorrow's, making love, marking time. They didn't speak of the future that loomed after the summer's end. They never talked of what they'd do the day after the treasure was found.

The treasure became their focus, something that kept them from reaching out when the other wasn't ready.

The day was fiercely hot as they prepared to dive. The sun was baking. It was mid-July. She'd been in Ocracoke for a month. For all her practicality, Kate told herself it was an omen. Today was the turning point of summer.

Even as she pulled the wet suit up to her waist, sweat beaded on her back. She could almost taste the cool freshness of the water. The sun glared on her tanks as she lifted them, bouncing off to spear her eyes.

"Here." Taking them from her, Ky strapped them

onto her back, checking the gauges himself. "The water's going to feel like heaven."

"Yeah." Marsh tipped up a quart bottle of juice. "Think of me baking up here while you're having all the fun."

"Keep the throttle low, brother," Ky said with a grin as he climbed over the side. "We'll bring you a reward."

"Make it something round and shiny with a date stamped on it," Marsh called back, then winked at Kate as she started down the ladder. "Good luck."

She felt the excitement as the water lapped over her ankles. "Today, I don't think I need it."

The noise of the prop-wash disturbed the silence of the water, but not the mystery. Even with technology and equipment, the water remained an enigma, part beauty, part danger. They went deeper and deeper until they reached the site with the scoops in the silt caused by their earlier explorations.

They'd already found what they thought had been the officers' and passengers' quarters, identifying it by the discovery of a snuff box, a silver bedside candleholder and Ky's personal favorite—a decorated sword. The few pieces of jewelry they'd found indicated a personal cache rather than cargo.

Though they fully intended to excavate in the area of the cache, it was the cargo they sought. Using the passengers' quarters and the galley as points of reference, they concentrated on what should have been the stern of the ship.

There were ballast rocks to deal with. This entailed a slow, menial process that required moving them by hand to an area they'd already excavated. It was time consuming, unrewarding and necessary. Still, Kate found something peaceful in the mindless work, and something fascinating about the ability to do it under fathoms of water with basically little effort. She could move a ballast pile as easily as Ky, whereas on land, she would have tired quickly.

Reaching down to clear another area, Ky's fingers brushed something small and hard. Curious, he fanned aside a thin layer of silt and picked up what at first looked like a tab on a can of beer. As he brought it closer, he saw it was much more refined, and though there were layers of crust on the knob of the circle, he felt his heart give a quick jerk.

He'd heard of diamonds in the rough, but he'd never thought to find one by simply reaching for it. He was no expert, but as he painstakingly cleaned what he could from the stone, he judged it to be at least two carats. With a tap on Kate's shoulder, he got her attention.

It gave him a great deal of pleasure to see her eyes widen and to hear the muffled sound of her surprise. Together, they turned it over and over again. It was dull and dirty, but the gem was there.

They were finding bits and pieces of civilization. Perhaps a woman had worn the ring while dining with the captain on her way to America. Perhaps some British officer had carried it in his vest pocket, waiting to give it to the woman he'd hoped to marry. It might have belonged to an elderly widow, or a young bride. The mystery of it, and its tangibility, were more precious than the stone itself. It was…lasting.

Ky held it out to her, offering. Their routine had fallen into a finders-keepers arrangement, in that whoever found a particular piece carried it in their own bag to the surface where everything was carefully catalogued on film and paper. Kate looked at the small, water-dulled piece of the past in Ky's fingers.

Was he offering her the ring because it was a woman's fancy, or was he offering her something else? Unsure, she shook her head, pointing to the bag on his belt. If he were asking her something, she needed it to be done with words.

Ky dropped the ring into his bag, secured it, then went back to work.

He thought he understood her, in some ways. In other ways, Ky found she was as much a mystery as the sea. What did she want from him? If it was love, he'd given her that. If it was time, they were both running out of it. He wanted to demand, was accustomed to demanding, yet she blocked his ability with a look.

She said she'd changed—that she was just beginning to feel in control of her life. He thought he understood that, as well as her fierce need for independence. And yet… He'd never known anything but independence. He, too, had changed. He needed her to give him the boundaries and the borders that came with dependence. His for her, and hers for him. Was the timing wrong again? Would it ever be right?

Damn it, he wanted her, he thought as he heaved another rock out of his way. Not just for today, but for tomorrow. Not tied against him, but bound to him. Why couldn't she understand that?

She loved him. It was something she murmured in the night when she was sleepy and caught close against him. She wasn't a woman to use words unless they had meaning. Yet with the love he offered and the love she returned, she'd begun to hold something back from him, as though he could have only a portion of her, but not all. Edged with frustration, he cleared more ballast. He needed and would have, all.

Marriage? Was he thinking of marriage? Kate found herself flustered and uneasy. She'd never expected Ky to look for that kind of commitment, that kind of permanency. Perhaps she'd misread him. After all, it was difficult to be certain of someone's intention, yet she knew just how clearly Ky and she had been able to communicate underwater.

There was so much to consider, so many things to weigh. He wouldn't understand that, Kate mused. Ky was a man who made decisions in an instant and took the consequences. He wouldn't think about all the variables, all the what-ifs, all the maybes. She had to think about them all. She simply knew no other way.

Kate watched the silt and sand blowing away, causing a cuplike indentation to form on the ocean floor. Outside influences, she mused. They could eat away at the layers and uncover the core, but sometimes what was beneath couldn't stand up to the pressure.

Is that what would happen between her and Ky? How would their relationship hold up under the pressure of variant lifestyles—the demands of her profession and the free-wheeling tone of his? Would it stay intact, or would it begin to sift away, layer by layer? How much of herself would he ask her to give? And in loving, how much of herself would she lose?

It was a possibility she couldn't ignore, a threat she needed to build a solid defense against. Time. Perhaps time was the answer. But summer was waning.

The force of the wash made a small object spin up, out of the layer of silt and into the water. Kate grabbed at it and the sharp edge scraped her palm. Curious, she turned it over for examination. A buckle? she wondered. The shape seemed to indicate it, and she could just make out a fastening. Even as she started to hold it out for Ky another, then another was pushed off the ocean bed.

Shoe buckles, Kate realized, astonished. Dozens of them. No, she realized as more and more began to twist up in the water's spin and reel away. Hundreds. With a quick frenzy, she began to gather what she could. More than hundreds, she discovered as her heart thudded. There were thousands of them, literally thousands.

She held a buckle in her hand and looked at Ky in triumph. They'd found the cargo. There'd been shoe buckles on the manifest of the *Liberty*. Five thousand of them. Nothing but a merchantman carried something like that in bulk.

Proof. She waved the buckle, her arm sweeping out in slow motion to take in the swarm of them swirling away from the wash and dropping again. Proof, her mind shouted out. The cargo-hold was beneath them. And the treasure. They had only to reach it.

Ky took her hands and nodded, knowing what was in her mind. Beneath his fingers he could feel the race of her pulse. He wanted that for her, the excitement, the thrill that came from discovering something only half believed in. She brought the back of his hand to her cheek, her eyes laughing, buckles spinning around them. Kate wanted to laugh until she was too weak to stand. Five thousand shoe buckles would guide them to a chest of gold.

Kate saw the humor in his eyes and knew Ky's thoughts ran along the same path as hers. He pointed to himself, then thumbs up. With a minimum of signaling, he told Kate that he would surface to tell Marsh to shut off the engines. It was time to work by hand.

Excited, she nodded. She wanted only to begin. Resting near the bottom, Kate watched Ky go up and out of sight. Oddly, she found she needed time alone. She'd shared the heady instant of discovery with Ky, and now she needed to absorb it.

The *Liberty* was beneath her, the ship her father had searched for. The dream he'd kept close, carefully researching, meticulously calculating, but never finding.

Joy and sorrow mixed as she gathered a handful of the buckles and placed them carefully in her bag. For him. In that moment she felt she'd given him everything she'd always needed to.

Carefully, and this time for personal reasons rather than the catalogue, she began to shoot pictures. Years from now, she thought. Years and years from now, she'd look at a snapshot of swirling silt and drifting pieces of metal, and she'd remember. Nothing could ever take that moment of quiet satisfaction from her.

She glanced up at the sudden silence. The wash had stilled. Ky had reached the surface. Silt and the pieces of crusted, decorated metal began to settle again without the agitation of the wash. The sea was a world without sound, without movement.

Kate looked down at the scoop in the ocean floor. They were nearly there. For a moment she was tempted to begin to fan and search by herself, but she'd wait for Ky. They began together, and they'd finish together. Content, she watched for his return.

When Kate saw the movement above her, she started to signal. Her hand froze in place, then her arm, her shoulder and the rest of her body, degree by degree. It came smoothly through the water, sleek and silent. Deadly.

The noise of the prop-wash had kept the sea life away. Now the abrupt quiet brought out the curious. Among the schools of harmless fish glided the long bulletlike shape of a shark.

Kate was still, hardly daring to breathe as she feared

even the trail of bubbles might attract him. He moved without haste, apparently not interested in her. Perhaps he'd already hunted successfully that day. But even with a full belly, a shark would attack what annoyed his uncertain temper.

She gauged him to be ten feet in length. Part of her mind registered that he was fairly small for what she recognized as a tiger shark. They could easily double that length. But she knew the jaws, those large sickle-shaped teeth, would be strong, merciless and fatal.

If she remained still, the chances were good that he would simply go in search of more interesting waters. Isn't that what she'd read sitting cozily under lamplight at her own desk? Isn't that what Ky had told her once when they'd shared a quiet lunch on his boat? All that seemed so remote, so unreal now, as she looked above and saw the predator between herself and the surface.

It was movement that attracted them, she reminded herself as she forced her mind to function. The movement a swimmer made with kicking feet and sweeping arms.

Don't panic. She forced herself to breathe slowly. No sudden moves. She forced her nervous hands to form tight, still fists.

He was no more than ten feet away. Kate could see the small black eyes and the gentle movement of his gills. Breathing shallowly, she never took her eyes from his. She had only to be perfectly still and wait for him to swim on.

But Ky. Kate's mouth went dry as she looked toward the direction where Ky had disappeared moments before. He'd be coming back, any minute, unaware of what was lurking near the bottom. Waiting. Cruising.

The shark would sense the disturbance in the water with the uncanny ability the hunter had. The kick of Ky's feet, the swing of his arms would attract the shark long before Kate would have a chance to warn him of any danger.

He'd be unaware, helpless, and then... Her blood seemed to freeze. She'd heard of the sensation but now she experienced it. Cold seemed to envelop her. Terror made her head light. Kate bit down on her lip until pain cleared her thoughts. She wouldn't stand by idly while Ky came blindly into a death trap.

Glancing down, she saw the spear gun. It was over five feet away and unloaded for safety. Safety, she thought hysterically. She'd never loaded one, much less shot one. And first, she'd have to get to it. There'd only be one chance. Knowing she'd have no time to settle her nerves, Kate made her move.

She kept her eyes on the shark as she inched slowly toward the gun. At the moment, he seemed to be merely cruising, not particularly interested in anything. He never even glanced her way. Perhaps he would move on before Ky came back, but she needed the weapon. Fingers shaking, she gripped the butt of the gun. Time seemed to crawl. Her movements were so slow, so measured, she hardly seemed to move at all. But her mind whirled.

Even as she gripped the spear she saw the shape that glided down from the surface. The shark turned lazily to the left. To Ky.

No! her mind screamed as she rammed the spear into position. Her only thought that of protecting what she loved. Kate swam forward without hesitation, taking a path between Ky and the shark. She had to get close.

Her mind was cold now, with fear, with purpose. For the second time, she saw those small, deadly eyes. This time, they focused on her. If she'd never seen true evil before, Kate knew she faced it now. This was cruelty, and a death that wouldn't come easily.

The shark moved toward her with a speed that made her heart stop. His jaws opened. There was a black, black cave behind them.

Ky dove quickly, wanting to get back to Kate, wanting to search for what had brought them back together. If it was the treasure she needed to settle her mind, he'd find it. With it, they could open whatever doors they needed to open, lock whatever needed to be locked. Excitement drummed through him as he dove deeper.

When he spotted the shark, he pulled up short. He'd felt that deep primitive fear before, but never so sharply. Though it was less than useless against such a predator, he reached for his diver's knife. He'd left Kate alone. Cold-bloodedly, he set for the attack.

Like a rocket, Kate shot up between himself and the shark. Terror such as he'd never known washed over him. Was she mad? Was she simply unaware? Giving no time to thought, Ky barreled through the water toward her.

He was too far away. He knew it even as the panic hammered into him. The shark would be on her before he was close enough to sink the knife in.

When he saw what she held in her hand, and realized her purpose he somehow doubled his speed. Everything was in slow motion, and yet it seemed to happen in the blink of an eye. He saw the gaping hole in the shark's mouth as it closed in on Kate. For the first time in his life, prayers ran through him like water.

The spear shot out, sinking deep through the shark's flesh. Instinctively, Kate let herself drop as the shark came forward full of anger and pain. He would follow her now, she knew. If the spear didn't work, he would be on her in moments.

Ky saw blood gush from the wound. It wouldn't be enough. The shark jerked as if to reject the spear, and slowed his pace. Just enough. Teeth bared, Ky fell on its back, hacking with the knife as quickly as the water would allow. The shark turned, furious. Using all his strength, Ky turned with it, forcing the knife into the underbelly and ripping down. It ran through his mind that he was holding death, and it was as cold as the poets said.

From a few feet away, Kate watched the battle. She

was numb, body and mind. Blood spurted out to dissipate in the water. Letting the empty gun fall, she too reached for her knife and swam forward.

But it was over. One instant the fish and Ky were as one form, locked together. Then they were separate as the body of the shark sank lifelessly toward the bottom. She saw the eyes one last time.

Her arm was gripped painfully. Limp, Kate allowed herself to be dragged to the surface. Safe. It was the only clear thought her mind could form. He was safe.

Too breathless to speak, Ky pulled her toward the ladder, tanks and all. He saw her slip near the top and roll onto the deck. Even as he swung over himself, he saw two fins slice through the water and disappear below where the blood drew them.

"What the hell—" Jumping up from his seat, Marsh ran across the deck to where Kate still lay, gasping for air.

"Sharks." Ky cut off the word as he knelt beside her. "I had to bring her up fast. Kate." Ky reached a hand beneath her neck, lifting her up as he began to take off her tanks. "Are you dizzy? Do you have any pain—your knees, elbows?"

Though she was still gasping for air, she shook her head. "No, no, I'm all right." She knew he worried about decompression sickness and tried to steady herself to reassure him. "Ky, we weren't that deep after—when we came up."

He nodded, grimly acknowledging that she was winded, not incoherent. Standing, he pulled off his mask and heaved it across the deck. Temper helped alleviate the helpless shaking. Kate merely drew her knees up and rested her forehead on them.

"Somebody want to fill me in?" Marsh asked, glancing from one to the other. "I left off when Ky came up raving about shoe buckles."

"Cargo-hold," Kate murmured. "We found it."

"So Ky said." Marsh glanced at his brother whose knuckles were whitening against the rail as he looked out to sea. "Run into some company down there?"

"There was a shark. A tiger."

"She nearly got herself killed," Ky explained. Fury was a direct result of fear, and just as deadly. "She swam right in front of him." Before Marsh could make any comment, Ky turned on Kate. "Did you forget everything I taught you?" he demanded. "You manage to get a doctorate but you can't remember that you're supposed to minimize your movements when a shark's cruising? You know that arm and leg swings attract them, but you swim in front of him, flailing around as though you wanted to shake hands—holding a damn spear gun that's just as likely to annoy him as do any real damage. If I hadn't been coming down just then, he'd have torn you to pieces."

Kate lifted her head slowly. Whatever emotion she'd felt up to that moment was replaced by an anger so deep it overshadowed everything. Meticulously she removed her flippers, her mask and her weight belt before she rose. "If you hadn't been coming down just then," she said precisely, "there'd have been no reason for me to swim in front of him.'' Turning, she walked to the steps and down into the cabin.

For a full minute there was utter silence on deck. Above, a gull screeched, then swerved west. Knowing there'd be no more dives that day, Marsh went to the helm. As he glanced over he saw the deep stain of blood on the water's surface.

''It's customary,'' he began with his back to his brother, ''to thank someone when they save your life.'' Without waiting for a comment, he switched on the engine.

Shaken, Ky ran a hand through his hair. Some of the shark's blood had stained his fingers. Standing still, he stared at it.

Not through carelessness, he thought with a jolt. It had been deliberate. Kate had deliberately put herself in the path of the shark. For him. She'd risked her life to save him. He ran both hands over his face before he started below deck.

He saw her sitting on a bunk with a glass in her hand. A bottle of brandy sat at her feet. When she lifted the glass to her lips her hand shook lightly. Beneath the tan the sun had given her, her face was drawn and pale. No one had ever put him first so completely, so unselfishly. It left him without any idea of what to say.

''Kate…''

''I'm not in the mood to be shouted at right now,'' she told him before she drank again. ''If you need to vent your temper, you'll have to save it.''

"I'm not going to shout." Because he felt every bit as unsteady as she did, he sat beside her and lifted the bottle, drinking straight from it. The brandy ran hot and strong through him. "You scared the hell out of me."

"I'm not going to apologize for what I did."

"I should thank you." He drank again and felt the nerves in his stomach ease. "The point is, you had no business doing what you did. Nothing but blind luck kept you from being torn up down there."

Turning her head, she stared at him. "I should've stayed safe and sound on the bottom while you dealt with the shark—with your diver's knife."

He met the look levelly. "Yes."

"And you'd have done that, if it'd been me?"

"That's different."

"Oh." Glass in hand, she rose. She took a moment to study him, that raw-boned, dark face, the dripping hair that needed a trim, the eyes that reflected the sea. "Would you care to explain that little piece of logic to me?"

"I don't have to explain it, it just is." He tipped the bottle back again. It helped to cloud his imagination which kept bringing images of what might have happened to her.

"No, it just isn't, and that's one of your major problems."

"Kate, have you any idea what could have happened if you hadn't lucked out and hit a vital spot with that spear?"

"Yes." She drained her glass and felt some of the edge dull. The fear might come back again unexpectedly, but she felt she was strong enough to deal with it. And the anger. No matter how it slashed at her, she would put herself between him and danger again. "I understand perfectly. Now, I'm going up with Marsh."

"Wait a minute." He stood to block her way. "Can't you see that I couldn't stand it if anything happened to you? I want to take care of you. I need to keep you safe."

"While you take all the risks?" she countered. "Is that supposed to be the balance of our relationship, Ky? You man, me woman? I bake bread, you hunt the meat?"

"Damn it, Kate, it's not as basic as that."

"It's just as basic as that," she tossed back. The color had come back to her face. Her legs were steady again. And she would be heard. "You want me to be quiet and content—and amenable to the way you choose to live. You want me to do as you say, bend to your will, and yet I know how you felt about my father."

It didn't seem she had the energy to be angry any longer. She was just weary, bone weary from slamming herself up against a wall that didn't seem ready to budge.

"I spent all my life doing what it pleased him to have me do," she continued in calmer tones. "No waves, no problems, no rebellion. He gave me a nod of approval, but no true respect and certainly no true affection. Now, you're asking me to do the same thing again with you.'' She felt no tears, only that weariness of spirit. ''Why do you suppose the only two men I've ever loved should want me to be so utterly pliant to their will? Why do you suppose I lost both of them because I tried so hard to do just that?''

''No.'' He put his hands on her shoulders. ''No, that's not true. It's not what I want from you or for you. I just want to take care of you.''

She shook her head. ''What's the difference, Ky?'' she whispered. ''What the hell's the difference?'' Pushing past him, Kate went out on deck.

Chapter 12

Because in her quiet, immovable way Kate had demanded it, Ky left her alone. Perhaps it was for the best as it gave him time to think and to reassess what he wanted.

He realized that because of his fear for her, because of his need to care for her, he'd hurt her and damaged their already tenuous relationship.

On a certain level, she'd hit the mark in her accusations. He did want her to be safe and cared for while he sweated and took the risks. It was his nature to protect what he loved—in Kate's case, perhaps too much. It was also his nature to want other wills bent to his. He wanted Kate, and was honest enough to admit that he'd already outlined the terms in his own mind.

Her father's quiet manipulating had infuriated Ky and yet, he found himself doing the same thing. Not so quietly, he admitted, not nearly as subtly, but he was doing the same thing. Still, it wasn't for the same reasons. He wanted Kate to be with him, to align herself to him. It was as simple as that. He was certain, if she'd just let him, that he could make her happy.

But he never fully considered that she'd have demands or terms of her own. Until now, Ky hadn't thought how he'd adjust to them.

The light of dawn was quiet as Ky added the finishing touches to the lettering on his sailboat. For most of the night, he'd worked in the shed, giving Kate her time alone, and himself the time to think. Now that the night was over, only one thing remained clear. He loved her. But it had come home to him that it might not be enough. Though impatience continued to push at him, he reined it in. Perhaps he had to leave it to her to show him what would be.

For the next few days, they would concentrate on excavating the cargo that had sunk two centuries before. The longer they searched, the more the treasure became a symbol for him. If he could give it to her, it would be the end of the quest for both of them. Once it was over, they'd both have what they wanted. She, the fulfillment of her father's dream, and he, the satisfaction of seeing her freed from it.

Ky closed the shed doors behind him and headed back for the house. In a few days, he thought with a glance over his shoulder, he'd have something else to give her. Something else to ask her.

He was still some feet away from the house when he smelled the morning scents of bacon and coffee drifting through the kitchen windows. When he entered, Kate was standing at the stove, a long T-shirt over her tank suit, her feet bare, her hair loose. He could see the light dusting of freckles over the bridge of her nose, and the pale soft curve of her lips.

His need to gather her close rammed into him with such power, he had to stop and catch his breath. "Kate—"

"I thought since we'd be putting in a long day we should have a full breakfast." She'd heard him come in, sensed it. Because it made her knees weak, she spoke briskly. "I'd like to get an early start."

He watched her drop eggs into the skillet where the white began to sizzle and solidify around the edges. "Kate, I'd like to talk to you."

"I've been thinking we might consider renting a salvage ship after all," she interrupted, "and perhaps hiring another couple of divers. Excavating the cargo's going to be very slow work with just the two of us. It's certainly time we looked into lifting bags and lines."

Long days in the sun had lightened her hair. There were shades upon shades of variation so that as it flowed it reminded him of the smooth soft pelt of a deer. "I don't want to talk business now."

"It's not something we can put off too much

longer.'' Efficiently, she scooped up the eggs and slid them onto plates. ''I'm beginning to think we should expedite the excavation rather than dragging it out for what may very well be several more weeks. Then, of course, if we're talking about excavating the entire site, it would be months.''

''Not now.'' Ky turned off the burner under the skillet. Taking both plates from Kate, he set them on the table. ''Look, I have to do something, and I'm not sure I'll do it very well.''

Turning, Kate took silverware from the drawer and went to the table. ''What?''

''Apologize.'' When she looked back at him in her cool, quiet way, he swore. ''No, I won't do it well.''

''It isn't necessary.''

''Yes, it's necessary. Sit down.'' He let out a long breath as she remained standing. ''Please,'' he added, then took a chair himself. Without a word, Kate sat across from him. ''You saved my life yesterday.'' Even saying it aloud, he felt uneasy about it. ''It was no less than that. I never could have taken that shark with my diver's knife. The only reason I did was because you'd weakened and distracted him.''

Kate lifted her coffee and drank as though they were discussing the weather. It was the only way she had of blocking out images of what might have been. ''Yes.''

With a frustrated laugh, Ky stabbed at his eggs. ''Not going to make it easy on me, are you?''

''No, I don't think I am.''

"I've never been that scared," he said quietly. "Not for myself, certainly not for anyone else. I thought he had you." He looked up and met her calm, patient eyes. "I was still too far away to do anything about it. If…"

"Sometimes it's best not to think about the ifs."

"All right." He nodded and reached for her hand. "Kate, realizing you put yourself in danger to protect me only made it worse somehow. The possibility of anything happening to you was bad enough, but the idea of it happening because of me was unbearable."

"You would've protected me."

"Yes, but—"

"There shouldn't be any buts, Ky."

"Maybe there shouldn't be," he agreed, "but I can't promise there won't be."

"I've changed." The fact filled her with an odd sense of power and unease. "For too many years I've channeled my own desires because I thought somehow that approval could be equated with love. I know better now."

"I'm not your father, Kate."

"No, but you also have a way of imposing your will on me. My fault to a point." Her voice was calm, level, as it was when she lectured her students. She hadn't slept while Ky had spent his hours in the shed. Like him, she'd spent her time in thought, in search for the right answers. "Four years ago, I had to give to one of you and deny the other. It broke my heart. Today, I know I have to answer to myself first." With her breakfast hardly touched, she took her plate to the sink. "I love you, Ky," she murmured. "But I have to answer to myself first."

Rising, he went to her and laid his hands on her shoulders. Somehow the strength that suddenly seemed so powerful in her both attracted him yet left him uneasy. "Okay." When she turned into his arms, he felt the world settle a bit. "Just let me know what the answer is."

"When I can." She closed her eyes and held tight. "When I can."

For three long days they dove, working away the silt to find new discoveries. With a small air lift and their own hands, they found the practical, the beautiful and the ordinary. They came upon more than eight thousand of the ten thousand decorated pipes on the *Liberty*'s manifest. At least half of them, to Kate's delight, had their bowls intact. They were clay, long-stemmed pipes with the bowls decorated with oak leaves or bunches of grapes and flowers. In a heady moment of pleasure, she snapped Ky's picture as he held one up to his lips.

She knew that at auction, they would more than pay for the investment she'd made. And, with them, the donation she'd make to a museum in her father's name was steadily growing. But more than this, the discovery of so many pipes on a wreck added force to their claim that the ship was English.

There were also snuff boxes, again thousands, leav-

ing literally no doubt in her mind that they'd found
the merchantman *Liberty*. They found tableware, some
of it elegant, some basic utility-ware, but again in
quantity. Their list of salvage grew beyond anything
Kate had imagined, but they found no chest of gold.

They took turns hauling their finds to the surface,
using an inverted plastic trash can filled with air to
help them lift. Even with this, they stored the bulk of
it on the sea floor. They were working alone again,
without a need for Marsh to man the prop-wash. As
it had been in the beginning, the project became a
personal chore for only the two of them. What they
found became a personal triumph. What they didn't
find, a personal disappointment.

Kate delegated herself to deal with the snuff boxes,
transporting them to the mesh baskets. Already, she
was planning to clean several of them herself as part
of the discovery. Beneath the layers of time there
might be something elegant, ornate or ugly. She didn't
believe it mattered what she found, as long as she
found it.

Tea, sugar and other perishables the merchant ship
had carried were long since gone without a trace.
What she and Ky found now were the solid pieces of
civilization that had survived centuries in the sea. A
pipe meant for an eighteenth-century man had never
reached the New World. It should have made her
sad but, because it had survived, because she could
hold it in her hand more than two hundred years later,

Kate felt a quiet triumph. Some things last, whatever the odds.

Reaching down, she disturbed something that lay among the jumbled snuff boxes. Automatically, she jerked her hand back. Memories of the stingray and other dangers were still very fresh. When the small round object clinked against the side of a box and lay still, her heart began to pound. Almost afraid to touch, Kate reached for it. Between her fingers, she held a gold coin from another era.

Though she had read it was likely, she hadn't expected it to be as bright and shiny as the day it was minted. The pieces of silver they'd found had blackened, and other metal pieces had corroded, some of them crystalized almost beyond recognition. Yet, the gold, the small coin she'd plucked from the sea floor, winked back at her.

Its origin was English. The long-dead king stared out at her. The date was 1750.

Ky! Foolishly, she said his name. Though the sound was muffled and indistinguishable, he turned. Unable to wait, Kate swam toward him, clutching the coin. When she reached him, she took his hand and pressed the gold into his palm.

He knew at the moment of contact. He had only to look into her eyes. Taking her hand, he brought it to his lips. She'd found what she wanted. For no reason he could name, he felt empty. He pressed the coin back into her hand, closing her fingers over it tightly. The gold was hers.

Swimming beside her, Ky moved to the spot where Kate had found the coin. Together, they fanned, using all the patience each of them had stored. In the twenty minutes of bottom time they had left, they uncovered only five more coins. As if they were as fragile as glass, Kate placed them in her bag. Each took a mesh basket filled with salvage and surfaced.

"It's there, Ky." Kate let her mouthpiece drop as Ky hauled the first basket over the rail. "It's the *Liberty*, we've proven it."

"It's the *Liberty*," he agreed, taking the second basket from her. "You've finished what your father started."

"Yes." She unhooked her tanks, but it was more than their weight she felt lifted from her shoulders. "I've finished." Digging into her bag, she pulled out the six bright coins. "These were loose. We still haven't found the chest. If it still exists."

He'd already thought of that, but not how he'd tell her his own theory. "They might have taken the chest to another part of the boat when the storm hit." It was a possibility; it had given them hope that the chest was still there.

Kate looked down. The glittery metal seemed to mock her. "It's possible they put the gold in one of the lifeboats when they manned them. The survivor's story wasn't clear after the ship began to break up."

"A lot of things are possible." He touched her cheek briefly before he started to strip off his gear.

"With a little luck and a little more time, we might find it all."

She smiled as she dropped the coins back into her bag. "Then you could buy your boat."

"And you could go to Greece." Stripped down to his bathing trunks, Ky went to the helm. "We need to give ourselves the full twelve hours before we dive again, Kate. We've been calling it close as it is."

"That's fine." She made a business of removing her own suit. She needed the twelve hours, she discovered, for more than the practical reason of residual nitrogen.

They spoke little on the trip back. They should've been ecstatic. Kate knew it, and though she tried, she couldn't recapture that quick boost she'd felt when she picked up the first coin.

She discovered that if she'd had a choice she would have gone back weeks, to the time when the gold was a distant goal and the search was everything.

It took the rest of the day to transport the salvage from the *Vortex* to Ky's house, to separate and catalog it. She'd already decided to contact the Park Service. Their advice in placing many of the artifacts would be invaluable. After taxes, she'd give her father his memorial. And, she mused, she'd give Ky whatever he wanted out of the salvage.

Their original agreement no longer mattered to her. If he wanted half, she'd give it. All she wanted, Kate realized, was the first bowl she'd found, the blackened silver coin and the gold one that had led her to the five other coins.

"We might think about investing in a small electrolytic reduction bath," Ky murmured as he turned what he guessed was a silver snuff box in his palm. "We could treat a lot of this salvage ourselves." Coming to a decision, he set the box down. "We're going to have to think about a bigger ship and equipment. It might be best to stop diving for the next couple of days while we arrange for it. It's been six weeks, and we've barely scratched the surface of what's down there."

She nodded, not entirely sure why she wanted to weep. He was right. It was time to move on, to expand. How could she explain to him, when she couldn't explain to herself, that she wanted nothing else from the sea? While the sun set, she watched him meticulously list the salvage.

"Ky…" She broke off because she couldn't find the words to tell him what moved through her. Sadness, emptiness, needs.

"What's wrong?"

"Nothing." But she took his hands as she rose. "Come upstairs now," she said quietly. "Make love with me before the sun goes down."

Questions ran through him, but he told himself they could wait. The need he felt from her touched off his own. He wanted to give her, and to take from her, what couldn't be found anywhere else.

When they entered the bedroom it was washed with

the warm, lingering light of the sun. The sky was slowly turning red as he lay beside her. Her arms reached out to gather him close. Her lips parted. Refusing to rush, they undressed each other. No boundaries. Flesh against flesh they lay. Mouth against mouth they touched.

Kisses—long and deep—took them both beyond the ordinary world of place and time. Here, there were dozens of sensations to be felt, and no questions to be asked. Here, there was no past, no tomorrow, only the moment. Her body went limp under his, but her mouth hungered and sought.

No one else... No one else had ever taken her beyond herself so effortlessly. Never before had anyone made her so completely aware of her own body. A feathery touch along her skin drove pleasure through her with inescapable force.

The scent of sea still clung to both of them. As pleasure became liquid, they might have been fathoms under the ocean, moving freely without the strict rules of gravity. There were no rules here.

As his hands brought their emotions rising to the surface, so did hers for him. She explored the rippling muscles of his back, near the shoulders. Lingering there, she enjoyed just the feel of one of the subtle differences between them. His skin was smooth, but muscles bunched under it. His hands were gentle, but the palms were hard. He was lean, but there was no softness there.

Again and again she touched and tasted, needing to

absorb him. Above all else, she needed to experience everything they'd ever had together this one time. They made love here, she remembered, that first time. The first time…and the last. Whenever she thought of him, she'd remember the quieting light of dusk and the distant sound of surf.

He didn't understand why he felt such restrained urgency from her, but he knew she needed everything he could give her. He loved her, perhaps not as gently as he could, but more thoroughly than ever before.

He touched. "Here," Ky murmured, using his fingertips to drive her up. As she gasped and arched, he watched her. "You're soft and hot."

He tasted. "And here…" With his tongue, he pushed her to the edge. As her hands gripped his, he groaned. Pleasure heaped upon pleasure. "You taste like temptation—sweet and forbidden. Tell me you want more."

"Yes." The word came out on a moan. "I want more."

So he gave her more.

Again and again, he took her up, watching the astonished pleasure on her face, feeling it in the arch of her body, hearing it in her quick breaths. She was helpless, mindless, his. He drove his tongue into her and felt her explode, wave after wave.

As she shuddered, he moved up her body, hands fast, mouth hot and open. Suddenly, on a surge of strength, she rolled on top of him. Within seconds, she'd devastated his claim to leadership. All fire, all speed, all woman, she took control.

Heedless, greedy, they moved over the bed. Murmurs were incoherent, care was forgotten. They took with only one goal in mind. Pleasure—sweet, forbidden pleasure.

Shaking, locked tight, they reached the goal together.

Dawn was breaking, clear and calm as Kate lay still, watching Ky sleep. She knew what she had to do for both of them, to both of them. Fate had brought them together a second time. It wouldn't bring them together again.

She'd bargained with Ky, offering him a share of gold for his skill. In the beginning, she'd believed that she wanted the treasure, needed it to give her all the options she'd never had before. That choice. Now, she knew she didn't want it at all. A hundred times more gold wouldn't change what was between her and Ky—what drew them to each other, and what kept them apart.

She loved him. She understood that, in his way, he loved her. Did that change the differences between them? Did that make her able and willing to give up her own life to suit his, or able and willing to demand that he do the same?

Their worlds were no closer together now than they'd been four years ago. Their desires no more in tune. With the gold she'd leave for him, he'd be able to do what he wanted with his life. She needed no treasure for that.

If she stayed… Unable to stop herself, Kate reached out to touch his cheek. If she stayed she'd bury herself for him. Eventually, she'd despise herself for it, and he'd resent her. Better that they take what they'd had for a few weeks than cover it with years of disappoinments.

The treasure was important to him. He'd taken risks for it, worked for it. She'd give her father his memorial. Ky would have the rest.

Quietly, still watching him sleep, she dressed.

It didn't take Kate long to gather what she'd come with. Taking her suitcase downstairs, she carefully packed what she'd taken with her from the *Liberty*. In a box, she placed the pottery bowl wrapped in layers of newspaper. The coins, the blackened silver and the shiny gold she zipped into a small pouch. With equal care, she packed the film she'd taken during their days under the ocean.

What she'd designated for the museum she'd already marked. Leaving the list on the table, she left the house.

She told herself it would be cleaner if she left no note, yet she found herself hesitating. How could she make him understand? After putting her suitcase in her car, she went back into the house. Quietly, she took the five gold coins upstairs and placed them on Ky's dresser. With a last look at him as he slept, she went back out again.

She'd have a final moment with the sea. In the quiet air of morning, Kate walked over the dunes.

She'd remember it this way—empty, endless and full of sound. Surf foamed against the sand, white on white. What was beneath the surface would always call her—the memories of peace, of excitement, of sharing both with Ky. Only a summer, she thought. Life was made of four seasons, not one.

Day was strengthening, and her time was up. Turning, she scanned the island until she saw the tip of the lighthouse. Some things lasted, she thought with a smile. She'd learned a great deal in a few short weeks. She was her own woman at last. She could make her own way. As a teacher, she told herself that knowledge was precious. But it made her ache with loneliness. She left the empty sea behind her.

Though she wanted to, Kate deliberately kept herself from looking at the house as she walked back to her car. She didn't need to see it again to remember it. If things had been different... Kate reached for the door handle of her car. Her fingers were still inches from it when she was spun around.

"What the hell're you doing?"

Facing Ky, she felt her resolve crumble, then rebuild. He was barely awake, and barely dressed. His eyes were heavy with sleep, his hair disheveled from it. All he wore was a pair of ragged cut-offs. She folded her hands in front of her and hoped her voice would be strong and clear.

"I had hoped to be gone before you woke."

"Gone?" His eyes locked on hers. "Where?"

"I'm going back to Connecticut."

"Oh?" He swore he wouldn't lose his temper. Not this time. This time, it might be fatal for both of them. "Why?"

Her nerves skipped. The question had been quiet enough, but she knew that cold, flat expression in his eyes. The wrong move, and he'd leap. "You said it yourself yesterday, Ky, when we came up from the last dive. I've done what I came for."

He opened his hand. Five coins shone in the morning sun. "What about this?"

"I left them for you." She swallowed, no longer certain how long she could speak without showing she was breaking in two. "The treasure isn't important to me. It's yours."

"Damn generous of you." Turning over his hand, he dropped the coins into the sand. "That's how much the gold means to me, professor."

She stared at the gold on the ground in front of her. "I don't understand you."

"*You* wanted the treasure," he tossed at her. "It never mattered to me."

"But you said," she began, then shook her head. "When I first came to you, you took the job because of the treasure."

"I took the job because of you. You wanted the gold, Kate."

"It wasn't the money." Dragging a hand through her hair, she turned away. "It was never the money."

"Maybe not. It was your father."

She nodded because it was true, but it no longer hurt. "I finished what he started, and I gave myself something. I don't want any more coins, Ky."

"Why are you running away from me again?"

Slowly, she turned back. "We're four years older than we were before, but we're the same people."

"So?"

"Ky, when I went away before, it was partially because of my father, because I felt I owed him my loyalty. But if I'd thought you'd wanted me. *Me*," she repeated, placing her palm over her heart, "not what you wanted me to be. If I'd thought that, and if I'd thought you and I could make a future together, I wouldn't have gone. I wouldn't be leaving now."

"What the hell gives you the right to decide what I want, what I feel?" He whirled away from her, too furious to remain close. "Maybe I made mistakes, maybe I just assumed too much four years ago. Damn it, I paid for it, Kate, every day from the time you left until you came back. I've done everything I could to be careful this time around, not to push, not to assume. Then I wake up and find you leaving without a word."

"There aren't any words, Ky. I've always given you too many of them, and you've never given me enough."

"You're better with words than I am."

"All right, then I'll use them. I love you." She waited until he turned back to her. The restlessness was on him again. He was holding it off with sheer will. "I've always loved you, but I think I know my own limitations. Maybe I know yours too."

"No, you think too much about limitations, Kate, and not enough about possibilities. I let you walk away from me before. It's not going to be so easy this time."

"I have to be my own person, Ky. I won't live the rest of my life as I've lived it up to now."

"Who the hell wants you to?" he exploded. "Who the hell wants you to be anything but what you are? It's about time you stopped equating love with responsibility and started looking at the other side of it. It's sharing, giving and taking and laughing. If I ask you to give part of yourself to me, I'm going to give part of myself right back."

Unable to stop himself he took her arms in his hands, just holding, as if through the contact he could make his words sink in.

"I don't want your constant devotion. I don't want you to be obliged to me. I don't want to go through life thinking that whatever you do, you do because you want to please me. Damn it, I don't want that kind of responsibility."

Without words, she stared at him. He'd never said anything to her so simply, so free of half meanings. Hope rose in her. Yet still, he was telling her only what he didn't want. Once he gave her the flip side of that coin hope could vanish.

"Tell me what you do want."

He had only one answer. "Come with me a minute.'' Taking her hand, he drew her toward the shed. ''When I started this, it was because I'd always promised myself I would. Before long, the reasons changed.'' Turning the latch, he pulled the shed doors open.

For a moment, she saw nothing. Gradually, her eyes adjusted to the dimness and she stepped inside. The boat was nearly finished. The hull was sanded and sealed and painted, waiting for Ky to take it outside and attach the mast. It was lovely, clean and simple. Just looking at it, Kate could imagine the way it would flow with the wind. Free, light and clever.

''It's beautiful, Ky. I always wondered...'' She broke off as she read the name printed boldly on the stern.

Second Chance.

''That's all I want from you,'' Ky told her, pointing to the two words. ''The boat's yours. When I started it, I thought I was building it for me. But I built it for you, because I knew it was one dream you'd share with me. I only want what's printed on it, Kate. For both of us.'' Speechless, she watched him lean over the starboard side and open a small compartment. He drew out a tiny box.

''I had this cleaned. You wouldn't take it from me before.'' Opening the lid, he revealed the diamond he'd found, sparkling now in a simple gold setting. ''It didn't cost me anything and it wasn't made especially for you. It's just something I found among a bunch of rocks.''

When she started to speak, he held up a hand. "Hold on. You wanted words, I haven't finished with them yet. I know you have to teach, I'm not asking you to give it up. I am asking that you give me one year here on the island. There's a school here, not Yale, but people still have to be taught. A year, Kate. If it isn't what you want after that, I'll go back with you."

Her brows drew together. "Back? To Connecticut? You'd live in Connecticut?"

"If that's what it takes."

A compromise…she thought, baffled. Was he offering to adjust his life for hers? "And if that isn't right for you?"

"Then we'll try someplace else, damn it. We'll find some place in between. Maybe we'll move half a dozen times in the next few years. What does it matter?"

What did it matter? she wondered as she studied him. He was offering her what she'd waited for all of her life. Love without chains.

"I want you to marry me." He wondered if that simple statement shook her as much as it did him. "Tomorrow isn't soon enough, but if you'll give me the year, I can wait."

She nearly smiled. He'd never wait. Once he had her promise of the year, he'd subtly and not so subtly work on her until she found herself at the altar. It was nearly tempting to make him go through the effort.

Limitations? Had she spoken of limitations? Love had none.

"No," she decided aloud. "You only get the year if I get the ring. And what goes with it."

"Deal." He took her hand quickly as though she might change her mind. "Once it's on, you're stuck, professor." Pulling the ring from the box he slipped it onto her finger. Swearing lighty, he shook his head. "It's too big."

"It's all right. I'll keep my hand closed for the next fifty years or so." With a laugh, she went into his arms. All doubts vanished. They'd made it, she told herself. South, north or anywhere in between.

"We'll have it sized," he murmured, nuzzling into her neck.

"Only if they can do it while it's on my finger." Kate closed her eyes. She'd just found everything. Did he know it? "Ky, about the *Liberty*, the rest of the treasure."

He tilted her face up to kiss her. "We've already found it."

* * * * *

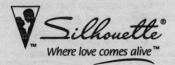

Eg

NORA ROBERTS

83592	LAWLESS	___ \$7.50 U.S.	___ \$8.99 CAN.
28505	REUNION	___ \$7.99 U.S.	___ \$9.50 CAN.
28504	WITH OPEN ARMS	___ \$7.99 U.S.	___ \$9.50 CAN.
28502	CHARMED AND		
	ENCHANTED	___ \$7.99 U.S.	___ \$9.50 CAN.
28501	ENTRANCED	___ \$6.99 U.S.	___ \$8.50 CAN.
28500	CAPTIVATED	___ \$6.99 U.S.	___ \$8.50 CAN.
21892	WINNER TAKES ALL	___ \$7.99 U.S.	___ \$9.50 CAN.
21803	TRULY MADLY		
	MANHATTAN	___ \$7.50 U.S.	___ \$8.99 CAN.

(limited quantities available)

TOTAL AMOUNT   \$_____
POSTAGE & HANDLING   \$_____
(\$1.00 for 1 book, 50¢ for each additional)
APPLICABLE TAXES*   \$_____
<u>TOTAL PAYABLE</u>   \$_____

(Check or money order—please do not send cash)

To order, complete this form and send it, along with a check or money order for the total above, payable to Harlequin Books, to:
In the U.S.: 3010 Walden Avenue, P.O. Box 9077, Buffalo, NY 14269-9077;
In Canada: P.O. Box 636, Fort Erie, Ontario L2A 5X3.

Name:_____
Address:_____ City:_____
State/Prov.:_____ Zip/Postal Code:_____
Account Number (If Applicable):_____
075 CSAS

*New York residents remit applicable sales taxes.
Canadian residents remit applicable GST and provincial taxes.

Silhouette®
Where love comes alive™

Visit Silhouette Books at www.eHarlequin.com

PSNR1204BL